War Babies

ANNIE MURRAY was born in Berkshire and read English at St John's College, Oxford. Her first 'Birmingham' novel, *Birmingham Rose*, hit *The Times* bestseller list when it was published in 1995. She has subsequently written seventeen other successful novels. Annie Murray has four children and lives in Reading.

PRAISE FOR ANNIE MURRAY

Soldier Girl

'This heartwarming story is a gripping read, full of drama, love and compassion' *Take a Break*

Chocolate Girls

'This epic saga will have you gripped from start to finish' *Birmingham Evening Mail*

Birmingham Rose

'An exceptional first novel' *Chronicle*

Birmingham Friends

'A meaty family saga with just the right mix of mystery and nostalgia' *Parents' Magazine*

Birmi

'A tale of passion
keep you hook

ANNIE MURRAY

War Babies

PAN BOOKS

First published in the UK 2015 by Macmillan

First published in paperback 2015 by Pan Books
an imprint of Pan Macmillan
20 New Wharf Road, London N1 9RR
Associated companies throughout the world
www.macmillan.com

ISBN 978-1-5098-3636-9

1 3 5 7 9 8 6 4 2

A CIP catalogue record for this book is available from the British Library.

Typeset by Ellipsis Digital Limited, Glasgow
Printed and bound by CPI Group (UK) Ltd, Croydon, CR0 4YY

Visit www.panmacmillan.com to read more about all our books
and to buy them. You will also find features, author interviews and
news of any author events, and you can sign up for e-newsletters
so that you're always first to hear about our new releases.

For Sam with love
xx

One

'It's a hovel. Nothing but a filthy hovel!'

The words forced out through Peggy Mills's lips, full of bitter resentment. Rachel, a sturdy five-year-old, clutching a floppy old doll, looked up at her mother with anxious grey eyes. Peggy was a slender woman of thirty, her frizzy brown hair fastened back under a hat with a narrow brim and a thin face with a waxen complexion. Her usually pretty features were soured with rage at the sight of their new home. In her arms, as they stood there in the winter dusk, she was hugging the last remaining bundle of their possessions.

'It's even worse than . . .' She whispered the words, but even so, Rachel could hear the intensity of her bitterness. 'Look at it – a *slum*. What can it be like inside – *verminous* . . . Oh!' There was a shudder in her voice. 'I can't bear to go in. My God, look what he's reduced me to. I'll be begging on the street next.'

It was the last in a row of mean back-to-back terraces, crouched hard up against one of the soaring, blue brick arches of the viaduct. As they stood there a train rumbled deafeningly overhead, raining down smuts. The window frames were caked in soot and grime and the bridge cast the place into permanent shade.

1

They had walked here, from the comfortable villa in which they had lived in Sparkhill, along the busy Stratford Road towards the middle of Birmingham. The further in they progressed, the more closely crammed together were the factories, the tiny, dark workshops and cramped, rotting dwellings. The air had thickened, smoke and fumes filling their nostrils. Along the streets, through the chill afternoon air, came the clang of metal against metal, the drone and roar of machines whose heat sometimes breathed, dragon-like, in their faces as they passed the factory doorways. Male voices could be heard shouting over the racket of machines and the wheels of carts clattered by on the road. The cold air was gritty and sour with a mixture of smoke and metallic dusts, sharp with chemicals, and ripe with the stench of horse manure trodden into the cobbles and refuse piled in the crowded back courts of houses. This was the old quarter called Deritend.

People passed them in the gloom, some eyeing them curiously, others with heads down, wrapped up in their own business. White breath streamed from them in the cold. Peggy flinched away from anyone who came too close. All she wanted was to get safely inside where prying eyes could not see her or guess that she might be the wife of that man named in the newspapers . . . But now that she was in front of the house, she hesitated, looking fearfully at it.

'I can't bear to open the door,' she said. 'God knows what's behind it – and I don't suppose there's even a nub of coal in this godforsaken hole.'

As they stood there, a man emerged from an entry along the street and moved towards them with an odd, shuffling gait. He was small of stature and dressed in black. As he drew near, Rachel shrank back closer to

Peggy, seeing that the man had a terribly misshapen face, distorted by a hare lip. Brown, angry eyes fixed on them from under his cap. Peggy tried to move away, reaching for Rachel's hand. The man addressed them, barking out a series of abrupt sounds that made no sense. Saliva hung in a string from one corner of his mouth.

'Get away from us,' Peggy cried, her voice shrill. Rachel felt her mother's fear in the sharp tug of her hand, pulling her frantically towards the house, which suddenly seemed like a haven. 'Come on – get in!' she hissed, shoving the door open.

Leaving the man still addressing them, mystifyingly, they almost fell inside and shut the front door – a row of parched, nibble-edged planks somehow hanging together – hard behind them.

After the shadowy street, the gloom was even greater inside, the cold even danker. At first there were the smells: long-dead ash, a rank, vegetable odour and underlying all of it, a stink of damp. Something scuttled and squeaked in the corner. Rachel shivered and gripped her mother's hand. As their eyes cleared they took in the filthy iron range, the ash and rubbish scattered all over the floor, the stained walls. Otherwise the room was bare except for a lopsided table and two chairs, one with the two back legs missing so that it was keeled over, resting on the back of the seat. Peggy stepped over, peered at the surface of the table and blew across it before putting her bundle down. Without removing her neat black coat, she went to the stairs. Not wanting to be left down there, Rachel followed her up the rotten treads. In the waning afternoon light, through the narrow windows of two mean rooms looking over the street, they saw that the only furniture, in the larger of the rooms, was a thin

3

mattress slumped up against a wall, covered in stained ticking. Peggy said not a word.

Downstairs, she sank onto the one useable chair, her hands bunched into fists. Her breaths came loud and fast as if she were an angry pair of bellows. Rachel felt her insides knot with dread. Mom looked as if she was going to burst.

Rachel stood still and waited. Already, during these terrible weeks, she had learned to keep a little secret part inside her locked away from her mother, to take her mind somewhere else because Peggy's rage and bitterness were so terrifying. She wanted to make things better for Mom but she did not know how and she was starting to feel as if she might burst herself. Her thoughts escaped to the horse she had seen further along the street, an enormous creature with a thick black mane, its face pushed into a nosebag. As they passed, the munching animal had lifted its head and stared at them – at her, she was sure. That horse is my friend, she thought. She wanted to go outside again and find it, to pat it and rub her cheek against its neck for comfort.

She knew to stand quiet, not to interrupt her mother's rages. It was something she had had to learn in these weeks since her father's disappearance, since the day his body was pulled out of the Grand Union below the Camp Hill locks. And that was only the beginning of the life they had known being snatched away from them.

'Look at me!' Peggy's words jolted from her. 'Look at what you've done to me, Harold Mills – made me into a pauper! Damn you . . . *Damn you!*' Her fist slammed on the rotten table. 'You stupid, feckless fool! As if I had anyone else to turn to – oh, I can't bear it!' She pulled herself upright, then turned suddenly on her daughter with a burning expression of loathing in her eyes.

4

'And you – always there like a millstone round my neck. I never wanted children, you know that, don't you? Oh no! I let him have one, just for the sake of it! One child! One rock – that's enough to drown you!' She gave a horrible, harsh laugh. 'If it wasn't for you, I could get away from here and have a life. Look at this place –' She looked wildly around the room. 'This is our life now – thanks to *your father*. Poor, outcast and living in a slum – that's our life now. So you'd better get used to it!'

I

Two

1932

'Get back, you silly girl – how many more times've I got to tell you?' Peggy snapped as Rachel tried to follow her up the path to the front door of the big house. 'Stay behind that wall out of sight.'

This outburst brought on another bout of Peggy's coughing. She leaned groggily against the wall for a moment, curling forward as her chest rattled and she gasped for breaths of the cold air.

Rachel, now a solemn-eyed seven-year-old, used to doing exactly as she was told to try and please her mother, shrank back into the gloom outside the imposing gate-posts. In her arms she held their little bundle of the day so far, wrapped in a sheet. As her mother's coughing died down she heard her give a low groan. Rachel wanted to put her fingers in her ears. Mom kept making these terrible, frightening noises. Her chest sounded so bad. Peggy had insisted that Rachel come with her after school, though when they set out she hardly seemed to have the strength to get along. Some of the people today had been so rude and nasty, so Mom was upset and angry as well as poorly.

They were outside another of the big Edgbaston houses which all seemed like palaces to Rachel. She

9

shifted so that she could see through the gate. The glow of electric lights through the long windows showed glimpses of the curves of deep red curtains fastened back at each side, the elegant symmetry of a china vase, its blue and white patterns lustrous, on the sill inside. It was all so grand and beautiful! How she longed to creep along the path and slip inside, to lie by the fire which she knew must be crackling in the grate in the big room, a soft hearthrug in front of it for her to relax into and feel her frozen limbs uncurl in the warmth . . .

In the front garden was a horse chestnut tree, its remaining leaves wizened into autumn colours and glowing in the dusky light like a shower of bronze. She wanted to gaze and gaze at it. Fancy having an enormous tree right outside your house! When they stepped out of their house it was straight onto the narrow street with not a blade of grass in sight. Until recently she had forgotten that there were such houses as this, or places where the air was not thick with smoke and factory smells. She thought they were only in stories, not in Birmingham.

She put the bundle down on the ground behind her. It was nice and soft and she thought about sitting on it but decided she'd better not. It was dark and growing colder, a late October evening with the mist beginning to seep along the streets. Rachel shivered. Under a navy gaberdine, so big it reached most of the way down her shins, she had on the little grey tunic which Mom had made for school. The sleeves of the gaberdine were too long and the cuffs frayed so Mom told her to keep them rolled up. Now, defiantly, she pulled them down to try and warm her hands, but the cold air seemed to slither its way up the sleeves and across her chest. After a moment she crossed her arms and pushed each hand up the opposite sleeve, hugging herself. She was a pale child, her grey eyes looming large in her face. Her mouse-coloured hair just reached her shoulders and was parted on one side and pinned back with two kirby grips. On her feet were scuffed black boots that they had been given at one of the houses. The soles were worn thin and they were too large as yet, so that she slopped along in them and it was hard to run in the school yard. But they were not *Mail* boots, handed out as charity by the local newspaper! Mom said over her dead body was she ever wearing those – she'd pawn her wedding ring first.

Rachel looked around her. The wide road was very quiet and clean compared with Deritend. Except for a couple of people whose steps she could hear further along the street, it was almost deserted.

One of them, a man, was trundling along towards her, pushing a barrow. As he drew closer in his shabby clothes, she saw that he was quite an old fellow, a knife grinder with his tools on the barrow, who must also have been working his way along the street. His head was lowered and he was mumbling to himself. He did not look up as he passed Rachel. She heard his muttering and the creak of the barrow, caught a whiff of stale sweat and then he was gone round the corner. She thought he sounded angry but she wasn't sure. He was another of those people Mom said she shouldn't talk to.

It was quiet enough to hear her mother's footsteps moving along the side of the house towards the servants' entrance. Don't let her start coughing again, Rachel prayed. It seemed wrong for a stranger to see Mom bent over, helpless like that. Rachel heard the door open and quickly hid herself again. There was a quiet exchange of women's voices, but even so, Rachel's innards tightened with dread. She was not used to this yet. They had only started out selling on the Rag Market just a few weeks ago, when they could get a pitch. She always went with Mom now, two or three days a week after school, to help carry things. They'd take the tram or a trolleybus out to one of the spacious suburbs and work their way along the streets of big houses. Mom always put on the most genteel voice she could and spoke very politely:

'I was wondering if you had any unwanted clothes or items to sell, madam. I'll give you a fair price.'

Last week at a house in Moseley, a man answered the door. 'You clear off!' he burst out, voice full of scorn at the very sight of them. 'I'm not having any of your sort round my place. You go back where you belong, you filthy gyppos!'

'Heaven damn him,' Peggy burst out once they were along the street. In a low voice she added, 'May they rot. Rot!' She stopped and stared at her shaking hands as if she did not know what to do with them. 'Do I look like a gypsy? *Do I?*'

Of course the answer was no. She was a neat woman, quietly spoken and as well dressed as she could manage in her precarious circumstances, in a black coat belted at the waist and her dark green hat with a peacock feather tucked in the brim. The comfortable life she thought she had been promised by her dead husband, Harold Mills, had been cruelly snatched away, both by his death and by the hard truths she found out about him afterwards – the gambling debts, the dreams he had spun in the face of hard reality. After two years of struggling with every kind of work she could do to stay home and out of the factory, cleaning and taking in laundry, outwork from factories like sewing pins or snap fasteners onto cards, she had hit upon an additional source of income – the markets. After all, they only lived a stone's throw away from them. So she had become a 'wardrobe dealer'.

Today they had been to several houses already. Some of the ladies had dismissed her abruptly – or at least, instructed their maids to send her packing. Rachel, waiting outside, heard front doors close with an emphatic bang and then her mother's hurried footsteps in her black shoes with their tidy heels, their strap and button.

'Right snooty little madam that one,' Peggy fumed as one of them ordered her to leave. 'Putting on airs. Anyone'd think she owned that brassy monstrosity of a house herself when she's nothing more than a skivvy.'

More often though, after being turned away as if she was something dirty, Mom would be silent, sprung taut as a mousetrap. Rachel could feel it in her, waiting for her to snap.

The air grew colder while she waited, hugging herself as a ghostly mist spread along the street. She hoped this would be the last one, that they could just go home and get in close to the fire . . . She stood hopping from one foot to the other, trying to keep warm. Her stomach was gurgling with hunger. What on earth was going on? She couldn't hear a sound. After what seemed an endlessly long time, she heard voices again. The door closed quietly and she heard her mother hurrying back down the path.

Peggy stepped out onto the street, a parcel in her arms. Rachel could hear the faint crackle of paper. But before she could say anything, her mother turned her face to the wall, the parcel clutched to her breast and her other hand over her eyes, and burst into tears. Her shoulders shook as the pent-up sobs forced their way out and her weeping made her cough and gulp. Rachel listened helplessly.

'Mom?' she dared to say eventually. Her voice came out sounding small and scared. Had this lady been nasty like the others?

'Oh!' Peggy managed, trying to control her tears and her coughing. And 'O-oh!' again, a long, distressed sound which twisted Rachel inside. She never knew what to do for Mom but she felt she must do something, because who else was there? It felt as if there was no one but her and Mom in the world. She clutched the long ends of her sleeves tightly in her hands, tears of helplessness rising in her own eyes.

But Peggy turned to her, tugging the backs of her wrists across her eyes, trying to stifle her crying.

'So kind!' she said, her voice still wavering like a child's. 'She was so kind. It was the mistress of the house herself came and spoke to me. Look –'

She hurried towards a street lamp a few yards away. Rachel picked up their bundle and scampered after her.

'Such lovely things – look.' In the circle of light Peggy was unfolding the paper from around the treasure inside. 'So pretty . . .'

Rachel saw a folded cream blouse with a collar of intricate lace and little pearl buttons. It was such a delicate, beautiful thing that she did not dare reach out and touch.

'And look –' There were several pairs of lacy bloomers in a peach colour. 'They're new – brand new! And this –'

At the bottom of the little pile of clothes was a silk garment, also in a blushing peach shade. Rachel did not know what it was, but it looked very pretty and Mom seemed so pleased that she said 'Ooh' and 'Oh!', infected by her mother's excitement.

Peggy turned her pale face towards her. There were

14

dark rings under her eyes which gazed at Rachel so intensely that she had to look away at the pretty armful of clothes with their indications of a soft, feminine life.

'She didn't take anything for them – not even a farthing!' Peggy laughed suddenly, a strange, overwrought sound. 'She said she didn't want money for them, she just wanted rid of them. These bloomers are brand new!'

Rachel smiled up at her, the tide of dread receding slowly. Mom was happy – oh, for once, Mom was in a good temper! Her mother's mood brought light into the world – or darkness, depending. What her father had done was beyond her understanding. But it was Mom who was always there, was here now.

'Come on. Bring the other stuff.' Peggy started to walk off rapidly along the street. 'We'll go down to the Bristol Road and get the tram. And once we get to town we're going to buy a tanner's worth of chips to warm us up, that we are.'

Rachel skipped along beside her. Never, in all the days since her father died, had things felt as good as this. It felt like the grandest celebration in all the world!

Mom insisted that they take the chips home. 'I'm not eating in the street,' she said. 'It's not ladylike.' Even though the smell of them through the newspaper, hot and tangy with vinegar, was making them both drool.

Peggy built up the fire with the last bit of kindling and slack and put the kettle on for tea. Both of them drew up as close as they could and Rachel turned this way and that, toasting first her front, then her back as she devoured her salty chips with what was left of the bread.

It was a front house that they lived in – one of two

dwellings under one roof, backing onto one another and consisting of merely one room downstairs with a tiny scullery and the two upstairs bedrooms. The house backing theirs opened onto a small yard, reached by a narrow entry between the houses. The shared toilets were in the yard, as were the shared tap and the dustbins. At the back of the yard, in a low cutting, the River Rea flowed almost unseen through the heart of the city, bringing added damp to the houses and sometimes bursting its banks. At the front was the constant shadow of the viaduct. Bit by bit, over the months, Peggy had done what everyone in these jerry-built houses had to do – make the best of it. She scrubbed and cleaned, fixed up what she could, stitched curtains and acquired a few sticks of furniture. But it was still a poor, damp, tatty place, prone to infestations of bedbugs and silverfish which had to be stoved with a sulphur candle. And the family who lived in the back house, facing the yard, were noisy and quarrelsome and only added to Peggy's rage and bitterness over her blighted life. But her anger did give her energy – the raging energy of one who wants, desperately, to get up and out of there.

Peggy coughed, groaning as the fit passed. But she seemed a little brighter now, thanks to the warm food and tea and the small victory of the afternoon. She sat with her hands warming around her cup. Rachel sat on the peg rug at her feet and stared into the fire. It was quiet for a few moments, with only the hiss of the flames which were quickly dying back for want of fuel. Just for a moment things felt good. Then there came a bang and shouts of raucous male voices from the house behind, the thud of boots on the wooden stairs.

'Dear God –' Peggy closed her eyes for a moment, waiting for the racket to die down.

The feet descended the stairs again. The voices carried on, but quiet. A woman had joined in. Peggy opened her eyes

'We'll go from this place,' she murmured.

Rachel did not know if she was talking to her. She kept very still. She wasn't sure she wanted to go somewhere else. There were things she didn't like about living here. She often saw rats in the yard at the back, where they had to use the lavatories. Every time she went, she was in fear of meeting one of the rats with their horrible fleshy tails. But from her point of view not everything was bad. She went to the little school along the road and played out with some of the children. She had become an adaptable child, tougher than she might have been had things been different.

'I'll not punish myself with this place much longer.' There was a silence, then in a voice full of venom, Peggy hissed, 'His fault. *His*. His vile habits.'

Rachel squirmed a little. By now she understood that her father, a vaguely kind, male shape, had piled up debts. He had a business as a portrait photographer which seemed to be prospering. But the gains from the business were nothing compared to the losses from his habit.

'Betting,' Peggy had told her. 'On horses. By God, he was good at picking losers!' Peggy had not known a thing about it until afterwards. 'Up to his neck,' she said. A debt so big it must have overwhelmed him. Everything they owned had gone towards paying it off. Any thought of her past marriage was stalked by betrayal.

Rachel was getting sleepy. She felt her mother's hand on her shoulder, bony but warm now.

'We'll be out of here soon. I vow we shall.'

Peggy's voice was gentler now, not blaming Rachel

for all her burdens. The young girl looked up and saw her mother's intent face, her eyes reflecting little orange furnaces of fire. She didn't mind where they lived, not really. She just wanted Mom to be well, not to be sick and angry and struggling, forever exhausted taking in washing and cleaning other people's houses until her hands were red raw. Perhaps now they were on the market everything would be all right. She closed her eyes and leaned against her mother's leg. And on that happy, memorable night, Peggy stroked her hair until she was almost asleep, then she took her hand and led her up to bed.

Three

It was the Saturday after that, at the Rag Market, that Rachel saw Danny Booker for the first time.

Market day was Saturday. By midday the fruit and veg traders who had set up early in the morning had cleared away. The place was swept up and it was time for the Rag Market to move in. The gates were closed while they set up, to keep the crowds out. Not everyone got a pitch. Some had permanent pitches in the market, but the 'casuals' had to queue up to see if there would be a pitch for them. It was a nerve-wracking business when you were desperate for the trade. For Peggy to line up amid the other jostling casuals, some of whom she was afraid of – sometimes fights broke out – only to be turned away was a huge disappointment and meant she would have to find other bits of work to get by for the week. Peggy was especially irritable with nerves on a Saturday morning and nagged Rachel for them to get out as early as possible. But she seemed to have endless energy, as if driven by rage and by her determination that she was owed a better life. She was getting quicker at reaching the front of the queue. If they did not get a pitch they waited, and sometimes managed to scramble into one if someone else sold out early and went home.

Every time Rachel passed through the immense iron gates decorated with the city's crest – an arm bringing down a heavy hammer, and the exhortation 'FORWARD!' – she brimmed over with excitement. Peggy felt that market trading was something she had had to stoop to, but Rachel loved everything about the markets.

Her first job was to go round to the stables at the back of a pub in Bromsgrove Street where for a couple of bob a week, the landlord allowed market traders to store their carriages with whatever leftover goods would fit in them. The 'carriage' was a big wicker basket on wheels. Rachel always felt very important, fetching it out of the dark stable building, and wheeling it round into all the bustle of the streets.

As she pushed the carriage over the cobbles and along Jamaica Row – Smithfield, the huge wholesale market on one side and the meat markets on the other – and into the Rag Market, all around her was the raucous, busy bustle of lorries and carts and banter of the trade. The air was full of voices calling out, the low rumble of the carriage wheels, the smells of roasting chestnuts and potatoes, of tobacco smoke on the winter air. And all around, amid the legs, skirts, bundles, carts, trestle tables, prams and hat stands, grew up piles of second-hand clothing for sale, rolls of cloth, ribbons and bows, hats and coats, all in a host of shapes and rainbows of colour. And other wares were laid out – crocks and glass, zips and buttons, cutlery, scent, food, sheets, toys, table linen . . .

When she found Peggy that morning, her mother – on her own as usual, not joining in the banter – was setting out the new clothing she had brought that week. Peggy was still not very well, troubled by her cough. But Rachel knew her mother always gave off this aura of self-contained isolation, almost as if there was a line drawn around her. I am not really here. I am above all this. Head down, under her sporty hat with the feather in it, she was laying out the sheets from her bundle on the ground to keep the clothing off the floor and arranging things folded to look as neat and attractive as possible.

'It's no good throwing them down any old how,' she'd remark sometimes. 'That's what Harold would say, I know he would.'

These were rare moments when she spoke of her dead husband with respect. Harold Mills's photographic business in Sparkhill had had a marvellous display window, full of his best portraits artistically arranged. 'Oh, Harold was very good at *appearances*,' Peggy would say in more bitter moods. The debts she had inherited were a worse shock than the loss of her husband itself. People understood grief – they gave sympathy. A body in the cut, as the canal was known locally, and a legacy of debt was another matter altogether. Harold took with him to his grave her trust and respect, buried them forever and left her with fear, bitterness and penury. She had left the neat villa where they had lived and the neighbours she could not look in the eye, found the cheapest place she could bear to rent and set out to earn her own living.

Peggy was laying out the clothes from the lady in Edgbaston, giving them pride of place. Rachel had wondered if her mother would keep the blouse. It was so pretty and she could see she was tempted. But no. There it was, carefully folded to show off the lace collar. The peach-coloured garment had turned out to be a beautiful, expertly tailored dress. Usually Peggy spent a long time with any clothes she bought, washing and pressing them so that they would look their best, in addition to the other washing and sewing she took in to keep afloat. But these clothes needed no improvement – they were new and of good quality.

'Why did 'er give 'em yer, Mom?' Rachel had asked as they went home that night, clutching their chips.

'She, not 'er,' Peggy said sharply. 'She. For the love of God speak properly, not like those urchins at school. She said they were her sister's. I never asked any more. P'raps they'd had a death in the family. It wasn't as if she'd tell me, was it?'

As they went to set up their pitch that morning – the day of Danny – in the middle of the market, Rachel saw, to her consternation, that another woman was with her mother and that an argument was brewing. She had seen the lady before and she was rather fascinating – tall and voluptuous and wearing a dress with rusty-coloured flowers all over it. Her broad, big-boned face was heavily powdered, the lips bright scarlet, and her thick blonde hair topped by a wide-brimmed hat.

'You just move over!' the woman boomed at Peggy. Beside her were bundles of clothes in disorderly heaps. 'You're on my pitch – look, you've pinched nearly a yard – I'm paying for this. You just clear off!'

Peggy had her hands on her waist and was standing tall, looking proud and disdainful. 'You just stop shouting at me,' she was saying. 'You only need to ask. There's no call to be so unpleasant.'

'Eh, eh, now, ladies . . .' a deep, tobacco-laden voice interrupted. Rachel saw the person they called the Toby Man, with his pouch at his waist, striding over towards them. He was a solidly built man with a bottle-green neckerchief tied in the opening of his shirt, and a cap resting at a sideways angle on his head, from under which looked out a fleshy face with brown, twinkling eyes. His manner was relaxed, as if dealing with squabbling women was a completely familiar part of the job. But he knew he was in charge. 'What's going on 'ere then?'

''Er's pushing onto my pitch . . .' the red-lipped woman began again. 'These casuals don't know how to go on. This is mine – up to 'ere, see?' Rachel could see her mother seething but she was holding her anger in. It would do her no good to get into a fight. 'Tell 'er to move over. I ain't paid for my patch to 'ave 'er moving in on it.'

The Toby Man eyed Peggy up and down. He stroked his stubbly chin for a moment, and considered the wares the two women were setting out.

'So far as I know,' the Toby Man retorted, 'you ain't paid for nowt yet today, Aggie, so yer'd best button it 'til you 'ave.'

''Ere's my money –' The woman rummaged about in her cleavage and slammed some coins into the man's outstretched hand. The Toby Man made a comical face.

'Flamin' 'ell, Aggie – where's this lot been?'

'Never you mind,' Aggie said tartly, rearranging her upper storey by yanking at her clothes so that her mountainous breasts lurched about. 'Now you tell that one –' she nodded her head towards Peggy – 'to pay up and shove over.'

'Here you are,' Peggy said quietly, holding out her own rent for the pitch. Her solemn face and neat, simple dress automatically gave her a dignified appearance.

'Ta.' The Toby Man looked intently down at the ground where the goods were laid out as if reading it in some way, then declared, with a wave of his hand, 'Move yerself over a foot this way, missis. Aggie's right – you're too far over.'

'Told yer, didn' I?' Aggie crowed. 'That's it – you shift yerself.'

Aggie stood, arms folded, and was obviously not going to move until Peggy did as she commanded. Without responding or looking at her neighbour, Peggy tugged at the edge of her sheets, easing the whole pile over.

'You just stay there,' Aggie said, with a self-righteous nod.

Rachel watched her mother's face, but it was a blank. As the Toby Man moved away, he patted Rachel's head. 'That's it, wench – you 'elp yer mother get settled.'

'Get the rest of the clothes out, Rachel,' Peggy said, calmly ignoring Aggie.

''Er's a proper snooty bit, that one,' Rachel heard Aggie mutter behind her.

Together they lifted the bundle of clothes out of the wicker carriage and laid those out as well. There were some very large bloomers and camisoles, a pair of gent's trousers which were on the small size and which no one had wanted last time, and a misshapen man's jacket with a paint stain on one sleeve. It smelt smoky and musty. Peggy folded it to make it look as good as she could. There were several hats that they had bought at a church jumble sale and Rachel enjoyed arranging those. Peggy had also acquired a set of embroidered table mats.

The queue of shoppers was building up outside. Excitement mounted before the gates opened. At last as they swung back, a tight crowd in hats and coats poured in, the ones at the front jostling good-naturedly, laughing and moving out all around the market. Some already had bags of meat from Jamaica Row or other goods they had bought; some were in deadly earnest looking for bargains, and others were there just for a mooch around. Soon the place was buzzing with crowds and activity.

It was a cold, overcast day. Rachel looked around her, watching one lady haggling for a nesting trio of pudding basins, another comparing the feel of skirt lengths. Customers approached her mother's pitch and immediately took interest in the new things she had on display.

'Ooh – look at that! How much is that?' a woman asked, pointing at the peach creation with its silken ruffles along the neckline. Rachel thought that such an enormous lady would never fit into the dress. Surely she didn't want it for herself?

'Three pounds,' Peggy said. 'It's brand new – never been worn. Very good quality. Made in Paris.'

'Three pound?' The lady chortled incredulously. 'I'll give yer ten bob and that's robbing myself.' Peggy shook her head with disdain.

'Huh!' Rachel heard the woman say as she turned away. 'She'll be lucky – three quid! This ain't Lewis's, you know.'

As the market got into full swing Rachel wandered back and forth among the crowds, taking it all in. A man stood in a gap to one side of a crock stall juggling plates, letting out banter at the same time. Rachel watched, smiling. Would he drop one? But he never did. One lady was selling cheap bottles of perfume and the sweet, heady smell filled the air. There were mouth-watering aromas from all around of roasting chestnuts and potatoes and meat and frying onions from the cafe by the gates. From the edges of the market came a cacophony of shouting. Only those who were lucky enough to have places along the walls were allowed to pitch their wares and they were almost always the regulars who had worked their way into the best pitches.

Gradually, as Rachel wandered back towards her mother, she became aware of a voice sailing upwards over the cries of other traders. It was high and strong and thrumming with energy.

'Come and get yer comics 'ere – get yer *Champion*, the Tip-Top Story Weekly! Get yer *Triumph*, yer Buck Rogers . . . ! A farthing each – three for a halfpenny! Never say I don't give yer a bargain!'

Rachel realized that the voice was coming from somewhere across from them where a woman called Gladys Poulter regularly had a pitch against the back wall. Gladys was a handsome woman with strong, high cheekbones, a sharp blade of a nose and piercing blue eyes. Rachel thought Gladys looked rather forbidding, with an air of strength and dignity which defied anyone to give her trouble. She wore her dark brown hair plaited and coiled up into a bun and dressed her wide, curvaceous body in dark, old-fashioned clothes, a black skirt, high-necked blouse and, in the cold, a black woollen shawl hugged round it.

There were some women at Peggy's pitch leaning down to feel some of the clothes and Rachel could see her mother watching them carefully.

'Those underclothes are brand new,' Peggy was saying to them.

Feeling she was not needed, Rachel wandered away again through the milling shoppers, amid the smells of people's coats, their sweat and perfume, towards Gladys's pitch. That voice was still coming through loud and clear. Through a gap she saw a young lad, about her own age, standing in front of Gladys's cascades of clothing, belting out his patter. He held one hand out like a seasoned professional. She smiled, impressed. The boy looked like a grown-up man who had shrunk. He too had striking blue eyes. He must be Gladys's son, she thought.

'Best comics!' he bawled. 'Come and get 'em – *Football Favourite*! Three for a halfpenny!'

The boy's electric energy drew Rachel in. He had a selection of comics laid out on the ground in front of him and a tobacco tin in which to keep his takings. He was a thin, wiry boy, with thick brown hair cropped very short, big blue eyes which looked out at the world very directly and a squarish face with a strong jawline.

'There's girls' comics as well,' he announced, pointing rather grandly, as soon as he saw she was interested. His patter did not include the girls' comics. *Tiny Tots* and *The Schoolgirl* were clearly not names he saw fit to be broadcast by someone as manly as himself.

'You've got a *lot*,' Rachel said, impressed. She loved comics, though Peggy could never spare the money for any. There were several piles of them, some of them looking very dog-eared.

'I've got a good supplier,' the boy said, folding his arms.

'You tell her!' Gladys said, laughing with another woman. 'Good supplier – what'll he come out with next?'

The boy was a little taller than Rachel and had on threadbare grey shorts, one of the front pockets torn, a shirt which looked several sizes too big and a green V-necked jersey with frayed cuffs. Rachel saw that he was wearing black *Mail* boots and that they were badly scuffed.

''E's been off round the jumble sales,' Gladys told her, coming round to speak to them. 'Found himself a new line of business, 'ain't yer, bab? Now you give 'er a good bargain mind, Danny. You've got to learn to keep your customers happy!'

'What d'yer want?' the boy said gruffly. His blue eyes looked very directly at her.

Gladys Poulter cuffed his head affectionately. '*What d'yer want?* What kind of way is that to speak to your customers? You tell 'em what you've got, you ask if there's anything they like the look of – and then whether there is or not, you show 'em summat they can't resist . . .'

The boy had such a compelling gaze that Rachel knew she could not just walk away. But she had only come to have a nose – she had not intended to buy anything.

'I've got a farthing,' she admitted.

'Well – tell yer what,' the boy said, folding his arms and considering carefully. 'I'll give you a special deal. Two for a farthing. How's that?'

'That's more like it,' Gladys chuckled.

Rachel felt herself become daring. At school she found boys were easier if you stood up to them. 'Three.' Eyes full of mischief she looked up at him. 'Make it three.'

She heard Gladys let out a hoot of laughter. 'What's 'er saying? You driving a hard bargain, miss, are yer?' She bent over and Rachel saw her dark lashes and the rough ruddiness of her cheeks. 'What's your name, bab?'

'Rachel Mills,' she said. 'My mother's over there.' She pointed in Peggy's general direction. She saw Gladys Poulter sizing up her mother.

'Oh ar – that new one,' she said. 'I've not seen much of 'er. Come on then, Danny. What's it to be?'

Danny looked pained. 'I'm crippling myself,' he said. 'I can't go lower than a halfpenny.'

'You're a one, Danny!' Gladys laughed. 'You got the whole box for tuppence!'

'I've only got a farthing,' Rachel repeated.

Danny let out a theatrical sigh and shifted his weight onto one leg as if in resignation.

'All right. Pick three. *Girls*' ones. And don't go spreading it around or everyone'll want the same.'

Rachel squatted down and went solemnly through the pile of comics. But she was more interested in Danny. She thought he was funny.

'How old're you?' she asked.

'Eight.'

'I'm nearly eight,' she told him, even though he showed no real desire to know. In fact she was not due to be eight for months yet.

'You're seven then,' he said with some scorn.

'I'll have these.' She held out the comics, their paper feeling fragile between her fingers as if they had been read countless times already. She handed over the farthing.

'Don't you go selling them on now,' Danny warned sternly.

'They're mine now,' Rachel said, tucking them under her arm. 'Mom says once you've bought summat it's yours.' She had no intention of selling them, but somehow the boy brought out a mischief in her.

Danny looked at her and grinned suddenly. 'Don't go selling them on anyway,' he said. 'Even if they are yours.'

'Want a humbug?' Gladys called to her, holding out a little white bag.

'Ooh, yes!' Rachel squeaked, unable to believe her luck. 'Please,' she added. She decided she liked Gladys Poulter, even if she did look fierce. The bag, held open in Gladys's hand, contained a sticky mass of tiny mint humbugs.

'Take a couple or three,' Gladys offered. 'They're not much.'

Rachel managed to pull two mints away from the others.

'Thank you,' she said shyly. She stood, uncertain, holding the sweets between her fingers, as her mouth watered at the smell. She wanted to talk to Danny more but she couldn't think of anything to say.

'Better go,' she said.

'Bring a halfpenny next time,' Danny advised.

Rachel skipped back to their stall across the way, feeling as if it was her lucky day.

Four

All that week, Rachel kept thinking about Danny. Would he be at the market again next Saturday? And would they get a pitch themselves? She was always disappointed if they did not, but now she was praying, *Please let us, and make him be there!* She had friends at school but there was no one as exciting as Danny. He had a sparkiness and force of personality that drew her in. He was not like anyone she had ever met before.

Now that Peggy was working at the market more, she was able to let up a bit on some of the other jobs she was doing. Many a night Rachel had fallen asleep knowing that her mother was still all the way round in the yard, in the brew house, the shared wash house which was usually being used by someone else in the daytime. She would be slaving over a copper of water full of dirty clothes and toiling away with the maiding tub and dolly by the light of a candle. Rachel didn't like having to go to sleep without Mom in the house and Peggy's hands were often red raw and itching from all the wetness and harsh soap. Now she could make better money on the market. The first things she had bought as soon as she could afford them were an old flat iron and a second-hand Singer sewing machine. She could make more money taking in sewing and mending things for the market. Now, the hot, scorching smells from the iron were from ironing her own wares, not from other people's laundry.

One day, after school that week, Rachel calculated that her mother's mood seemed quite good. She was an expert now at reading Peggy.

'Mom,' she said, through a mouthful of bread and margarine, 'can I have a halfpenny this week – just once?' Mom sometimes allowed her a farthing, for a few sweets.

Peggy was standing at the range in her apron, stirring a pan of soup. She frowned. 'What's got into you? You're not going to spend it on those old comics again, are you?'

Rachel gazed back at her, head on one side as she finished chewing. Mom said it was rude to talk with your mouth full. With her eyes she pleaded with her mother to agree.

'It's *reading*,' she wheedled, once she had swallowed. 'You like me reading.'

Peggy gave a sigh of exasperation. 'You're a determined miss, aren't you?' She brought her cup of tea over and sat at the rickety table, giving a rare smile. 'You're a little monkey. All right – just this once. But I don't want you coming home with those dirty old things every week.'

She had sold the silk dress for eighteen shillings – less than she had dreamt of, but a high price for the market and eighteen shillings for nothing was a good profit. The blouse and pretty underwear had also fetched in more than she had ever taken at the market before.

Rachel could feel lightness and hopefulness coming from her. Though she did not know it now, these were some of the sweetest hours she would ever spend with her mother.

'D'you know,' Peggy said, holding her cup in both hands, 'I really do believe that soon we shall be able to look for a new place to live. We can get out of this rat-hole and start again.' She looked at Rachel, sat a little straighter, a fierce pride burning in her eyes. 'And I've done that – all of it. Kept us out of the clutches of the parish and those means-test harridans. I haven't taken a penny from anyone!'

As Rachel trundled their basket-carriage into the market the next week, there was no sign of Danny. But while she and Peggy were setting up, she saw Gladys arrive, a powerful figure in her black dress, pushing her own carriage. Danny was striding along beside her, holding a cardboard carton in his arms. Rachel saw that his shorts were so patched and darned they looked like several garments in one. She didn't laugh – her heart fluttered at the shame of it. Why didn't his mom dress him a bit better when she had all those clothes to sell? They must be very poor, she thought. But Danny strutted along in his *Mail* boots as if he was dressed to kill.

Once the market opened, Danny's strong voice rang out through the high space amid the other hawkers. 'Come and get yer comics! Nearly new comics – half-penny for three! Get yerself a bargain!'

After a time she could not resist going over to look. There were a couple of boys there, looking down at the comics. Rachel recognized one of them from school and shrank back. He was a bully with a face she thought looked like a pig's. The girls always kept out of his way in the school yard and she didn't want anything to do with him now. But the boys were taking no notice of her.

''Ow much?' The pig-faced boy pointed at the pile of boys' comics. His voice sounded sneering.

'A farthing,' Danny repeated. 'Three for a halfpenny.'

'They'm all mucky. Give us three and I'll give yer a farthing.'

Rachel listened carefully. This was the deal Danny had allowed her last week. She wanted to think she was special and that Danny wouldn't do the same for just anyone.

'Nah,' Danny said, pushing his hands deep into his pockets and standing up very straight. Once again he reminded Rachel of a little man. A hard man at that. 'Can't do that. Three for a halfpenny or nowt.'

''S too much. Fight yer for it.' The boy raised his fists.

Rachel felt her heart thump harder. He was always fighting, this boy. It was the main thing she remembered about him. He was a strapping lad. Danny would never win a fight against this heavily built bully. She glanced at Danny's mom for help, but Gladys was surrounded by a gaggle of customers all fudging through her piles of clothes and she was talking to them, hands on hips, watching them like a hawk. Thieving was a constant danger in the market and you had to keep alert.

There was a silence between the two boys for a moment, their eyes locked together. Rachel stood clenching her hands. She desperately didn't want to see Danny humiliated by this great lump of a boy.

'Nah – I ain't fighting yer,' Danny said, casual sounding. 'That's the price. If you don't like it you can clear off. Take it or leave it.'

'But *I said* . . .' The boy moved towards Danny.

Rachel could stand no more. She marched up to

Danny's row of comics and said, 'I want to buy some! I'll have three. Look – here's my halfpenny.'

She didn't look at the other boy. She acted as if he wasn't there.

'All right,' Danny said, turning his attention to her as if to a proper customer. 'Pick 'em then.' To the other boy he said, over his shoulder, 'Come back when you've got the right money.'

Rachel bent over the comics, choosing the ones that had the most words in them and would last her the longest. The back of her neck tingled with the sense of pig-face boy behind her and she waited for the fight to break out over her head. But nothing happened. She was aware of Danny standing over her, his bony knees close to her. When she raised her head, the story comics clutched in her hand, the boy had gone. She stood up.

'I'll have these.'

Danny pocketed her money. 'Ta. So yer got the right money this time.' He had a brisk, distant air, but she thought she saw a smile trying to escape round his lips.

Rachel nodded. She couldn't think what else to say. She wanted to say something, anything, to give her an excuse to stay there.

'That boy's in my form at school,' she said. 'He's stupid. Thick as a brick.' She'd heard someone say that and she thought it was funny.

Danny didn't smile. 'Looks it,' was all he said.

'Eh, bab!' Gladys called to her. Her customers had temporarily thinned out. 'You buying our Danny out again, are yer? Want one of these?'

She was holding out another sweetie bag. Inside this time were sherbet pips, what seemed liked hundreds of them.

'Go on, take a good few – and take our Danny some while you're at it.'

'Ooh, thank you,' Rachel said. Fists full of little sweets she went back to Danny. ''Ere – these are for you.' She emptied one hand into his palm. 'Your mom's *nice*.'

'She ain't my mom,' Danny said as they both tipped the little sweets into their mouths. 'That's my Auntie Glad.'

'Oh,' Rachel said. 'Well – she's nice.'

She never knew quite what to say to Danny. As the weeks passed and Christmas drew nearer, the market was at its busiest. School broke up and in the week before Christmas the market was open on more days. Peggy didn't always manage to get a pitch, but she made sure her name was always on the Toby Man's list and more and more often, she was successful.

Whenever Peggy and Rachel walked into the market, the first thing Rachel did was look for Danny. Her heart jumped faster whenever she saw him there in his raggedy clothes and big boots. If she had any money she bought comics which she read avidly afterwards as if the comics themselves were an extension of him. And Gladys usually had her supply of sweets.

'She says it's either them or fags,' Danny told Rachel one day. 'And 'er likes sweets better.'

They had brief, gruff conversations. She didn't think Danny had much time for girls, but at the same time she had the impression he was pleased to see her, flattered perhaps by her devotion, even if he only showed it by not telling her to go away. He treated her in a lofty, amused way as if she was a faithful dog whom he could choose whether or not to pat.

She tried asking him questions and got very short answers.

'Where d'you live then?'

'Down Ladywood. Summer Hill.'

'Where's your mom then?'

He looked away, suddenly very distant, not answering.

'When's your birthday?'

'It's the day I were born.'

She got out of him that he was about a year and a half older than her. It seemed far more. He felt aged, like a granddad.

''Ve you got any brothers and sisters?'

'Three sisters.'

'What – no brothers?'

'No – I'd've said if I had, wouldn't I?'

'What about your dad?'

'What about 'im?'

It was hard work getting anything out of Danny.

Times were very hard: the depths of a depression; three million unemployed. The government had introduced the means test the year before, shredding the already poor even poorer. No one could have public assistance before any last possession worth anything had been sold, whether it be the piano or the sewing machine.

The well-to-do might take their children to Lewis's department store to see the winter wonderland and Father Christmas. But in the markets, everyone could mingle among the crowds amid the festive atmosphere. Late on these cold winter afternoons the place was lit by naphtha lamps and everyone went out of their way to make it cosy and festive. Streamers hung high across the wide space; some of the market people had brought oil lamps and wrapped red crepe paper round them to create a warm glow; others decorated their pitches with tinsel and lametta, winding strands of it round their hair and hats. Sprigs of mistletoe made an appearance and kisses were begged and granted or laughingly refused.

The sights, sounds and smells filled Rachel with excitement. The market seemed louder, more vibrant and busy than ever. Horses and carts were lined up outside the gates, the animals' steaming breath swirling in the freezing air, their warm smell mingling with the smoke from all the factories, with manure and the musty smells of the old clothes. Mixed in with all these were the enticing aromas of chestnuts roasting and other whiffs of hot, delicious food. And there was all the vendors' shouting and the chatter and bustle! It was so exciting, so much better than being at home, and Rachel could see that despite her scruples about being there, Peggy had grudgingly learned to enjoy some of it too.

But Gladys seemed very quiet that afternoon. It was the one thing that put a dampener on the day. Every so often, she shouted, 'Buy yerself a Christmas treat! Come on, ladies – gloves and scarves – keep the cold out!' But compared with normal, her heart wasn't in it. There was a visible heaviness to her, as if something was dragging at her. She seemed shut away with her own sad thoughts. Disappointed, Rachel kept out of her way.

Peggy had a pretty array of table linen that she had bought from a widow in Handsworth.

'My mother-in-law gave it to us when we were first married,' the woman had confided in Peggy. 'I never saw eye to eye with her at all and I hid it away in the sideboard and only used it once or twice when she came round. I'm glad to see the back of it to tell you the truth. You can have it, dear, and good luck to you.'

Peggy was hoping someone would like it to give as a Christmas present and she had ironed it all carefully and laid it right at the front.

Rachel skipped back and forth between her mother's pitch and Danny's, sucking the barley sugar Gladys offered her and standing beside Danny, hoping everyone would think they were running the comic business together. She had not bought anything from Danny lately because she was saving her farthings to buy a present each for Mom and Danny for Christmas. The trouble was she only had a penny halfpenny even now and there didn't seem much you could buy with that. She noticed that Danny, like his aunt, seemed especially distant today and his shouting had a harsh, angry edge to it. She wondered if she had done something wrong.

'Get yer comics here!' he bawled into the general racket, ignoring her. 'Get yer Christmas comics – two for a farthing!'

The price had gone down as the day waned, Rachel noticed. Darkness had fallen and the place was lit up now that it was getting on for closing time. Cigarette smoke tingled in her nostrils. She shivered under her jumper. Her feet in her little boots felt like blocks of ice, but she didn't care. Gazing round at all the animated faces in the crowds, at Danny, his swaggering way of standing, his voice singing out, she was full of happiness – even if Danny was in a mood. She loved the decorations and the feeling of Christmas coming. And life was so much better than when Mom had just been slaving away on her own!

And then it happened. She didn't see it coming. She

was standing near Gladys and Danny. The man was just another stranger, burly, in dark clothes like all the other men, pushing through the crowd. She couldn't tell that he was drunk and in a rage. Shoving his way through, he was suddenly upon them.

Afterwards she did not know what happened first. Rachel saw the man's wide fleshy face, thick, dark brows under his cap, a merciless expression. Gladys's voice shrieked, 'Oh no, you don't – you get away from 'ere, you bullying sod you!' And Danny, who saw him too late, twisted round and tried to duck away. But the man seized him by one ear, yanking cruelly at it.

'You – come with me, yer little rat . . .' he slurred. 'You're coming along with me – *now*.'

In those seconds she could see Danny was in pain and that he was trying not to cry out. He was helpless as the man twisted his ear, then grabbed him by the arm.

Gladys shot out from behind her wares and was game to fight the man with all she had. 'He's staying with me –' She started punching his chest, pulling on him, but he was so big, he just shoved her away.

'Get off, you meddling bitch . . .'

All in seconds, as Gladys staggered backwards and other people around exclaimed in protest, Danny was disappearing with the man across the market, squirming and struggling, but defeated. The two of them merged with the crowd and disappeared.

Gladys stood watching, panting, hands on her waist, a terrible bitter expression on her face. Rachel was rocked to the core, seeing Danny like that. In the seconds as the man grabbed him, she saw an anguished, despairing look cross Danny's face. He was suddenly young. Very young and scared. Her legs were shaking.

'Who was that?' she asked Gladys, her voice trembling.

Still staring across the market, Gladys said, 'That's his father. Married to my sister. Poor cow. Was, that is.' Gladys sagged then. "Er's just passed away, Wednesday. Heaven help them all.' Her voice crumbled. She drew a clenched fist into her body, as if to quell a spasm of pain, and she turned away shaking her head. Rachel knew she could not ask any more.

Every time she went to the market from then on she looked for Danny. Nothing was the same without him and she could not shake off the memory of his face that day, the helpless fear in his eyes. His mom had died and he had not said a word. Her heart turned leaden at the thought of it.

'Is Danny coming back?' she asked Gladys once or twice. Gladys's strong faced filled with anguish. 'They've gone away, that's all I know. As for them coming back – I don't know, bab. I really don't.'

II

Five

May 1938

'So – here is our new home.'

Rachel raised her head, resentfully, at Peggy's triumphant announcement. After following her mother with dragging feet from the bus stop on the Coventry Road, she found herself in front of a shop with a sign over the door which read, in curling script, HORTON'S DRAPERS & HABERDASHERS.

'We'll be living upstairs, over the shop,' Peggy said as they hesitated outside with their bags and bundles. Her voice was purring with excitement. 'It's quite roomy and Fred's got it very nice up there.'

Rachel looked up at the sizeable brick terrace, its gables decorated with ornate, bottle-green barge-boards. Like every other house in the city it was dusted with soot. But the windows looked newly washed and reflected the morning sun. Compared with the houses they had lived in so far, it was a step up indeed.

Only at this moment, though, as they stood in the warm spring air, did Rachel take in fully what this meant, what Peggy's wedding yesterday to a man called Fred Horton – at the big church, St Cyprian's in Hay Mills – implied. It meant that both of them had to change their names. That Rachel had to leave her school, leave the neighbourhood. Mom had only told her a week ago.

Rachel, now twelve, dressed in her best Sunday frock, turned her face upwards with a stony expression.

'I don't want to live here,' she muttered. 'I don't like it. I want to go home!' She felt helpless, as if she had been tricked.

'What d'you mean?' Peggy laughed. There were new, happy lines on her pale face. 'Of course you want to live here. Look at it – after the other ratholes we've been in! This is my chance for some *life*. A new start – and nothing's going to get in the way of it – not you, nor anyone else . . . Now don't you go making trouble for me, or . . .' Whatever she was going to say, it died on her lips as the shop door swung open.

'There you are at last, Peggy, my dear!'

Fred Horton was a man of barely more than five feet tall, his mouth beaming pink under a clipped moustache, gingery-brown hair slicked back on each side of a middle parting, freckled cheeks, pink and bunched like tiny plums under his ginger-lashed eyes.

'Come in – come in!' He gave a silly little bow and his jacket swung open to display a tightly fitting weskit beneath, and a watch chain. 'Your home, my dear!' There was something aged about Fred Horton. Although in his forties, seven years Peggy's senior, he seemed very old to Rachel. Old and peculiar and stinking of tobacco. She wrinkled her nose at the very look of him.

'Fred – yes, here we are, with our few chattels,' Peggy said in a jolly tone. It felt to Rachel as if they were being taken in like beggars, taken pity on. But of course her mother was now this man's wife. And she had a step-brother seven years her senior, who she had disliked on sight. It felt strange and all wrong. 'Come along now, Rachel. This is our new home, thanks to Fred.'

'We'll take your things upstairs,' Fred instructed. He had put on an expansive air, as if showing them around a palace on behalf of the king. 'We don't want to clutter up the vestibule.'

They passed along the hall and Rachel glimpsed the shop through the first door to the left. The stairs led straight up in front of them, covered with a runner of moss-green carpet. Soon they were on a narrow landing.

'There's a small storeroom downstairs, and the back kitchen. We conduct most of our life upstairs, though,' Fred told them. Rachel looked the other way as he talked. Why should she be interested? And Mom had already been round the house, though she seemed happy to be shown it all again and exclaim over it as if she was seeing it for the first time, which just seemed silly.

'Our room will be at the front of the house, Peggy dear.' Fred spoke in a voice that made Rachel shudder. Already she loathed him, for existing, for marrying her mother. 'We'll save that one for later. Now – this is the parlour.' They peeped into what might once have been a bedroom, in the middle of the house, with a narrow window overlooking the yard at the back. It was a glum-looking place. The floor was covered in brown linoleum. To one side, dark brown leather chairs were arranged stiffly around a little lead fireplace; to the other, away from the window, was a gateleg table with no covering on it and four chairs, squeezed up towards one corner. It felt chill, even in the spring weather. The only thing on the narrow mantelshelf was a photograph of what seemed to be Fred, standing beside a woman in a wedding dress. The woman was not Rachel's mother.

'You see, Peggy,' Fred said. 'The place is badly in need

47

of a woman's touch. Our little daily only does the very basics. But now you're here, my dear.'

Rachel saw one of his stumpy, freckled hands move across her mother's back. Fred leaned in and pressed his lips to his new wife's cheek. He was barely half an inch taller than Peggy. Rachel felt herself shrink inside. She felt alone, as if there was no one else with her in the world. She didn't want some strange, freckly man laying his hands on her mother.

But there was nothing she could say. Peggy was quite closed off to her. There was no choice. They were to live in this house, owned by Fred Horton, whose business, 'Horton's Drapers & Haberdashers', was thriving on the Coventry Road. During the past three years Peggy had moved out of the 'hovel' as she called it, in Floodgate Street, to a bigger – though still small – terrace in Bordesley, not too far from the markets. That had not been a rathole. It was ordinary enough, and Rachel had liked it. But now Peggy was onto greater things. She was going up in the world, to comfort and security, to the station in life she felt she was due and with a man to look after her. But Rachel would have done anything to stay in that little house with Mom and Mom alone – even if her mother was often harsh and unhappy.

Peggy had met Fred Horton in his shop. One day, as she was in the area looking to buy clothes, she had gone into Horton's to see if he had any remnants for sale which would suit her to make up into garments. She was a good seamstress and had had a lot of success selling her own clothes. That was how it started. Fred's first wife Alice had died a year earlier and he was on the lookout. Within three months the two of them were engaged – but not before Peggy had been introduced to this house and all that went with it. And she had not said a word to Rachel – not until the last minute.

'He's got a maid!' she'd said, excited. 'Imagine!' Harold Mills had never run to domestic help. Now Peggy knew why – all his money was being sucked off elsewhere.

The dark corridor seemed to Rachel to stretch for a very long way between the front and back of the house. After the parlour Fred Horton showed them a bathroom – with running water! Peggy exclaimed with excitement again.

Stairs turned off the landing to another floor. 'The attic – that's where my son Sidney's going to be now. He's moved out of his room specially to give it to you, you see.'

And as they progressed to the back of the house, Fred announced, 'And here's where you'll sleep, little Sally!'

'Rachel, dear,' Peggy corrected. 'Not Sally.'

'*Rachel*. I *do* beg your pardon.' Fred turned in the passage, forcing them all to stop rather abruptly. 'Rachel – of course. I don't know why, but you look just like a Sally to me.'

Rachel withered further inside. She did not trust his oily apology. She wanted to run outside into the sunshine, to run away, back home – except home had gone. There was nowhere she could run to. She made a face at Fred's back.

'Here we are – this is all yours,' Fred said, opening the door grandly.

The room was tiny, barely bigger than a boxroom. At that moment it was advantageously bathed in sunlight, the one thing which gave it a cheerful look. The bed was to the right of the door, though there was nothing on it but a mattress covered in dusty-looking ticking. Along the left wall next to the door was a dark wooden chest of drawers with a tatty white crocheted mat on it. The floorboards were bare, except for a square offcut of brown carpet by the bed.

'We'll soon get your bed made up,' Peggy said, cajoling as she saw Rachel's mutinous face. The sunlight could not disguise the stained distemper and smell of damp in the room. But it wasn't the room she minded – that was certainly no worse than other rooms she had slept in – it was that she didn't want any room in this house, with this man who she did not like.

'But it's so far away,' she whispered. She reached for her mother's hand, but Peggy shook her off as they followed Fred Horton's dumpy figure.

'Oh, our room's only just along here,' Peggy said in a determinedly cheerful voice. 'Not far away at all. And you're a big girl now – you don't need to sleep near me, do you?'

That Sunday they spent unpacking their few belongings. Rachel's took up very little space in the dark chest of drawers. She went to look out at the back, wondering if there was a garden, but there was nothing but a scrubby brick yard with weeds pushing up between the cracks.

In the evening the four of them sat at the table in the parlour above the shop. Rachel's feet did not touch the floor and the seat of her chair had sunk in its frame so that she felt as if she was sitting on a lavatory. Fred was at one end of the table and Peggy the other. Opposite Rachel was Sidney Horton. He was nineteen years old, with the same looks as his father, muddy red hair and eyes which Rachel hardly saw throughout the meal because he never looked up for long enough. His brow was clenched in a permanent frown. He worked at Webster & Horsfall's, the wire factory in Hay Mills. He was silent and graceless and ate with loud slapping, squelching sounds, paying no attention to Rachel, as if she wasn't there, which suited her well enough because she wished she wasn't. But his smell wafted over to her, sweaty, metallic and alien.

The meal, which 'Ettie' the maid had evidently cooked, was of rubbery liver and onions and boiled potatoes which had gone grey. Rachel saw her mother trying to look as if this meal was satisfactory, enjoyable even, but it was a struggle. No one needed to say much because Fred Horton could talk the hind leg off any animal you put in front of him and on his very favourite subject, broadly speaking: himself.

Peggy, at rare intervals in Fred Horton's endless flow of talk, tried to involve her new stepson in conversation.

'I hear you're doing very well at the wire factory,' she said to Sidney.

Sidney, his mouth full, nodded and grunted in reply.

'A great firm,' Fred said. 'They made the first trans-atlantic cable – thirty thousand miles of it. Think of that!' He seemed considerably more impressed with this than Sidney himself did.

'I always think it's marvellous to be apprenticed somewhere very good like that and to move up through the firm,' Peggy said, trying hard. 'It gives you such a firm base.'

'I wasn't apprenticed,' Sidney said, with obvious hostility.

'Just a factory hand, I'm afraid,' Fred said.

Rachel saw Sidney look directly at her mother for the first time, with an insolent stare. Chewing slowly, he emptied his mouth, then said, 'So, you're a market trader?'

Rachel felt her stomach lurch at the tone of his voice. She knew how much Mom loathed rudeness. She pushed the tough bits of liver round her plate. The sharp tone of Peggy's reply was unmistakeable.

'I have a little business, yes – as a wardrobe dealer.'

'Had Peggy, *had*,' Fred insisted. 'But those days are over now.'

'I had a good little business,' Peggy defended herself. 'I built it all up myself.'

'Oh, very fine – of course,' Fred laughed, humouring her. 'But you can put all that behind you now. Peggy's a fine little seamstress and buyer. She can make up things to sell – and on some days she'll help me in the shop.'

'Funny,' Sidney said, looking insolently round the table. 'I remember *my mother* saying that the market people were rough as dirt – nothing better than gypsies.' He turned his sludgy eyes on his father. 'I don't re-member you disagreeing with her.'

There were frozen seconds of silence.

'That's enough of that,' Fred ordered. Rachel saw that her mother's face was flushed with fury and she was pressing her lips together. 'No more of that talk.' To Peggy he said, 'Alice didn't know much about the work – the noble work – of the markets. She'd led rather a sheltered life.'

'But they are a bunch of gyppos, aren't they?' Sidney said, addressing his remaining potatoes with a sup-pressed snigger. 'Everyone says so.'

Rachel heard her mother's voice snake across the table, low with rage. 'I'll thank you to find some man-ners and not keep on about things you know nothing about. I'll have you know, I've been perfectly capable of earning my own living and I'll do so again if necessary. No one's doing me any favours, young man, and don't you forget it.'

Rachel's heart was banging hard. She kept her head down, wondering what on earth was coming next.

'Leave the table, Sidney.' Fred's voice was heavy with anger as well. 'And don't come back unless you can find yourself some manners. Go on!' he shouted, as Sidney showed no signs of moving. 'You're old enough to know better than to talk to a lady like that. And this lady is my wife, so you'd better get used to it, or you can find somewhere else to hang your hat!'

Sidney got up slowly, smirking.

'Go on – get out, you idle little bugger!' Fred bawled at him. His son slouched from the room and slammed the door.

There was a terrible silence. Rachel's blood was thudding. She had never heard such shouting and carry-on in her own home. She stared into her lap, her fingers clasped round the tassels of the pale green chenille table-cloth. She heard Fred move his chair back.

'I'm sorry, Peggy,' he said, sounding very contrite as he moved round the table to her. Rachel was surprised by the gentleness of his voice.

'I won't be spoken to like that!' Peggy snapped. 'We need to start as we mean to go on.' Rachel could hear that she was close to tears as well. She tilted her head to look at her mother and saw that she was quivering with emotion. Fred Horton was leaning over her, his arm round her shoulders.

'I've had enough,' Peggy went on, 'of being treated like that by people who . . .' The tears came then. She couldn't hold them back. 'Oh God!' she cried, hands over her face.

'He'll come round,' Fred said. 'I suppose he hasn't got over his mother. He's not a bad lad really.'

Peggy didn't reply and Fred held her, trying to give comfort. 'It's all right, my dear, my darling Peggy. Don't take any notice. All that matters is you and me, isn't it?' He lowered his head and rested his cheek against Peggy's. 'No one else – just us two?'

Rachel slipped from her seat and left the room. She looked about anxiously to see if Sidney Horton was outside the door but there was no sign of him. Then she tore along the shadowy landing to her bedroom at the end. Peggy had made the bed up for her and she lay down in the dusky light, on an eiderdown that stank of mothballs. She hated everything about this new life she was being forced into. Everything was wrong – it even smelt wrong. And she had to live with these horrible, rude men. But most of all she kept hearing Fred Horton's soft, persuasive voice – 'All that matters is you and me . . .' She knew that she counted for nothing. She felt the big, alien house around her and she had never felt more lonely and bereft. She curled tightly on the cold sheen of the eiderdown and let the sobs begin to shake their way out of her.

Six

October 1938

'Rach – wait for me!'

Rachel was on the way to school along the Coventry Road. It was a blustery morning, filthy puddles in the gutters, the carts and cars splashing through them. She turned, face screwed up in the mizzling rain, to see a thin, pale girl called Lilian struggling towards her. Rachel smiled, cheered by the sight. Over these past miserable months, the arrival of Lilian and her family was by far the best thing that had happened.

Lilian caught her up, wheezing and pressing a hand on her chest. 'Don't go so fast – I can't keep up,' she complained.

Lilian was a sweet, sickly little thing with long, white-blonde hair which clung flat to her head and was tied up loosely behind. She was wearing a brown tweed coat which was too big for her and a felt hat, and she had very white skin through which you could see mauve veins at her temples. There were blue shadows under her pale blue eyes. She was thin as a twig. And she was nice. Like Peggy, Lilian's mother had been widowed and remarried, and Lilian had just one baby brother, ten years younger. Unlike Rachel she had a mother and stepfather who were kindly people and went out of their way to look after her and pay her attention.

Mrs Davies stayed at home to look after the little boy, Bobby, and they were happy for Rachel to come round any time she wanted to. She had taken Lilian back to Fred Horton's house once to meet her mother, but now they always went to Lilian's. She would do anything to get out of Horton's – as she called it to herself, never 'home' – as often as possible.

The girls scuttled from one shop awning to another, trying to dodge the rain.

'Stop a minute,' Lilian begged, when they'd dashed under another one. She stood propped against a box of pears on the greengrocer's outside display, her lungs heaving.

'You feeling poorly?' Rachel asked. Lilian's chest sounded really bad.

'I'm all right. Just need to catch my breath.'

As they set off again, Rachel said, 'Can I come round yours later?'

Lilian's mother, Mrs Davies, was a blonde, homely woman, who always gave Rachel a warm welcome and was glad to have company for Lilian.

Lilian shrugged. 'Course.' She peered at Rachel. 'Why don't you ever want to go home?'

It was Rachel's turn to shrug. 'I just don't, that's all.'

Stepping inside Horton's filled her with dread. It was like moving from light into darkness.

Ever since Peggy married Fred Horton, she had given up her hard-earned regular pitch on the market and worked alongside him in the brown surroundings of the shop. She was good at selling, cutting lengths of cloth with long-bladed scissors, measuring strips of lining or ropes of brocade with tassels, doling out threads and pins, tailor's chalk and needles, spools and zip fasteners. She also let it be known that the business now offered a tailoring and alteration service. When she was not in the shop, moving around on the swell of Fred's patter, she was occupied in the back room of the house. She had cleared out the storeroom and put a table in there for sewing. The needle of the sewing machine seemed to *chuk-chuk* up and down almost without stopping. And she hated any interruption.

Peggy was in Fred's thrall. As a young child, Rachel had sensed that her mother did not relish her company, but after Harold Mills's death, neither of them had anyone else. Nowadays, her mother gave off an impatient air of busyness and boredom at the very sight of her. She had far too much to do to be bothered occupying a child – important business demands. What's more, she had something she had never had before – a devoted husband.

Fred adored Peggy. He adored her so much it was sickening. Slobbered over her, Rachel thought. The picture of his first wife Alice in its decorative silver frame, which had been in the parlour upstairs when they arrived, had since disappeared. Fred needed a woman. Peggy was queen. Rachel could see, jealously, that this dumpy man held genuine affection for her mother. This she could not deny. But this new coupling was so tight at the joins that it left no room for anyone else. Their evenings were spent sitting comfortably in the back room, the wireless on or reading the newspaper. When she came into the room they looked up as if to say, 'Oh – are you here?' They wanted no one else.

'Off you go – run and play,' she was told constantly.

Either that or 'Sit quiet for a bit,' or 'It's time you were in bed.' But who, in this dark, soulless house, was she meant to play with, and where? Meals were almost the only times she saw her mother. She had less and less of Peggy's attention.

Several times, after they had all gone to bed, Rachel crept along the dark passage wanting her mother, even just to hear the sound of her breathing and know she was there. She moved as lightly as she could, stopping at the door of the front bedroom and pressing her ear to the wood. Mostly there was silence. Once she heard Fred Horton snoring. Another time, both their voices and strange, blurred grunting sounds. She never did dare to call out. Each time she slunk back to bed, uncomforted.

It was no better in the daytime.

'Leave me in peace, Rachel, for goodness' sake,' Peggy would snap at her. 'I've got an order to finish.'

Rachel sometimes stood down at the door of the back room. She watched her mother's neat form busy at the sewing machine in her powder-blue dress, or her dusty pink dress, each made by her own hands. Peggy's hair would be pinned back out of her eyes. Her body would rock slowly as her foot worked the treadle of the machine. Sooner or later, when Rachel could not resist making a slight noise to let her mother know she was there, an arm would shoot out to shoo her away. Peggy did not even turn round. 'Go on – off you go. Find something to occupy you.' Even her back seemed to give off a forbidding message. *Don't bother me.*

The only time her mother looked after her with her eyes fully on her was for a couple of days when Rachel was in bed with a stomach upset. Then she had sat with her a while and been kinder and more motherly. But mostly it felt as if Peggy was moving away from her down a long, gloomy corridor, further and further until she would be gone altogether. Rachel imagined this sometimes – the colour of her mother's dress fading away into dark nothingness – and fear would stop her breath.

She could have borne all this: feeling she was a nuisance. Mom was there, at least. Fred treated her well enough, for a stepchild; not unkindly. She was fed and clothed, had a bed to sleep in. He was not cruel as such. He just had no interest in her at all. But at least she had a friend in Lilian.

She could tell Lilian some things – that she did not like her stepfather, that her mother was forever busy. What she could not put into words was the way Peggy had betrayed her when it came to Sidney Horton.

Seven

In the beginning, Sidney, who was nineteen, had been as interested in Rachel as in a speck of dust under his feet. But by the time they had been living there for a few weeks, his gaze had swivelled round and fixed on her. She was now a thirteen-year-old and with her mother's big-eyed, pretty looks, though she was fleshier than Peggy, pink cheeked, with straight, shiny brown hair cut in a bob to her jaw.

When she passed him in the hall, or upstairs, he started saying, 'Hello, *Rachel*,' in a funny way she didn't like, mocking, sneering. She would just whisper back and hurry past, never looking at him. She started to feel him eyeing her while they were listening to his father droning on about the day's business. Evidently Sidney was just as bored as she was.

One afternoon, at the end of a very close, hot day, she was sitting on the stairs. She often sat there, on a step near to the top, because she didn't feel comfortable or at home anywhere else. Peggy told her to move if she came across her there.

'It doesn't look good for the customers, you sitting there. And they can see your knickers.'

But Rachel didn't care. She did it all the more.

She was reading a book of girls' stories, about saints and heroines. Caught up in a tale, she was only faintly aware that someone had come in at the back door through the kitchen, his boots clumping along towards the stairs. Through the banisters she saw his sludgy hair come past, the thick neck and slouching shoulders. Her heart slammed with panic. Don't let him be coming upstairs! It was too late to move away.

Sidney put his foot on the first step, his left hand on the banister. His sleeves were rolled in the heat, to show hairy arms. He always looked dishevelled.

'A*ha* – what's this then?' He spoke in the tone people used for telling stories, when the fox spots the chicken, or the wolf claps eyes on Little Red Riding Hood.

Rachel's heart banged in panic. She folded her arms across her, leaning forwards and shuffling as close to the wall as she could get.

'You can go by,' she said, looking down at the carpet, the dusty treads.

'Oh ar – I'll go by when I'm good and ready,' he said. She could feel him staring at her. She felt very silly and vulnerable in her ankle socks, with her bare legs and skirt not even covering her knees. The hairs on her arms were standing on end. She could just hear the tick-tick of the sewing-machine needle behind the door of the back room.

'You waiting for me then, are yer?'

She had to look up. 'N-no – I was just reading.'

'Why're you sitting on the stairs if yer not waiting for summat then, eh?'

'I dunno. I just . . .'

'*Eh?*' His face was right up close suddenly. He stank of the wire works and of sour, oniony breath.

Rachel shrank back, staring down into her lap, the

white cotton frock decorated with a pattern of little blue squares and triangles.

'Well, I think you're waiting –' His voice was barely above a whisper. 'You're a little liar. Here you go then – I bet this is what you're after.'

He pushed his hand between her legs. She cried out at this hard, hairy arm forcing along the tender skin of her thighs. His fingers met the gusset of her knickers. She whimpered as he poked about, hard, hurting her. Her mind could barely take in what was happening. After a few seconds he yanked his hand away and was off and away up the stairs. She heard him climbing up to the attic – and his laugh, like a braying mule.

That was only the beginning.

That night, lying in bed, she thought she heard someone moving with secretive, stealthy steps towards her room. She stiffened in the dark. The adults had not yet gone up to bed – it was too early.

The footsteps stopped at her door. There was a long silence. She strained her ears, hardly breathing. The bedcovers felt like ropes around her. Finding that her chest was almost bursting, she took a gasping breath. The blood was banging round her body. Who was out there? Why didn't they say something, or go away? The tension of not knowing grew unbearably in her. But she did know. She knew it must be Sidney Horton.

The silence went on for so long that she began to wonder if she had imagined the noises. Maybe Sidney had gone up to his own room after all and she had misheard? Her blood began to slow gradually. She dared to shift in bed, her eyes open into the dark. Gradually her eyes began to want to close.

There was a tap on the door, not loud, but definite. She jerked wide awake again, her body revving up in fear. Again it came, and then she heard him calling in a low, sing-song voice, 'Rachel. Ra-a-achel . . .' The tone was both mocking and cajoling.

There was no lock on the door. He must know that. And he must know that she knew that he knew it.

'Rachel. You're not asleep. I know you can hear me.'

She had no idea what he was about, what he wanted, but she was rigid with terror. There was a menace in him, in his horrible silky voice. She thought she might burst with fear. It was impossible to move. She lay in bed like a stone statue while the blood continued to thunder round her body.

There was a little sound. The doorknob was turning. It was slightly loose and rattled when you touched it. She heard it move back and forth, waiting any second for the door to open. Her breathing was a shallow flutter and her stomach sickened. Those seconds seemed to last for hours.

Sidney turned the doorknob back and forth several times. After what seemed an eternity she heard his footsteps moving away and he retreated up to his own room. She gasped for breath, shaking all over. It took her a very long time to get to sleep, convinced that if she did she would open her eyes and find him in her bedroom. For what, she did not know, but the thought terrified her.

It became a hobby of Sidney's to torment her. In the daytime, if they ever ran into each other in the house, he almost always laid a hand on her somewhere in passing. It might have been only on her shoulder as she dashed past him, on her thigh at the table when no one else was looking, or a pat on the head. She never stayed long enough near him for him to repeat his first groping up her dress. But it was as if every time he saw her he was warning her – *I can do what I like when I like. I'm biding my time and don't you forget it.*

Rachel was too young and innocent to have any real idea what he might do, but his air of threat sent her into a constant state of vigilant fear. One afternoon she could not bear it any longer. She went to Peggy in the back room, and found her leaning over the table, cutting a piece of green cloth.

'Mom?'

'Umm – I'm very busy, Rachel, as you can see.'

'I . . .' Her throat closed with tears and she could not speak. As she stood at the door, wiping her eyes, Peggy looked up.

'Oh dear –' Her tone lay somewhere between sympathy and impatience. 'Whatever's the matter?'

'It's . . .' It was hard to find the right words for the nightmare of her bedroom hours now. 'It's Sidney,' she blurted. 'He keeps . . . He keeps coming and bothering me.'

'Sidney?' Peggy was listening now, the scissors held down at her side. 'What d'you mean?'

'He keeps coming to my bedroom.' Nothing could capture the terror of it. Her words seemed tame. 'Saying things.'

'What – into your bedroom?' There was a note of alarm.

Rachel shook her head. 'No, but he keeps saying things.'

'Oh –' Peggy was a bit puzzled – none of this seemed serious. 'Well, he's your brother now, sort of. You've never had brothers to deal with before. I'll ask him not to tease you too much – but you need to toughen up a bit, dear. Girls who have brothers get used to this sort of thing.'

Did they? Rachel wondered. How did Mom know? She had no brothers. And Lilian didn't have to get used to this, did she? Her brother was only little.

'Just tell him to stop teasing you. He's a silly boy that one.'

Rachel could see her mother's eyes drawn back to the cutting out. She drifted away, with a desperate, lonely feeling inside.

She realized that her bedroom door opened inwards and using every bit of strength, when she went to bed, she managed, bit by bit, to haul the end of the chest of drawers up close to it. Every morning she had to shift it again but it made her feel safer. At least he could not get the door open.

But it did not stop him standing at the door, torment-ing her.

'Rachel – I'm here. You can hear me, I know you can.' There would be that rattle of the doorknob. 'Shall I come in? You want me to, don't yer? You're a dirty girl – I know you are. Shall I come in and play some games with you?'

The names he called her got worse. She often didn't know what he was talking about but his talk made her feel sick and soiled. She was being accused of things, labelled with things. Was she dirty? What did that mean?

'You're a dirty girl, aren't yer? Eh? A dirty little ho. I know what you're up to . . . I'm going to come and show you what's good for yer . . .' On and on he rambled, night after night, his hand on the doorknob, turning it as if he was about to break into the room.

This went on, most nights, for almost three weeks.

And one night, at about nine o'clock when Peggy and Fred were still downstairs, he did try to come in.

'Are you there, Rachel?' He had been standing at the door for some time, his low, wheedling voice going on and on. It completely wracked her nerves, even though she had the chest of drawers in the way. 'Well, Rachel,' he said, as she lay, tense and silent. 'I think it's time I paid you a visit.'

Rachel gasped. The handle turned and there was a bang as the door hit the side of the chest of drawers. Foul language came from outside. Sidney could not seem to make sense of why the door would not open. He was losing his temper. He pushed on the door again and again.

'Whatever's going on up there?' Rachel heard Fred Horton's voice down in the hall, followed by her mother's: 'Is everything all right, Fred?'

They were both coming up the stairs. Light appeared on the landing.

'What's all the banging, lad?' Fred demanded. Evidently Sidney had not run away upstairs. 'It sounds as if someone's trying to knock the house down.'

Peggy came straight along and tried to get into Rachel's room. She was met with the same obstacle.

'Rachel? What's this blocking your door?'

In the background, as she climbed weakly out of bed, Rachel heard Sidney making excuses about 'the kid having a nightmare' and him trying to get in.

'Rachel?' Peggy's voice was high with annoyance.

Rachel pulled on the chest of drawers with her whole weight, shifting it enough to get out through the door. Her mother leaned in, switched on the light and looked around.

'The chest of drawers – what's it doing there?'

'I moved it.' Rachel felt very small with the three of them staring at her. She tried to control her shivering. Looking at Sidney she said, 'He tries to get in.'

Sidney let out a guffaw of laughter. 'I was trying to get in because she was yelling,' he said.

'Was it a bad dream?' Fred said in a sugary voice.

'No,' Rachel said mutinously. 'I wasn't asleep.'

'You can't keep shifting the furniture about like that,' Peggy admonished her. 'What if there was a fire? Come on now – we'll move that back to where it belongs and you get into bed again.'

The men drifted away. Peggy shifted the chest of drawers back and Rachel got into bed. Peggy stood looking at her, arms folded. 'This has got to stop,' she said sternly.

'But Mom . . .' Her voice was high and desperate.

'No more silliness and making up stories, all right? It's not nice.' She was turning away.

Rachel looked up at her, silenced. She knew that whatever she said, Peggy was not going to believe her. In that moment the wedge that was beginning to force itself down between her and her mother slammed in deep. Peggy would hear what she wanted to hear.

Rachel lay down and closed her eyes, feeling as if her chest might burst with hurt and anger.

'Now you get to sleep – no more nonsense.'

As soon as Peggy had gone, she leapt up and with all her force, moved the chest back against the door. She couldn't rely on Mom. She was on her own.

The next day when Sidney came home, Rachel was in the kitchen, standing around as her mother cooked, hoping to catch her attention. Peggy had got rid of the maid, saying that she ate money and her cooking was terrible. Dealing with her, Peggy had said, was more trouble than it was worth. She would do the cooking herself.

Rachel saw Sidney outside and she fled out of the kitchen and up the stairs. But he had seen her.

As she reached the top few steps he was up, taking them two and three at a time.

'Oi, you – where d'yer think you're off to? Running away from me, are yer?'

She was forced against the banister, the rail hard against her back. They were both standing on the top steps of the staircase. Rachel started to feel that her legs would not hold her much longer. But her hatred of him put steel inside her for just long enough. Her face contorting with loathing, she said, 'You're bad you are. I'll tell them.' Even as she said it she knew it was hopeless.

Sidney stood back, giving an exaggerated shrug and laughing as if she was the village idiot. 'Tell them? Tell 'em what? Eh? They're not going to believe a little babby like you, are they?' He moved his face close again, the way he liked to bully her. 'Dain't believe yer last night, did they?'

Shrinking inside, she knew he was right. Mom hadn't believed her. She made herself look back at him. She couldn't think of anything else to say and Sidney stared her out until she was forced to look down.

'Huh.' He made a contemptuous sound and she thought he was going to move away upstairs. But as she looked up again, he was up close, a mocking expression on his face. He reached out and rubbed one hand across her chest, her flat, undeveloped breasts, then drew his hand back with a gesture of disgust.

'Wasting my time there,' he said scornfully. 'Flat as cowing pancakes, yer little runt.'

He strode off then and she heard him whistling as he went along the landing.

Every night after that she moved the chest of drawers against the door. But he didn't try to get in again.

Eight

November 1938

Whenever she could, Rachel escaped to the Davieses'. They lived in a small two-up two-down terrace and it was the loveliest house she had ever seen. The Davieses did not have much money, but they knew how to make a home. Mr Davies had a job in a factory. Mrs Davies had lost one husband and had lived in a run-down house on a yard before. She knew when she was well off.

'This is my little piece of heaven,' she'd say. 'Me and Bill have been given another chance. Sometimes I can't believe how lucky I am.'

Mrs Davies, slender and energetic, kept her newly acquired corner of heaven immaculately clean and was forever scrubbing, dusting and polishing the furniture and the little knick-knacks she liked to collect. One day there might be a new china bird on the mantelpiece in the front room, some paper flowers or a picture of somewhere deep in the countryside, with streams, meadows or bluebell woods. Bill, unlike the men who had gone to war in France and returned – if they returned, changed and ruined – had been in the factory throughout. He was small, birdlike and jovial, who always came in with a chirpy greeting – 'All right, wenches – noses still on yer faces, are they?' – which never seemed to require any answer but a smile. He would go and pick up little Bobby and fling him about as he gurgled. He was a man who had also been widowed young and like his new wife knew he was in luck.

Mrs Davies still cooked on a range in the back kitchen. She was not in favour of 'those new-fangled gas contraptions'. The room was always very hot and usually smelt of something cooking. When the girls came back there after school she would get out the toasting fork and hold wedges of white bread in front of the fire until they were amber coloured and crisp; then she scraped butter onto them and held out a plateful. Rachel could always feel a pool of saliva collecting in her mouth as the smell drifted towards her from the fire. Occasionally Mrs Davies bought crumpets and they were the most delicious of all.

Mrs Davies never asked Rachel anything directly about her home life but she seemed to sense that there were things amiss, that Rachel needed a bolt-hole, and she was happy to embrace this sweet-looking, rather solemn child who was a friend of Lilian's.

One day, looking at one of the newest of Mrs Davies's ornaments – a china Alsatian dog, lying down with its tongue hanging out – Rachel asked her where she had bought it.

'Off the market, of course,' Mrs Davies enthused.

''Er likes a good bargain, that one,' Mr Davies commented, passing through the back room where they were sitting, with his boots in his hand. He rolled his eyes in affectionate despair. 'There's no stopping 'er.'

'Ooh, I like a good mooch around the market, I do,' Mrs Davies said with relish. 'Most Sat'd'ys we go, don't we, Lilian?'

The market! Since they left the Rag Market, Peggy

71

had never been back. She did her shopping locally and never felt the need to go into town. It was months since they had set foot in the place and now Rachel realized how much she missed it: the bustle and chatter, the sights and smells.

'Oh!' she cried, hardly thinking. 'Can I come with you?'

'Can she, Mom?' Lilian cried.

'Doesn't your mother ever go round the market?' Mrs Davies said incredulously. Rachel didn't answer. She knew Peggy didn't like people knowing she'd been a market trader. 'Well, of course you can, bab. Bring a penny for the trolleybus and we'll have a little outing. How's that?'

Peggy handed over sixpence, only too glad to have someone else take her child off her hands for a Saturday afternoon.

Rachel stood on the packed trolleybus beside Lilian and her mother as they trundled along the Coventry Road, through Small Heath and onwards into Birmingham. She kept slipping her hand into the pocket of her coat to feel for the sixpence and polishing it against the soft inside of the pocket. She imagined that the dull, tarnished thing might come out looking new minted if she polished it enough. Mrs Davies had paid for her ticket, saying she could pay her back later.

She could see nothing outside. The bus was stuffy, smelly with hot bodies and old clothes. Her face was up close against the back of a woman in a black and white dog-tooth coat and it kept tickling her nose. She wrinkled her face up at Lilian, who giggled. There were murmurs of conversation around her, about shopping and day-to-day things, about somewhere called Czechoslovakia and how Chamberlain and that fiddling little bit of paper weren't going to stop Hitler. A woman just behind Rachel said, 'I can't stand the sound of them rattle things. Makes my blood run cold, that noise.'

'Better than being gassed,' another offered, close to Rachel's right ear.

'Hmm – I s'pose . . . But the stink of those respirators. I can't stand the smell of rubber, makes me gag . . .'

'My brother Sid was gassed during the last lot. Only lasted a year after the war . . . That one was s'posed to have put a stop to all this. You can't believe anything they say, can yer?'

There was going to be another war. It looked more and more like it. All around, people seemed to be saying so these days. They had all been allocated their black, rubbery gas masks. Fred and Peggy had cleared out the cellar, in case there were bombs, they said. Rachel took no notice. And now all she could think of was going back to the market. She realized how much she missed it and some of the people who worked there.

Most of all she missed Gladys Poulter, Danny's aunt. Even when Danny left and never came back and Gladys was quieter, sadder than before, she was good to Rachel. She always had a kind word and offered her something from her inexhaustible supply of sweets. After that afternoon when the man dragged him away, it had changed her view of Danny. His father looked so rough and cruel. But she had not been able to take in that Danny would not be back. Week after week she went in with Peggy to set up, thinking that one day, there he would be, beside Gladys Poulter with his box of comics, swaggering along, crying out across the market in his strong voice. But he never was. Eventually she plucked up courage to ask, approaching Gladys timidly one day during a quiet moment. Gladys was folding up items in her clothing pile.

'Mrs Poulter?' she said. 'Is Danny ever coming back again?'

To her surprise, Gladys Poulter's face quivered and her eyes filled with tears. She wiped them away almost angrily.

'I wish I knew, bab.' She finished folding a pale yellow blouse with expert fingers, seemingly trying to decide whether to say any more. Then she looked round at Rachel. 'I was trying to look out for him, and his sisters. But Wilf – Danny's Dad – he's taken the four of them and . . .' She looked down for a moment, then up at Rachel again with tears in her eyes. 'Oh, I'm sorry to have to say this because it shames me, but I don't know where they are – none of them, including *him*, their father.'

Tears rose in Rachel's eyes as well. She could see how upset Gladys Poulter was. Seeing Danny's father had given her no confidence that whatever had happened to his children would be kind or good.

'I don't know where to start even,' Gladys went on in a desolate voice. 'I don't know if 'e's gone off with 'em to Australia or summat or if they're still here in Birmingham.' Rachel could see she was suffering over it every hour of the day. She reached out and patted Rachel's head. 'But one day I swear I'm going to find out – somehow.'

This news sat inside Rachel like lead, the memory of Danny and all his liveliness so fresh in her mind. But weeks passed, months, and still there was no sign of him. Now and then she asked Gladys Poulter again, but all she got was a shaken head in reply and she stopped asking. She had stopped expecting ever to see him.

The bus lumbered up Digbeth to the Bullring and they all streamed off to join the crowds already milling around the fruit and veg and flowers in Spiceal Street.

'We'll go to the Rag Market first,' Mrs Davies said, to Rachel's joy, as they struggled down past St Martin's Church, towards Jamaica Row. 'We'll come back to the Market Hall for veg – I don't want to cart them around and we might get some bargains if we go later.'

'Ooh look, it's just the same!' Rachel exclaimed as they passed through the tall gates into the Rag Market among the crowds. She breathed in the smells. Cigarette smoke made her nostrils tingle. And she could not resist adding, 'Mom and me used to work here!'

'*Did* you?' Mrs Davies's head whipped round. 'You never mentioned that before.'

'You lucky thing,' Lilian said. She coughed again. Now winter was back she had a bad chest, as usual. 'I'd *love* to work here.'

'Come on,' Mrs Davies said gamely. 'Let's see what they've got for us. Hold hands, you two, and don't get lost. I don't want you running off – specially you, Rachel. What would your mother say?'

Rachel had a feeling her mother would not say much, that it often felt, in fact, as if Peggy rather wished she might disappear. But she smiled vaguely back into Mrs Davies's kindly face.

They worked their way round all the pitches, the little tables or old prams with knick-knacks crammed on them, crocks and toys and shoes, the piles of old clothes and hats, the dresses and men's old jackets. There was a smell of musty cloth and mothballs tinged with sweat, all so familiar that Rachel lapped it up, happy with the memory of it all. And on the cold air, once again she sniffed the smell of hot potatoes and chestnuts and her mouth started to water.

'Smell that!' Lilian said, poking her in the ribs. Lilian always seemed to be hungry. 'Shall us get some? You've got some money.'

'You've only just had yer dinner!' Mrs Davies argued. 'Wait for later and then we'll see.'

It didn't take Rachel long to spot Gladys Poulter's strong features across the market, standing tall and proud, inviting people with her eyes and every now and again with her deep, carrying voice.

'Best quality – get your bedding here, sheets and towels!'

Gladys's voice seemed to vibrate through Rachel. She moved towards her immediately, pulling Lilian along.

'Let's go here,' she ordered.

'But Mom said . . .' Mrs Davies was drifting in the opposite direction. Lilian dragged reluctantly behind her.

'Quick – we'll go back to your mom in a tick –' Having to hurry made Rachel bolder. Suddenly nothing mattered except reaching Gladys. Drawing nearer to her pitch she stood on tiptoe, trying to see if Danny was there. She couldn't hear him. There was no sign of him.

Lilian was getting cross.

'Rach – come *on*. Mom told us not to go off –' She broke away. 'I'm going back to her. Come with me or you'll get lost.'

Lilian folded herself back into the crowd, but Rachel ploughed on. When she reached the Poulters' pitch, Gladys showed no sign of recognition at first. Speaking quickly, before the woman sizing up a black dress could get there first, Rachel said, 'Mrs Poulter?'

Gladys looked at her, and a smile spread over her face.

'I'm Rachel – Peggy's daughter,' Rachel said.

'Course you are. It's been a while since I've seen you – you've grown up a bit, ain't you, eh?' Although it was only a few months since they had stopped working on the market and gone to Fred Horton's house, it felt like a lifetime to Rachel. 'How's your mother?'

'She's all right,' Rachel said. Gladys and Peggy had never really got on. Rachel knew that her mother looked down on Gladys. And she didn't want to talk about Mom – there was something far more important to ask. 'Did Danny ever come back?'

'Our Danny? Oh – there's a tale.' There was angry grit in her voice. 'He did, bab – two months ago. He's working with me now, Sat'd'ys, taking on more of the gents' clothes . . . Look, there 'e is – just coming over.'

Heart racing with excitement, Rachel looked round, seeking out the bold little lad she remembered. Gradually, a tall, thin, wiry figure jostled towards them through the crowd, carrying a bundle of dark clothing. She realized with a lurch inside her that this must be him. She was thirteen, so Danny must be getting on for fifteen now. His face was no longer round and cheeky-looking but gaunt, so that his eyes seemed bigger than she remembered. While he looked pale and stretched tall now, there was still something of the sparking energy about him that she remembered. But as he came closer, she could see that there was something very different about him, a hard, closed-off look. She felt immediately both excited and very shy.

'Eh, Danny,' Gladys Poulter said. 'This is little Rachel – d'you remember her? Used to come and buy your comics off of you.'

Rachel felt Danny's big blue eyes fasten on her, blankly at first, then with a slight sense of recognition.

He gave the faintest nod and started to turn away again, completely aloof from her.

'D'you remember?' Gladys asked. 'You and your comics?'

'Yeah.' Danny nodded. He obviously didn't want to speak to her.

'He's not much of a talker these days, our Danny,' Gladys joked, but there was a sadness in the way she said it. 'We're trying to teach him how to do it again!'

'I'd better go,' Rachel said.

'Come and see us again when you're about,' Gladys said. 'We'd like that, wouldn't we, Danny?'

He was facing the other way, undoing the bundle. He made no response.

''Ere – have one of these.' Rachel found a little bag of red cough candy held under her nose. She reached for one of the pungent sweets. 'Take one for your little pal as well.' She nodded at Lilian who had turned back to find her. She was waiting, looking bewildered.

'Thank you, Mrs Poulter,' Rachel said.

'Nice to see you, bab. Ta-ra-abit. See you again.'

'Come *on*,' Lilian urged her, her cheek bulging with cough candy. 'We got to find Mom. Who was that?' She sounded resentful.

'Just someone,' Rachel said. Her mouth was too crammed full for any explanations, and she did not feel like giving them anyway. This was hers. Suddenly it mattered more than anything – more, even, than Lilian. She kept turning back as they jostled their way across to Mrs Davies. She saw Danny bending down, sorting through his pile of clothes. See you again, Mrs Poulter had said. This warmed Rachel, made her feel she had a friend. She'd be back to see them. To see Danny. And one day, maybe eventually he'd look at her and speak to her.

Nine

It took a long time before Rachel managed to get more than the barest nod or half-smile out of Danny. That voice he had had on him before he was sent away still rang out when it came to hawking his wares, but he seemed to have forgotten how to talk face to face with anyone.

Rachel's happiest times were going to the market with Lilian and her mother. At home, she felt alone. The fact that Sidney Horton was now very deliberately ignoring her was the greatest blessing. He came in and out and moved around her as if she was a shadow. And he seemed to be courting some girl though he was very secretive about it. But she could never feel at ease when he was in the house. She loathed him. If he came near her the hairs on her body stood on end and she could not relax when he was around. What if he started on her again?

She could never have said she was not cared for, not in the basic things of life. Fred and her mother made sure she was fed and clothed, and Peggy was always happy to give her a few pennies to go out with the Davies family. But now that her mother was with Fred Horton and taken up with him and his business, she had almost no time to spare for her daughter and barely more than a passing interest in her.

'I've got a proper life now,' she said occasionally. She had the safety and comfort she deserved after all the impoverished suffering and striving of her years as a widow. And nothing and no one, she seemed to imply, was going to get in the way of it.

Through the winter Rachel went to the market almost every Saturday with the Davieses. She would slope over to Gladys Poulter as soon as she could and Danny was always there too, looking busy and remote. There was never much time so she could not stay and she started to resent going with Lilian and her mother. She felt disloyal for feeling that, but the pull of Danny was so strong. There came a day when Mrs Davies and Lilian were not going to town, but Rachel told Peggy they were. The lie sat in her throat like a toad but she made it jump out just the same and received sixpence from Peggy. She knew what to do now. She was not afraid of going into Birmingham by herself.

Before going to the bus stop, on a February afternoon from which the fog had barely lifted, she went into a newsagent's on the Coventry Road. She spent two of the precious pennies on a present for Danny, which she tucked inside her coat to keep it dry. She did not question whether he would like what she had bought. Somehow she knew he would, even though he looked so grown up and distant. He had to like it!

Soon she was jumping down from the trolleybus and hurrying across the Bullring. As she walked into the Rag Market a surge of happiness filled her. She was here! And, much as she liked Lilian and her mom, she didn't have to trail around with them – she could go just where she liked.

Before many seconds had passed, she made out Danny's voice: 'Gents' clothing – all good quality – nothing over ten bob! Come and have a look – don't be shy!'

Her heart picked up speed. Something about Danny's belting voice had always thrilled her, since the first time she heard it. She stood in the crowd, watching from a distance. Gladys was at one side, with the women's clothing and bedding. She had made room for Danny to trade at the other end. He seemed to be standing on something; he looked so tall, a black jacket hanging from his thin shoulders, his eyes alight and intent.

'Come on now – come and have a look! Best gents' suits – don't miss a bargain!'

He might not be very talkative, she thought, but he can certainly still holler! The other times she had been all she had managed to get out of him was a grudging 'All right?' or ''Ullo.'

'Come on, our Danny,' Gladys would tease. 'Spit a few more words out – we won't charge yer.' But Rachel saw that when she said things like that, her eyes were sad and she wondered why. No one had told her where Danny had been all this time and she was afraid to ask. It was as if Gladys Poulter felt ashamed, or just could not bear to talk about it.

And Danny would half-smile and turn away with the air of a very busy man. The more she saw of Danny, the more determined she was to get him to talk to her. It was not just nosiness – her heart seemed to be hooked onto him somehow.

Rachel walked towards them, her heart thudding. She made a great show of looking at some of the women's clothes, a pile of bloomers in varying colours, a coat in dark red wool, a blouse with a lace-trimmed collar. She was just behind Danny who, she saw, was standing on a wooden box. His thin body was full of urgency.

'Oh – you're back again!' Gladys Poulter turned to her when she had finished dealing with her customer. 'You don't give up easy, do yer?' she laughed. Rachel blushed. She had not realized that it was so obvious she came to the stall to see Danny. 'Eh, Danny!' she called. 'Your little friend's here again!'

In that second Rachel made a decision. If Danny turned now and saw her just standing there she would feel silly, the way being a girl was somehow silly if all she did was to wait there with her face glowing red, as if it was all up to him to come and see her or not. So she leapt into action and strode towards him.

'Hello!' she offered, planting her feet side by side.

Danny stepped down off the box. Rachel saw a pink flush spread across his cheeks as well and it changed everything. Maybe Danny wasn't so tough after all.

''Ullo,' he said, sticking his hands in his jacket pockets. He seemed to droop suddenly, unsure of himself. She got the feeling that he was holding something in his pocket, as if for comfort.

'I brought you something,' Rachel said.

Danny looked suspicious, his brows pulling into a frown. Now that his face was thinner, she saw that he had prominent cheekbones and a strong jawline. 'What d'you mean?'

'It's nothing much –' She tried to sound casual. 'I thought you'd like it.' From inside her coat she brought the folded comic she had bought. It was a new one that had only started coming out a few months ago. She felt afraid then. Would Danny think he was too old for comics? 'Here –'

Danny took it. He seemed wary, but then another

expression came into his large eyes – a wondering interest. 'The *Beano*.' He stared at it, then opened it up. A
chuckle made its way out of him. 'It's good, that is.
Funny.'

Rachel beamed. 'Tin Can Tommy,' she said.

'Ping the Elastic . . .' Danny gave a sudden cough of
laughter. 'Comics are the *best*.'

'What you got there, Danny?' Gladys asked.

'The *Beano*,' he grinned, then his face sobered again,
unsure. 'This ain't for me?'

Rachel was so happy at the sight of his smiling face –
she had made him smile! – that she was grinning all over.
'It is.' She shrugged. 'Yes. For you.'

'Well, that's nice, Danny.' Gladys laughed. 'There was
a time she had to come and buy them off you! Tell you
what – have a break, lad.' She fumbled in her pocket. 'Go
and get yourself and this young lady some chestnuts –
and bring me some back while yer at it.'

Danny looked uncertain, but Rachel said, 'Ooh,
thank you, Mrs Poulter, can we?'

Danny fished around at the back of the pile of sale
clothes for his cap and put it on at a jaunty angle. As
they turned to walk towards the man with the barrow
selling chestnuts she heard Gladys Poulter say, 'Cheeky
little minx.'

They bought three twists of paper full of hot, delicious-
smelling chestnuts and hurried back to give Gladys hers.
'Right, you two,' she said, taking them. 'Get lost for a
bit.'

They walked out of the market. The street was full of
carts, some parked by the kerb, their horses munching
out of nosebags, the warm animal smells steaming out

into the cold. Others were cramming in and out of Jamaica Row and crowds of people were weaving in between them and jostling along the mucky pavements. Rachel and Danny, without consulting each other, moved out away from Rag Alley and the main market bustle, along towards the bottom of Bradford Street. The slaughterhouse was near the bottom of the hill, close to the meat markets. The air was rank with the stenches of blood and fat and offal, and the bawling of animals carried out into the street. Rachel felt her stomach turn. It was horrible to hear.

'Not here.' Danny nodded that they should go further. They turned into a side street, stopping by the wall of a factory. Other metallic screeching sounds replaced the agonies of beasts. The smell of the chestnuts crept out into the chill, smoky air. Danny shelled one and ate it eagerly.

'Nice,' he said through a mouthful.

Rachel was encouraged by this sudden outburst of communication. She was enjoying the sweet taste of her chestnuts as well, but she was more eager to talk than eat.

'That your auntie then?' she said, although she knew perfectly well that Gladys was his mother's sister.

'Yep,' Danny nodded, digging into another chestnut.

Where have you been? she wanted to ask. Where did you go all this time? She watched him while his head was down. There was a light sprinkle of freckles across his nose. Feeling her gaze on him, Danny raised his head and looked hard into her eyes. Rachel did not look away, though she was intimidated by his gaze. The blood rose in her cheeks. Danny did not smile. He stared as if he was looking for something.

'Why'd you bring me a comic?' he asked eventually. His voice sounded wary again, almost hostile.

Rachel's pulse thudded. It felt as if he might run away if she gave the wrong answer. Looking into his eyes, she said, 'When you went away – before – it was never the same. I just thought you'd like it.' A truck came past at the end of the street, labouring up the hill, sending out clouds of black fumes. When its noise had passed far enough away, she asked quietly, 'Where did you go? Did you run away?'

'No!' Danny replied sharply, as if startled by the question. He shifted so that he was leaning his back against the wall. He bent his right leg and rested his foot on the sooty bricks. His oversized jacket hung limply on his thin body. Once more he fingered something in his right-hand pocket. 'Run away? No.' Looking beyond her, back along the street, he said in a flat voice, 'He put me in the home. My old man. After our mom passed on. Me and my sisters – only they were put somewhere else. I dunno where they are. Auntie's trying to find out.' He looked her in the eye then. 'I've got three sisters – somewhere. Jess, Rose and Amy.'

'The home?' Rachel said, not quite understanding.

'Orphanage.' Danny lowered his head as if washed in shame. 'You know, for kids. It was a long way from here, over the other side of town. Our mom passed on to the angels – she were an angel, our mom . . .' Rachel felt a lump rise in her throat. 'And our dad dain't want us so he got rid of us, once she'd gone.'

He said all this in a flat tone, almost as if it was about someone else. It was Rachel who had tears in her eyes.

'Sent you away? How *could* he send you away?' She thought of her own mother. Whatever else, Mom had never done that.

85

Danny shrugged. He looked at her, then again more closely, frowning. 'You blarting?'

'No.' She looked down. A tear slipped from her cheek and onto the ground.

'You are,' Danny insisted. 'Why're you blarting?'

'Because it's sad.' She looked up at him, wet-eyed. 'That your mom passed away and then . . .'

He stared at her again. 'Is that sad?'

'Yes – course it is.'

To her astonishment, Danny smiled suddenly, a twisted sort of half-smile, but the most wholehearted she had ever seen on him. 'You're nice, you are.'

'D'you want to be friends?' she asked eagerly. She felt bonded to him somehow, in a way she could not explain, but it was a bond which reached across between his loneliness and hers.

He pushed himself off the wall and began to turn away. 'Yeah – all right,' he said, almost dismissive now. 'If you like.'

She looked at his strong back as he turned down Bradford Street again, its posture bristling with toughness and bravado. Such a lad. So strange to her. But friends – he said so, and a warm feeling moved through her chest.

Ten

January 1939

'Mrs Poulter?' Rachel stood before Danny's aunt with pleading eyes. 'Can I come and help you, proper like, on Saturdays?'

Rachel had come hurrying into town on this grey, freezing Saturday from which the fog had still not lifted. The fumes from the traffic and everyone's breath steamed out into the air. Gladys was still only just setting up. There was, for the moment, no sign of Danny. Gladys was stooping over a tottering pile of white bed linen, coughing. It was a freezing day and she had a black woollen shawl wrapped round her, over her black skirt and boots. Her hands were covered by black, fingerless gloves. Rachel wondered if Gladys ever wore pretty dresses. Gladys straightened up, wincing, one hand pressed to her back.

'I could do that, see, to save you bending!' Rachel offered eagerly.

Gladys stood, considering for a moment. 'You seem to be 'ere all the time any road, bab.' She paused. 'I can't pay you, or not much . . .'

'No – I don't want pay!' Rachel said. The thought had never crossed her mind. Peggy always gave her more than enough for her fare. She was not after money. She wanted . . . What did she want? To be part of it all, officially – the market. To enjoy Gladys's welcome. To have something to do and to get out of the house. And Danny – she wanted to be near Danny.

'I can go and pick up your carriage for you,' Rachel offered eagerly. 'I used to do it for Mom – I know what to do. And I can help – whatever you like. Now Danny's not here.'

Danny had a proper job now, as a porter over on the fish market. He seemed to enjoy the raucous, bantering atmosphere with other lads and the hard, physical work of pushing around catches of fresh and saltwater fish to be displayed in their gleaming beds of ice. The fish market was not far away and he often popped across during his break.

Gladys folded her arms and put her head on one side. Rachel quailed under her gaze. She still found Gladys Poulter intimidating. She was so strange and interesting-looking with her dark hair and piercing blue eyes. 'Well,' she brought out eventually. 'Another pair of hands never does any harm. Ain't you going to work soon? When d'you leave school?'

'Not 'til the summer,' Rachel said. 'My birthday's August.'

Gladys digested this. 'What about your mother?'

'She thinks it's a good idea,' Rachel fibbed.

'Well.' Gladys released her arms again, obviously intending to get back to work. 'I don't see why not if you want to. You need to get 'ere before midday, once they've cleared up.'

'Oh, thank you, Mrs Poulter!' Rachel said, overjoyed. The market felt like the best home she had now and it wasn't a very big fib about her mother. Peggy didn't seem to care what she did either way.

*

One day, just after school began again after the Christmas holidays, Rachel had come home to find her mother, once again, seated at her sewing machine. But instead of turning the handle in her usual relentless way, Peggy had her head in her hands.

'Mom?' Rachel stopped, worried, at the door.

'Oh – you're back,' Peggy said, trying to make her voice normal, but it was still full of tears. She wiped her face on a scrap of pink cotton and stood up. 'I didn't hear you come in.'

She obviously did not want Rachel to know she had been crying and Rachel did not like to ask. But Peggy cried so seldom that the thought of it sat like a tense wire of dread inside her. By the time they all sat down to eat in the evening she looked calm and normal again. Things in the household had moved on. Sidney was courting seriously now and was hardly ever there, to Rachel's relief. She had grown more used to Fred Horton. He was not a nasty man and he loved her mother. He just spent his whole life thinking about his business and very little else. That evening Peggy sat facing the two of them calmly; they talked about the day and it was as if nothing had happened.

But within a couple of days, for the first time, she overheard a frightening outburst between the two of them. It was after she had gone to bed but their voices carried through the house. She crept along the corridor to their bedroom and stood listening, one hand pressed to the cold wall. Her mother was crying and sounded distraught. She could catch scraps of their argument.

'How can you have been so careless?' Fred's voice came furiously to her ears. 'After all, you're the one who—'

'Careless!' Peggy wailed. 'What have I done that's

careless? It's you who . . .' The rest of the words were muffled and Rachel could not make them out.

Within days of this, one afternoon when Rachel returned from school, she found her mother waiting for her, looking pale and strained. Sitting sideways on her sewing chair, she put her hand groggily to her forehead.

'I don't feel very well, as you may have noticed,' she began.

Rachel began to think she understood. Mom was ill. She must have done something to make herself ill. She looked down at her mother's slender, crossed ankles, her feet in stylish black shoes.

'The thing is – you'll have to know sooner or later.' Peggy swallowed with a wince, as if she had a bad taste in her mouth. Tears began to run from her eyes. 'Oh – it's no good. It's not something I can hide for ever. I am with child.'

Rachel stared at her.

'A baby,' Peggy said. 'I am carrying a child. You will have a brother or sister.'

'But –' Rachel was astonished by this. 'Aren't you . . . too old?' That was what Mrs Davies said sometimes. She'd had little Bobby and Mr Davies joked about having another six. 'Oh, I'm too old for all that,' Mrs Davies would say.

'I am almost thirty-nine years of age,' Peggy said sniffily. 'There are children born to women a good deal older than me, I can assure you.'

'Oh,' Rachel said. She had no idea what to say next. None of this felt as if it was anything to do with her. But, just in case, she added, 'That's nice.'

'It may be for you,' Peggy snapped. 'But it's not for me and Fred's none too pleased either.'

Rachel found herself wondering about Danny,

whether she would see him this week. In any week that was the best thing ever to happen.

'Well,' Peggy was saying. 'Now you know. But you'll need to be a help round the house. I shan't be able to manage anything.'

'All right,' Rachel said. Leaving the room, she shut this abstract news entirely out of her mind. It was just another reason why the place where she lived did not feel like home.

Most Saturdays when she was helping Gladys Poulter, Lilian and Mrs Davies would come to the market. Rachel knew that Lilian was disappointed that she no longer came into town with them. The two girls saw plenty of each other at school and at other times, however, and Lilian wasn't one to bear a grudge. She was impressed by Rachel's post in the Rag Market. It was lovely, standing there in the crowded market, suddenly to see their familiar faces coming towards her, smiling and always stopping for a natter. Mrs Davies and Gladys became quite friendly towards each other.

'Ooh, I'd've liked your job,' Mrs Davies told Gladys during a lull one morning. Rachel was making herself busy tidying the clothes while Lilian watched enviously. 'Beats factory work hands down – that's what I've always done.' Mrs Davies had worked in the jewellery quarter before she was married the first time. 'Still – I've got my little Bobby now and Bill likes me to stop at home, so I can't grumble.'

'I started off after the war,' Gladys said. 'Had to do summat and it was on top of another job in them days.'

'Your husband . . . ?' Mrs Davies asked carefully.

'He passed away in 1916.'

Rachel watched Mrs Davies's sympathetic face and listened to her 'Oh dear's and 'How dreadful's. Rachel loved it when the two women chatted. It felt as if both of them were her aunties. Best of all was when Danny came across, sometimes on his break in the afternoon. There wasn't a lot of talking, all through that time. They were young and awkward with each other. He'd nod to his aunt who'd tease him – 'Oh my word, you stink like a lobster pot, Danny!' – and she'd give him a sweet from her little bags of treats and ask him how trade was doing in the fish market. And he and Rachel would mainly look at each other. Rachel always gave him a smile, putting everything she felt into her eyes. And he'd say, 'All right?' to her and maybe they would say a thing or two. And Danny just seemed to like them both being there and would hang around for a while and go reluctantly back to work, saying, 'Ta-ra – see yer.' Rachel would watch him stride off across the market, tall and lithe, and the sight of him always gave her a twinge of excitement inside and she wanted to call to him, 'Don't go!'

She was happiest away from home, and whatever was going on there seemed to have nothing much to do with her. This was where she wanted to be.

Eleven

'A *filing clerk*?' Peggy said. But she had not the energy to be as snooty as she would have been a few months ago when she was saying, 'My daughter will never go into a factory.' Rachel left school at the end of the summer term and Peggy was heavily pregnant and too languid and tired to get worked up about anything, even if she had hoped for something more glamorous, like Lewis's department store. 'Well, that's a start, I suppose,' she sighed.

Rachel had perversely decided that working in a factory was therefore exactly what she wanted to do. Lilian had got herself a job learning to be a bookkeeper for a firm making cricket bats and she seemed happy enough. Going to the Labour Exchange with her references, Rachel was told that she could go and work as a filing clerk and trainee office junior – at the Bird's Custard Factory in Gibb Street.

Rachel was pleased with the job. She liked the huge Devonshire Works off Digbeth, not too far from where she and her mother had previously lived, with its sweet, vanillary smells. The job would keep her out of the house for most days of the week. Miss Pike, the lady who was in charge of her, seemed even-tempered enough. She was in her thirties with her hair swept up into a neat pleat. When Rachel started the work, learning to sort piles of filing in the offices of the vast red-brick building, she found it quite easy. And best of all, the Works were not far from the Markets – and Danny.

As that spring turned into a long, hot summer, all the talk was of war, of Hitler's 'sabre-rattling' as people kept calling it.

'They're on about sending the kids off – evacuating them,' Fred said one stifling evening as they sat round the table in the dark upstairs room. Eyeing Rachel with richly insincere concern, he said, 'Maybe you should send this one off – keep her safe.'

'No, I'm not going!' The words rushed out of Rachel's mouth before she could stop them. She wasn't being packed off anywhere on his say-so!

'No, Fred – they're only talking about the young children,' Peggy said in a weary voice. Her pregnancy was very much on show now and she was tired and resentful. None of it seemed real to Rachel – not that there was actually a baby in there. 'They don't send away the ones who're out of school.'

How much Fred Horton would love to be rid of her, Rachel thought! He wouldn't have to bother with her then, the cuckoo in his nest who had to be fed and clothed. And now, with another child on the way who was actually his flesh and blood, how very much more she was in the way. But he wasn't going to be able to!

'Huh,' he said. 'I s'pose we'll have to find her a decent job somewhere. There's no need to look at me like that, wench – find some manners!'

Her thoughts must have been written on her glowering face. *Anywhere, so long as it's away from you.*

Within days of her starting at Bird's in August, there was an air-raid practice. When the howling alarm went off, they all trooped down into the enormous basement which was now to be an air-raid shelter.

'Ooh, sign of things to come,' one of the women said as they stood waiting in the dank underground space. 'I hope they're going to bring something down to sit on.'

War was coming daily closer it seemed and the factory was even busier than usual.

'Orders are pouring in,' Miss Pike said. 'You've never seen anything like it. Everyone's stocking up in case of shortages.'

The days were very busy and Rachel found that time flew without her needing to watch the hands of the big clock on the office wall. There was not much time to think of anything else as she put papers and documents in order in the huge filing cabinets. By the end of each day, despite the sensible black lace-up shoes Peggy had insisted on buying, her feet were aching and she was longing to sit down. But she liked the job – it was all right. Anything was better than hanging around at home.

At the end of one afternoon, once she had picked up her things and gone down the stone steps out into the late-afternoon sunshine, she saw a figure standing a little way along Gibb Street. Her heart picked up speed. Tall and thin, leaning up against the wall in a way she instantly recognized: Danny.

As she drew closer along the narrow street amid the other hurrying workers, she saw him spot her. He immediately slouched even more against the wall, as if trying to look nonchalant. He pulled his cap down further and pretended to examine his fingers.

'Hello!' she said. 'What're you doing here?' Surely

there was no other reason he could be here? Was he really waiting for her?

He looked up, solemn-faced. 'Oh, hello,' he said, as if he had not especially been expecting to see her there, though he must have been. Suddenly he dragged his hat from his head. 'All right, are yer?'

'Yes. I'm doing all right. Working here –' She held her arm out towards the Bird's works.

'Auntie said.'

'I'll still be coming to the market Sat'd'ys,' she said.

Danny seemed to take this in, and gave a nod. There was a silence. A stream of other people were moving past them. The silence went on. Danny seemed to have stalled. Why was he here? But Rachel sensed that something had changed. Now that she had left school things felt different. These days, they were both in the grown-up world of work.

'Do you . . .' he brought out eventually. 'D'you like fish and chips?'

'Do I . . . ?' Rachel laughed. 'Yes! Why?'

'Well, I thought we could get some.'

'Haven't you had enough of fish?' she teased.

Danny gave her a look. 'We don't eat it. We just push it about. D'you want some or not?'

Rachel thought. Her mother would be expecting her home for her tea. Mom's moods were very uncertain these days. But Danny meeting her, asking her to come with him – of course she would go with him. Nothing could stop her!

'Yes. All right,' she said.

Without discussing it they headed out to Digbeth, the main road to town. It had been a very hot day and the sun was now sinking low, burnishing all the soot-blackened buildings with copper light. They passed the

Digbeth Institute and the old pub. The street was noisy with trams, trucks and carts and they did not talk. She was just aware of him beside her, fractionally in front, hands in his pockets. He often kept his hands in his pockets, especially his right hand, as if he had hold of something. He had grown fast and was almost a head taller than her now. His head tilted forward slightly as he walked. She looked down at her black lace-up shoes. They might have been practical for standing a lot of the day but they were ugly so-and-sos. But she did not think Danny was paying any attention to her shoes.

Danny had come to find her! That was all she could think. With him beside her, every part of her body felt more awake and alert. He kept swimming in and out of her mind. Sometimes Danny was all she was aware of, the fall of his feet in his big boots, the angle of his thin shoulders, the line of brown hair along his neck beneath his cap, the brown mole just below his left earlobe. While caught up in him she was oblivious to anything else. A moment later the sounds and smells would burst in on her.

The Bullring was busy as ever, all its sights and smells rich to the senses. People milled around the stalls looking for late-in-the-day bargains. A thin fountain of sparks dropped from a knife-grinder's stone. Amid the cries of the fruit and veg vendors echoing along Spiceal Street, she became aware of a deep, ponderous voice raised in song. Glancing back she spotted the man in front of the statue of Nelson, arms held out, his mouth a black, moving shape in his face:

'That day of wrath, that dreadful day,
When heaven and earth shall pass away,
What power shall be the sinner's stay?
How shall he meet that dreadful day?'

They passed further away so that she could no longer make out the words.

'There's going to be a war,' Danny said.

'Yes,' she said. 'People say so. I don't know.'

'I wish I could go,' he said fiercely.

Startled, she turned to him. 'Why? You're too young.'

'I know. I *know*.' He sounded frustrated. He stopped and looked around as if wishing he hadn't spoken. 'Let's get some grub. I'm starving.'

'I've got no pay yet,' she pointed out. 'I've got enough for a few chips.'

Danny gallantly paid for both of them. They carried their newspaper-wrapped bundles, went back down towards the church and found a place to settle close to the church wall. The man seemed to have stopped singing for the moment. Rachel peeled off the outer layer of newspaper before the grease could seep through and laid it on the ground to sit on.

'We can both squeeze on there,' she said. 'I don't want to dirty my skirt.'

They sat very close together, their bent thighs just touching. Rachel pulled her navy work skirt carefully over her knees, but even so they received some disapproving looks from passers-by. As she opened the packet of fish and chips her mouth began to water and she realized she was very hungry. Danny wolfed his down as well.

'Nice,' he said, in between mouthfuls.

'Yeah. Lovely. Ta,' she said. 'That was nice of you.'

Danny turned his head slightly. 'S'all right. I'm getting wages now.'

'So'm I. Or I will be when I get paid anyway.' There was a pause, then she said, 'Have you found your sisters?' She did not really think they could have done or Gladys would surely have told her.

'No,' he said. 'She's trying to find out – Auntie, I mean. She's been round a few places in Birmingham, but no one seems to know.'

He sank into silence again, tapping his feet. He was forever on the move, like something wound up.

'D'you like your job?' she asked.

'Yeah. It's OK. I have to start early – it's hard to get up.'

'Why d'you want to go – to war?'

'I dunno.' Danny stared ahead of him. 'It'd be different from here. Seems like you'd go places. It wouldn't be boring.'

'How d'you know? It might be.'

'Yeah. I s'pose. But it'd be a different sort of boring.' He turned a sudden grin on her.

Rachel laughed. 'I s'pose that's one way of looking at it! Now you say it I wish I could go too.'

They quickly finished the food and threw the paper away.

'Can I walk home with you?' Danny asked.

Rachel was completely taken aback. 'What, you – with me?'

He shrugged. 'Yeah.'

'But it's miles, Danny!' Gladys's house was in Aston – across the other side of town. She knew she ought to catch the bus: she was already going to be much later home than her mother was expecting. But if she could walk with Danny . . .

'Doesn't matter. It's only a few miles out my way. I've got nothing else to do.'

This last comment was a bit of a dampener, but she tried not to mind. 'You're a case, Danny, you are,' she said. But she knew she was blushing. She and Danny could walk together all that way!

They set off in the balmy evening, along Digbeth, out of town.

'This is where we used to live,' she said, leading him into Floodgate Street. She showed him the house in the shadow of the railway arch.

'You lived here?' Danny looked up at the great blue span of the bridge and down at the scruffy little house. He seemed surprised.

'We did. Not any more. Mom always wanted to get out of here to somewhere better.' She thought bitterly of Fred Horton but she didn't say anything.

'It's just like where we lived,' Danny said. He seemed reassured somehow. 'Before our mom passed on, I mean. And it's a bit like Auntie's. We live on a yard – off of Alma Street.'

He sounded very young when he said that. For a moment Rachel felt like taking his hand but she thought better of it. They wound their way through Deritend, across to the Coventry Road.

'D'you remember your mom?' she asked. 'I can only remember my dad a bit – I was very young when he passed on.' *Passed on*. The silence of shame clung to her father's death, but it seemed so remote from her that she scarcely ever thought of it. Peggy never mentioned him.

'Course I can remember,' Danny said, so fiercely that Rachel was taken aback. 'She was the best, our mom. I'd never forget her.'

'What was she like?' she asked, encouraged that he seemed so keen to talk.

'Well, she was – you know – a proper mom. Nice and kind. It was the old man who spoiled everything. He always did, the drunken sod.'

Rachel remembered the frightening man who had dragged Danny away all those years ago.

100

'Have you seen him? Since you came back, I mean?'

'No,' Danny almost shouted. 'And I don't want to! I'll kill 'im if I set eyes on 'im – I swear to God I'll finish 'im off!'

'I don't blame you,' she said gently.

'Don't you?' He gave her a sharp look.

She returned his gaze, steadily. 'No. I don't.'

He made a sound of annoyance. 'What would you know, any road?'

'I don't know,' she said carefully. 'But I don't blame you, that's all.'

There in the street, on some dusty bit of the Coventry Road, he stopped abruptly and turned to her.

'I want to show you summat.' His hand was gripping the thing in his pocket, whatever it was, and he seemed unsure whether to bring it out.

'What?' she said, trying to sound encouraging.

Danny hesitated for a moment, his eyes wide, searching her face as if to be sure of something.

'Come over 'ere.'

They were at the corner of a road with rows of houses. Leaning up against the low wall, Danny pulled from his pocket a cheap little notebook with a worn, dark green cover. The spine of it had been reinforced with a strip of black cloth about an inch wide, glued round it.

'I found this in the home,' he said. 'There was a cupboard, with a few old books in and this fell out from under them when I was having a look. I tore out the pages which had writing on.'

Rachel watched, feeling it better not to say anything. Danny opened it and showed her, turning the pages which were worn soft and old. Each page was covered with little drawings, done with a not very sharp pencil, many of them smudged. The drawings weren't very good, but over and over again she saw the same thing. There was a boy in a hat – it looked like a straw hat – pulled down low, wearing raggedy trousers and no shoes. At his side was a little dog with perky ears, one sticking up, the other lying down. Half of the dog's face was black, the other white, and he had a black splotch on the back of his otherwise white body. The boy and the dog both had big, sad eyes. Looking at them as Danny turned the pages, Rachel felt herself react in a strange way. Something about the boy and the dog – even badly drawn – tugged at her. She felt for them, tenderness for their sweetness. It was as if she fell in love with a cartoon boy and a daft-looking dog. Tears prickled in her eyes.

'Who are they?' she asked, trying to make her voice sound normal.

'Jack and Patch,' Danny said, in a voice which made it sound as if he was talking about characters he knew well. 'Patch is the dog,' he added, unnecessarily.

She could hardly find words for him. Looking up at him, she could not hide the tears in her eyes. 'They're lovely, Danny. Did you do them?'

She saw him take in her reaction, a flare of feeling in his eyes as if something had kindled inside him.

'Yeah. I kept them with me. If anyone'd tried to take it off me I'd've laid 'em out. I had to once – they left me alone after that. Look – d'you like this one?'

He found a page where Jack and Patch were standing side by side, seen from behind, Patch's tail tipped with black and curving over his back. All she could see beyond were squiggles.

'Jack and Patch at the seaside,' he said, his voice full of proud longing.

'Oh – yes!' she said. 'That's the sea, is it? Have you ever seen the sea? I've never.'

'Mom and Dad took us once,' he said. He closed the book again and slid it into his pocket, not removing his hand, as if he had to check constantly that it was safe. 'It was before our Amy come along. Our mom'd had our brother, William. He died – he was only a week old. And we went on a trip – to perk her up, I think. Dad decided we would. It was the best thing he ever did. We got on a train at Snow Hill and we went all the way down south to the sea. It was magic.' There was a smile in his voice even though it did not quite reach his face. 'I couldn't tell you where it was now, but it was the best thing ever. The sun was hot and Jess and Rose and me all went in the sea. And Dad was all right, that day. It made our mom smile. I never knew there were places like that.'

He stopped suddenly as if he was embarrassed or had just run out of words. Turning towards her, for a tense second he stood looking at her. She wasn't sure what she could see in his face, whether he was angry even. Had she said something wrong? He was breathing fast, as if full of emotion. With a force which took her by surprise, he stepped towards her and wrapped his arms roughly around her, pulling her close. Rachel hardly dared breathe. She was so taken aback she could think of nothing to do or say and she did not have time to relax in his arms or think clearly about what was happening. She was sure she could feel the violent beat of his heart, though she couldn't be sure that it was not her own.

Before she could return the embrace he let her go, without speaking. They walked the rest of the way to Hay Mills in a silence that was full of feeling but not uncomfortable. She felt bound to him, as if there was a cord between them.

'This is where I live,' she said at last, pointing at HORTON'S DRAPERS & HABERDASHERS. 'Don't come in,' she said. 'My stepdad's there.'

Danny looked up at the building as he had at the house in Floodgate Street. 'What's he like – your stepdad?'

Rachel wrinkled her nose, shrugging. 'All right. I s'pose.'

Danny seemed to understand. 'Can we . . .' he began, his strong hands in front of him, moving uncertainly. 'Can I come and meet you again?'

She gave him a smile. 'Yes,' she said. Yes didn't seem enough to say, but it was all she meant. She wondered for a second how she looked to him, standing there in her new work clothes, blue skirt, white blouse, her shoulder-length hair pinned back at one side.

He smiled. A happy smile. 'I've . . .' He stopped. 'Come and see me and Auntie one day? At home, like?'

Rachel nodded. 'If you like.' But she was pleased, fizzing inside.

Danny kept looking at her. He seemed to find it hard to leave, and eventually began walking backwards before he turned away. 'All right. See yer soon.'

She watched him walk back along the road and wondered if he would catch a bus or walk all the way. She could still feel the force of need in his arms as he held her to him, and clasped the little notebook in his pocket.

Turning to the house, she was caught by another emotion – dread. She was so late getting home! There would be trouble. But she didn't care in the slightest. All she cared about was Danny.

Twelve

September 1939

'Rachel?'

She woke, startled, from a deep sleep, hearing her stepfather's voice through the bedroom door, quavery with panic.

'Rachel – it's your mother. The pains've started. I'm going for Miss Lofthus, I think her name is . . .'

Wide awake now, she almost fell out of bed. Opening the bedroom door, she heard a muffled groan from the other end of the house. It was disturbing – she did not know anything much about babies being born.

'You stay with her,' Fred instructed. There was no arguing, though the idea of being left on her own with these strange sounds made her legs turn to jelly.

He was off down the stairs. Rachel crept along the landing and stood outside her mother and Fred's bedroom door. She heard nothing for a few moments, then there was a low whimper and she heard her mother say, 'Oh dear God.'

Trembling, she tapped on the door and went in. A dim light glowed on the bedside table. All she could see in the bed was a humped shape under the bedclothes. As she went close she saw that Peggy was facing down onto the mattress, on all fours in the bed. This was even more disconcerting.

'Mom? You all right?'

Peggy turned her head. Her hair was hanging loose, unbrushed in a wild, frizzy mass. There was a tense expression on her face as if she was listening to some other sound that Rachel could not hear. 'Yes . . . I'll be . . . Oh!' she cried. As the wave of pain began to sweep across her she gasped, 'Go down and put the kettle on – and a pan of water . . .'

Rachel dashed out to obey as the unnerving groaning sounds began to take over, relieved to be out of the fuggy bedroom and down in the back kitchen out of earshot. She filled the kettle and the biggest pan she could find, lit the gas under them and stood, her heart pounding, willing Fred to come back.

'What's going on?'

Sidney's voice startled her horribly. He was at the kitchen door, bare from the waist up, his hair rumpled. She shrank away from his fishy white body with the shadow of thick hair on his chest, not even looking at him properly.

'It's my mother. She's having the baby.'

Sidney grunted. 'Oh Christ . . .' He slouched off upstairs again.

Rachel listened to the kettle's whisper, wondering what was supposed to happen next. The last thing she wanted was to go upstairs herself.

Eventually she heard the front door open, and the sound of voices. As Fred Horton led Mrs Lofthus up the stairs, she heard the woman say, rather grumpily, 'Let's hope it'll be on its way very soon. It's not as if it's her first, is it?'

It was only then that Rachel fully took in that a new person was about to arrive in the house.

It felt like an endless night. Contrary to what Mrs Lofthus had predicted, the baby was not in a hurry to be born. Fred Horton spent the night in the parlour, alternately smoking and snoozing and demanding cups of tea. Rachel stayed almost all the time in the back kitchen. Her job became that of supplying tea to Fred and Mrs Lofthus, a heavy woman with thick chins and swollen ankles who stayed on the chair by the bed, mostly dozing with her head on her chest despite the groans of pain from beside her.

The first time Rachel crept upstairs and into the bedroom carrying a cup and saucer, she found Mrs Lofthus swigging out of a little brown bottle which she hurriedly corked and slipped into the pocket of her vast, grubby-looking apron. Over the bodily smells in the room was a heady reek of spirits.

'Oh!' Mrs Lofthus exclaimed. 'You startled me, you did.' She narrowed her eyes under their bushy brows. 'What's that you got?'

'A cup of tea for you,' Rachel said.

'Ah – well, I could do with that,' Mrs Lofthus said, pulling herself more upright. 'Got plenty of sugar in, has it?'

'Yes,' Rachel fibbed. She'd put half a spoon in.

'Anything to eat? I could do with a bite to eat, bab,' she wheedled. 'Sitting up all night like this.'

'I'll look,' Rachel said. Peggy started to stir then, as if another of the pains was beginning, and Rachel hurried away out of the room. As she did so, she heard Mrs Lofthus say, 'That's it – come on, hurry along now will yer, madam. Push the thing out and let's get it over with.'

By the time a thin dawn light appeared there was still no sign of the baby. On and on it went as the sun rose and the day grew warm and fine. Fred moved restlessly in and out of the shop, even though it was a Sunday.

'I can't stand all this waiting,' he said to Rachel as their paths crossed. 'When's it going to end? Alice didn't take long.' He was biting at his fingers and smoking one cigarette after another. 'Oh my word, I do hope she's going to be all right.'

Rachel tidied the kitchen, trying to keep busy and fill her mind with something other than her mother's struggles. She thought about Danny, about the drawings in the notebook. She felt the emotional tug of them again as if they were the key to understanding Danny. The boy in the drawings, Jack, had looked solitary but happy. She wondered why Danny had drawn him wearing a straw hat.

As the morning progressed the sounds from upstairs became more intense. By midday, sitting at the kitchen table muzzy-headed with exhaustion, Rachel heard a sound which made her heart crash in her chest: the cracked, outraged cry of a newborn baby. She sat up straight with astonishment. The next moment she heard Fred's feet pounding up the stairs, but she waited for a little while before following him.

Knocking on the door, she walked in to find Fred perched on the side of the bed, his eyes looking wet and adoring as Peggy lay back, utterly spent, with the little wrapped bundle in her arms. Rachel stalled at the door, immediately feeling as if she was intruding.

'A little wench,' Miss Lofthus said, seeing her. Her voice sounded distinctly slurred. 'All well with her – though she took her time, that one did.'

'Oh, my dear,' Fred was saying. 'My poor little pigeon –' He laid his arm protectively round Peggy's head, with her damp hair plastered down on it.

'Go and see yer sister then,' Miss Lofthus said to Rachel, since no one else took any notice. 'And then, bab, I'll need more water. There's a bit to do yet. And another cup of tea wouldn't go amiss.'

Rachel went and peered at the tiny pink face of the baby. She was lying with her eyes closed, and very still.

'Say hello to your little sister,' Fred said. 'This is Cynthia. A proper little princess, that's what she is.'

Rachel thought she looked more like a broiled rabbit. Her mother half-opened her eyes for a moment and murmured something before closing them again.

Rachel slipped away. At the door she looked back at the three of them: Fred, her mother and this new being who had arrived. Fred Horton had his own daughter now. There they were, all together in a perfect triangle. Feeling cold and tired she went downstairs to boil yet more water.

It felt as if she had been imprisoned in the house for days. She stepped out into the scrubby backyard and immediately heard voices, a gaggle of the neighbours over the wall, all talking excitedly. The air smelled mouth-wateringly of Sunday dinners roasting.

The woman next door leaned over the wall and called to her, 'How's your mother, Rachel – did I hear summat from in there?'

'She's all right, ta, Mrs Hodge,' Rachel said, squinting in the sudden light. Shyly she added, 'She's had the babby – a little girl.'

'Ooh, has she?' Mrs Hodge, a lean, handsome, copper-haired woman, called over her shoulder to the others, 'Hear that? A new babby next door – a girl!'

Everyone made noises of approval. There was talk of wetting babies' heads.

'What a day to arrive!' Mr Hodge said, appearing beside his wife, blonde and pink skinned. Rachel never thought they looked well suited: what with her hair, they clashed, colour-wise.

'How d'you mean?' Rachel asked. She felt stupid with tiredness, as if nothing quite made sense. She had been in another world.

'Have you not heard, bab?' Mrs Hodge said. 'Oh my word, I s'pose you'll've missed it. We're at war! Eleven o'clock – on the wireless – our Mr Chamberlain. He said if the Germans dain't clear out of Poland we'd be at war and they ain't – so we're at war.'

Rachel ran back inside and up the stairs.

'We're at war!' she cried into the thick air of the bedroom. 'They said next door. The war's started – Mr Chamberlain said!'

Miss Lofthus was wringing out a cloth over a bowl. Peggy raised her head from the pillow for a second.

'Oh, Lord above,' she said.

'Rach – hang on, wait for me!'

Lilian came charging along as Rachel set out for work a few days later on a cool, misty morning. Her cardigan was flying open and her hair already working its way out of the coil of a bun she had attempted to pin it back into. Rachel smiled, seeing her skinny friend tearing along. Lilian grabbed Rachel's arm and clung onto her.

'My God, it's good to see you!' she cried.

Rachel smiled, surprised. 'What's up with you?' she said as they walked up the Coventry Road amid the other hurrying morning workers.

'Hey –' Lilian didn't answer the question straight away. 'Has your mom had the babby yet? She must've by now?'

'Yeah,' Rachel said.

'Well, you don't sound very excited. When Bobby was born I thought he was the best thing ever! What is it then?'

'It's a baby,' Rachel said flatly.

'*Rach!*' Lilian tugged on her arm.

'All right – it's a girl. Cissy. Well, Cynthia but they call her Cissy all the time. She's little, she's got two arms and two legs and two of everything else except a head –'

'What about nose?'

'One nose. And one hell of a gob – she never stops blarting. *Wah wah wah* all flaming day – and night.'

These days Rachel felt even more pushed away by her mother, who existed walled in by napkins and the baby sucking away at her, and Cissy's yowling.

'Oh, Rach, you're awful – I bet she's lovely.'

'She's all right,' Rachel conceded. 'When she's asleep.' She did stand sometimes and marvel at the little girl's flickering eyelids and her little sucking mouth. She'd nothing against Cissy. She was a sweet little thing. But what she couldn't stand was the way Fred slobbered over the baby. 'Ooh, look at my little princess – the most beautiful thing in the world – ooh what a little darling.' It was enough to make you sick.

'Rach,' Lilian was saying, still clinging urgently to her arm. 'I've got to get out of this job. It's going to drive me out of my wits I'm so bored. What can I do?'

'I thought you said they were nice?'

'They are, but I don't know why I went to do it – I never liked arithmetic or numbers or anything when we were at school. And there's only so much you want to know about cricket bats. The firm's all right, it's the *job* – it'd be the same wherever I was. And now with the war and everything . . .'

There were signs of it everywhere, the changes that had come one by one. There were sandbags stacked up all over the place which all the dogs seemed to enjoy cocking their legs against, silvery barrage balloons tugging on their cables above the city and white-painted edges along the pavements to make it safer in the dark. Fred was doing a roaring trade in blackout material and it took them ages every evening, blacking out the house so that not a crack of light showed from any window. Posters were appearing with urgent messages on them: 'FREEDOM IS IN PERIL, DEFEND IT WITH ALL YOUR MIGHT!'

'Well, there're jobs going,' Rachel said. 'What with the lads joining up. Why don't you come and work at Bird's?'

'Could I, d'you think? Oh, Rach, I'd work anywhere almost, except doing this.'

'I'll ask for you. You'd be in the factory, I expect – we're ever so busy,' she added importantly.

Within a fortnight, Lilian was established in the basement of the Devonshire Works where the packing was done. She was happy enough.

'They keep telling me the custard's made up at the top,' she told Rachel at the end of the first day. 'You know, the powder and that. And it comes down to us. I keep thinking there's this big river of custard pouring down the stairs!'

Rachel laughed. 'Think of it – all bright yellow!'

'Oh, it's so much better here,' Lilian said, 'instead of

being in that poky little office where I was. Even if everything is covered in yellow dust! We can have a chat and a laugh here. And the wages aren't much different anyway.'

Rachel was very happy to have Lilian around. But there was one problem. Lilian expected that every day the two of them would meet after work and go home together, if their shift patterns allowed it. But some days, every now and then, Rachel came out of work to find Danny waiting for her.

'The thing is, Lily, he waits for me to walk me home when he can,' she explained to her friend.

'Oh, I see,' Lilian said rather huffily. 'So you're going to ditch me again for some boy . . . It's that market boy, isn't it? The one with the eyes.'

Rachel blushed. 'I like him, Lily. There's summat about him.'

'Well, I don't want to play gooseberry,' Lilian said. 'If he turns up I'll clear off and leave you to it.'

Rachel gave her a playful punch on the shoulder. 'Ta, Lily. You're a pal. He's quite shy, see, and it's easier if it's just me and him.'

'I get the message,' Lilian said, long-sufferingly. 'So –' She looked at Rachel with a mischievous glint in her eye. 'Danny boy, eh?'

III

Thirteen

April 1940

All these months it had felt as if they were waiting for it to begin properly. The Phoney War, as it came to be called, went on all through that winter. The Russians were fighting across Finland and Poland; the Germans – 'the forces of darkness', Fred Horton called them – forcing their way into country after country: first Poland, now Denmark and Norway. There seemed to be nothing that would stop them.

Rachel had seen her mother become more and more nervous as the news piled upon them. The Germans appeared to be drawing daily closer. With the new baby she seemed to feel everything more intensely.

'Don't you worry, Peggy,' Fred kept trying to reassure her. 'We've got our cellar if anything happens and it's quite cosy down there. We'll be quite safe.'

'Not if they invade we won't!' Peggy sobbed, cradling Cissy in her arms and looking woefully down at her. 'They'll soon have us surrounded! And it's bad enough stumbling about in the dark and having all this stuff stuck across the windows making you think of bombs falling on us every time you look out. And as for those horrible masks! Oh, my little darling, what kind of a world have I brought you into?'

Rachel held back from reminding her mother that she had once upon a time brought her into the world as well and that she was still here. But Peggy was also strangely more upset that Sidney Horton had been called up than his father was. She had thought that his job might be a reserved occupation, but apparently it was not. Sidney who was twenty-one had to go.

'These poor boys,' Peggy said. 'It's all wrong. It's just like the last time. This should never have happened again – it's wicked, that's what it is. Just like poor James. And what good did it do anyone?'

Rachel had been rather enjoying the possibility that Sidney might meet with physical misfortune somewhere along the line – a serious injury at the least. And she realized that what was really upsetting her mother was the memory of her own brother, James, who had died in France. All Peggy's emotions seemed to be heightened and she went to pieces at the slightest thing. Rachel wondered what had happened to the mother she used to know who had seemed strong enough to stand up to anything.

The first time she visited Gladys's and Danny's house was a Sunday afternoon in April. As she turned up at the Rag Market week after week to help Gladys out and see Danny as often as possible, gradually they had all got used to each other. Gladys now seemed to take it for granted that she would be around.

'Come and have a cup of tea with us tomorrow, bab, will you?' Gladys invited while they were in the market. 'I'm having a little do for my pal Dolly. It's her birthday.'

Rachel was excited to be asked. Only slowly had she come to realize how alone in the world Gladys was.

She was such a strong, attractive personality, so capable and friendly, that Rachel had somehow imagined that she had a home full of family and a husband, even though she knew full well that Gladys was a widow. It sounded as if her friend Dolly was very important to her and she was happy to be included.

'Get the number six tram, then walk along to Summer Lane,' Danny said, as Gladys moved away and picked up a man's jacket to inspect it. 'We're in Alma Street – a bit further along.'

'Come and see the palm trees swaying,' Gladys sang over her shoulder. She smiled at Rachel's baffled expression. 'It's a song, bab –' She continued singing, her voice deep and strong:

' . . . See the folks a-singing at the "Salutation",
No snow in Snow Hill,
There's no need to catch a train,
To your southern home where the weather is warm,
It's always summer in Summer Lane!'

She finished off, laughing, as a couple of other people joined in beside her and there was clapping. Gladys took a joking bow.

'So you get the tram. Get off by the nail works and Danny'll meet you – oh yes, you will, Danny – about three, all right?'

When she arrived in Summer Lane she was still half-expecting to see palm trees but this illusion was quickly dispelled. Danny was waiting when she got off the tram and she saw his grin as he leaned against a wall. They were both growing up, she could feel it. Danny had turned sixteen and he was taller, broader in the shoulders, like a man. And she sensed that he looked at her more as a man would look. She was wearing a new pale pink frock that Peggy had made for her and some white shoes, her hair, now shoulder length, neatly pinned back each side. She hoped Danny would like the way she looked and when she saw his eyes drinking in the sight of her, she could see that he did.

'Hello you,' she said shyly, and the way he smiled back, his cheeks turning pink, she realized how much small things pleased him, and that he was happy to see her. 'You gunna show me the way then?'

'Come on then,' he said.

Summer Lane, a shabby vista, stretched ahead of them, lined with factories, warehouses and shops, with warrens of houses packed everywhere in between. The smell of coal smoke was very strong for it was a breezeless, heavy day, the sun straining to shine through pale clouds. The street was crowded with children who'd all been turfed out to give their weary moms and dads some peace. Rachel had to dodge to get out of the way of kids whirling round the lamps on remnants of rope or dashing back and forth with hoops or makeshift carts. A lad was scooping horse muck into a bucket with a wafer of plywood and seemed to be falling out with another who wished he had got there first. The gutters were still wet and mucky from recent rain.

'What's that – Crocodile Works?' Rachel asked, seeing the imposing, brick-faced works as they progressed along Alma Street. 'Don't tell me they make crocodiles!'

Danny chuckled. 'Nah – knives and such. Bayonets – and big machete-type things.' Further along, he said, 'Here – in here.'

He led her up an entry and into a yard of five houses, three of them backing onto the houses facing the street, the other two onto a wall which divided the yard from a similar one next door. At the far end was the higher wall of a factory. It was very like the yard where they had had to go round to the toilet in Floodgate Street, only wider, and less squalid. Rachel looked around. The toilets and miskins, or dustbins, were at the far end. In the middle of the yard were both a lamp and a common tap, dripping into a drain in the ground. The blue bricks of the yard were swept very clean – she could see where the bristles of the brush had passed over the muddiest patch near the tap. A hard-faced woman with a scarf on her head was standing in her doorway, watching as they passed.

'Got yerself a girlfriend then, Danny?' she said. When Danny didn't answer she added, 'Not got a tongue in your head then, lad?'

'That's Ma Jackman, lives next door,' he whispered. 'Nosey old bag she is.'

Rachel giggled.

Gladys lived at number three of the five houses in the back court. Hers was in the corner, the last in the row backing onto the houses facing the street. When they got to the door there seemed to be a crowd inside and Danny said:

'Oh – they've got started then. This lot weren't here when I went out!'

There was a low cheer as he and Rachel came in the door. Round the table in the middle of the room, on which sat a large cake, was a crowd of people: one a dark-haired, pretty woman, who Rachel realized must be Dolly, and a gaggle of blond-haired little boys who at first sight all looked the same. Rachel made out Gladys among them, who raised an arm in greeting.

'Come on in, bab, if you can get in!'

Gladys was wearing a short-sleeved shirtwaister frock in a soft sage green with white spots which showed off her magnificent curves. It must have been her best dress, Rachel thought, and it made her look younger suddenly, though she still had her hair plaited and coiled up in its rather old-fashioned style. It was the first time Rachel had seen Gladys not dressed in black or without her arms covered. They were pink and plump and comfortable-looking, though her hands were work-worn.

'It's our Mom's birthday!' One of the little boys announced as Rachel and Danny stepped into the little downstairs room. 'It were yesterday!' He seemed very excited. 'There's cake – look!'

Rachel looked around her in wonder. As she remembered the poor, bare house in Floodgate Street – how long ago that seemed now – Gladys's downstairs room was another world. It was like walking into a cosy, immaculately clean little palace, Rachel thought. The walls were painted pale blue and there were neatly tied curtains in the window in navy-and-white gingham. The range was polished to a black sheen with well-scrubbed pans arranged on it, though thankfully, in this warmth, it did not seem to be lit. All along the mantelpiece, over which was draped a cheerful piece of crimson, flowery cloth, was an array of knick-knacks: jugs and ornaments, china animals and candlesticks, a wooden-cased clock and two palm crosses atilt in a pewter cup. Rachel saw a china country cottage which also seemed to be a teapot and at the far end was a photograph in a frame. Despite the reflected light on the glass she could just make out the man in it, who she realized must have been Gladys's husband. On a dark sideboard on the left-hand wall, she saw a wireless with a polished wooden case.

'So you're the famous Rachel – we've heard all about you,' the other woman said. She was slender and energetic-looking with black wavy hair pinned back from her face and lively brown eyes. She was so pretty! Rachel thought, especially with the touch of red lipstick which matched the flowers in her frock. Rachel liked her straight away.

'Don't tease her, Dolly!' These words came from a stocky, jolly-looking man sitting near the range. For a moment Rachel wondered if he was the woman's father, but then she saw that he must be her husband. He had a very pink face and the blond hair which he seemed to have passed on to every one of his sons, though his own hair was now faded almost to grey, as was his bushy moustache. He sat in his braces, leaning forward on his thighs, a cigarette in one hand. 'Look. You're making the wench blush. But then, as we know –' He tapped his bulbous nose with the hand holding the cigarette so that ash dropped down on his trousers. Curses followed.

'Mo!' Dolly cried, exasperated. 'You'll have holes in those trousers again! Here – pass me one ...' She reached for the packet of cigarettes and lit up. 'Ooh – and look at all this. This is so nice of you, Glad!'

Gladys waved this away as if to say it was nothing.

'As I was saying,' Mo addressed Rachel, with dignity. 'You're like a film star around 'ere – least you'd think so, the way Danny carries on.'

Rachel blushed even more. What on earth was he talking about?

'Now who's teasing her, Mo?' Gladys said. 'Come on – time for some char.'

'Yes,' Dolly added. 'And you boys can keep yer

thieving little mitts off that cake 'til anyone says you can have some or I'll send you out to play up the far end – got it?'

There was a big teapot on the table covered with a crocheted cosy in varying shades of green. Beside it, a jug full of pink sweet williams and the cake with white icing, ringed with glacé cherries. The little boys – Rachel counted five of them, in descending size – were all swarming round it. Danny pointed them out and told her their names – Eric, Wally, Reggie, Jonny, Fred the youngest, only just able to stand – but by the end of the afternoon she still could not tell which of the elder four was which.

'Hands behind yer backs,' Dolly ordered. 'Wally – if I have to say it once more, you're out!'

'I've been saving my rations,' Gladys said, smiling as she poured tea into pretty china cups, with a pattern of pink dog roses winding round each. 'I've had those bits of cherry since before the war – I knew they'd come in useful one day and it's time we had an excuse for a get-together. Come on – sit down – those who can find a chair.'

'Not you, Reggie –' His father hoicked him from the seat of a chair by one ear. 'Age before impudence.'

Danny and Rachel sat on a couple of stools just inside the door. Danny leaned over and whispered close to her ear, 'Dolly is Auntie's best friend.' Rachel smiled and nodded. She could already see that.

Danny explained that Mo's real name was George but he was always called Mo after their surname, Morrison. And that the pair of them had been good friends to Gladys, ever since she moved into the yard nearly twenty years ago. They seemed very nice, Rachel thought. Dolly, Danny whispered, was half-Italian. Rachel could see why Dolly and Gladys had been drawn together as friends, each with their dark, interesting looks. Of the two, Dolly was the more straightforwardly pretty with her long black hair and dancing eyes. Rachel already felt at home with them all. She gazed round at the scrubbed tiles of the floor, the neat cleanness of the few plates on the shelves and the dark red chenille cloth on the table. She looked up again at the photograph, which she now noticed had black crêpe arranged lovingly around it. From it smiled the face of a thin, dark-haired man. She could not make out the face very well. It did not seem to stand out. She found herself wondering what sort of man had been married to Gladys.

Before anyone could say anything else, a little lad about seven years old with curly red hair and freckles all over his nose appeared in the doorway, holding in his arms what appeared to be a round bundle of newspaper tied with string. At first he did not seem to notice all the other people in the room.

'Mrs Poulter,' he gabbled urgently, 'can I ask Danny . . .' He spotted Danny then, by the door. 'Danny – you gonna come and play out? I've gorra new football, our dad's done it and everyone's out the front and they want yer to come . . .'

The boy stopped, at last, taking in the unusual sight inside. He stared at Rachel. He stared even more at the cake, with wide eyes, a gaze which he then turned with desperate appeal on Gladys.

'He's not coming out for a while yet, Ernie,' Gladys said. 'We're just having a bit of tea.'

Rachel could almost see the saliva rising in the boy's mouth.

'I'll come out a bit later, Ern,' Danny told him.

The four older Morrison boys were shoulder to shoulder in front of the cake as if guarding it with their lives.

'Oh, go on, let him have a bit,' Dolly said, laughing. To Rachel she added, 'He ain't even from this yard, he's from next door!'

Gladys winked at Ernie. 'Oh ar – I s'pect we can spare you a bit, lad. You come back in a few minutes when I've cut the cake and you can have a little slice.'

'Ooh, ta, Mrs Poulter!' He tore away again on skinny legs. Rachel was amazed. It was impossible to imagine her own mother sharing what she had with anyone who was not her own. And she liked the friendly, easy feeling between Gladys and Dolly and Mo Morrison.

'Well, many happy returns, Dolly,' Gladys said when she had poured the tea and they had stirred in a tiny ration of sugar. She raised her teacup as if in a toast.

'Happy birthday!' everyone chorused.

Dolly blushed and laughed. 'Oh, ta all of you – stop it, I'm starting to fill up!' Rachel saw she had tears in her eyes and she wiped them, laughing at herself at the same time. 'This is nice, Glad – and look at your cake.'

Gladys didn't seem to know what to say and Danny called out, 'So, when are we going to eat some of it then?'

'Oi you!' Gladys retorted, pointing the knife at him. 'Just remember, I've know you since you was in napkins,' she added sternly.

As if by some form of mind-reading, as soon as she put the blade of the knife to the top of the cake, Ernie's ginger head was back at the door, accompanied by a whole gaggle of small children, all eagerly trying to see in, elbowing each other and giggling.

'Oi, you lot!' Mo boomed at them. 'What d'yer think you're all doing 'ere – eh? Clear off, the lot of yer!'

Gladys looked up, a moment's dismay turning to amusement.

'Brought a few pals, 'ave yer, Ernie? Did I say the whole street was invited?' She waited, smiling at them. They all tittered and looked hopeful.

'Well – you've got quite a party now, Dolly – shall we give 'em some cake? We can't eat all this on our own, can we? Right – now you just hang on, you lot, 'til we've had some.'

Once she had given a slice of sponge to everyone in the room, she turned to the excited crowd at the door. 'Right – one at a time – hold yer hands out. Then out yer go, and there won't be no more, right?'

Soon a sticky procession of children had passed through the room and out again, nuzzling their faces into their hands ecstatically to eat the finger of pale yellow cake. Their laughter floated in from outside.

'Well – there you are, Dolly,' Gladys said. 'You've made a lot of people very happy on your birthday.'

Dolly laughed, still eating. 'Little sods,' she said, indistinctly.

'Mrs Poulter?' Rachel said a little later, choosing a moment when everyone else was talking. She moved her stool closer to speak to Gladys and Danny followed.

'Why don't you just call me Auntie?' Gladys suggested. 'It makes me feel peculiar you calling me Mrs Poulter all the time.'

Rachel smiled. 'If that's all right.' She was delighted, loving Gladys's approval and acceptance. 'I was just wondering why Danny didn't just come and live with you – after his mother, well, passed away?'

Gladys gave a harsh laugh. 'Me? I'll tell you why, wench. Danny's father, Wilf – oh, he hated me like

127

poison. I could see the way he was and I'd tell him so. I know he was never the same when he came back from France – but he was alive, which was more than any of 'em. Instead of coming back and making a life, all he could think of was the bottle. Downhill all the way, he was. The way he treated Mary – I'd've happily seen him hang and that's the truth.'

Rachel saw that Danny was looking down into his lap and she was sorry that she had raised the question.

'If my poor sister Mary hadn't gone the way she did, things would've been different, I'd've seen to that, somehow – you know, made sure Danny and the others were all right, whatever their father got up to. But Wilf Booker would've drowned those children rather than let them come anywhere near me. That's the sort of man he was. And God alone knows where he's gone . . .' She shook her head. 'I'm sorry, Danny – I'd like to be able to speak better of your father but you know it's the truth.'

Danny nodded, looking glum.

'That's enough of that anyway,' Gladys said. 'What's done's done. Want another bit, Dolly?' She reached to cut the last bits of cake.

'Sorry,' Rachel whispered to Danny, 'didn't mean to be nosey.'

'S'all right,' he said, but he couldn't quite meet her eyes at that moment. Rachel looked around the room, watching Gladys and Dolly chatting easily, Dolly smoking away and Mo falling into a snooze in the best chair. Dolly looked affectionately at him.

'They've been drilling up the park,' she said. 'Poor old sod, it's taken it out of him. They've got uniforms at last though!'

Rachel realized, as they talked, that they meant the

LDV or Home Guard. She also noticed again that Dolly was a good deal younger than her husband.

Now the last of the cake had been polished off, their boys had all run outside and peace descended on the room. Danny looked round at Rachel, reached out his hand and took hers for a moment, giving it a squeeze. And at that moment Rachel thought there could not be anyone in the world happier than she was.

It was already growing dark when Danny walked her back to the tram stop. Once the Morrisons drifted off home and the afternoon turned chilly, Gladys closed the door and lit the fire and the lamps. The room became warm and fuggy. While she reminisced about Danny when he was very small and the mischief he used to get up to, Danny sat leaning forward, elbows on his thighs, looking up sometimes with a shy delight that filled Rachel with tender emotions.

Now, they walked together, as they had done over the past few months, whenever they could manage. But tonight there was an extra feeling between them.

They passed along the side street off Summer Lane. Now it was dusk they had to strain to make out each other's faces. Cooking smells and smoke filled the air.

After the happy afternoon, silence grew between them suddenly.

'Today was the best,' Danny said eventually. He added, ''Cause you came.'

She flicked a smile sideways at him. 'I really liked it. Your auntie's ever so nice.'

Danny nodded, pleased. 'Yeah.'

It felt as if the walk was not long enough. As soon as they reached the end of the street they would be almost at the tram stop. Danny slowed to a halt, near the opening into an alley between two factory buildings.

'C'm'ere – will yer?' He beckoned her into the shelter between the walls. They stood awkwardly close together for a moment, until their arms wrapped round each other and they were standing looking into each other's faces. Rachel could just see the lustre of Danny's eyes in the gloom and the shape of his face. He was quiet and serious. She felt his lean, skinny body close to her, marvelling at how strong he felt while looking so slight. One of his hands stroked tentatively up and down her back.

'You're lovely, you are,' he said. 'Can I kiss yer, Rach?' His voice was uncertain.

She nodded her head. Her heart was pounding: Danny, so close to her, in her arms. She held him, feeling so much for him. She closed her eyes as their lips met, clumsily, neither quite sure what to do, feeling their way into their first kiss in the dark chill of the evening. She felt the tickle of his tongue against her lips and for a few minutes they explored each other before drawing apart. Rachel knew she ought to get home.

They looked into each other's eyes, holding on for a moment. Rachel smiled.

'What would Jack and Patch think?' she said.

Danny grinned. 'Oh, they'd be happy as anything.'

'I'll have to go,' she said. Danny took her arm as they moved out to the street again. At the tram stop, he turned and took each of her hands in his. 'Will you be my girl?'

In the gloom, as the tram came rocking and clanking towards them, she nodded her head.

Fourteen

June 1940

She would never forget the sight of Danny's face as she stepped out of the Bird's that Friday night. He came tearing towards her, trouser legs flapping round his skinny legs, his face full of tense excitement.

'What's going on?' she said, amused, as he skidded to a halt.

'Auntie's had a letter,' he panted. 'From . . . I dunno who from. It's my sisters – they're coming next week! They're coming back! And Auntie wants you to—'

'Your sisters?' Rachel could hardly take all this in. 'But where are they?'

'Somewhere down south.' Danny's voice had thickened and Rachel realized with a pang that her tough boy was fighting back tears. 'They're coming up on the train. Auntie's to meet them.'

'Oh, Danny, that's wonderful,' she said softly, smiling up at him. 'You'll have some of your family back together again.'

'You will come – tomorrow, won't yer?' he insisted. 'Auntie says . . . Well, she says you're almost part of the family, and what with them being girls and everything . . .'

Rachel felt honoured. A warmth spread through her.

Part of the family! It felt true – things had changed over these months.

'You've made a big difference to our Danny,' Gladys said to her one day, while they were working together on the market. 'I could hardly get a word out of him when he first came back. Now the floodgates've opened!'

Since their first kiss, Danny seemed hardly able to let go of her whenever they were together. He wanted to be close to her, feeling her touch. Rachel basked in his adoration, in the need he had for her. No one in her life had ever wanted her the way Danny did and she adored him back. They were completely caught up in each other. She thought of him constantly, aching to be near him whenever they were apart. And she felt very happy and gratified that Gladys wanted her to be there to meet Danny's sisters. It also dawned on her that Gladys, though she always seemed capable of everything, might be nervous about welcoming back these girls who they had not seen for so long.

'Course I will,' she said.

Rachel stepped from the glare of the boiling afternoon into the shade of the entry off Alma Street. Even in this weather it was still dank, the blue brick path, which had been wet and slimy all winter, only just drying out.

She knew her way easily now, into the yard and along to Gladys's house. She was very nervous today though. On Friday, Gladys had been to meet Danny's sisters, Jess, Rose and Amy. They would all be in the house. They're only little girls, Rachel told herself. What's to be worried about? But her stomach was fluttering all the same.

The doors of all the houses were flung wide in the

heat and the yard tap was still dripping, its droplets catching the sunlight. There was a nasty smell of refuse coming from the end of the yard, but as ever the place looked well kept up and tidy. In the doorway of number four, one of the two houses at the side of the yard, a very old lady dressed all in black sat dozing on a wooden chair in the shade, her head sunk onto her chest.

As Rachel reached Gladys's door, she heard the murmur of voices and then a high shred of laughter. Her stomach tightened even further. She felt she was intruding. Danny had not seen his sisters for eight years and it meant so much to him. She was nervous on his behalf as much as her own. But they had asked her to come . . .

She knocked timidly on the open door and stood back.

'That you, Rachel?' Gladys called. 'Come on in, bab, don't be shy!'

Her eyes adjusting from the brightness outside as she went in, she felt them all watching her. Four pairs of eyes. Four? Shouldn't there be five? Gladys was at the table, Danny on a chair near the cold fireplace, a cigarette in his hand. A girl who Rachel guessed must be the eldest, Jess, was seated on the third chair facing him. The other child was on a stool close beside her. Rachel's first thought was that they were older than she had expected. In her mind they were still very little girls.

Both of them had severe haircuts, cropped roughly just below their ears and with very straight fringes. Jess was the fairer of the two, with a distinct likeness to Danny. She had the same honey-brown hair, almost fair at the temples as his was, and a sprinkling of freckles across her nose. The remains of guarded amusement were still evident on her face. The younger girl was swarthier in looks, with thicker, darker hair. She looked across at Rachel with wary eyes, her brows gathered into a frown. Was this Amy, or Rose? They both had a distant air to them, as if they were holding themselves outside everything.

Danny took a drag on the cigarette, put his head back and puffed out a succession of smoke rings, which made the older girl titter again. But in the tense atmosphere Rachel sensed a desperation in his clowning. She could see that Danny was trying to win his sisters back.

'Ain't yer going to say hello, Danny?' Gladys ticked him off. 'Where're your manners?'

'All right, Rachel?' Danny said, obviously shy.

'These two are Jess and Amy, Danny's sisters,' Gladys said. 'This is Danny's friend, Rachel.' No one mentioned the third sister, Rose, and Rachel did not like to ask.

'Hello,' she said, making herself smile, though there was something forbidding about the two sisters, especially the younger one.

Jess said a wary 'Hello' back. Amy said nothing.

'Cup of tea?' Gladys asked. 'Come on, Danny – give her your chair.'

Rachel pulled the chair closer to the table. Jess, who she realized must be thirteen, as she was three years younger than Danny, though she looked about ten, did take some interest in the conversation and she smiled at Danny's antics. Amy sat stonily staring ahead of her and would not eat or drink anything, despite Gladys cajoling her. Rachel thought it might be better just to leave them alone and let them get used to things.

'They had a proper time of it on the journey,' Gladys said as they drank their tea. She had done her best to greet them with a spread, despite rationing and the plain dryness of the cake she had made. 'They put them on a train packed full of the lads coming back from France!

When I got to Snow Hill it was – oh, I've never seen anything like it.'

The country was riveted by news of the evacuation of troops from Dunkirk, forced to the coast by the advancing German troops, the flotillas of boats all braving the channel to bring them in. It had been going on for days now.

'The platforms were packed like tins of sardines,' Gladys told Rachel. 'They've turned the hotel dining room into a sort of hospital. And there were people calling out to the train as they came in, blokes hanging out of all the windows, people trying to find their lads and the lads all shouting out as well. Oh, they did look a sight – filthy – and you could see, well, they just looked all in, the poor devils. What a thing – it's a miracle they've got so many out, praise God for it. And they had people from some of the bakeries there handing out sandwiches and cake for them and cups of tea. What a thing – they must be so glad to be getting home.'

There was a silence which grew longer after she had finished. No one seemed sure what to say. Nothing in the room felt easy. Driven to break the silence, Rachel said to Jess, 'Are you two going to be living with your auntie now then?'

Amy's large eyes turned on her sister, her face full of some desperate, imploring emotion. Rachel was not sure what she was trying to say. Jess gave a helpless lift of her shoulders. 'I think so.' She looked at Gladys.

'Course you are. You're Mary's flesh and blood and Danny's sisters – I've know you since you were babbies. Your home's here and welcome,' Gladys said with a tremor in her voice. She looked round at Rachel. 'It was Jess remembering where I lived that got them here. You didn't know the number, did yer, love, but she remembered Alma Street and Aston and they found it all right. I've lived here for years. God knows what would've happened if I'd moved. They're emptying out the home, see – it's out in the country somewhere, in Essex, I think. Probably to make a hospital out of it for the lads coming back. So the war's done us a favour in its way.'

Rachel wondered, looking at the girls' sombre expressions, whether this was what they really felt.

'What was it like – where you were before?' she asked Jess. She saw Danny watching intently. She could almost feel his longing for things to be right, to have back the little sisters who he remembered.

Speaking very quietly, Jess said, 'It was big. There were fields and trees. And cows,' she added as an afterthought, before adding bleakly, 'not like here.'

Rachel saw a troubled look cross Gladys's face. Aston was going to take some getting used to.

By the time they left the house, Rachel was at bursting point with the questions she wanted to ask. Danny walked her to the tram again through the warm evening, holding her hand so tightly that it almost hurt. He kept his head down, obviously upset. Once again she was struck and touched by the contrast between the clowning, joking Danny and the need in him.

'Danny – what about Rose?' she asked as soon as they were along the street. 'You said you had three sisters. I thought when I got there she might be in the lav or something, but . . .'

Danny was shaking his head. 'They never told us!' he burst out. 'When Auntie got there to meet Jess and Amy, there they were, in all that crowd, with some woman who'd brought them up on the train. She handed them over like a couple of parcels. And Auntie said, "There's s'posed to be three of them – where's their other sister Rose?" The lady said she dain't know about any Rose, there was only the two of them, and it seemed as if she really hadn't known anything, she was just delivering them. When she'd gone, Auntie asked Jess, "Where's Rose then?" and she said Jess started crying and said that Rose had been poorly, some time ago, last year. She had a fever and dain't know who anyone was and they took her away somewhere so's the rest of them dain't catch it. They never saw her again.'

Rachel felt herself swell inside with pity and outrage. 'D'you think – well, did she pass away, Danny? Why wouldn't they say?'

He gave an angry shrug. 'Must've done. They never told Jess or Amy.'

'How old was she then?'

Danny frowned. 'Last year? She'd've been . . . ten.'

'Oh, the poor little things – all of them. You must be so glad to have Jess and Amy back home.'

'Yeah.' He put his head down and she could not see his face properly. There was something so sad in the way he said it and she saw that he had his hand in his jacket pocket again, as if holding on tight to his little notebook. She thought of all the lost years in between now and when he last saw his sisters. This reunion had been nothing like what he had hoped for. Instead of the familiar sisters he had longed for, he found himself confronted with two shocked, frightened strangers. As she was thinking this, Danny said, 'Amy was only a babby. She doesn't know who we are – not really.'

She squeezed Danny's hand and he raised his head

and looked round at her. 'Rach, can we go somewhere – just you and me? I just want to be with you.'

'What, now?' she said, startled. She was having enough trouble convincing her mother that she was spending all this time at Lilian's house. Mom must not know about Danny. She could just imagine how snooty Mom would be about the idea of her having anything to do with anyone from the markets now. So far as Peggy was concerned, she had raised her station in life. She'd have a fit at the thought of Rachel walking out with Danny.

'No, not now. I just mean, on a day off, on Sunday. Just get out somewhere, you and me. Away from all of it.'

She was puzzled for a moment. Danny had only just got his sisters back and now all he wanted was to get away! But he looked at her so imploringly, and she liked the idea as well.

'Yes,' she said. 'We could go on the tram – have a proper outing. Will Auntie mind?'

'I doubt it.'

'Next Sunday then?'

Danny nodded. His eyes were suddenly intent and serious. Once again he drew her into the alley off the street and stood with his arms round her, clutching her tightly to him.

'Rach – I . . . I think I love you,' he said.

She was moved as much by the stumbling way he said it as by the words themselves. He was subdued and fragile. And he loved her – Danny Booker, her lovely Danny!

'Oh, Danny – I love you too,' she said with a tremble in her voice. It seemed such a big thing to say. But she felt it welling up in her, wanting to pour out over him, to comfort him. For the moment that was all she needed to know. It felt as if Danny was fast becoming her home, her world and everything she needed.

They stood kissing, lost in each other's warm lips and hands, not caring that they were in a dark alley with scraggy weeds round their ankles. Heat came at them in waves off the bricks of the factory walls. Danny hugged her close and they stood silently for a long time.

'Don't ever go off and leave me, will yer?' he said into her neck.

'Danny?' She pushed him away gently and looked into his eyes, disturbed by the pain in his voice. 'Why would you say that? I'm not going to go off, am I? Where d'you think I'm going to go?'

He looked down between them at his feet, seeming embarrassed by his own vulnerability. 'I dunno,' he mumbled. 'I just want to know that . . . Well, that you're there.'

'Silly.' She pulled him close and kissed him again. 'I'm not going anywhere. You're the one, you are. The one for me.'

As she sat on the tram heading back into Birmingham, she was full of a loving glow. The memory of the feel of him pressed close to her, still so fresh, filled her with happiness so that she could have danced along the street. Danny loved her!

He's my man, she said to herself, solemnly. This seemed very grown up. He's *the one*.

She thought about home, the bleakness of the flat over Fred Horton's shop. After all, who else was there? She knew she loved Danny, that she almost always had. Her Danny, with his little book of happy dreams of Jack and Patch. Jack, the boy he wanted to be. He was the one person in the world who she wanted with all her heart.

Fifteen

They rode the tram out to the Lickey Hills the next Sunday afternoon, sitting on the top deck, full of excitement as it swooped out along the Bristol Road. The tram was not too crowded because they had set out so late. Most of the families out for the day had left earlier, to make the most of it.

'I can't get out of having dinner at home,' Rachel had told Danny. 'Not on a Sunday.' She made a face at the thought of Fred Horton. 'The old man, head of the table – they'll want to know where I'm going. I'll get into town as soon as I can after. Meet me in Navigation Street?'

It was a warm, bright day. Rachel had on the pink frock, a white cardigan and her black work shoes. Danny wore his usual grey trousers, had his shirtsleeves rolled up. At the sight of him waiting for her, seeing his smile, she had leapt inside with excitement. An afternoon to themselves!

She knew things were not easy at Gladys's house now, with Jess and Amy there. Both of them were playing Gladys up. Jess was angry and defiant. She and Amy were sharing a mattress in Danny's old room. Gladys had cleaned up the attic, where she usually stored stuff for the market, for Danny to sleep in. Both girls were finding the adjustment to this new place very difficult and Amy wet the bed every night, which enraged Jess so much that she would slap Amy and make her howl. Neither Gladys nor Danny knew what to do for the best.

'Does Auntie get cross?' Rachel asked him.

Danny shook his head, staring out of the window ahead. 'Nah. She's all right with 'em. Dolly keeps coming round – and Mo. He keeps larking about, trying to get them to come out of themselves.' Rachel smiled at the thought of Mo's burly figure and cheerful face. It would be a tough person who would not smile at Mo Morrison. 'Jess'll talk a bit – to me. Only all she talks about is the home . . . I said summat about our mom, her passing and . . .' He looked away for a moment. 'I dunno if she remembers her. She dain't seem to.'

Rachel could see why Danny was keen to get away from it all for a bit.

They were halfway along the tram on the left, with Rachel next to the window. As Danny sat beside her she could feel that he was in one of his tense, restless moods. He made jokes and fooled around all the way out to Rednal, making her laugh with his whispered observations about some of the other people on the tram – 'Look at that hat. You could turn that upside down and use it as a po!' – and cracking jokes. And she did laugh, but she also hoped that sooner or later he would calm down. His endless joking also felt like a way of shutting himself, and what was troubling him, far off, away from her.

He pulled his small canvas bag on to his lap and opened it. Rachel heard the faint clink of bottles. 'Look, Auntie's sent me off with some tea and butties – jam.'

'God, Danny, don't you ever think about anything except your stomach? We've only just had dinner!'

Danny grinned. 'Not much, no. A man has to eat! We'll get hungry later – and if you don't, I'll have yours!'

They got down at Rednal and everyone headed off into the Worcestershire hills known as the Lickeys. The two of them strode on quickly, overtaking some of the straggling families, and climbed up Beacon Hill. At the top was a little fort-like construction on which you could stand to look at the view all around. They stood amid a gaggle of people looking out. Rachel felt different standing up there. It wasn't like being down in the streets where you could not see out. She looked at Danny, loving the sight of him as he stood gazing around him in the sunshine, taking in deep breaths. Birmingham lay spread in the distance, barrage balloons swimming like little fish above it in the blue sky. It felt lovely to be getting out of town. It was like getting away from the war as well, from the shelters and sandbags and all the rest. But when she said so to Danny he pointed across the green.

'Not quite – look. Guns.'

The high vantage point was a good place for gun emplacements and spotlights. There was no escaping it completely.

'Come on.' Danny prodded her gently. 'Let's go. Get away from all these people.'

As they walked off along one of the wooded tracks across the hills, he said, 'You can breathe up here. I hate being shut in – walls around you you can't get out of.' He gave a shudder. She thought he was going to say more, but he clammed up. The walk away from the tram seemed to have altered his mood. He was quieter, seemingly involved in his own thoughts. It felt as if there was a different sort of wall around him – of things she did not understand.

'Danny?' she said, as they wandered in the coolness of the trees. 'What was it like where you were – in the orphanage?'

He walked with his eyes on the ground for a moment, apparently so closed down to her that she thought he might not answer. Like a reflex, he put his hand in his pocket where he kept the notebook. 'What d'you think? Walls all around you. Other kids. People ordering you about.'

'Were you naughty?' she asked.

Danny considered this. 'No, not much. Wasn't worth it.' He stopped abruptly as if thinking, then took her hand. 'Come on – let's go in here. Get away from everyone.'

They could already hear laughter along the path behind them. On this lovely day it felt as if there were always other people not too far away. Holding Danny's hand she followed him into the woodland glade among the pale green growth on the trees, dry leaves and soft mulch under their feet. They came to a place where there were two bushes close together, screening them from the path.

'Let's sit here,' Danny said.

They both realized then that they had brought nothing to sit on. Rachel looked down at her soft pink dress.

'Never mind – it's quite dry,' she said and settled herself on a bed of old leaves. Danny sat beside her and fumbled in his bag.

'Want a bit of tea?'

'Go on then.'

He handed her an old stera bottle – it had had sterilized milk in it – full of now cold tea, with a piece of cork plugging the top. She pulled it out and swigged some of the slightly sweet tea. She felt suddenly light-hearted, but when she looked at Danny, sitting tensely forward, leaning on his bent legs, he seemed enclosed in sad thoughts. She was not sure what to do or say. After a moment she put her hand lightly on his back and felt him flinch slightly before settling under her touch.

'Penny for them,' she said softly.

Without turning his head, Danny said, 'You asked me what it was like. No one's ever asked me that before. I was thinking about it. Six years I was in that place, nearly. When our – when my father – stuck me in there I thought it was . . . I dunno. I just dain't know anything. I thought he was coming back to get me. He never said he was, but that's what I thought. It felt like a mistake. One minute we was all there at home with Mom and everything. The next – everything'd gone. The old man was always hard. He was a wreck, Mom said, because of the war. She never said what happened to him and he looked all right – nothing missing, you know, not in his body, any road. But she said he'd never been the same. And then –' His voice took on a bewildered tone. 'It was all right when Mom was there. She stuck with us. She was an angel, our mom. She got between the old man and us, when she had to. But then he'd . . .' Danny lowered his head. 'I'd have a go at him, whenever he started on our mom. I tried to fight him . . . She said I shouldn't, I should keep out of it. And then . . .' He kept getting stuck, as if he could not get the words out. She heard the strain in his voice, the tears he was fighting.

'Oh, Danny,' she said. She shifted closer, cautious, sensing that he could not stand too much sympathy. She rested her arm along his back.

'Then she'd gone and everything . . . Nothing was the

same . . . And he . . .' He broke down then for a moment, hanging his head. 'I wish someone else could remember, not just me – Jess *must* do, but she won't say . . .' He shook his head and a sob came from him. Rachel felt his shoulders heave. She was overflowing with feeling for him. All she wanted was to take him in her arms and hold him. But she held back and stayed close, her hand on his warm back, waiting.

'In there, in the home, they don't like you talking. Whatever you do or say, they tell you to stop it, to shut it. Speak when you're spoken to – or not even then. Keep quiet. So you do, in the end. Course we whispered to each other and played about. But why say anything much? There's no one to say it to. It's better to tell jokes and think up silly things like that. At least you can make someone else laugh for a minute or two. It was us and them. They were nasty really. It was better to make out that you weren't very with it – you know, a bit slow. They dain't like anyone who could think a bit, as if you were against what they were doing. Some of 'em'd beat you if you so much as looked at them a certain way. There was this room they'd take you to . . . It was as if they thought we was rubbish, sort of thing. Lowest of the low. As if it was all our fault.'

'The people in charge?'

He nodded, face twisted into a bitter expression.

'Why didn't you run away, Danny?'

'I thought of it. I s'pose I was scared. For a start I dain't know where I was. It sounds stupid but I never even knew we was so near Birmingham. And I dain't want to run back to our dad. He said to me if I was any trouble they'd send the peelers after me and have me in jail. He put the fear of God into me. I dunno whether jail'd be any worse really but I'd built it up into a bogey

sort of thing in my mind. All those years locked in there
I just felt as if I was somewhere else altogether. Another
world. Devil's Island or somewhere. And the longer I
stayed there the more it felt like that. I dain't know
where Jess and the others were. Time just went by and I
dain't know what to do . . .' He stopped, thinking for a
moment. 'A few of the others went away. I think they
went to families – fostering they call it. I dunno why or
who decided who'd go but no one ever picked me.'

'So you did your drawings?' she said gently.

Danny nodded. 'There was a dog a bit like Patch back
where we lived, in Ladywood. He used to look at you
and his eyes were all bright. Cheeky, like. And Jack – he
did all the things I wanted to do . . .'

'And then they let you out?'

'I was old enough to go to work. I told them I had an
auntie even though I had no idea whether I did by then.
Auntie told me she was trying to find me on and off all
that time but no one seemed to know anything about
me, or the girls.' After another pause, he went on, 'I
knew I'd get out one day. I said to myself, when I'm
ready I'll get out. I'll just walk away.'

He sat silently for so long that she thought he was not
going to say any more. But suddenly, in a low, fierce
voice, he said, 'If I ever have kids, I'll *never* be like my
dad. Never.'

'I missed you,' she said, her throat aching. 'When you
went.'

Danny turned. In his eyes she saw uncertainty, fear,
hunger.

'Come here.' She held out her arms. A moment later
she was on her back on the bed of leaves, Danny pressed
close beside her. They held each other tight. He felt
warm and powerfully strong.

'Rach?' He leaned on an elbow and looked down into her eyes.

She looked back, full of feeling, but he didn't say any more. He moved his lips closer to hers. They tightened their arms round each other and clung together, kissing and touching as the afternoon drifted by. Rachel was dimly aware of voices passing in the distance, of birdsong and the changing angle of the sun through the leaves. Sometimes they stared into each other's faces and said, 'I love you.' Sometimes they said nothing. Rachel was lost in Danny's blue eyes, in the feel of his body pressing against hers. Nothing else mattered. When they had to get up and brush off their clothes to go and catch the tram, it was like waking from a dream.

Sixteen

'The Battle of France is over . . .' The new prime minister Winston Churchill's voice growled from the wireless that June evening. If necessary, Britain would fight alone.

Rachel heard the news at home, in the upstairs parlour, with her mother and Fred. The war was moving closer. The Maginot Line, built to keep the Germans out, had failed completely. The French had signed the armistice, surrendering only six weeks after the Germans had invaded.

'My God,' Fred said, clicking the wireless off. 'They even made them sign it in the same railway carriage – that's where they signed the armistice in nineteen eighteen. What a disaster!'

Peggy had wept a month ago when Mr Churchill made his first speech in the House of Commons as prime minister. 'Our poor Mr Chamberlain! But oh, what wonderful words – I feel better already for hearing him!'

This did not seem to last long, however, and she was soon full of woe again. 'We're going to be invaded, I know we are. Overrun! Those horrible Germans will be striding down our streets, doing terrible, savage things . . .'

It was a tense, frightening summer as the Battle of France became the Battle of Britain, fought out over the south-east by the air force and the ground defences. By the late summer it was becoming clear that they had fought off the invasion, but all through those months, rumours were flying. At work, Rachel found, there were stories of secret German invasions, of spies in exotic disguises. Shortages of everything increased and everyone was being asked to hand in pots and pans to be melted down to make aircraft. There was a sense of unease and panic.

It was all coming closer, and there was the worst tension of waiting for the unknown. What was going to happen – and when?

When the air-raid sirens first went off, Rachel felt a few moments of relief. Now it was coming – it was beginning. This soon turned to panic and terror. They had heard the sirens before, of course. There was a daylight raid in Erdington, to the north of the city, earlier in the month, but hearing it that night in late August, the sound made every nerve in her body jump and jangle.

'Down in the cellar everyone!' Fred commanded.

They had prepared it down there, even though it was a cold, dank hole. Fred had got hold of a couple of old mattresses and they had a torch and an oil lamp ready as well as some blankets to take down.

There was confusion at first, none of them used to this.

'I ought to bring Cissy some milk!' Peggy cried, dithering at the top of the steps with the sleepy child in her arms. Cissy was the only one of them who was calm.

'Just get down in there where it's safe,' Fred bossed.

'You go with her, Rachel. We don't know how long we've got.'

Rachel followed her mother down the steep cellar steps, still just able to hear the horrifying yowl of the siren outside. Fred followed and in that moment Rachel realized another thing – if this was going to happen a lot she would end up spending nights in the company of her mother and stepfather.

'Hold your sister while I get sorted out,' Peggy commanded.

Rachel scrambled onto one of the cold mattresses while Fred lit the tilly lamp. She held out her arms and Peggy lowered the plump child into them. Cissy, now almost a year old, had gingery hair like her father's but luckily, so far as Rachel was concerned, she did not look like Fred in any other way. Her hair fell in loose curls, she had a pink-and-white complexion and big blue eyes which she opened now, looking round in bewilderment. Seeing her sister's face above her, she made a little happy noise and smiled sleepily.

'S'all right, Cissy – you go back to sleep,' Rachel said. She cuddled the little girl close. She hadn't had much to do with Cissy when she was a small baby. All she'd done then was eat, sleep and scream, and Rachel kept resentfully out of her way. But nowadays Cissy was more settled and was starting to know who everyone was, and she had a sunny personality. She adored her big sister and immediately reached her arms out towards Rachel whenever she saw her.

She's all right, Rachel thought, with a rush of fondness for the little bundle in her arms. She is half my sister, after all. It was comforting now they were experiencing this first real, frightening raid, to have someone smaller than herself to look after, especially someone so warm and sweet.

Peggy sat down on the other mattress beside Fred. He had arranged them at right angles to each other, along two walls. There was a bitter smell of coal dust and it was very dark but for the light of the lamp flickering shadows across their faces. The night was warm, but the cellar always felt chill, and the damp from the cold bricks seeped into her back. Rachel wished she had a blanket behind her and shivered, thinking what it would be like down here in the winter.

'Right – I'll have her back if you like,' Peggy said.

'It's all right, she's settled,' Rachel said. 'She can stay here with me for now.'

'Huh – that's a turn-up for the books, you taking an interest in your sister,' Peggy began. But she was silenced by Fred.

'Shh, wench – listen. That's them coming!'

Peggy was too aghast even to protest about being called 'wench'. They could barely hear the sound of the planes' engines down there but the distant thumps and explosions were not lost on them.

'Oh my Lord,' Peggy said. 'We could've all died in our beds.'

They lapsed into a tense, listening silence, all trying to hear what was going on outside.

As it quietened a little, Fred muttered, 'Those buggers – we should've finished 'em off good and proper the first time.'

Rachel did not see it until after work the next day, but she heard. The Market Hall. The news spread. One of

151

the best-loved parts of Birmingham, the Market Hall had received a direct hit.

She went to look after work, with Danny. Taking their turn they peered in through a hole in the side wall. Everyone gasped as they looked in. It was bad enough that you could already see the roof was missing, that the place was nothing but a shell. But inside was still a shock.

'It looks terrible,' Rachel said, staring at the mass of twisted metal, the charred beams lying at angles over heaps of rubble. It was hard to believe that only yesterday it would have been full of stalls and shoppers in all its usual bustle and colour, full of fruit and veg and flowers, of meat and poultry and fish. A couple of little Union Jacks had been stuck into the desolate sea of destruction.

Danny was silent, seeming stunned. The fish market, where he worked, was just next door.

'The clock's gone,' a woman's voice said behind them. There had been an ornate clock in the Market Hall, with a striking bell and moving figures round it. 'Burnt to ashes, they say.'

The two of them moved away from the shell of the wrecked building, leaving others space to look. There was a sober, shocked atmosphere all around them and that was how they felt too. It was the first time for them that the war had come up really close. When they had moved a little further away, Danny took Rachel's hand.

'It seems daft that they've sent Jess and Amy here when the other kids're being sent away,' he said.

No one ever mentioned Rose any more. What else was there to say but to mourn her quietly?

'Mind you,' he added sadly, 'Auntie's thinking about sending Amy away again. She don't seem to like it here.'

Gladys had tried bringing the two girls to the Rag Market on Saturdays. Jess seemed to enjoy it, but Amy remained silent and sullen, however much Jess and Rachel tried to cheer her up. It was as if she had shut everyone out and was in a sad, angry world of her own.

'I'm at my wits' end with her,' Gladys said. She looked more tired and drawn in the face every time Rachel saw her. 'I ought to get them into some sort of school – but how are they going to deal with Amy, the way she is?'

All that summer, Gladys struggled to help the two girls adjust to being back in their family. Jess was quiet, eager to please, but somehow quietly wretched. Amy remained mutinous and disturbed.

'I've never seen a child like it,' Gladys reported wearily one Sunday afternoon when Rachel was at the house. It was September, but still very warm. Jess and Amy were out in the yard, the rest of them inside with the door open. Smells of smoke and ripe whiffs from the dustbins and lavatories drifted in. Flies blundered into one of the sticky flypapers Gladys had hanging up. 'Yesterday – I heard this noise from upstairs, thump-thump. When I went up, there she was, in the bedroom, just sat there, banging her head on the wall.' Gladys's eyes filled with tears. 'I'm nearly at the end of my tether.'

People in the yard had been kind – or some. Ma Jackman, who seldom had a good word to say for anyone, gave the two arrivals hostile looks and kept saying, 'They're not right, those two.' Which Gladys said was quite something when you considered how odd Edwin Jackman had turned out – and who wouldn't with a mother like that? Rachel had caught sight of Edwin a few times. He was a pale, expressionless lad a couple of years older than her.

The Morrisons kept trying to help. Dolly was kind and motherly with the two girls. Mo would sit down in the yard, call them over and do little tricks of his. He'd blacken the back of a plate with smuts on the fire and let them draw pictures with a matchstick. And he would tell them jokes, his wide pink face stretching into a grin. Jess would smile, but even he could not get Amy to crack her face. She would back away from him angrily.

'You gonna take her to Uncle Albert?' Danny asked miserably. Rachel felt so sad for him. Getting his family back together had only caused more heartbreak. It was almost, now, as if he wished them gone again.

Gladys looked uncertain. 'My brother Albert and his wife live out at Sutton,' she explained to Rachel. 'He's done all right for himself he has. He was our mother's little afterthought. He was too young to join up when the Great War came and he works in insurance. They won't be able to call him up – he's bad with his chest. He can hardly breathe sometimes.' She took a thoughtful sip of tea, holding the cup in both hands. 'They've got two of their own – about Amy's age. Albert's never been one for putting himself out much but Nancy, his wife – well, she's all right from what I remember. I thought she was very nice. I think I'd better write to them.'

'Amy might like it out there,' Danny said. 'With their kids.'

Gladys nodded, but she looked worried. 'If she goes on like this, I wouldn't wish her on anyone. But I've not brought up young ones that age, like Nancy has – I don't know where to begin.'

Rachel thought of Amy's hard, angry expression and wondered if she would get on anywhere.

'I hope they'll help out, I really do,' Gladys said desperately. She got up from the table. 'I'll do it – later. I'll drop them a line.'

Rachel could see how upset Gladys was. She had been unhappy and ashamed that she had not been able to find the girls earlier, but now they were here, she couldn't manage. She felt she had let everyone down.

Jess and Amy drifted back inside then, so the conversation ended.

'They keep telling her to go away,' Jess reported. Amy had not been welcomed by the other children in the street. Her permanent look of sullen misery and angry outbursts of temper had probably not helped.

'C'm'ere, bab,' Gladys beckoned her and pulled the child onto her knee, which to Rachel's surprise Amy agreed to as if she was much younger than her years. She leaned her head miserably on Gladys's shoulder. 'Shall I cut you a piece, bab – are you hungry?'

Amy shook her head. Rachel could feel the child's deep unhappiness coming towards her in waves. Her heart ached for her, remembering how she had felt when her mother moved in with Fred Horton, how lost and pushed out. How much more sad and bewildered Amy must feel.

'Top up the pot, wench, will yer?' she said to Jess, who got up, seemingly glad to be asked, and brought the pot to the table. As she poured the tea, Rachel thought how pretty she was, with her sweet, freckled face.

'If we went for a visit to Uncle Albert's house,' Gladys said quietly to Amy, 'would you like that? There's a big park there, with a stream. Not like here.'

Amy gave a little nod into her shoulder. 'Don't like it here,' she said in a voice so small they could only just make it out. 'It's dirty and horrible.'

'All right, bab,' Gladys said softly. 'I know. But we're

your family and we're what you've got in the world. We're going to have to see what we can do – if they can let you stay. We'll go out there and see, as soon as we can. But you'd have to try hard to settle down. D'you think you could do that?'

Amy pulled back and looked intensely into her face. After a second she gave an uncertain sort of nod, before cuddling up to Gladys again. Gladys looked at Danny over her head and gave him a look as if to say, 'Heaven help us.'

Seventeen

November 1940

Rachel walked wearily along Alma Street, hugging her coat round her, collar up against the damp and cold. Under it she had on a green tartan skirt and a cream jumper. In the bomb-damaged streets around her, children were careering about, laughing and yelling, but she hardly noticed them. Passing into the yard, she tapped on the door of Gladys's house and opened it.

'Danny?'

He was sitting staring into the fire as if in another world. He jumped at her voice, and looked round. The room was tidy as ever and the house felt quiet and bereft.

'They've gone then?' Rachel shut the door and took her hat off, shivering.

'Yeah,' he said in a flat voice. 'Soon as Auntie was back from church.'

She peeled her coat off. As Danny sat up straighter, she saw that he was holding his little notebook and the stub of pencil.

'Have you been drawing?' she asked carefully. She knew it was because he was upset.

Danny gave a sheepish smile. 'Yeah.' He held the little page out to her. She saw another of his rough sketches. Jack and Patch, both sitting down.

'Where are they?'

'Oh, at the top of a big hill, covered in grass,' he said. 'Somewhere like the Lickeys where you can look down – only higher. You can't see out when you live in a place like this. One day I want to climb a big mountain – the biggest I can find.' He closed the book and put it in his pocket, as if the conversation was over.

'So is Jess staying as well?'

Danny shrugged. 'Depends.'

Gladys had written to Albert and Nancy and waited in trepidation for an answer. When it came, it was much warmer than she'd feared. At the time the family had two evacuees from London's East End living with them in Sutton Coldfield. It was not proving a success.

'It sounds as if it's driving them all round the bend,' Gladys said, when the letter came.

Nancy had written:

All they really want is to go back home to mother, bombs or no bombs. And who can blame them? The mother is a tough nut but fond of them. She wants her boys back – they want to go. They're nine and seven and they're miserable – and so are John and Margaret. These Cockneys are fish out of water here in such a country place. So the long and short is, they're going. Two girls would be a relief after that and they are Albert's nieces after all. Poor little things. We do really want to do our bit for the war any way we can, so let's give it a try. And what with all the raids you're getting, they're best out of there. Bring them here and we'll do our best to make them welcome.

It was true: the bombing had intensified and there had been some terrible raids. The sirens would often go off in the evening when they were eating. For Rachel this meant finishing off her tea in the cellar. Danny, Gladys and the others ran round to the shelter at the back, or into the cellar of the wire-spinning works at the end of the yard. Even bombers that were not heading for Birmingham often flew overhead, on their way to wreak havoc on Liverpool or some other city, and it was impossible to know whether it was their turn until they had passed over.

Everyone was getting more and more tired and living on their nerves.

'These girls are in a bad enough state as it is,' Gladys said. 'I'm going to get them out of here.'

So Danny had said goodbye to his sisters again that morning, not knowing if or when he was going to see them again.

Now he stood up and came over to Rachel once she had her coat off and had laid it on a chair. He put his hands on her shoulders, looking for her to return his gaze. Their eyes met and she placed her own palms lightly each side of his waist, feeling the warm hardness of his boy's body. Man's body, she thought. He's a man now.

'Give us a kiss,' he said, with a half-begging smile. He seemed very raw in himself, and hungry for her to be close.

They cuddled, kissing and warming each other in silence for a while. Despite the sadness of it, both of them knew what this afternoon meant: for once, just for once, they had a little bit of time by themselves.

'Are you going to make me a cup of tea?' Rachel said eventually. 'I'm starving, I am.'

'If you want. I thought you'd had dinner?' Danny said, going to the range. He put the kettle over the fire.

'I could still do with a cup of tea.'

He came back to her, taking her in his arms again. The kettle began to murmur. The air smelt of coal dust and something sweet, spicy and mouth-watering.

'Has Auntie been baking?' Rachel asked.

'Yeah – she made buns to take over there. She left us a couple.'

They drank tea and ate the spicy buns at the table. Danny kept reaching over and stroking her hand. He seemed caught up in her, as if he could think of nothing else. Even when she told him snippets of news, little things Cissy had done or that she had chatted about to Lilian who was once more bored to tears at work, he hardly seemed to be listening and hurried down his tea. He seemed distracted and restless, one knee twitching up and down.

'What's up?' she asked eventually, although she knew really. His family, or what was left of it, was being scattered once again.

'Nothing.' He gazed at her, then held his hand out. 'Come here, to me.' Pushing his chair back, he drew her towards him. She felt excited by his demand, as if something new and more adult was happening between them. As she stood over him, he looked up at her and patted his leg. 'Come and sit here.'

She settled on his lap, giggling, smoothing the skirt over her thighs. 'God, Danny, d'you think the chair'll stand it?'

Without answering, he buried his head against her and she cuddled him close, stroking his face. His hand moved up and down her back. He raised his head and his lips reached for hers.

They sat for some time, kissing, their exploring growing bolder. Rachel did not know, for sure, how this might continue. But she knew her body felt alive and more awake all over than ever before, that each time Danny's hand smoothed over her breasts she wanted the feel of it to go on and that there was a melting ache of longing between her legs. There were no words for it. She could only follow the feelings, this being here with Danny, so close to him, his powerful need, and hers.

'Come upstairs with me.' He surfaced, looking at her, but he seemed half in a trance.

'Upstairs?'

'Yes . . . Yes . . .' He took her hand again, leading her up the twist of the first staircase.

'God, it's dark up here,' Rachel said at the top of the first flight of stairs.

'I know,' Danny said. 'Auntie always keeps her door shut – she dain't like anyone going in there.' He pushed open the door of the other room where the girls slept and they could suddenly see a bit better.

'Why?' Rachel asked.

'I dunno,' Danny said. 'I s'pose she just likes to be a bit private.' He was not interested in this conversation. With both hands on Rachel's waist, he steered her up the bare treads of the attic stairs.

There was a bed up there now, Danny's single, black iron bedstead, a chest of drawers and chair and a bright peg rug on the floorboards. The light was cobweb grey and it was very cold compared with downstairs, air seeming to force itself in around the windowpane. Rachel was already shivering.

Danny pulled her close. 'I want to see you, Rach. I can't think of anything else – please, let me. I need you . . .'

'See me?' she said, doubtful.

Danny made a gesture with one hand that took all of her in, top to toe. 'See you – all of you.'

His eyes held an intense expression. She was astonished and gratified that she could make him feel so much, make him need her so much, it seemed, by just being there. She was full of tender emotion, wanting to hold him and care for him. She barely understood where this was leading, except in the vaguest terms, but she felt she would do anything for him. Overcoming her misgivings she gave a little nod of her head.

His trembling fingers were not used to the delicate buttons of her blouse and she had to help him. Danny undid his own shirt and slipped his hands in under the muslin grey of her blouse, pressing their bodies together. She could smell him more strongly now, his salt-sweat, boy smell. She pushed back the shoulder of his shirt and kissed his bare arm, the rounded hill of muscle. But she was beginning to shiver violently.

'Come into bed.' He pulled back the sheet and tan-coloured blanket.

The sheets felt icy on her skin at first. She stayed sitting up, pulling the bedclothes round her, only in her panties now, her hair tickling loose on her shoulders.

'I wish we had a fire,' she said, through chattering teeth.

Danny seemed not to notice. He was pulling off his clothes. He came and knelt on the bed, gazing at her. His fingers curled into the top of her panties and began to tug them down.

'You're so bloody lovely,' he said. Then, in a tone not rough, but urgent, he said, 'Lie back.'

And he fell forward into her embrace with a sound like a sob. Pure instinct made her raise her legs.

*

It was afterwards that she would always remember. The act itself was strange, his hardness jabbing his way into her, the burn of pain at first, before the feelings of pleasure grew in her. She was moved by the urgent explosion of his pleasure. But then, as he surfaced, endearments tumbled from his lips, things she would never have thought of Danny saying: 'I love you ... You're my woman, my sweetheart ... I need you. Nothing feels right without you.' And he was soft and curled in her arms and she felt a melting love for him overwhelm her. 'I'm frightened you'll go – that one day you won't be here,' he said into her neck, as he lay in her arms. She held and stroked him. 'I'm here, Danny,' she whispered, her own softness also taking her by surprise. 'I love you like no one else. I'm not going away. You're all I want in the world, my love. I just want to be with you.'

He drew closer, holding her like something utterly precious, his hand on her belly. Rachel drew the covers closer around them like a warm cocoon. With one hand she ran her finger over the fair trace of hair above his upper lip, her other trailing the strong runnel of his spine with her fingers. She shifted so that their eyes were level and they wrapped their gaze around each other.

'I don't want to go home,' she said, nuzzling against him. 'I don't ever want to go anywhere ever again.'

'Don't then. Stay here.'

'Don't be daft – I've got to.'

'I want you here.' He looked seriously at her. 'I feel safe with you, Rach. It feels as if you've always been here. You make life feel right.'

She kissed him. 'So do you.'

'What'll we do?'

She drew back a fraction. 'What d'you mean?'

'To be together.'

163

'Well . . .' She giggled. 'Danny, I'm only fifteen. Give us a chance. We shouldn't be doing this, for a start.' Only now was she realizing exactly what they had done: *that*. The disgraceful 'thing' that was so forbidden, so shameful unless you were married. Panic rose in her at the thought. 'What if anyone found out?'

'Sod 'em,' Danny said.

'Danny!' She raised her head, indignant now. 'You can't just say that! As if no one else exists.'

'They don't,' he said obstinately. 'Not for me. Just you.'

'And Auntie.' She was about to add, 'And Jess and Amy.' But she lay down again. She could hardly preach to him. His sisters had gone and left him, hadn't they?

He rolled over and looked down at her, kissing her lips, then her breasts. 'All I know is, this has been the best afternoon of my life and . . .' He paused. 'Yep – that's all I know.' He rested his head on her stomach and they lay quietly, until they grew so cold they had to get up.

All the way home she felt wrapped in the smell of him, the feel of him. She felt like a different person. She knew that she was promised to Danny Booker. And her mother did not even know he existed.

Eighteen

The first time it happened was a December morning, after what had felt like an endlessly long night raid. Even in the safe haven of the cellar it was impossible to sleep, lying there, listening to the thuds and bangs outside. As she set off for work, Rachel felt her nausea rise up and take over. She had to rush and gag over the gutter.

'Been a bad night, ain't it, bab?' a woman said kindly as Rachel straightened up, groggy and embarrassed. 'We're all a bit churned up after that.'

It was the day the King came to Birmingham, to have a wander about and inspect the damage. Rachel had been awake almost all night – she thought her sickness was just because she was exhausted.

The next day, she was standing on the Coventry Road waiting for the trolleybus. There was a cold wind blowing which seemed to bring the promise of snow. Her stomach already felt nasty and acidic. As she stood there a man walked past, smoking. The drifting tang of the smoke caught in her nostrils and she felt suddenly very sick and had to breathe and swallow hard to try and stop it. At home, the smells of stew and cabbage in the passage had the same effect.

I must be coming down with something, she thought.

Either that or it's all these nights up and down. It did not even occur to her what was really going on.

On Saturdays she still went with Gladys to the Rag Market. There were just the two of them again. Jess and Amy, on seeing Albert and Nancy's place in Sutton Coldfield, had immediately chosen to stay there. Rachel could see that Gladys was relieved, even though feeling that she had failed them. 'They're better off with Nancy,' she said. 'She's a kind soul and I could see they felt a bit better as soon as they got there. Amy looked as if she was thawing out like a block of ice when she saw the garden and all the trees.'

Even with the war on and the nights of bombing sapping everyone's energy, all the people in the Rag Market tried to create a good atmosphere in the build-up to Christmas. As the afternoon darkened outside, the lights came on and the barrows and racks and anything else that could have tinsel or holly twined round it was decorated.

That day was very cold, steam pluming from the horses' nostrils outside and all the traders stamping their feet and wearing all possible layers of coats, scarves and shawls. Rachel had on her grey coat and a navy felt beret she had bought from the market a few weeks before. Gladys had her shawl wrapped over her coat and a colourful scarf over her head, tied under her chin. A lady had come to inspect some of the bed linen that Gladys had for sale. She had insisted on opening out all the sheets and pillowcases 'to see they're not full of holes'.

'Well, that one was an old tartar,' Gladys remarked, riled. 'Thinking I'd try and palm off any old tat on 'er! Those sheets're brand new! She never even bought anything after all that. Fold 'em up tidy again, Rach, will you?'

Rachel started to sort out the tangle of bed linen. But the frowsty smell of clothing in the market which normally she hardly noticed, the smoke from cigarettes and fumes from passing traffic, all seemed suddenly unbearable. As she stood up from picking up one of the sheets, she was suddenly overcome with heat. She was fighting to take off her wool scarf when she saw dots of light at the edge of her vision.

'Ooh, I do feel queer,' she was saying as the lights flashed more intensely, before everything went black.

'Rach?' Gladys's voice echoed in from somewhere. 'Rach – are you OK?'

The next thing Rachel knew, Gladys was on one side of her and another of the market traders on the other, and she was being picked up from the floor. Someone brought a box. Feeling exceedingly groggy, Rachel managed to sit on it.

'Ooh, she looks poorly,' their neighbour said. 'I'll go and get her a cup of tea.'

Other people were gathering round. 'Is she all right? What's up, wench?'

Gladys squatted beside her. 'Keep your head down 'til you feel better,' she instructed. After a few moments, with the blood thumping back into her head, Rachel sat up, feeling sick and peculiar, but conscious. Her right elbow hurt and she realized she must have banged it as she fell.

'You fainted,' Gladys said. Rachel saw a troubled look in Gladys's grey eyes. 'You should've said if you was feeling poorly.'

'I wasn't,' Rachel said. 'It just came on, suddenly like. I have been feeling a bit funny, on and off.'

The woman came back through the crowd and handed her a cup of tea. 'Here y'are, bab – get that down you if you can.'

'Ta,' Rachel said. Her hands were shaking a little. She sat sipping the tea and everyone else drifted away. After a time the sweet tea restored her and she went back to work.

'I want a word with you, miss.'

A week later, on the Sunday afternoon, Rachel had gone over to Aston. Just for once, she wished that Danny could make the journey over to her and she could stay lying on her bed. She felt tired to her bones and the queasiness came and went. What on earth's the matter with me? she thought. I'm turning into an old lady. Looking in the mirror she saw how pale her cheeks were, and the dark circles under her eyes.

But she longed to see Danny! She got up and dragged herself over there, half-dozing on the tram out of town, praying she would not be sick. She'd not long arrived when Gladys started on her.

'What d'you mean?' she said, through a yawn. All she wanted was to sink into a heap by the fire.

'Come with me.' Gladys wiped her hands on a rag and led Rachel out into the cold yard again.

'Auntie!' Danny protested. 'What's going on?'

She quelled him with a look over her shoulder, then stopped and turned. 'If you need to know, you'll know soon enough. Now go inside, lad.'

Rachel followed Gladys's strong figure, wrapped in her old black shawl. She looked at the hairpins holding Gladys's thick plait in its old-fashioned bun, at the worn heels on her old black shoes below the hem of her skirt, at her walk which was just beginning to be a rock from one foot to the other through the stiffness of her joints. She was an impressive woman and, at this moment, at her most forbidding.

'Come in 'ere a tick.' She pushed open the door to the brew house, a small brick building at the end of the yard. It was gloomy inside. They squeezed in beside the mangle, a green, galvanized thing, and the shared copper under which a fire was lit to heat water for washing clothes. Each household in the yard took its turn in there. Rachel thought of her mother, slaving all those evenings away in the brew house in Floodgate Street. It felt very damp and smelt of ash and rough soap.

Gladys shut the door and turned to face her, arms folded. 'Keep your voice down,' she warned. Rachel saw her jaw clench. Her blue eyes were very solemn and never had their gaze seemed more intimidating. 'Right, miss – what's going on?'

'What d'you mean, Auntie?' Rachel said, in genuine bewilderment.

Gladys shifted her weight from one foot to the other. Rachel thought she saw her soften slightly, a kinder light come into those piercing eyes. She stood, considering for a moment.

'You're not looking too well,' she observed.

'I do feel bad – off and on,' Rachel said, adding hurriedly, 'but I don't want to let you down, Auntie – I can come to the market and help. I'm all right. I've just had a bit of an upset stomach.'

Gladys continued to look at her, her mind clearly working. 'Just tell me one thing,' she went on. 'Last month, when I went to my Albert's . . . With Amy and Jess . . .'

169

Rachel could feel a blush begin to rise in her neck as Gladys spoke. But she still did not fully understand.

'You came to see Danny?'

'Yes, Auntie, I did . . .'

Gladys's eyes widened slightly. She swallowed, and it seemed an effort to bring out the next words. 'Did you and Danny . . .' She looked down, embarrassed. Rachel had never seen her look like that before. 'You know what I mean? Did anything happen?'

The blush flooded across Rachel's cheeks and she lowered her head. *Did anything happen?* Oh yes, something happened all right. She thought of Danny's naked body moving against hers. It sent a thrill through her, just for a second. How did Auntie know?

'I see.' Her blushes seemed to tell Gladys everything she needed to know. Struggling to remain calm, she said, 'And when did you start feeling bad?'

'The morning after that very long raid . . . I thought it was just that I was tired, but . . .' Tears rose in her and her throat hurt with it. 'Come to think of it I felt funny before that, for a day or two – a bit sick when I woke of a morning. I just took no notice. Auntie – what . . . What does it mean?'

'Heaven help you – the penny still hasn't dropped, has it?' Gladys said. 'You've been feeling bad for a couple of weeks or more? It looks as if . . . Well, as if you're expecting, bab.'

Rachel stared back at her, the words not making sense.

'It's early to tell, but by the look of things, you're going to have a babby. If . . . Well, if you don't lose it on the way. It can happen.'

Rachel's heart was pounding so hard that her breathing could scarcely keep up. 'But . . . Is that . . .? Is that how it . . .?' She shook her head. 'I never really knew, how it happens.' Then she looked at Gladys in disbelief across the gloom. 'But we only did it once – ever!'

Gladys shook her head. 'Once can be enough. You're both young and . . .' She rolled her eyes and looked upwards for a moment. The anger had gone out of her. 'Oh dear God.'

They stood in silence for a moment. Rachel gazed at Gladys, her eyes begging Danny's auntie to say something, to tell her what to do. Gladys unfolded her arms, clasped her hands to her waist and drew in a deep breath.

'Right,' she said, with an effort. 'What's done's done. Whatever I say can't undo it now. We'll go back in the house. Time to do some talking to Danny. He's half of this – more than half if I know anything about men. And the little bugger can take his share of it – there's no reason why you have to carry it all on your own. Come on.' She ushered Rachel out and across the yard.

Danny looked up as they both appeared back inside. He seemed to feel a bit left out and looked puzzled and fed up. His eyes searched their faces.

'Sit down, Rachel,' Gladys said. As Rachel obeyed, not looking at Danny, Gladys stood over them, her feet apart, arms folded again.

'Danny,' she said in a forbidding tone. 'Listen to me.'

Danny looked understandably apprehensive. 'What?' He looked from one to the other of them.

'Danny – you're sixteen years old and you're a babe in arms, d'you know that?' Gladys said. In that moment the harsh tone left her voice. She released her arms and leaned forwards, her hands on the table. To Rachel's astonishment she saw that Gladys's eyes were full of tears. 'I remember the day you were born, lad. Loved you like my own, I did.'

Rachel watched his face, that face she loved. He glanced at her in confusion, then back to his aunt who was struggling to compose herself.

'It looks as if our Rachel here's in the family way, Danny.' She spoke more gently now, but with a clear insistence that this was gravely important. 'That means she's going to have a babby – yours, Danny.'

Rachel would never forget the look of utter astonishment that came over Danny's face. If a bolt of lightning had struck him he could not have looked more stunned.

'A babby? What d'yer mean?'

'You and her – remember?' Gladys pointed at each of them in turn. 'That's how babbies are made, Danny.'

'Rach?' He turned to her. The thing she never forgot was that never, not once, did he look horrified, nor angry. There was just amazement. His mouth hung open.

'I've been feeling a bit funny, Danny. And Auntie says . . .'

Danny closed his mouth. He swallowed and glanced at Gladys, then back at Rachel.

'I s'pose that means we'll have to get wed then – doesn't it?'

Nineteen

January 1941

Rachel sat in her sagging seat, in the Grange Super Cinema in Small Heath. She and Danny were holding hands. His leg rested reassuringly against hers as they watched the Pathé newsreel. British and Commonwealth forces had taken the airport in Tobruk in North Africa . . . This was all Rachel took in before her mind wandered again.

She sat clutching Danny's hand. They had only been to the pictures once before and that had been interrupted by an air raid. This time, although no sirens had gone off so far, she just could not keep her mind on the picture. She was starting to feel sick. The air was growing thick with smoke as people puffed their way nervously through the action. It felt as if the seat was closing in around her and she had to quell an urge to get up and fight her way out. On top of that, real life was the most pressing, frightening thing now. She could not escape into the story of the picture. She sat stroking a hand over her as yet flat stomach. If it were not for the fact that she felt so odd and different in herself, it would be impossible to take in that anything had changed. How could there be a baby in there? There was nothing to see at all.

It only takes the once, Gladys had said. Even so, she

still had doubts that she was really carrying a child. Sometimes when she was playing with little Cissy she would gaze at her thinking, no! It couldn't be that she was going to have a little child like her! She would go through periods of forgetting and be jolted back into remembering. I'm expecting . . . Oh my God.

She shifted restlessly in her seat, the acrid air burning her nostrils. Looking along the shadowy row of people she thought with dread about trying to get out. But what if she was sick in here? Sensing her restlessness, Danny turned to her. In the flickering light from the screen, she was struck by how young he looked. Another twinge of panic seized her. He *was* young. They both were. Help me, she thought. Don't leave me, Danny. She leaned forwards, resting her head in her hands.

She felt Danny's hand on her back and his breath on her ear. 'What's up? D'you want to go out?'

She hesitated, then nodded.

Amid the annoyed tuttings, they shuffled out. Rachel could no longer hold back her tears. The lady in the ticket office looked curiously at them so they hurried out into the freezing, blacked-out night. 'Shut that door!' she called after them. 'That warden'll be after me.' Danny put an arm round Rachel's shoulders.

'Oh, Danny,' she burst out as soon as they were in the Coventry Road. 'What're we going to do?'

Danny stopped her. 'C'm'ere.' He put his arms round her, hugging her to him. Both of them were shivering, the icy air biting into them.

'We can't just go on as if nothing's happening,' she sobbed. She tried not to make too much fuss but she felt like crying her heart out.

She had struggled on, still going to work and getting through Christmas. She told her mother she was feeling a bit off colour. Fortunately, what with the exhausting nights of the raids and having to tend to Cissy's needs, her mother had no energy to notice that there was anything different about her.

'Rach, we're going to be together, just you and me – that's all that matters,' Danny said into her hair.

'But what're we going to do?' She pulled back and tried to see into his face in the darkness. 'You won't leave me, will you? You'll stand by me?'

It was not the first time they had had this conversation but there was so little time together, what with work and everything else. And Gladys had suggested that for the moment they wait and see and think things through.

'The babby won't be showing for a bit yet. Let's see if it takes – wait 'til you're three months gone at least, before you make any rash decisions.'

Rachel felt, rather than saw, the serious way Danny was looking at her.

'Did you mean it – about getting married?' she asked in a small voice. It wasn't the first time she had asked. She just kept needing reassurance.

'Course I did – I keep telling yer,' Danny said in his gruff way. 'Look, Rach – I know this shouldn't've happened like this. And we're hardly more than kids ourselves.' Even so she was surprised by how grown up he sounded at that moment. 'But you're my girl. You're what I want – nothing else. Does it matter how old we are? We can get wed and look after each other. I love you, girl –'

She sobbed at the tenderness of his words, all her fear and worry pouring out. She felt as fragile as a little seed pod, blown by the wind.

'D'you mean it, Danny – do you really? I love you

too, but I don't want to . . .' She could not speak for crying.

'What?' he asked, stroking her back.

'I don't want to force you into it.'

'No one's forcing me. Not you and not Auntie. Look, Rach –' His voice became nearly as emotional as hers. 'It's terrible not to have anyone. It's the worst. And now I've got you – and you're all I want.'

Moved by his words, she cried even harder. When she could speak again she said, 'Oh, Danny – I'm so scared. But you're all I want as well. We'll be together, won't we?' She let go of him and wiped her eyes, feeling stunned suddenly with exhaustion. 'I just don't know what Mom's going to say.'

They walked slowly along the road, Danny's arm around her. After a moment's thought, he said, 'I'll come home with you now. We'll tell her – tonight.'

'Now?' she gasped. 'But Danny . . .'

'Come on.' He grasped her hand. 'Now. The two of us together. I'm not leaving you to do it on your own.'

'This is how people must feel before they go in front of a firing squad,' Rachel said as they made their way along the blackness of the Coventry Road. The night was clear and cold. White pinpricks of stars and the occasional shaded lamps of a bus were the only light. She let out a giggle. Now they were on their way to tell her mother she felt a relieved, devil-may-care lightness coming over her. She kept wanting to laugh hysterically one moment and burst into tears the next.

'We'd better go and get it over with,' she said.

Danny was solemn and determined. 'Any problems with your old man and I'll sock him one,' he promised.

'He's not my old man. He's nothing to me,' she said. 'What's it got to do with him?' But her light-hearted bravery seeped away as they neared the house. Fred Horton would damn well think it was his business as the man of the house, even if he took very little notice of her the rest of the time.

'I can't,' she said. Standing outside the blacked-out windows of the shop she seemed to feel the cold, smoky night air weigh down on her. She clung to Danny's arm. 'Let's not do it now – let's leave it 'til I'm showing, and then we'll have to . . .'

'No.' Danny seemed to be puffed up with all the determination that had deserted her. 'Let's tell them. We'll tell 'em we're getting married.'

'Are we allowed to get married?' she said, suddenly appalled by her lack of knowledge about this, or anything.

'Auntie says you have to have permission if you're not twenty-one.' Before she could say that Peggy would never give permission in a month of Sundays, he said, 'Got your key?'

Inside, she could hardly get up the dark stairs, her legs were trembling so much. It was still only about eight o'clock, though so dark and wintry that it felt like the middle of the night. The passage smelt unpleasantly of boiled fish. Everything was quiet. Cissy must already be asleep.

'Is that you, Rachel?' she heard her mother's voice come sleepily from the sitting room upstairs. Mom thought she had been to the pictures with Lilian, who in fact she only snatched quick chats with at Bird's in their breaks. She had not seen her in the evening for weeks.

'Yes.' She forced her voice to sound normal.

They stood on the landing together in confusion.

Danny indicated that they should go in. Rachel shook her head desperately. She was so shaky and terrified she could hardly stand. He took her hand.

'Go *on*.'

They stepped into the room. Fred was asleep in the armchair near the glowing embers of the fire, feet splayed apart on the rug. He had loosened his shirt collar and fly buttons and his mouth was slightly open. Peggy was bent over a piece of hand stitching, squinting in the poor light.

'Mom.'

Peggy looked up. It took her a second to register that someone else was there and she sat up straighter in indignation. Her crinkly hair was still fastened tightly back and she looked hard faced and forbidding.

'Who's this? Rachel – what're you thinking of, bringing some strange person into the house at this time of night. Fred – Fred, wake up!'

Fred Horton righted himself with a snort, said, 'Uh – what's the matter? Who's this?' A second's realization later he hastily buttoned up. 'What's going on? A man can't sit in his own house . . .'

'Mother – this is Danny,' Rachel said as they stood before her. She deliberately did not speak to Fred.

'Hello, Mrs Horton,' Danny said stiffly.

'Rachel, what's going on?' Peggy said with growing annoyance. 'How dare you bring some stranger in here at this time of night. You – go on with you. Out you go.'

This was not a good start. Danny stood calmly, upright and dignified. 'I'll go in a minute,' he said. 'But I've summat to say to you, Mrs Horton.'

'Have you now?' Peggy said in a tone of heavy sarcasm. 'I've got something to say to you too – what d'you think you're doing here with my daughter?

Rachel – who is this . . . This . . .' She waved her arm, not seeming to be able to find the right word.

'I've come to ask you,' Danny said carefully. He struggled to find the right words as well and when they came out, even Rachel could hear how rough and awkward he sounded. 'Thing is, Rachel and me . . .' He was clumsy now. 'We want to get wed.'

Peggy gaped at him. Rachel saw Danny through her Peggy's judging eyes, his workaday clothes, his skinny body and unrefined voice. She could see the snooty contempt growing on her mother's face. Finally Peggy burst out laughing. 'Oh – you want to "get wed",' she mocked. 'The pair of you no more than children and I've never even set eyes on you before, whoever you are. I don't know you from Adam and you're certainly not having anything more to do with my daughter, who, *when* she gets married, will be finding a *professional* person to marry – someone with a lot more prospects than you, I can tell you! Rachel, I don't know what you're thinking of but please get rid of this person.' Her anger was growing now. 'I take it you've been telling untruths about where you've been, you deceitful little hussy . . .' She looked to her husband. 'Fred – make this . . . this little guttersnipe leave our house, will you?'

'Right –' Fred was pushing himself up out of his chair. 'Now you – get on your way . . .'

'No!' Rachel cried. 'Mom – you've got to listen!'

Fred subsided, temporarily.

'Mom, this is Danny. I've known him for ages – he used to be on the market with Gladys Poulter – d'you remember? Ages ago. And we're friends – well, more than . . . And . . .' She started to grow tearful again. 'We want to get married.'

'Oh, you want to get married!' Peggy's mockery

flared into anger. 'I don't care what you want!' She laughed again, in an outraged way. 'Have you gone out of your mind? You walk in here with some factory Jack I've never seen before . . .'

'But Mom, I told you—'

'When you're barely old enough to boil an egg by yourself, and you expect me to agree to . . .'

'Time to go, lad.' Fred got up again, attempting to exert some sort of authority. He went to lay a hand on Danny's shoulder, but Danny shrugged away from his reach.

'Mom,' Rachel burst out. 'You've got to listen! I'm in the family way. I'm having a baby – and it's Danny's.'

The air froze into silence. After an endless, thunderstruck pause, Peggy hissed, 'You'd better be having me on, Rachel.'

'No, Mother.' She shook her head, defiant now. 'I'm not.'

Peggy looked from one to the other of them, seeing the seriousness of their announcement. She got to her feet in a terrible, threatening way, her eyes never leaving Rachel's face. Rachel took a step back. Danny reached for her hand. Fred Horton stood quite still, without any apparent clue what to do.

'Is this true?' Peggy asked hoarsely.

Rachel nodded. She looked down then at the rug under her feet, her cheeks burning.

'Get out.' Her mother's voice lashed her. 'You filthy, dirty girl. Get out of my house and don't you ever come round here again. You're no daughter of mine. And you, you little –' She could not seem to bring to mind a bad enough word. 'You've corrupted her – *sullied* her. Well, on your head be it. Don't involve me in your disgusting carry-on. She's yours now!' She looked at Danny as if she was about to slap him. 'Both of you. You've made your own foul bed – you can lie on it. Now get out!'

Twenty

Rachel was dry eyed now and explosive with rage as they waited for the bus on the Coventry Road. She could not even look at Danny, even though her fury was not directed at him. Her feelings were too confused. She hugged her arms around herself, looking away along the dark street.

'Rach?'

She didn't reply.

'Come on – don't be like this.' He sounded wretched and tried to take her in his arms but she thrust him away. She wanted his comfort but could not accept it, not then.

What was she doing out here in the cold, cast out by her mother? Did Mom really mean it – didn't she have any pity or love in her heart? But Rachel had always known that her mother did not really want her. Some of the horrible things Peggy had said to her over the years flooded into her mind. *You've always been a millstone round my neck . . .* She's got what she wants now, Rachel thought bitterly. Me out of the way so she doesn't have to bother with me. Just her and Fred and Cissy – a neat little family, no mess. And what about Danny? In her fragile state, even her own feelings about Danny were cast into doubt. Here she was throwing her lot in with him. How well did she really know him, when it came down to it? How did she know for sure that he would stand by her and not just take off and disappear the way his own father had done?

Danny withdrew and stood in silent misery beside her, as if her pushing him away had forced him right back into himself. She could not see his face in the darkness, but he lowered his head, hands in his pockets. She knew this stance – how dejected he could be – but she felt so bad herself that she did not have it in her to do anything about it at that moment.

A bicycle passed, the front lamp covered except for a tiny slit. Soon afterwards they heard the bus in the distance. They boarded in silence and sat hunched up together. It felt as if they were hundreds of miles apart.

They had only gone a mile, to Small Heath, when the shrieking sound of the sirens rose up outside. The driver gave a shout of frustration and the bus slid to a halt.

'Right – here we go again! Everybody off. Get yerselves into a shelter – there's one not far, along there.'

There were only a handful of people on the bus and they all climbed off into the howling racket. Danny clasped her hand. The noise battered Rachel's ears and made every nerve in her body jangle. As they stumbled along the pavement, the white beams of searchlights prowling the sky above, they could hear a voice shouting, 'Over here – come on, get yerselves under cover. Quick!'

A finger of light moved towards them and they saw one of the ARP Wardens, a middle-aged man with a dark little moustache.

'Down here – come on, look sharp. There's room for a few more sardines in here.'

There was another man behind them and the three of

them stumbled their way down the brick steps into the basement under a factory, into an atmosphere already fuggy with the collective miasma of a crowd of people, some of whose faces they could just make out in the light of an oil lamp. There must have been close on a hundred people in there.

'That's it, bab,' a lady called, 'come on in and get the door shut. Don't want those cowing Jerries seeing our light. Shove up, lads – look, there's still some space near the door.'

The woman, who had a hairnet on over a head bumpy with curlers, seemed to be in charge. Somewhere in the murky depths of the shelter a child was crying, a ragged, grating noise which quickly made Rachel want to scream herself. 'Shh now, Terry,' a lady kept urging. 'That's enough of that racket – just close yer eyes.'

'Are they after Small Heath tonight? Bets on, eh?' the older lady said.

There were plenty of firms in Small Heath – Singer, Alldays & Onions and others. They'd already hit the BSA, where they were turning out armaments, back in November, flattening part of the factory.

There were a few chairs and benches. Some people had brought bits of bedding for children and a few others were lying down, but most sat up. Rachel and Danny sank into a small space on a wooden bench right by the door. Next to Danny was a large man with his head back against the wall, apparently fast asleep against all the odds, with the general carry-on going on around him. He was a big fleshy fellow, with cropped brown hair, his open mouth emitting little snores. Rachel eyed him enviously. If only she could just go to sleep like that!

The fact that they were close to the door was both good and bad. It meant more fresh air leaking around the door to combat the growing stench in there, but it was also freezing cold.

'Here –' Danny took off his jacket and covered them both with it.

'But the wall's freezing,' she protested, seeing him sit back in only his shirt.

'S'all right,' he said. 'Come on – just lean on me.'

She felt suddenly utterly drained and queasy. The thought of the cold night ahead sitting in here was almost too much to bear. Dimly she heard the rumble of the planes' engines. Later there were muffled bangs. Rachel imagined the incendiaries, falling through the darkness like candles. Everything went quiet. The child stopped crying as if someone had unplugged him. But the bangs were muted compared to the racket of some raids. When the planes had passed over, the grizzling and the buzz of conversation resumed.

'Ooh – well, that wasn't too close . . . Some other poor bugger's getting it . . .'

'. . . there was a bloody great crater full of water, right outside the shelter,' Rachel heard, as she tried to doze. Another voice said, 'We know, Dor, we was there as well, remember?'

'. . . and I said to 'im, I ain't standing 'ere on these bunions for nothing but a half-pound of tripe – I've been shopping with 'im for the past thirty years . . .'

'. . . and that barrage balloon come down and the cables dug up all my leeks, right along the row . . .'

'Anyone want a biscuit? I've got a flask of tea but it won't go far . . .'

At some stage as she dozed against Danny's warm chest, there was an outbreak of singing: 'We'll Meet Again . . .' and 'Daisy, Daisy . . .' Danny put his arms round her and rested his chin on her head. For a while, both of them slept.

She woke in the dim light. Her back was very stiff and she moved to ease it. All was quieter, except for snores and the odd moan as someone shifted position. She listened. Surely the all-clear hadn't sounded, had it? That would have woken her, she was sure.

'Rach?' Danny woke as she shifted to sit up. Her feet were so utterly frozen in her black work shoes that they were aching and she felt stiff as a rusty bicycle. But she did not, to her surprise, feel sick, despite the smell in there. She was clearer in her head.

'Just need to sit up,' she whispered. They rearranged themselves side by side with the jacket over them, their heads close together.

'Rach?' In the gloom she could see his breath on the freezing air. 'You angry with me?'

She felt different now. Sleep had changed things. She laid her hand on his chest under the jacket, feeling the bony warmth of him. 'No. I was angry with Mom. Am angry. And I'm scared, Danny. I don't know what it's like having a baby and what will everyone say and I'll lose my job and how are we going to live?' She started feeling overwhelmed again at all these thoughts, but she was determined not to cry.

He clasped her hand. 'I'll look after you. I *will*. I can work and Auntie'll let us live with her, at least to start.'

'Has she said so?'

'No. Not as such. She's asked me what I think I should do and I just say we should do the right thing and get married. Beyond that . . .' He shrugged. 'I dunno. But Rach –' He turned to face her and she could see the gleam of his eyes. 'I don't mind. I know we're starting young, but family's everything – we'll be family. Auntie says –' He hesitated.

'What?'

'She says I'll have to make a man of myself. I want to be a man – proper like. Not like my father. Not just give up on everyone. Whoever's in there . . .' He stroked her belly. He seemed more able to believe in the baby than she did. 'That's family.'

'Oh God, Danny – I feel too young.'

He nodded. 'I know. But what's to do?'

'If it's a girl, d'you want to call her Rose, after your sister?'

'No. That'd be sad. Let's call her summat . . . modern.' He thought. 'Melanie.'

'Melanie? Like in *Gone With the Wind*?'

'I s'pose so. It's pretty – I think anyway.'

'What if he's a boy?'

Danny chuckled. 'Tommy. Like Tommy Trinder – he's funny he is.'

'Not Jack?' She thought of the sweet, happy boy in his sketches.

Danny thought for a moment, then said quietly, 'No, not Jack.'

'Melanie or Tommy.' Just for a second she was caught by excitement.

It was possible for a while to forget how cold it was. They sat holding hands under the jacket. The big man beside Danny stirred, opened his eyes and fumbled in his pocket for a cigarette. 'All right?' he said blearily, nodding at Danny as he lit up. Danny nodded back. The man said nothing else.

'Danny?' Rachel whispered. 'We're going to have to get married, aren't we?'

'Yeah.'

'I don't even know what to do. Mom'll have to agree to it.'

'I have to ask you, don't I?' Moving closer to her ear, Danny whispered, 'Rachel Horton, will you marry me?'

She looked into his face, their noses almost touching. She knew she was where she wanted to be, whatever else. Her home was with Danny. 'I will,' she said. 'I love you, Danny. I just want to be with you. I want us to have a nice little house with running water and a bathroom and a garden for the children . . .'

'And you'll be Mrs Booker,' he said. 'Like our mom was.'

'I will, won't I?'

He kissed her solemnly. 'Rachel,' he said in wonder. 'Rachel Booker.'

The next day was utterly exhausting. The all-clear sounded at last, just before dawn. By then there was no point in trying to get to Aston. It was nearly time to go to work. They stayed in the shelter even when a lot of the others turned out to go back to their houses. Cold air slid down the stairs and cleared the atmosphere a little. The lady in the hairnet came round with a kettle full of tea and gave them a cup each. Rachel drank it, then had to rush up outside to be sick.

'Oh dear,' the lady said. 'That's being up all night for yer. You going to work?'

Rachel nodded groggily.

'Well, look – have another cup and see if you can keep it down.'

'You're ever so kind,' Rachel said.

'It's no bother, bab,' she said, pouring the last of the

tea. 'All you people've got to get to work – and you look all in.'

'Come to ours after,' Danny instructed her as they parted for the day. He kissed her gently. 'We'll talk to Auntie. She'll be all right.'

It seemed astonishing to her after every raid that when she got to Digbeth, the Devonshire Works were still standing, still producing custard powder despite all the struggles with rationing. Some of the streets around had been badly smashed up in other raids, mess and rubble everywhere. Such a large factory right in town seemed fair game, but so far, though the gutters were littered with spent incendiary canisters, the air thick with smoke, Bird's stood intact. She worked all day in a daze of tiredness and it seemed forever before it was time to go.

She stepped thankfully outside, her whole body aching with exhaustion. At the corner of Gibb Street she saw, not Danny, but a woman in a camel coat and dark green hat waiting with a toddler in her arms. It was a moment before she took in the baby's gingery hair and excitement at seeing her, and realized that it was her mother and Cissy.

'Way-chaw!' Cissy was shouting, waving her arms. That was the best she could do in saying Rachel's name.

Warily Rachel approached them. She took Cissy's hand, smiling at the little girl who bounced and gurgled with pleasure. Their mother's stony expression softened a fraction.

'She was asking for you,' she said.

Rachel shrugged. Trams rumbled along Digbeth. She waited to hear what Peggy had to say. It was typical of her to use Cissy as a reason for coming.

'I don't know what to say,' Peggy came out with eventually. As this obviously didn't get them anywhere, she added, 'I was hasty last night – what I said.' She still sounded on the edge of anger and she spoke without looking at Rachel. Her eyes fastened on the other side of the road.

'I don't want to cast you off.' This did not sound wholly convincing and she stalled for a moment. 'You're going to marry him – that . . . that creature?'

'His name's Danny,' Rachel flared. 'Danny Booker. You knew his auntie, remember?'

Peggy looked down at her feet. 'I don't want any of this anywhere near Fred.'

Any of this? Rachel's thoughts burned inside her. Well, it wasn't my choice to be anywhere near Fred in the first place. But she kept them to herself.

'Where will you live?'

'With Mrs Poulter – in Alma Street.' She hoped to God this was true.

Her mother nodded. She seemed helpless.

'Will you come to our wedding, Mom? We will get married – but it won't be much.'

'I don't know.' Peggy's voice was desolate, on the edge of tears, but she seemed, as ever, to be feeling sorry for herself. 'I'm losing a daughter.'

'Only if that's what you want,' Rachel retorted.

Peggy's head shot up and the tears did not come. She seemed startled. 'I need time to think,' she said abruptly.

'Mom –' Rachel was near tears herself now. 'I'm expecting. I *am*.' She still had to struggle to make herself believe it. 'We'll get married, Danny and me. Only you have to say we can . . .'

Peggy gave a sharp bark of a laugh. 'A shotgun wedding. Oh – just what I've struggled for all these years, scrimping and slaving to bring you up nicely so you could marry well.'

Rachel continued to look at her. 'Better a wedding than none. He could've run off and left me. He's good, Danny is, Mom. He *is*.'

Her mother seemed to pass through a moment of unbearable tension. 'Very well,' she snapped eventually. 'Marry him then. You've made your bed – you can lie on it. But don't expect any help from me. I've had enough of sacrificing myself for you.'

Rachel watched as her mother walked self-righteously away from her in her neat winter coat, along Digbeth. Guilt and shame mingled with her hurt and anger. She wanted to cry after Peggy, 'I'm sorry, Mom – I know you're ashamed of me, but please don't go! Please just stay with me and be my mom!' And, as her tears started to come, her inner cry turned to, 'Can't you be nice? Can't you think of someone except yourself – just for once?' But within seconds, without looking back, Peggy had disappeared, merging in among the crowds along the pavement.

Twenty-One

On a snowy February afternoon, Rachel and Danny stood side by side in front of the altar. The church was cold and dark and outside, the sky was so low it seemed to brush the spire. Rachel had put on everything she possessed in the way of clothing under the pretty silk dress they had bought from the Rag Market, the colour of almond blossom. Even so, her feet, in a little pair of fawn court shoes, were numb with cold. She was carrying a bunch of pale cream narcissi.

Peggy had softened enough to let her come into the house and collect some of her things.

'I can't have you here for long,' she said, tight-lipped at the door. 'You must understand that.'

'I'm getting married,' Rachel told Peggy haughtily. 'So I wouldn't be here anyway.'

She packed her clothes and a few belongings and defiantly took her leave. But she felt so miserable getting on the bus along the Coventry Road, her mother's only positive words, thrown at her back, being, 'You might as well let me know when the wedding is.'

Rachel was surprised to realize just how happy Gladys was to have her moving in. She had lost Jess and Amy. Nancy reported that though there was still a long way to go – Amy was still wetting the bed – the sisters were happier and more settled out there than they had ever been in Aston. As well as feeling that she had let them down Gladys was happy to have another girl in the house.

'If it wasn't for your mother I'd've said wait a bit until you get married,' she told Rachel. 'Just to be sure. But now . . .'

'But we want to get wed anyway, Auntie,' Danny protested. He was all for it, eager as a puppy, as if it was just the thing he had been waiting for.

Gladys gave him a tight-lipped look, as if to say, *You've no idea, son.* 'But now you're here,' she went on, 'I'd best go and see the vicar and get the banns read. Get things done proper. And Danny – until you're wed, Rachel'll sleep in the room next to me. You stay up in the attic.' She gave him a fierce, meaningful look.

'All right, Auntie,' Danny said.

'And you can wipe that grin off yer face an' all, lad,' Gladys retorted.

And now, without too much fuss, the day had arrived.

'I now pronounce you man and wife.' The vicar smiled valiantly at them, as if trying to chase an expression of sceptical doubt away from his features.

We must look like children to him, Rachel thought, feeling the strangeness of the brass ring which Danny had bought, encircling her finger. We aren't much more. And he's probably guessed that I'm in the family way even though it doesn't show. A blush of shame spread across her cheeks, but she smiled up at Danny, so smart today in a suit. His blue eyes met hers and he looked happy and fizzing with excitement. He took her hand.

'Wife,' he whispered, in amazement. 'You're mine now. Mrs Booker. Family.'

Behind them, on one side of the aisle stood Gladys, in a grey woollen dress with a spray of red silk roses pinned above her left breast, and Dolly Morrison – who would always go to a wedding, given the chance – in a fuchsia-pink frock and teetering navy high heels. On the other was Peggy, alone apart from Cissy, who kept calling Rachel's name. She stood very upright, wearing a smart navy coat and hat, with an air of trying to rise above everything that was going on.

They did not have an organist or any hymns. Two lit candles on the altar gave the only light apart from pale daylight falling through the windows. Afterwards, they trooped quietly back down the aisle, this tiny wedding party, and stood just inside the church, the freezing wind gusting in through the open door. Rachel held Cissy and made a fuss of her. Peggy had dressed her up very nicely in a little pea-green wool coat and hat and her plump cheeks were rubbed pink from the wind.

'Waych!' Cissy kept saying excitedly. Rachel melted with fondness at the sight of her. She was going to miss living with her baby sister.

'This is Danny,' Rachel told her. Cissy beamed.

'Danny!' she cried, clapping her hands.

Danny laughed. 'She's got my name better than yours.'

'She can't say her r's yet,' Rachel laughed. 'Can you, Ciss?'

'I remember you from the market,' Gladys was saying to Peggy.

'Oh, that was a long while back,' Peggy replied dismissively.

Rachel saw Gladys sizing her mother up. She observed the strength in Gladys, her determination not to be talked down to. Rachel felt, once again, very annoyed with her mother. When it came down to it, Peggy and Gladys did exactly the same sort of work. Why did Mom always have to act as if she was so superior?

'Well,' Gladys said, 'whatever we might think, these two're man and wife now. You're our Danny's mother-in-law and you're welcome in our house whenever you'd like to visit. In fact we're going back there to toast the pair of 'em now, if you want to join us.'

'I see,' Peggy said. 'No, I don't think . . .'

Rachel could see she was extremely uncomfortable with Gladys's directness and everything else about her. She had started referring to Gladys as 'that gypsy woman'.

'And you can come if you want to visit your daughter and your grandchild, when it arrives,' Gladys went on bluntly. 'Unless they're welcome at yours.'

'We'll have to see.' Peggy spoke resentfully. 'You seem to have taken over everything,' she added. 'I can't see that I shall be needed. I think I'd better be going now.' She turned and started out, down the church steps.

'Mom!' Rachel said, hurrying after her, suddenly close to tears. This was her wedding day after all. And she was still holding Cissy, as Peggy realized when she reached the pavement and had to stop. 'Don't be like that with Auntie . . .' She held her sister tight as Peggy went to wrench Cissy from her arms. Cissy began to squawk in protest.

'Auntie?' Peggy said savagely, hauling Cissy away from her. 'Since when has that woman been any auntie of yours?' Once again she was about to walk off.

'When will I see you?' Rachel said. She felt cold and low now. Was this how it was always going to be? And today, when she needed her mother to be with her, to be on her side, Peggy had spoiled everything.

Cissy was squirming and screaming so much in Peggy's arms that her hat fell off. Rachel bent to pick it up from the cold tiles, a wave of nausea passing through her as she did so. For a second she felt like giving up on her mother and never seeing her again, while knowing at the same time that she needed her. And she wanted to see her baby sister. She handed Cissy's hat to her mother.

'You can call in.' Peggy almost had to shout over Cissy's howls. 'This isn't the moment . . . Goodbye.' And she turned away, without looking back, along the snowy pavement. Rachel watched. She could hear Cissy crying from all the way along the street.

It was only when she moved into number three with Gladys that Rachel started to get to know the area better and took more notice of their yard, off Alma Street. Aston had smells of its own. As well as the metallic and oily smells from the factories, and wafts of ale and smoke as you passed the pubs, there were certain aromas that belonged especially to the area – the whiffs of vinegar which floated from the HP factory and the strange, sour, hoppy scent of Ansells brewery at Aston Cross. As for the yard, of course she was familiar with it, with the tap and brew house, and the high wall of Taplin & May, the metal-spinning works at the end, from where you could hear the throb of machinery and thin screech of metal. They seldom saw the workers because they used an entrance round in the next street, but the murmur of voices or occasional shouts came through the wall.

A few of the faces were familiar: Ma Jackman at number two, whose son Edwin, an odd, sullen lad, still lived at home and worked in a nearby factory. She knew the Morrisons, of course, with all their boys. Mo, she discovered, worked as a road tester at the Norton works and was in their Home Guard unit. Sometimes at the end of the working day, the roar of a motorcycle would be heard in the yard and Mo would appear astride a Norton 16H round which his sons would gather begging for rides.

'Gerroff, you lot – out of my way!' he'd bellow. 'Don't flaming touch that or you'll get me in big trouble. Ernie,' he'd instruct the oldest boy. 'You make sure this lot keep their grubby mitts off it while I have my tea, right?'

Of course this was a lost cause and the moment he parked the thing the lads were all over it. After downing his meal, Mo would come out, yell them all off it and jump astride the bike, off for a night's work as a despatch rider for the Home Guard – all before breakfast and back to work the next day.

At number four were the Parsonses, a very old couple. Mrs Parsons, a tiny twig of a person who dressed perpetually in black, lived in terror that she and her husband would have to 'throw ourselves on the mercy of the parish'. Into the workhouse, she meant. Gladys, for one, often did their shopping and everyone lent a hand to make sure this did not happen.

At the end, at number five, lived Lil and Stanley Gittins. Lil, a glamour-puss of about forty, wore her mop of faded blonde hair piled on top of her head and frocks which displayed her cleavage to the best advantage. She was a cheerful soul, except in drink, when she had a tendency to punch people. Gladys described Lil as having 'a heart of gold but not much going on in the top storey'. But she seemed to have taken Danny and Rachel into that golden heart and saw them as if they were something out of a romantic tale from *Woman's Own*.

Just the other day, she had come teetering on her high heels across the uneven bricks of the yard, breaking into snatches of 'South of the Border' in between puffs on her cigarette. Rachel smiled, hearing her as she sat just outside Gladys's door, taking a few minutes to rest. It was one of the first days with a hint of spring warmth.

'All right are yer, you two lovebirds?' she called to Rachel.

'Yes, ta, Mrs Gittins,' Rachel said shyly.

'Ooh, I remember when me and Stanley were like you two. We got wed good and quick, I can tell yer – I had our Marie at about your age!' She gave a gurgling chuckle. 'Happy days!' Lil reached her door, humming another snatch of 'South of the Border', and turned with a flick of her bouncing blonde hair. 'Littl'un all right?'

Rachel nodded. 'Think so. She's moving about a bit.'

'Think it's a girl, do you then?' Lil called, pushing the door open. 'A mother always knows. Oooh,' she cooed. 'If my Stanley was 'ere I'd have another an' all.'

Stanley Gittins, who had worked as a railway goods checker, had been called up the year before and was a radio operator in RAF Fighter Command. Rachel had never met him, though she had seen one of their married daughters coming and going.

She smiled as Lil Gittins disappeared tunefully into her house. Lil was good at jollying everyone through air raids. And it was nice when people were just glad for her about the baby, instead of acting as if it was something to be ashamed of, like her mother. Even though she and Danny were now married and everything was above board, she felt self-conscious about the round bulge that was growing in front of her. But Lil Gittins treated her as if it was the most natural and happy thing in the world, and it cheered her up.

It was a good yard with mostly kindly neighbours, but Rachel also saw that Gladys was the gaffer. It was Gladys who got behind either Danny or Edwin to sweep muck away in the yard, who made sure everyone did their fair share of cleaning in the lavatories and sorted out when the washes were to be done in the copper in the brew house. Gladys also collected the didlum money, a fund everyone paid a little into to save for Christmas, or for any unexpected emergency, so that they all had a bit put away.

Gladys was full of energy. When she was not on the Saturday Rag Market she was out acquiring things to sell – from houses or other outlets and sales – or she was sorting her wares and calculating how much they might fetch. She also sewed sheets and pillowcases to sell. The smallest bedroom next to hers had bundles of her stock stored in bags and boxes. The two other things Gladys did religiously, every week, were go to church on Sunday and to the cinema, either the Globe or her favourite, the Orient at Six Ways, one afternoon in the week.

'I pay my respects to the Lord,' she told Rachel, 'and the pictures is my treat.'

'You do quite well just on the market, don't you, Auntie?' Rachel asked soon after she moved in, when they were folding clothes together in the downstairs room.

'Well, it's not bad, even with the war on,' Gladys said. 'I'm not selling stuff that's on the ration. But I've done plenty to keep body and soul together in my time. Cleaning, taking in washing – you name it.'

'Like my mother,' Rachel said. But Gladys's hands

were in a worse state than Mom's, the knuckles swollen.

Gladys paused in the middle of folding an embroidered tablecloth and looked at her. 'You lost your father,' she stated.

'When I was five,' Rachel said. She didn't feel like going into how or why. 'There was just the two of us after that.'

There was silence for a second. 'She had it hard then, your mother,' Gladys said.

Rachel didn't know what to say. She kept her eyes on her work, feeling the gaze of the soldier in the photograph looking down at them and her heart contracted with sadness, but she was too shy to say anything to Gladys about it. Gladys was so dignified and in a way, forbidding, that she could not imagine ever asking her about anything. She had an aura about her of both strength and a deep reserve. Rachel thought of the bedroom door upstairs, always closed. Once she'd asked Danny if he'd ever been in there. Danny had shrugged.

'No. Why should I?'

Rachel knew that she would never go against Gladys's wishes. Gladys was the queen of the house and they both owed her so much. Rachel already loved and respected her. But she also realized in that moment that she knew barely anything about this woman who had taken her into her home.

Twenty-Two

The longer Rachel stayed in Aston, the more Danny and Gladys seemed like her real family. Gladys was in charge in the yard and in her own home and there was something reassuring about the way she was boss. Rachel soon learned the way she liked things done in the house: the places where she kept her crocks and kitchen things, the fact that her bedroom was private with the door always kept shut, the fact that she liked good manners around her. She was also very hard-working, forever mending or ironing something or out getting goods to sell on the market. All these things became details that Rachel never questioned. She felt at home.

And it was wonderful that she and Danny could be together now, properly, even if that did mean nights squashed in side by side in Taplin & May's cellar, or the air-raid shelter at the back of the next-door yard.

The city was taking a terrible pounding. Everyone was bonded together by long nights of fear and sleeplessness. Sitting in the shelter with Dolly and Mo Morrison and the boys, and with Lil Gittins, they drew closer as neighbours. Except Ma Jackman whose response to sharing anything with her neighbours was, 'You're not having any of mine . . .' Old Mr and Mrs Parsons refused to get up.

'Me and the old girl'll stay abed of a night,' Mr Parsons had told Gladys when the bombing started the year before. 'If it's our time to go, we'll go. We'd take so long to get in the shelter, my old girl and me, the raid would be over by the time we'd got there. Don't you go worrying about us, Mrs Poulter. We'll take what comes.'

Just before Easter there came a raid as long and destructive as any that had gone before. They staggered out of the shelter in the morning wondering if anything could still be standing. There was no water in the taps and the air was rank with the smell of burning.

'I wonder if Mom and Cissy're all right?' Rachel said as they limped stiffly back across the yard.

Rachel had reached an arrangement with Peggy whereby she called in every week or two. Sometimes she longed for her mother's approval and support; at others she thought, I'm a married woman now and she'll just have to get used to it. At least it meant she could see Cissy, who was always overjoyed when she visited. She wanted her little sister to know she cared about her and wanted to be with her.

Danny put his arm round her. 'Best go and see after work,' he said. 'If you can get there. God knows what'll be running after all this.' Areas were often cordoned off where there was the worst damage, a landmine or an unexploded bomb.

'How much more of it?' Rachel said tearfully, exhausted by the very idea of a day's work after the night of howling bombs, the ground shaking around them.

'At least we're all here today, that's the main thing,' Gladys said, walking beside them with a couple of blankets folded in her arms. 'Let's be thankful for that.' She started humming one of her hymns. 'Praise my soul the King of heaven . . .' Gladys found a lot of comfort in hymns.

As the exhausting day passed and the terrible damage across Birmingham became known, Rachel stopped feeling so sorry for herself and knew Gladys was right. A lot of the burning smell, they discovered, was from Summer Lane which had been bombed from end to end, and there was damage to St Martin's church in the Bullring and many other places.

Once again, against the odds, the Devonshire Works stood unscathed amid the destruction all around. Rachel struggled through that day at work as if in a dream, feeling queasy and worn out.

That afternoon, when she finally got back to Aston, she had a shaming disagreement with Gladys.

Walking into the cosy little house, queasy with exhaustion, she threw herself down at the table, resting her head on her arms, feeling she might never get up again. Danny was not home yet. The room smelt of ironing and Gladys was at the table, peeling potatoes in a bowl and humming again.

'Did you see your mother?' she broke off to ask.

'Yes,' Rachel mumbled to the tabletop.

'House all right, is it?'

'Yes.' She did not mean to be rude, she was just so weary. She became aware of a movement near her and turned her head to see Gladys standing over her.

'What's up with you, miss?' she enquired tartly.

Rachel was beginning to realize that if there was one thing that was like a red rag to a bull with Gladys, it was people feeling sorry for themselves. But she *did* feel sorry for herself at that moment. She'd sat up all night, had been working all day – and she was expecting a baby. She was all in!

'Nothing,' Rachel said, still slumped over the table. 'I'm just tired, that's all.'

'In case you dain't notice,' Gladys said, a dangerous tone in her voice, 'we was all in the shelter all last night, listening to the same Jerry bombs falling from the sky. We still have to keep going, you know – the tea won't cook itself.'

'But I'm more tired than you,' Rachel retorted. 'I've been at work all day, and I'm the one who's having a baby!' She heard her voice turn high and whiny. 'How would you know what it's like? You haven't got any children.'

There was a silence so profound that she slowly pulled herself upright, filled with a plummeting sense of dread. She had never seen Gladys look anything like this before, not with her, anyway. Her jaw was clenched and her eyes bored into Rachel.

'How do you think you're in any position to say what I know or don't know, miss?' Gladys's voice was low and hard.

'I . . .' She stuttered. 'Well – you don't, do you? Have any children, I mean?'

In the tense seconds before Gladys could speak again, there were footsteps along the yard and Dolly's voice called out, 'Glad – you in?'

Gladys softened the grim expression on her face. 'Where else'd I be?' she called. 'Come in, Doll.'

Dolly's face appeared round the door. She had on a red flowery blouse and red lipstick. As ever she looked pretty and rather exotic. 'All right?' she said. 'Ooh, 'ello, Rach – how's the babby?'

'All right,' Rachel said shyly. She felt intense relief that Dolly had turned up when she did. Her heart was still beating fast after the way Gladys had looked at her. She'd better be careful in future. Gladys obviously thought she was getting above herself and she had never realized before that Gladys was so bitter about not having had children.

Dolly stood leaning on the door frame. 'One of my little buggers's come home with nits!' she complained. 'I bet the whole lot of 'em 've got them now – I'm going to have to see to them tonight. I bet it's that Carter boy Reggie knocks about with. He gets everything, he does – impetigo, fleas, you name it . . .'

'Cuppa tea?' Gladys asked, stemming the flow of indignation.

'All right, ta.' Dolly sank down at the table, pulling her cigarettes out of her pocket. She giggled. 'I'll laugh if Mo's got them an' all. We'll never hear the end of it, 'specially if it goes all round the factory!'

Gladys chuckled as well and Rachel felt relief seep through her. She hoped nothing more would be said about the disagreement.

'I'll get the boys to clean up that pram for you now the weather's picking up, Rach,' Dolly said. 'It's in the coal hole so it's a filthy mess, but it's not had anything nasty in it. It'll clean up nice. And I'm not planning on filling it again!' She gave her chesty laugh.

Rachel smiled and nodded her thanks.

'Now,' Dolly said, coming over all motherly. She looked intently at Rachel. 'How far on are you? About five months? When you've had it, you want to get yourself down to the clinic – it ain't far. I know some of 'em don't hold with it but I went with the last two and they was good to me. They'll find you a few bits and pieces for the babby if you need it. And they'll see everything's all right . . .'

Rachel saw Gladys watching them.

'Should I, Auntie?' she asked, looking very humbly at Gladys. Both of them knew it was a way of apologizing for the words they had had earlier.

'Dolly should know,' Gladys said, still speaking rather tartly. She took a seat beside her friend and started pouring tea. 'If she says go, you go.' Rachel took this as her cue to leave. The friends wanted to chat. But she also felt that she and Gladys had begun to make it up.

'Danny – what the hell're you doing?'

Rachel lay on their attic bed on a sweltering hot summer night as Danny pranced around the room.

As soon as they were married, they had taken up in the attic. The two of them shared Danny's bed, a three-quarter-sized frame which was not too bad. Rachel had made the room as homely as possible with some clippings from magazines – girls in pretty frocks and hats and a seaside view taken in Cornwall. 'That's for Jack and Patch,' she had teased Danny as she gummed it to the wall.

Going to bed and cuddling up with Danny was Rachel's very favourite moment of the day, especially on those blessed nights when there was no raid.

'You're so nice and warm!' she exclaimed, the first time they slept a whole night together. 'It's like sleeping next to the fire.'

But now a fire was the last thing she needed and Danny was jumping about like an excited flea.

'Stop it!' she hissed. 'What're you doing?'

She knew perfectly well what he was doing – he was

boxing his own shadow, as if there was an opponent coming at him through the door.

Danny took another lunge, dancing light on his feet. Rachel watched him miserably. She was so hot and uncomfortable, her belly distended further than she could have believed was possible. Her skin itched, her legs and back ached, and she was forever having to go and spend a penny.

'Littl'un in there must be pressing down on you,' Dolly told her. Whenever Dolly said something about the discomforts of carrying a child, it was always with a knowing smile.

'Oh – you should've seen me when I was carrying Fred,' she would begin. Fred or one of the four other lads. Then a whole catalogue of horrors would follow – swollen ankles, heartburn, piles – oh dearie me, those piles. And that was before they got on to the birth itself. Don't tell me! Rachel always wanted to scream. She would leave the room, upset and furious. She wanted them to give her sympathy, not fill her head full of terrifying ideas about what might be to come!

Then this weekend the Morrison boys and a few other hangers-on had hauled their old perambulator out into the yard and spent a happy hour sloshing water over it – and each other, naturally – and polishing it up, with Mo trying to supervise the proceedings and getting almost as wet as them. When Rachel saw it sitting out to dry in the sun, it had made her stomach turn with a mixture of excitement and dread. A pram – for a real baby!

'Danny,' she said miserably. 'Come 'ere, will you?'

Danny directed a vicious right hook at some invisible opponent. Rachel watched him. It was one of those moments when she was filled with bitter envy. It might be that Danny was this baby's father, but what difference did it make to him? His body was just as it had been before and his life would just go on as it had. She was the one having to put up with all this discomfort and not being able to lie comfortably in bed. Let alone walking about all day at work.

'*Danny*.'

'Wha'?' He lunged again.

'I want you.'

'Oh . . . All right.' He bounced onto the bed. 'What's up?'

'I just feel . . . I'm scared, Danny.' The tears came then. 'I don't know what it's going to be like. Feel it –'

He placed his hand on her. Arms and legs were lurching about inside her drum of a belly. Their eyes met. She snuggled closer to him.

'It's a bit like having a bomb inside you,' she said tearfully. 'You never know when it's going to go off and what it's going to be like.'

'Don't be daft,' Danny said. Though she sensed that he too was frightened. He was about to be a father and he had only just turned seventeen.

'You'll be all right,' Danny said. 'You're good at things, you are. And you'll be all right at that an' all.'

She pressed her cheek against his warm chest, a little comforted. 'That's a nice thing to say,' she said. 'We'll have to see, won't we?' She looked at him with big eyes. 'Give us a cuddle,' she said. 'I need you near me.'

So he took her in his arms and they held each other close. Rachel kissed his salty neck, feeling, in those moments, as if she had everything she needed in the world.

Twenty-Three

August 1941

'Don't forget your change, bab!'

'Oh – ta.' Rachel turned back with her bag of shopping to take the coins the woman was holding out to her in the baker's shop.

'You must be well off,' a woman joked in the queue. 'I'll 'ave it off yer if you don't want it – not that there's much to spend it on these days!'

The other women laughed and Rachel smiled vaguely.

'That's how you get when you're that far on,' someone else commented. 'You can't remember if you're coming or going.'

Rachel had now given up work as the baby was due any day. She felt self-conscious walking the streets, all big at the front and wearing a baggy floral dress that Dolly had lent her.

'I know it ain't pretty,' Dolly said as both of them eyed the frumpy frock with sludge green leaves all over it. 'Makes you feel like a sack of taters – but it's comfy enough. I'm hoping never to need it again but I daren't give it away – it'd be tempting fate!'

Gladys kept telling Rachel that she wasn't having her sitting around being waited on hand and foot – she could get out and do something useful if she wasn't bringing in any wages. So Rachel had taken on some of the shopping.

Before she finished work, leaving Bird's sadly behind her, she went to visit her mother. Every time she saw her, Peggy looked at her with disdain.

'The state of you,' she had remarked several times. She seemed ashamed and embarrassed by the sight of her pregnant daughter.

Rachel told Cissy that she might not see her for a little while but that soon she would be giving her a new little friend to play with. Cissy, at least, looked entranced at this news.

These days Rachel felt neither happy nor sad about the baby. She just felt as if she was in a haze most of the time and all she wanted to do was lie down and sleep. She was just heading into the greengrocer's when she almost collided with someone else in the doorway.

'Oh!' Rachel cried, startled, one hand instantly protecting her body and the baby.

'Sorry!' the other girl cried. She was a frail-looking, mousey-haired, blue-eyed person, not much older than Rachel, with a rather sweet face and dressed in a mauve shirtwaister dress that hung loosely on her skinny frame. Her wispy brown hair was dragged back any old how. She also seemed to have been in another world.

'Oh – sorry,' she said again. She stared at Rachel's prominent belly, then into her face. Tears came very abruptly and ran down her cheeks. She turned away and could not seem to stop crying. Rachel was not quite sure what to do.

'You all right?' she asked awkwardly. 'Did I hurt you?'

The girl turned back, wiping her face. 'Yes. No. I'm all right – only, I was expecting as well and my baby died, just last month. I was well on but it wasn't moving and the doctor said . . . They made me have him, but there wasn't a breath of life in him . . .' She crumpled into grief again. 'And now they've called up my Francis, God love him, and – well, I don't know when I'll see him and I just . . .' She broke down again. 'I just want a baby – that's all. God, all I need is to hold a baby in my arms!'

Rachel felt her throat begin to ache in sympathy with the other girl, who looked not much older than herself.

'I'm sorry for you,' she said. 'That's a terrible thing to happen.'

'I've just got to get over it,' the girl said. 'Only with my Francis going as well – and I'm moving back in with my mother – what's the use in paying two lots of rent? And I just . . .' She shook her head, unable to go on.

Rachel wasn't sure what to say. She just stood there, feeling sorry.

The girl pulled herself together eventually and told her that her name was Netta Fitzpatrick. They parted, wishing each other luck.

Afterwards she could not stop thinking of Netta and her distraught grief after giving birth to a dead child. Feeling her own baby's vigorous movements, she realized that she had a lot of luck already.

It was sometime in the middle of the night when it began. Rachel, lying restlessly on her left side, trying to get comfortable, woke as a warm gush of liquid arrived suddenly in the bed.

Ugh, she thought. I've wet myself. How can I have done that? She struggled out of bed to get away from the wet sheets. As she stood up, her abdomen clenched like a vice and she doubled up over the bed.

'Danny!' she gasped. 'Wake up – I'm having it!' This

ended in a wail as the pain reached its peak, then died off.

'What?' Danny shot up in bed. Seconds later, he was down the stairs and shouting, 'Auntie! Help!'

'Rachel?' Gladys came in with a candle. She took one look at her. 'Get off the bed, wench, so I can change it. Danny's gone to fetch the midwife.'

Gladys stripped back the bedclothes with their thin, bloody smell. Rachel stood helpless by the bed, a heavy, dragging feeling inside her. She heard the crackle of news-paper: copies of the *Birmingham Evening Despatch* which Gladys was laying over the mattress.

'I've got the water on,' Gladys was saying, more to herself than anything. 'Plenty of water . . . Thank the Lord there's no raids . . .'

As she moved swiftly round the room arranging things so that they were in place for the birth, they heard footsteps thundering into the house and up the stairs. Danny came charging in.

'Rach – you all right? I've been and got the mid-wife . . .'

'Well, where is she?' Gladys demanded.

'I told her,' Danny panted. He stood by the chair and put his hand on Rachel's shoulder. 'Then I came back.'

'Oh, for heaven's sake,' Gladys erupted. 'Go and meet her – the poor wench'll never find this house on her own in the pitch dark!'

Danny tore off again. By the time two sets of foot-steps were approaching, Rachel was back on the bed on a square of old sheet laid over the crackling newspaper, in the throes of another clamping bout of pain. She knelt, pressing her forehead into the pillow, and try as she could to keep quiet, groans of pain escaped her.

'There you go,' a brisk voice said beside her as she

surfaced. She had not been aware of anyone coming into the room.

'You – off downstairs,' she heard Gladys saying.

'But Auntie!' Danny protested.

'This is no place for a lad. Go on – hoppit.'

'How are we doing?' the voice said again.

Rachel moaned. 'All right,' she managed to say.

'Can you turn on your back for me?' Things were being brought out of a bag beside her, the midwife putting them on the chest of drawers. 'I'll need to have a little look at you.'

'You look young,' Gladys said. 'Not much older than her on there.'

Rachel looked up into a pair of brown, smiling eyes, the face topped by black curly hair.

'I'm Nurse Biggins, student midwife,' the young woman said. 'And I'm going to look after you. I don't think I've seen you at the clinic?'

Rachel was bewildered. What was she talking about?

'No,' Gladys said quietly.

'How old are you then . . .?'

'Rachel,' Gladys put in.

'Rachel?'

'Sixteen . . .'

'Ah – I am a little older than you after all,' she said, smiling.

Rachel could feel the first rumbles of another pain coming and she drew her legs up and murmured, 'Oh no . . .' Surely with it hurting this much there must be something terribly wrong?

The young woman said, 'Oh – I see. We'll wait until that's over . . . You've got water on the boil downstairs?' she said to Gladys. 'Thank you – you seem to have done a marvellous job in getting prepared.'

Once the next pain had passed the midwife examined her. Rachel gasped with shock as Nurse Biggins pressed her fingers up inside her. She had had no idea there would be all this. It would normally have felt very odd and embarrassing but just at the moment she did not really care.

'You're quite well on,' the midwife said. 'Lucky for a first one – it can take a long time. And everything's looking very normal.'

'Would you like a cup of tea, nurse?' Gladys asked. There was respect in her voice, awe almost.

Tea! Rachel thought, outraged as the pain surged through her again. Here she was, in agony, and they were all talking about drinking tea!

She dozed, and then massive claws of pain would seize her again and she would lift herself onto her knees, groaning and fighting with it.

'That's it,' Nurse Biggins kept saying. 'You're doing well. Just take nice big breaths, that's it. Won't be long now.'

Gradually she realized a new day had arrived. The sun was shining and it grew hotter. Her whole body was a slick of sweat. Gladys chased flies from the room. Every so often a sound would reach her, the clang of a pail outside, a door shutting or a voice; Gladys and the midwife talking beside her in low voices. At one stage she thought she heard Gladys talking to someone out of the window.

'Danny,' she murmured. 'Where's Danny? I want him.'

'He's had to go to work, bab,' Gladys told her. 'It's gone ten o'clock, you know.'

The pain built and built until Nurse Biggins was saying, 'Come on now, Rachel, you're almost there – you're going to have to start pushing the baby out.'

Suddenly the midwife and Gladys were on each side of her, holding her, and she felt as though she was going to split in half.

'I can't!' she wailed. 'I can't do it. I want it to stop.'

'It'll stop,' the midwife said gently. 'It'll stop soon – but you've got to get the baby out . . .'

Rachel's body was in charge and at last, feeling she was going to crack completely in two, she pushed out her child, a scream coming from her as she did so, however much she did not want it to. It seemed as if the noise was coming from someone else. After the final slither of the body, it was over.

'There!' Nurse Biggins said.

But Rachel became aware of a silence that went on. She raised her head and saw the midwife and Gladys leaning over the end of the bed, whispering to each other. She caught a glimpse of Gladys's expression, her face taut and solemn.

'What's going on?' Her voice was high with panic. 'What's wrong?'

A thin wail came from somewhere near her feet and the whole atmosphere in the room relaxed. Gladys's face lifted, transformed into a smile. Rachel felt the dread inside her seep away and a feeling of exultation take its place. With all of her being she realized she wanted to see her baby.

'There we are!' Nurse Biggins said, wrapping the baby in the pieces of sheet Gladys had saved. 'Just had to clear the airways a little bit. You've had a lovely little girl – here she is.'

And a warm, moist shape was laid in her arms, its

mouth open to let out a loud, cracked-sounding wail. Through the open window, suddenly, she heard the sounds of cheering and clapping.

Gladys laughed through her tears. 'They've been waiting for news out there,' she said. Going to the window she called out, 'It's a girl!' There was more cheering and she returned, smiling, but the tears were still running down her cheeks. 'Oh, bab, she's lovely – a perfect little girl! Oh, thank heavens that's over with! I felt every bit of it with you!' For a moment she put her hands over her face and sobbed with relief. The sight of Gladys, more emotional than Rachel had ever seen her before, brought tears to her own eyes. Gladys seemed overwhelmed with emotion as she gazed at the squalling new arrival in the family.

Rachel looked into the now pink, yelling face of her little girl. 'Hello, Melanie,' she said.

'Melanie?' Gladys said, wiping her eyes.

'That's what Danny and me decided,' she said. 'Melanie.'

'That's pretty,' the midwife said.

'I s'pose it is,' Gladys agreed. 'Very modern.'

'Right – well, I'm going to need the little one back now, to give her her first little wash,' Nurse Biggins said.

'And I,' Gladys said, rolling up her sleeves as if to pull herself together, 'am going to make you another cup of tea.'

Rachel woke later, feeling movements on the bed. She became aware of her sore body, of something thick tucked between her legs and of a feeling of utter exhaustion. Opening her eyes she found Danny looking down at her, or rather not at her but at something the other side of her on the bed.

The baby! She half-leapt up, her nerves jangled. 'Is she all right?' Melanie had had her first feed and the two of them had then slept and slept.

'Looks all right to me,' Danny said. On his face was a look of shy wonder. He sat on the bed beside her and she lay back and looked at him, relishing the moment. 'A little wench then.'

'Melanie,' Rachel said. 'Gladys says she looks like you. Don't wake her, will you?' she added, as Danny leaned over to look at his little daughter. In his expression she could see a mixture of pride, wonder and fear.

'She's all right, ain't she? Auntie's full of her,' he said. He looked at Rachel, seeming bashful with her, as if in awe of her. 'I can't believe she came from there – inside of you.'

'Oh,' Rachel laughed, then wished she hadn't as a twinge of protest went through her muscles. 'I can!'

'You all right?' he said.

'Think so. It was hard though. I'm never doing that again.'

Danny lay back beside her, the other side of her from the baby. His eyes started to close.

'Danny!' she protested. 'Don't just go to sleep on me!'

'I'm done for,' he murmured. 'After all I've been through today.'

'After all *you've* . . .?' She turned to look at him and chuckled. 'I'll say this for you – I've never seen anyone get into their trousers as quick as you did last night!'

IV

Twenty-Four

February 1942

Rachel was standing by the range in Gladys's house, Melanie on her hip, stirring a pot of thin soup made of odds and ends of vegetable.

'Well, that's not going to fatten *or* feed, is it?' Gladys had remarked when she came in earlier. 'I'll go along to Norris's and see what he can give me.'

Rachel had offered to go to the butcher's for her, but Gladys had just been to the pictures and was in a good mood. She sometimes quite liked to get out and go round the shops, even if it did involve exhausting queuing with ration books.

It was cold and already dark, the hands of the clock on the mantel crawling towards five o'clock. With the blackout curtains pulled shut, the house felt swathed in darkness. Even so, Rachel sensed the dank of the fog seeping its way in through the cracks in the door and windows. With a big metal spoon in one hand she jiggled Melanie on her other hip, singing, 'To market, to market to buy a fat pig, home again, home again, jiggety-jig!' At the last jiggle, Melanie gurgled with pleasure and waved her arms.

'Did you like that, Melly? Auntie will be back soon.'

Melanie chuckled. She was six months old now and

everyone said she was the image of her father. She had Danny's strong-boned face, his big blue eyes and neat brown cap of hair. She was an easy-going, sweet-natured child who had had her mother's constant attention and that of Gladys, Danny and lots of other people besides.

The time ticked by. There was a knock and Dolly's slim figure came round the door.

'Glad not back yet?' She came and made a fuss of Melanie, her dark eyes full of affection. 'Ooh, girls are lovely. Still, I'm not having another just to try for one. Over my dead body – or his!' She went out laughing. 'Tell her I popped in – I'll see her tomorrow.'

More time passed and Rachel was really beginning to wonder where Gladys had got to when the door opened again. Gladys, swathed in her black coat, hurried in and shut the door to keep the cold out and the light in. For a few moments Rachel didn't notice the state Gladys was in. She put her bag down and peeled off her coat.

'There's tea in the pot,' Rachel said. 'Those leaves have been round a few times though.'

Gladys made a weary sound. When she came and sat at the table, Rachel saw that she was very pale in the face and her hands were shaking.

'Auntie? Are you all right?'

'I'm all right – don't mither me,' she said irritably, seeming almost shamefaced at the state she was in.

Melanie had dozed off on Rachel's shoulder. She held the baby with one arm and poured Gladys a cup of tea with the other.

'Ta.' Gladys grasped the cup with both hands and peered into it. 'God, look at that maid's water. I could do with a nip of summat stronger, I can tell you.'

'What's the matter?' Rachel sat down opposite her, cuddling Melanie on her lap. She was startled by the strength of feeling in Gladys. Their conversations were nearly always of a practical nature – food, shopping, what they would take to the market. It was unusual to broach anything emotional.

Gladys took a deep breath. 'It's daft me being so shook up – but it were a close-run thing. I was in Newtown Row, just come out of the butcher's, finally. We'd been stood there I don't know how long. And a few of us went to cross the road. It's a proper pea-souper out there now and dark as pitch, but I looked back and stepped out and – God alone knows where it come from – there was a van, just came out of nowhere. It was just behind me – I mean, I heard the noise and I ran like mad across the road – heaven help me if there'd been summat coming the other way . . . But one of the ladies behind me went under it.' She shook her head. 'I heard the breath go out of her.'

'Is she . . .?' Rachel asked, horrified. 'I mean – what happened?'

'They called an ambulance,' Gladys said. 'Course, they take their time coming in this dark – you can hardly see a hand in front of your face. I didn't stick around – there was enough of a crowd round her already. But she wasn't making any noise after it, that I can tell you.'

'Who was she, Auntie? Did you know her?'

'I'd seen her before, in the butcher's. She's got a son in the navy, that's all I know.' Gladys sat back, shuddering. 'It just all happened that fast . . . It really shakes you up. Never saw it coming. It just seems . . .' Rachel was startled to see she was battling tears. 'All these young lads of ours being killed and Hitler and all these Japs overrunning everywhere . . . Something like this, nothing really to do with the war – it's just so *unnecessary*.'

There was a silence. For a moment Rachel thought Gladys was really going to break down and cry and she was surprised by how much it seemed to have affected her. She was not sure what to say.

'That's horrible, Auntie,' she said eventually.

Gladys tried to rally herself. 'I'll just have to thank the good Lord it wasn't me,' she said. 'Though I don't know what He's got against that lady – she wasn't doing any harm. Pass me that bag, Rach – I got some off-the-ration bits. Offal.'

Rachel groaned slightly.

'You may not like it but it's good for you,' Gladys said sternly.

By the time Danny came home from the markets, blowing on his hands, Gladys appeared back to normal. Seeing him come in, tall and energetic, made Rachel's day, every day. My husband, my Danny . . . The words ran through her head like a miracle and her heart was beating at the sight of him. She felt her face light into a smile as he came over to kiss her. By now she had laid Melanie down to sleep upstairs.

'How's my girls?' he said gruffly as he bent to peck her on the cheek. Rachel smiled. Sometimes there was something about Danny that reminded her of an old man, even though he was still so young. He had grown quickly into being a man, broader in the shoulders and gruffly responsible – except, of course, when he was acting like a big kid with the Morrison boys outside! All Dolly's lads adored Danny.

'We're all right,' she said. 'She's been a good girl today.'

'What about you – have you been a good girl?' he teased.

'That's for me to know and you to find out,' Rachel said. 'What chance do I have to do anything bad anyway?'

'Oh, you'll soon get your chance,' Gladys said, from the range, where she had taken over the cooking. The soup had been transformed into a stew now and the smell filled the room, along with boiling cabbage. 'Once that littl'un's weaned.'

They had agreed that once Melanie could be weaned, Rachel would go back to work.

She seemed quite confident that she could manage. Gladys loved having a baby in the house and was very good with her. Rachel had been quite surprised by how automatically she seemed to know what to do.

'You're very good with babies, Auntie,' she said once, when Melanie was very small. She was such a help and it was reassuring to have her there with advice.

'Ah well, there's always been babbies around,' Gladys said, tucking Melanie's nappy around her as if she had been doing it all her life. 'I've seen Dolly through all hers – and helped look after the little buggers sometimes.'

Once again, Rachel thought how much better a mother Gladys was to her than her own mother. She trusted Gladys completely. It seemed a sad thing that she had never had any children of her own.

Over these last six months, Rachel felt she had grown up fast. Melanie was an easy baby. As everyone said, 'She's so *good*. What a lovely babby!' She did the things everyone seemed to think she should do – she fed well, after the first weeks of fractured sleep she slept well, and she was easy to pacify. She gave every appearance of being a happy little soul and Rachel soon learned the things that every mother needs to know to respond to her baby's cries and was happy as well.

However, it was still a shock to realize that she was a married woman and a mother. She was always at home, though she did not miss work all that much. But one day she had particular cause to feel as if she was cut off from things. Her old pal Lilian, who she had barely seen since living with Danny, came round to see her and the baby. Already, when Lilian came bouncing into the house, Rachel began to feel they were growing so far apart as to inhabit different worlds. Lilian was very admiring of Melanie, but she had an announcement to make.

'I'm changing trades!' she said, beaming. 'I'm off to work at the Nuffield at Castle Bromwich, doing the rivets on the plane wings – Spitfires!' She told Rachel that the firm would find them lodgings up there. She was not likely to be around for a bit.

Rachel looked at her sitting at the table, sickly little Lilian of their schooldays, who was now tall and rather pretty in a pale way, with her blonde hair cut to her shoulders, pinned back in the fashionable style and turned under at the ends. She seemed confident, full of life and ready for anything.

'Crikey, Lil – what does your mom say?'

Lilian laughed. 'She thinks I've gone off my head. But that's war work for you. And I was bored . . . She doesn't really mind so long as I come home as often as I can. There's lots of girls working up there now.'

As Lilian left later, still full of it, Rachel said, 'Good luck – and keep me posted, won't you? Don't forget us.' But as she said goodbye, she knew she wouldn't be seeing much of her friend. She could already feel Lilian moving away from her into a quite different life. Here she was, married and – for a moment she had a pang – stuck here.

The person she did see now, though, was Netta Fitz-patrick. They had run into each other several times in the neighbourhood and over the months they had struck up a friendship. In a way Rachel could not understand why Netta wanted to see her. Netta's husband was able to come home on leave now and then from the Pay Corps and she had conceived and miscarried a second baby since they first met. Though it was much earlier on this time, at three months of the pregnancy, it was still very upsetting for her. Rachel thought the sight of Melanie must make her feel sad and jealous. But Netta was a sweet girl and it became a habit of hers to pop round after work sometimes or at the weekend. Rachel had met her mother, a little birdlike Irish lady called Mrs O'Shaughnessy, who had been very welcoming when she went to their house.

'Are they Catholics?' Gladys asked suspiciously when she first heard about Mrs O'Shaughnessy. Catholics to her were a foreign lot – the Italian mission to the Irish.

'Yes, they are,' Rachel said. 'But they're ever so nice, Auntie.'

It had been odd at first, seeing Mary O'Shaughnessy's sacred hearts and the crucifix and little glass stoop of holy water she kept nailed up by the door. It felt like walking into a foreign land, even though the house was on a yard not far away and almost identical to the one she lived in herself. After a while, though, she realized that these things were so taken for granted by the family – Netta and her mother and brothers – that she took no more notice of them either. Mrs O'Shaughnessy was always very kind and welcoming towards her.

With Melanie to keep her occupied, with new friends

and the support of the yard's neighbours, Rachel was contented enough, even though they were living through some of the darkest, most desperate days of the war, when everything seemed stacked against them and victory impossible.

The raids had petered out the summer before, when Germany turned its attention to the invasion of Russia in June 1941. But since then there had been little in the way of good news. Convoys crossing the Atlantic with food supplies from North America were sunk in horrifying numbers. All across the western desert, across the east, since the Japanese entered the war in December, the news came of defeats, one after another.

Once the bombing stopped, from Rachel's point of view, caught up as she was with her first baby, the war seemed mostly a faraway business. Apart from the black-out and rationing and all these day-to-day struggles, little of it touched her personally. Even in their yard only two people had gone into the forces. There was Stanley Gittins, Lil's husband, a tall, dark man Rachel had seen when he came home on leave from the RAF. And Edwin Jackman had gone into the army. Ma Jackman made frequent noises about how her family were the ones *doing their bit*.

'As if none of the rest of us are,' Dolly said to Gladys in annoyance after suffering another of these self-righteous remarks. 'I hardly see Mo these days what with work and the Home Guard. He's so tired he can hardly stand up. He's too old to join up anyway.'

'Oh, just ignore her,' Gladys said. 'You know what she's like.'

'I do,' Dolly fumed. 'But I don't have to like it, do I?'

Rachel basked in the attention she and Melanie received. With Dolly having produced so many boys it was a long time since a little girl had been born in the yard. And she loved living with Danny and Gladys. Once Melanie was a couple of months old she had started taking her to the Rag Market, at least for a bit of the day, to get out and have a change. She propped the little girl on a cushion at the side of Gladys's pitch where she alternated between sleeping and receiving a lot of attention.

'That's our little mascot,' Gladys would say proudly. 'Growing up in the trade, she is.'

Peggy had deigned to see Rachel and her granddaughter and they went over there about once a fortnight, to sit and drink tea stiffly together. Rachel always went in the weekdays, when Danny was at work and Fred Horton was in the shop. She didn't particularly want to see him. He wasn't interested in her nor she in him.

Cissy, who was now a very energetic two-and-a-half-year-old, was besotted with Melanie.

'Well, she is a healthy-looking child,' Peggy had to admit. 'And she'll be a bit of company for Cissy. You can bring her over and let them get to know one another. I find it hard going keeping her occupied.'

'As long as it suits you, Mother,' Rachel said, in just a neutral enough tone for her sarcasm not to be fully evident.

Beyond that, Peggy was no help at all, neither financially nor in any other way. So far as she was concerned, Rachel had made her bed and now she had to lie on it.

*

Danny seemed to thrive on having everyone dear to him under one roof as well and they had a harmonious few months playing – sometimes it felt like that – at being husband and wife. But then they were not playing, because they were actually married! Sometimes Rachel sat up in bed with Melanie in her arms and Danny's long body lolling beside her and said in wonder:

'I still can't believe it, Danny – you're my husband!'

'Well,' he'd say, with mock pompousness, '*wife* – you'd better get used to the idea, hadn't you?'

The Sunday morning after Gladys's near miss with the van, they were sitting up in bed together, Melanie lying across their laps. Rachel leaned against Danny, close and warm. She kissed his cheek. 'I'm so happy being with you.'

Danny reached for her hand. 'You're my missis, you are. You're everything to me. I don't half love you, Rach. I dunno how to say it really.'

She squeezed his hand. 'You said it.' She reached up and kissed him, then giggled. 'You've still got freckles – loads of them!'

'Have I?' Danny smiled back lazily, and rubbed his nose. He loved her paying him close attention.

Rachel looked down at Melanie who was snoozing, warm and content. 'I wonder if she'll have them too? Oh, look at her – she's the best ever. How many kids shall we have, Danny?'

He prodded her ribs so that she squirmed. 'I thought you said you were never doing that again?'

Rachel laughed. 'I'm getting like Dolly.' She leaned over and kissed his neck. 'I might just *think* about it. It'd be a shame for her not to have anyone to play with, wouldn't it? So how many?'

'Don't they just sort of come?' Danny said, bemused. 'I mean, you can't say really, can you? Four? Six?'

'Six! I'll be an old matron with my belly dragging on the ground if I have six!'

'Tell yer what – let's make another one now . . .' He made as if to grab hold of her, half-joking.

'Danny, no! What're you playing at – and you'll wake her up! You're crazy, you are. I didn't mean now! I'm not having another one for *ages* yet – not 'til the war's over anyhow. Danny –'

'Umm?' He was stroking her shoulder, his nose nuzzling her cheek.

'One day I s'pose we'll have our own place to live – we can't always stay with Auntie.'

At the time this felt frightening. They were both so young, like two lost waifs together, clinging to a rock – and Gladys was that rock on which they rested and depended.

'One day,' he said. 'But she likes having us here.'

Rachel lay back, warm and contented. She had never expected to be married with a baby at her age, but just at that moment she would not have swapped it for anything else.

That February day, the news came through on the wireless that Singapore had fallen to invading Japanese forces. The mood everywhere was sombre. Everyone was finding it hard to take in the speed with which the Japanese were moving across island after island. The horrors of the war seemed to be bleeding right across the globe and there was nothing any of them could do about it.

A few days later, a letter arrived which cut right through all Rachel's sense of happiness and safety.

They hardly ever received letters. When it came, that morning, Gladys was folding clothes at the table, getting ready for the Rag Market. She held the official-looking envelope out in front of her, squinting to see who it was for.

'Oh dear.' Her voice struck a chill in Rachel, who had Melanie on her lap and was spooning milky slops into her.

'What, Auntie?'

Gladys turned slowly, as if dreading to look at her. 'It's for Danny.'

Rachel frowned. 'Danny?' She realized later that they had never talked about this. Both of them had put it out of their minds as a possibility, or at least she had. Danny had turned eighteen the previous month.

Gladys brought it over and put it on the table. Rachel could just see Danny's name in typed letters.

'I can't open it – it's not for me,' said Gladys. 'But I'd say it's his call-up papers.'

'No!' Rachel cried. 'No, it can't be!' She was so alarmed and stiff suddenly that Melanie started to cry. She could not take in what this meant, not at all. 'They can't call him up, can they – not Danny?'

'Why not?' Gladys said. 'He's no different from anyone else, is he? And he's the right age.'

'Oh, they can't make him go!' she wailed over the baby's cries. 'There must be some way he can stay!' She stood up, Melanie in her arms, trying to quieten the little girl as her own tears began to flow. It felt like an utter calamity, as if her world, her security, was suddenly shattered in pieces. 'Oh, I hate this war – it ruins everything for everybody!'

Twenty-Five

March 1942

'Oh – I dain't realize you were in here, bab,' Dolly said, bursting into the brew house with an armful of washing as Rachel stood at the sink. She seemed wound up and annoyed.

'I've nearly finished,' Rachel said hurriedly. 'I know it's your turn today, Mrs Morrison – I just started early to get a few things done.'

'That's all right,' Dolly said, appeased. 'It never ends when you've got a babby, does it?' She put her bundle down and looked more closely at Rachel, who was feeding clothes through the mangle. 'Here – I'll give you a hand with those, get it done sooner. Eh – are you all right, Rach?'

'Yes.' But Rachel's voice cracked and she kept her head down, trying to hide the tears which came as soon as Dolly showed sympathy.

'Oh dear – you'll be missing your Danny. It's a rotten shame, that it is, you poor thing. My old man's too long in the tooth, but if he had to go I'd be in pieces too.'

Danny had gone to begin his basic army training two weeks ago. The days before he left were terrible – the dread of him leaving almost worse than when he actually went.

'You told them to call you up . . . You've always wanted to go . . . You've done this on purpose!' she raged at him when he came home that night and opened the letter. She was beyond reason in her panic at the thought of him leaving, sobbing with hurt and fury.

'I never!' Danny protested. He looked very shocked as well.

'You just want to go off and see the world – that's what you said!'

'No, I don't!' Danny interrupted. 'That was then – everything's different now. I never asked them to call me up.'

'I don't believe you. I bet you did! You *want* to go and leave me and Melly behind.' Rachel sank down at the table, head on her arms, and sobbed until Gladys intervened.

'Wench,' she said, standing over her. 'Pull yerself together. You're not being fair on the lad. Danny's eighteen now – they've called him like all the others.' Her voice wavered and Rachel quietened and looked up, startled. Only then, amid her self-absorbed unhappiness, did it occur to her that anyone else might be upset about Danny having to take the King's shilling.

Danny stood with his jacket hanging open, looking suddenly scared and somehow smaller.

'Oh, Danny.' Rachel got up and walked into his arms. 'I don't want you to go. What about Melly? I'll have to bring her up without her daddy.'

'Many a woman's had to,' Gladys said quietly. 'You won't be the first.'

Rachel sobbed even harder then, but she knew from that moment that she was going to have to accept it.

She stayed awake with him all the night before he left, holding him, crying intermittently and talking, clinging to his strong, slender body, trying to memorize every part of him. In the morning, the rest of the yard waved him goodbye.

'You send those Jerries packing, Danny boy!' Dolly said, hugging him. 'And you behave yourself while you're at it.'

'Look after yerself, lad,' Mo boomed. He sounded emotional. 'No more than a babby himself,' he muttered.

'Oh my – look,' Dolly said to the little crowd in a hushed tone. They turned to see old Mr Parsons standing creakily to attention at his front door, his old khaki Boer War uniform jacket buttoned over his scrawny frame. Silently, he gave a slow salute. Danny nodded solemnly at him. 'Ta, Mr Parsons,' he called.

'Bless the old feller's heart,' Dolly said, sounding tearful.

Gladys was holding Melanie who waved her little arm but did not know what was happening.

'Goodbye, m'lad,' Gladys said gruffly. 'Get yourself back here as soon as you can.' She pulled Danny roughly against her for a moment with her spare arm, before pushing him away again. Head down, she carried Melanie into the house.

Rachel caught hold of Danny's arm, determined not to be separated from him until the very last moment. He turned, with her on one arm, his bag on the other shoulder, and gave a wave before they set off along the entry. But as they travelled from Aston on the tram, Danny suddenly seemed cold and shut off from her, just when she needed him to be warm and close. He sat staring out of the window as if he was already miles away. By the time they got to New Street and found the right

235

platform, he had still not said a word and she was well-ing up.

'Danny!' She pulled his arm in the milling crowd of uniforms and civilian clothes all jostling together. 'Don't be like this. We might never see each other again!' And she was in a storm of tears.

Danny, looking wretched, pulled her to him and they held each other tightly, as if there was no one else in the world.

'I love you,' she said passionately. 'I'll always love you.'

Danny held her even tighter. 'I love you too,' he whispered. She saw then that he could not speak because he was afraid he might cry. 'Gotta go,' he said. 'Look after our little Melly.' And he pulled away, out of her grasp, as if he could bear it no longer.

Rachel would never forget the sight of his sad face looking through the train window, the trail of smoke and steam obscuring it as the engine got up speed and pulled away. He gave a last wave, then withdrew inside. She felt as if she was being torn in half. She walked back to the tram stop after leaving the station, the sounds of the city coming back to her now that she was not wrapped up in him. She felt desperately alone and empty.

Ever since, she had ached for him, a feeling like a heavy weight in her chest. She had been miles away, doing her washing, until Dolly appeared.

'Terrible, all these young'uns going off,' Dolly was saying, stoking the fire under the copper for her washing water. 'But then they need age on their side. I said to Mo the other night, "Eh, husband of mine, why don't we go out – have a bit of a dance? We ain't been out to the dance hall for ages!" And he sat there in his chair and said, "Dance? I can hardly get myself up the stairs to bed these days, let alone flaming dance!"' She turned, grinning. 'That's my old man for you – no good sending him off to war!'

Rachel couldn't help laughing, and pegged out Melly's clothes in the chill wind of the yard, feeling a bit cheered up.

Life now consisted of looking after her daughter and sitting in with Gladys night after night. Gladys, as ever, had busy hands, sewing and mending clothes she had acquired to sell, ironing and folding, and Rachel helped as much as she could. But she could not hide her misery at missing Danny. Gladys, she realized, had long worked out her own collection of comforts – her sweets, her trips to the cinema and her religion. She sang hymns to cheer herself up, but it didn't work for Rachel, who had scarcely ever been to church anyway.

'You ought to come out with me,' Gladys suggested. 'When I'm buying stuff. It'd get you out of yourself.'

'Well, I can't get that thing on the bus.' She nodded at the pram. 'I could come with her and carry her, I suppose . . .'

'Hmm.' Gladys pondered a moment, hands on hips. 'It'd be good to have the pram – we can put stuff in it. It's hardly worth going anywhere walking distance.' 'Most of the areas within reach were as poor as their own. "Cept Erdington maybe . . .' Her face lit up. 'I know – we can't get it on the bus but we might get it on the train. How about we go out to Sutton and do the rounds a bit – and we could call in on Nancy and Albert and see the girls?'

*

The train chugged out from Aston between the miles of soot-stained factories and lines of cramped houses, all covered in a pall of smoke, even on this quiet day. Gladys had hurried back from church and off they went to the railway station. Rachel found she was excited to be on a journey. North of Erdington everything started to open out and become more spacious and green. Rachel sat with Melly on her lap, looking out through the grimy window at the bigger houses with gardens, most with their curved, corrugated-steel Anderson shelters and the rows of allotments, some with people in them bent over, digging. It quickly began to feel like another world.

She looked at Gladys opposite her, with her dark hair plaited and coiled round her head today, her striking blue eyes and black coat. She was so used to Gladys now that she seemed very normal, but seeing her out here, and the curious stares of some of the ladies in the carriage, she remembered that Gladys was unusual and exotic to other people.

'Here –' Gladys passed her a sandwich with a thin filling of cheese and raw onion. 'Get this down you.'

'We'll stink if we eat that!' she protested in a whisper. She did not want to attract attention. There was a woman in a fancy hat opposite her giving the pair of them appraising looks.

'Well, it's all we had,' Gladys murmured back. 'So take it and stink, or leave it.'

Rachel was far too hungry to leave it and they would be doing a lot of walking. Despite feeling self-conscious, she quickly ate the piece, trying not to make faces at the strong taste of the onion. As they were swallowing the last mouthfuls, the train pulled into Sutton Coldfield.

*

They walked out through the gracious old town in the direction of Four Oaks, stopping along the way to knock on the doors of big houses. Rachel felt her heart beat faster each time they waited for a door to open, remembering the stinging rejections her mother had sometimes suffered. Sunday afternoon was not a good time to be disturbing people, but it was the only time they had. And there was something about Gladys, her striking looks, her dignity and air of knowing what she was about that did not seem to provoke this. By the time they were getting closer to the edge of town and Gladys's brother's house, they had Melly sitting propped up at one end of the pram and a neat pile of garments and linen at the other.

'I'll have to come out here again,' Gladys said, seeming pleased. 'It's worth the fare, all right. Having madam's carriage to put it in is a help too.'

Once they had eaten the rest of the sandwiches sitting at the edge of Sutton Park, they made for Gladys's brother's house.

Gladys had not prepared Rachel for Albert and Nancy. The door, one in a row of country terraces strung along the road, flew open to reveal a plump, beaming man in brown trousers, shirtsleeves and stockinged feet, the socks a bilious shade of green, one hand brandishing a brown teapot.

'I was passing the door and you knocked!' he announced. His lips looked very pink under a rather overgrown, tobacco-coloured moustache. 'Come in, sis – oh! Pram! Baby! Young woman! You've brought every possible thing of loveliness, Gladie!'

'Hello, Albert,' Gladys said.

'Is that them, Albert?' they heard from upstairs, in a

slightly strained tone, as they waited in the narrow hall on grey linoleum.

'It's them!' He started to disappear towards, presumably, the back kitchen, crying out, 'I'm filling the pot!' But he stopped and came back, still with the pot in his hand. 'Come in. All the girls are somewhere. Well, except the one who's a boy – but then of course, he's not here!' He laid a hand on his chest. Rachel heard the crackle as he breathed. Only then she remembered he suffered badly from asthma. 'Go into the back room. Chairs. Sit . . .' He vanished, with a mention of biscuits along the way somewhere.

Rachel left Melanie asleep in the pram, which was blocking most of the hall, and followed Gladys. The back room overlooked a long strip of garden. Gladys went to the window immediately, fastening her eyes on the sight of the two girls out on the grass. Rachel followed her gaze. The lawn near the house gave way to a long vegetable patch and at the far end was the Anderson shelter, covered in grass and weeds. It took Rachel a moment to realize that one of the girls playing there was Amy, because her dark hair had now grown long and was flowing free down her back. The other girl, also with dark, but finer hair, she had never seen before. The two of them were playing clap-hands games and in the quiet, you could just make out that one was singing the rhyme.

'Looks all right, doesn't she?' Gladys said. Her breath fogged the window. There was a wistful but relieved tone to her voice.

They heard feet thudding hurriedly down the staircase and a voice saying, 'Oh, I'm sorry to be so long and not down here when you arrived! Hello, Gladys, love – and you must be Rachel?'

Rachel turned to see a small, plump woman with a haphazard bun of black hair, bright blue eyes, pink cheeks and a snub nose. Smiling, homely, friendly, it was a face that it would be impossible not to warm to.

'We're all at sixes and sevens,' she chattered on. 'But then when aren't we? Now Albert – Albert?' she shouted. 'Are you making that tea?'

'Ye-es . . .' came a doubtful reply from the invisible kitchen.

'Well, are you or . . .?' She lowered her voice. 'Sorry – I'd better go and see what he's up to. You never know with Albert. He's likely got into the bag of seed potatoes – he was talking about them this morning . . .'

She disappeared for a time, during which there was a muffled altercation from the kitchen and then she re-appeared, squeezing round the pram with a tray and cups, flustered, but beaming.

'Lovely baby!' she remarked. 'Here we are – tea! Now I know you want to see the girls. I'll call Jess down in a tick. And our John's out, I'm afraid – off playing football with some other lads.'

'Amy looks well,' Gladys said.

Nancy's face clouded slightly for the first time. 'She is, I think,' she said, arranging the cups, which had painted strands of ivy round them. 'Oh, she was a sad little thing when she came – well, you know she was. At least now, she's –' she whispered this – '*dry at night*.' She passed Gladys a cup of tea. 'She and our Margaret are almost inseparable. They're in the same form at school and . . . Well, it's helped Amy. Sometimes I think it might be a bit much for Margaret, but she says, no, it's all right. After all, she and John have never been close. Anyway, Jess is getting along all right. Nancy crossed the room to the bottom of the stairs. 'Jess love!' she called. 'Come on down! Your auntie's here!'

'You've been a godsend,' Gladys said. Rachel knew just how heartfelt this was and she also smiled gratefully at Nancy, as she sat down again.

'Well, those poor little girls – and oh, I can't tell you how much better it's been since those London boys left. They were just children really but they were fish out of water. And some of their habits! I've never seen the like – ooh, I wouldn't want to start on it, not at tea. But we do what we can and I'm ever so fond of these two – they're like our own now. Ah – here's Jess.'

'Hello, Auntie,' Jess said, smiling as she came in. 'Hello, Rachel.' She spoke in a soft, shy voice but seemed pleased to see them.

'You've grown up again, my girl,' Gladys said. Jess had the top portion of her honey-brown hair brushed back from her face and pinned up at the back, while the rest hung loose. She was sweet-faced and pretty. 'Quite a young lady now, aren't you?'

'Ah, Miss Jess!' Albert said, appearing at last in his quaint way. 'What a very fair infant someone has left lying about out here!'

Rachel smiled. Suddenly she seemed to be permanently smiling. 'If she's still asleep, I'll leave her there.'

Nancy went and called the other girls in and at last the two ten-year-olds appeared, Amy holding Margaret's hand. Margaret, a dark, snub-nosed, sensible-looking girl, like her mother, said, 'Here are your visitors, Amy.'

Amy peered out unsmiling from under her heavy fringe.

'Hello, bab – come and see me,' Gladys said. Amy stood her ground. It took a while, as they all drank tea, for her to sidle over and at last settle close to Gladys.

Melanie woke and Rachel brought her in, and even Amy agreed to hold her. When Melly got hold of a hank of her hair and tugged on it, Amy's face broke into a grin at last, showing big, square teeth.

'Stop that, Melly,' Rachel said. 'You'll have her hair out by the roots!'

'It's all right,' Amy said, watching as Melly sucked messily on a biscuit. She seemed fascinated by her.

The adults all talked about the war, the endless shortages and the food Albert and Nancy were growing. They wanted to know how Danny was.

'Still doing basic training,' Rachel said, happy to hear him talked about. 'He might come home after that – for a bit of leave.'

'I hope he's writing to you,' Nancy said.

Danny had written a couple of short letters, telling her little bits of what he had been doing. But on each, in the top corner, he had drawn a little picture of someone she recognized – Patch the dog. She noticed, after Danny left, that he had taken his notebook with him. It had lain untouched in a drawer for months, but now, it seemed, he had decided he needed it again.

They left Albert and Nancy's house after a couple of hours and headed back towards the railway station. Rachel felt warmed by the visit to this chaotic but kindly household.

'I think they're all right, don't you?' Gladys said as they walked through the falling dusk, Rachel pushing the pram. 'I fear for Amy – she's an odd child. But she did seem a bit better.'

'Yes – it's lovely for them here, Auntie,' Rachel said. 'And Nancy's so kind. But you did your best while they were with us.'

'Yes,' Gladys said. After a moment she added, 'Bit

different here though, ain't it?' And in her voice, Rachel could hear an ache of longing for the life and family her brother and his wife had, out here in this green, spacious place.

V

Twenty-Six

May 1943

The morning the new neighbours moved in, Netta Fitzpatrick was round at the house. She and Rachel saw quite a lot of each other, and especially now because, within a week or so of each other, they had found out that they were each expecting a baby again and both babies were due in September.

Netta sat with her hand constantly pressed to her five-month swell of belly as if she could protect its fortunes by thinking about it at every moment of the day. All through the pregnancy so far she had been alternately tearful with dread and excited.

'I can't believe I've got this far – not after last time,' she said, her eyes filling at the memory. She had miscarried the second baby at three months.

'I hope to God this one's all right,' Rachel sometimes said to Gladys. 'How will I face her if she loses another one?'

'Every day I wake up and I think – oh, praise God, it's still there,' Netta went on, her pale eyes full of longing. 'Oh, Rach – I don't know what I'll do if . . .' She shook her head and looked away.

'You're looking well, you know,' Gladys said, glancing

up from her ironing. The hot, singeing smell of it filled the room.

'Mammy's saving every drop of milk she can for me, heaven bless her,' Netta smiled. 'To make a nice strong baby.'

'I expect you'll be all right, Nett,' Rachel encouraged her. 'Third time lucky, eh?'

She had grown very fond of Netta, who was a sweet-natured, if timid, girl. Beside Netta she felt her own strength. Netta was so frail, like a little stick with her wispy brown hair and watery blue eyes. And Francis, who she had met when he came home on leave, was not much better. Francis's mother, like Netta's, was Irish and a widow. He had one older sister who looked after their frail mother, who was an invalid. Francis was a pale, solemn lad, like something grown with no light, and with an unworldly look in his eye. No wonder the army had kept him in the Pay Corps, Rachel thought.

'Mammy says I should give up work any day now,' Netta said. 'I know she's right but we need the money and—'

She was interrupted by a great clatter of falling wood from outside, accompanied by a string of earthy, male curses.

'Hark at that!' Gladys said. 'Someone needs to wash his mouth out. Still, I don't think this one heard any-thing.'

She nodded at Melanie, now twenty-one months old, who was sitting on the floor playing with a tangle of bits of off-cut material, muttering to herself and in a world of her own. She was a pale, solid little girl with soft brown hair and a steady nature.

Rachel followed Gladys to the door from where they saw a hefty, dark-haired bloke bent over three wooden chairs which he was trying, without much sign of success, to stack together. One was upside down and resting its seat on the bottom one; the third he kept trying to balance on top of them.

'Ow, *bugger* it,' he stormed as the chair toppled off again to lie on the mucky bricks of the yard. It had rained overnight and the sky was only just clearing.

'Why doesn't he just take them one by one? They'll be matchwood in a minute if he carries on,' Gladys observed. She stepped outside, pulling her shawl around her. Rachel and Netta crept to watch from the doorway.

'Who're you?' Gladys demanded.

The man turned to show a strikingly handsome face with a black moustache and glossy black hair. He wore a white shirt, the sleeves rolled, and black trousers with black boots. For a few seconds he turned an aggressive stare on Gladys, then, taking in the sight of her, seemed to think better of it. His face cleared and he gave a smile which exuded calculated charm.

'Mornin'!' He gestured as if raising his hat, though he was not wearing one. 'I'm Ray Sutton – moving in at number four. My missis is following on with the kiddies.'

Gladys nodded soberly. Rachel could sense that she was both suspicious of and charmed by this ebulliently masculine stranger.

'Cart's out in the road,' he said, pointing down the entry.

'If you knock at number one, chances are Mo'll give yer a hand,' Gladys told him. 'Though come to think of it, he might be off with the Home Guard today.'

'Ah – it's all right,' Ray said, turning back towards the chairs. 'We ain't got a lot and my brother's with me. He'll be along in a tick.'

They had known someone would be coming. The Parsonses had both died at the end of the winter. First Mrs Parsons had succumbed to pneumonia and her husband had followed not long after. As Gladys said, 'Well, at least we kept them away from the Archway of Tears.' Thanks to their neighbourliness, the Parsonses had never had to consider turning to the workhouse.

A moment after they had gone back inside, Dolly was round, an apron over her navy work dress and her hair tied back in a navy scarf.

'Is that the new ones at number four?' she asked. 'Oh hello, Netta, bab – how're you?'

'I'm all right, ta,' Netta said, smiling.

'That's the husband,' Rachel said, giggling. 'Doesn't he look like Rhett Butler!'

'Clark Gable, ain't it?' Dolly said, pulling out a packet of Craven A and lighting up. 'He's the actor . . .'

'D'you think his wife'll look like Scarlett O'Hara?' Rachel said.

Dolly inhaled a long pull of smoke, then blew it out. 'Like the back of a bus, more likely.'

'Always the optimist, you,' Gladys laughed.

They did not have to wait long to find out. Gladys was at the Rag Market later on, but Rachel had stopped going for the moment. Once Melanie started toddling, she had become a handful to manage and now Rachel was expecting another child it was all too much.

'I'll stay home and do things in the house,' she promised. She felt guilty not working and always wanted to make up for it somehow. 'And I'll get the dinner.'

It was the second week of May and what Gladys called the 'hungry gap'. The new crops of fruit and vegetables were not yet grown and last year's stocks were dwindling. There was not much to be had. Rachel had taken to listening to the wireless to try and learn what she might do to eke out a parsnip and a couple of spuds, or whatever they had managed to find. She was forever hungry, especially now she was expecting. She found herself thinking even more about food than about Danny's letters, for which she lived.

Later on, she had just finished scrubbing the floor while Melanie had a nap upstairs. Going out into the yard she tipped out the pail of dirty water into the drain and was just turning back towards the house when she heard a booming woman's voice coming closer along the entry: 'Get out of the 'ass road – how many times've I gorra tell yer?' The voice drew a bit nearer. 'Shirley, get 'ere or I'll give yer a threapin', that I will!'

Rachel hurried back inside and shut the door. Who on earth was this coming now – and what an accent! Tiptoeing across the wet floor, the pail still in her hand, she stood peering out through the window. Seconds later, two little girls with scruffy brown hair ran into the yard. They were followed by a voluptuous blonde woman, who from the shape of her belly and the rocking, leaning-back way she was walking, Rachel could see, was well on expecting a baby. Even though the woman sounded so loud and strange, Rachel was pleased by the sight of the two little girls. Up until now there had been no girls on this yard to keep Melanie company. She saw Ray, the dark-haired man, appear at the door of number four and then they all disappeared inside.

'So – what're they like?' Gladys asked, hungrily tucking into the scrag end Rachel had cooked with mashed, woody parsnip. 'You've met the wife now, have you?'

'Oh yes, I have!' Rachel laughed. 'She doesn't look like the back of a bus, that I can tell you. She's blonde—'

'Out of a bottle,' Gladys interjected.

'How d'you know that?' Rachel asked.

'I got a look at her too. Dark eyebrows.'

'She's quite nice to look at,' Rachel said. Everyone in the yard had gone out to say hello. The woman was a looker: plump, pink skinned with a head of thick, blonde hair, rolled into waves which, whether out of a bottle or not, made her look like a film star. Her brown eyes looked striking against the pale hair. Come to think of it though, she did have dark brown eyebrows. She wasn't exactly friendly but Rachel just thought she looked harassed. With two kids and another on the way she could see why.

'Her name's Irene and they've got two girls, Rita and Shirley. She doesn't half bawl at them – proper yowm-yowm she is an' all. That's what Dolly said – that Black Country talk. Not him, just her. He's in some factory or other. The way she talks about him you can see she thinks the sun shines out of his . . .' She eyed Gladys who eyed her back. 'Out of somewhere of his anyway. Ray this, Ray that. *My Ray* . . . But she said in the end, she comes from Netherton – as if you couldn't tell.' They all laughed, the Black Country and Birmingham seeming about as much the same country as England and Scotland. 'And she's expecting as well, about the same time as me and Nett, I think – must be something in the water!'

'You should tell her about that clinic,' Gladys said.

Gladys, who had previously been scornful of any 'interference' by 'them' into the health of expectant mothers, had been converted in her views by talking to the midwife and the health visitor who had come to see Rachel and Melanie. The health visitor was a friendly young woman who had explained to them all the childhood conditions and problems that could be averted by catching them early.

'I wish we'd had better advice back in the old days,' Gladys said. 'For the mothers, I mean. Ooh, I remember the babbies dying of the diarrhoea and all sorts – terrible it was. I know some people think they're busybodies, but she's all right, that young woman. They've been very good to Dolly. You go – and take the advice they give you. They've had some education about it, which is more than the rest of us ever had.'

'I'll tell her,' Rachel said. 'I'm not sure she's the sort who'll listen though.'

The morning after Irene and Ray Sutton moved into number four, there was an upset in the yard – raised angry voices.

'What's that racket?' Gladys said, hands in a bowl of washing-up water. 'Sounds like trouble.'

Rachel got up from the table to open the door. 'Sounds as if it's coming from the brew'us.'

Gladys cocked her ear. 'That's Ma Jackman. I'd know her screeching anywhere.'

'I think she's having a barney with that Irene woman,' Rachel said.

Before she could even sit down again, Ma Jackman's gristly figure came striding along the yard and banged on their door.

'Glad Poulter? Come and tell 'er to get out the brew'us – it's my turn this morning. 'Er's gone in without a by your leave, filling the copper, no thought of asking, and now 'er won't shift!'

'All right, Ethel!' Gladys called. To Rachel she whispered, 'Better go and sort 'em out. You never know with that one – she might clobber her.'

Gladys pushed her feet into her old black shoes and took off along the yard. Rachel heard raised voices again before they quietened. Soon after, Irene Sutton came huffily out of the brew house and crossed back to her house, clutching a bundle of washing.

'You're all right, bab,' Gladys called to her as she came back. Her tone was kind but firm. 'You can go in later when Mrs Jackman's finished hers.'

She came back into the house, rolling her eyes, and returned to her washing-up. She nodded her head towards number four. 'Got some lip on her, that one.'

Rachel thought Irene Sutton looked intimidating, but at the same time she felt a bit sorry for her. It was never easy being in a new place, with new faces and new ways. And she wanted to get along with her. It would be nice to have someone else in the yard with really young children. The little one did not look much older than Melly – they could be company for each other.

Irene strode out of the yard tugging her two little girls along a bit later, seemingly going shopping. But later in the afternoon, Rachel saw the girls playing out, bent over a puddle of water that had collected outside the brew house. The Morrison boys were out in the road instead of roaring about the yard so it was quite quiet. Slowly she led Melly, who was just beginning to walk, over to the girls. Melly was clutching a little peg doll that Gladys had made for her. Sounds of sloshing water were coming from inside the brew house and Rachel caught sight of Irene's pale hair behind the grimy windowpane.

'Hello,' Rachel said to the children.

They looked up warily at her. The eldest had long, straggly brown hair and a thin, blue-eyed face. She was not a pretty child. Her eyes were narrow and close together, but she had a steady gaze. Close up now, Rachel could see that the younger one was stockier, with a darker shade of brown hair and eyebrows. Her hair just reached her shoulders. Each of them was wearing a little dress in the same pale yellow material, grubby and smeared with dirt.

''Lo,' the older one said. She stood up and swivelled slightly from side to side, in shyness.

'This is Melanie,' Rachel said. She saw Melly hug the peg doll close to her chest as if afraid one of them would pinch it. 'She's come to play with you. What's your name, bab?'

It was almost the first time she had ever called anyone 'bab'. She suddenly felt old.

'Rita,' the girl said.

'That's nice. How old're you, Rita. D'you know?'

After more rocking, her eyes cast down, the girl whispered, 'Three.' When Rachel asked about her little sister she said her name was Shirley. Rachel guessed the child must be two.

'Who's asking?' a voice said from behind her. Turning, Rachel saw that the blonde woman was standing in the doorway of the brew house, leaning her left side against it, her left knee bent, toe resting on the ground. Her belly was pushing out the front of an ugly grey frock with a bit of lace at the neck. Rachel saw that her shoes were brown, with a low heel and very scuffed. Her manner was pugnacious and forbidding.

Seeing Rachel looking at her, she said, 'This ain't how I dress – I'm doing my washing.' She pushed herself off the door frame and stood upright, a hand laid resentfully on her belly. 'Not that I can fit into anything decent, sticking out the front like this.'

'I thought they might play.' Rachel made her voice as friendly as possible, though Irene seemed hostile. 'Nice to see some more girls – it's all been lads in this yard.'

'Yeah, rowdy little sods that lot are,' Irene remarked, nodding towards the Morrisons' house. Rachel felt riled by this criticism of Dolly's boys but she said:

'Oh, that's the Morrisons – they're all right, they are. Very nice. They'd do anything for you.'

Irene stared back, apparently unimpressed by this information. 'That's Rita and Shirley.' She nodded at the girls now. 'Shirl!' she bawled suddenly. 'Don't yow go getting wet – get her out of there, Rita!'

Rita dragged Shirley away from the puddle so roughly that Shirley started to grizzle. Melanie stood quietly taking all this in.

'Yow can pack that in or yow'll get a threaping – the pair of you!'

Melanie pulled away from Rachel's hand and went to the other two who seemed interested in her presence. Shirley stopped crying and the three headed off to squat by the wall of the metal spinning works. Rachel kept an eye out but they seemed happy enough.

'Where've you moved from?' she asked.

'Oh – over from Long Acre way,' Irene said. She appeared to relax a bit and stood upright, folding her arms over her belly. 'My Ray's at Kynoch's, on the guns.' Here she goes again, Rachel thought. The way she said *my Ray* was as if to say, *I've got the best-looking man around and don't you forget it! He's a cut above anyone else!* She tried to imagine saying *my Danny* like that. Even though she loved Danny and missed him with an endless ache, she just could not imagine talking about him like that. It made her want to laugh.

'Oh, I've heard them,' Rachel said. You could hear the bangs in the park, the guns being tested. 'My feller's in the army.' She heard the pride flower in her own voice. 'He's just gone out east.'

'Oh, I'm glad my Ray's reserved,' Irene said with a smugness that rankled. 'I wouldn't want him going off. Keep 'em close, I say.'

All very well, Rachel thought to herself. Not as if I had a choice. But she didn't want to get into a quarrel.

'How long've you got to go?' She nodded at Irene's belly. 'Mine's due September.'

'Yeah. Mine too. It'd better be a lad this time. I've had enough of wenches. Blokes always want a lad, don't they?' The way she said it was 'blowkes'. 'Best thing you can give 'em.'

'I s'pose,' Rachel agreed. In fact Danny said he was quite happy with girls. He was used to having sisters about. He said he'd be happy with anything, they were all family, and she loved him for it. It wasn't as if she could do anything about it!

She left Irene to her washing, keeping an eye on the girls. She hadn't warmed to Irene much at all. She seemed rough and big for her boots and not very friendly.

Twenty-Seven

Danny had come home for the first time once his basic training was over, after Easter in 1942. Though it had only been a few weeks, it felt an eternity to Rachel. When she heard he was coming she could hardly keep still for excitement.

'Your dadda's coming home today!' she kept telling Melanie, who was full of smiles, seeing her mother's happiness.

Just as they were sitting down to tea, they heard a shout along the entry. 'Hello! Anyone in then?'

'He's here!' Rachel shrieked and tore outside. Coming round the corner was a strong, fit-looking young man with cropped hair, in khaki uniform. His blue eyes blazed with excitement as he saw her and he tore off his cap and ran to her.

'Danny! Oh, Danny!' She seized hold of him, laughing and crying at the same time.

He pressed her tight to him. 'Hello, my wench.'

'Danny – you're all muscles!' She squeezed him. He did look the very picture of health.

Melanie was shy of Danny at first, but she soon came round once he had swooped her up onto his knee.

'That's my girl,' he said. 'Ooh – you're getting heavy,

Melly!' He bounded her up and down. 'Here – horsey-horsey . . .' Melanie looked round at him, unsure at first, then started to cackle with laughter.

Tea consisted of pease pudding, cabbage and a crumb of cheese.

'I s'pose you're getting better grub in the army?' Gladys said. She too looked delighted to see him. He was her son, Rachel thought, looking at her happy face. Near as, anyway.

'Nothing's as good as yours, Auntie,' Danny said, grinning at her.

'Oh, go on with you.' She cuffed his head. 'By the look of you they're feeding you like a turkey cock.'

As they ate, they heard all about Danny's new life. He described the tent he had been living in and the square-bashing, the other lads and some of the pranks they got up to. Rachel realized, with a sinking feeling that she tried not to show, that he seemed to be enjoying it.

When they went up to bed, alone at last after settling Melanie, they were in a fever for each other.

'God, girl,' Danny said, steering her to the bed. 'Get those clothes off – I can't wait any longer for you.'

He was on her immediately, hungry for all he had missed. They made love quickly, she excited by his urgent need of her. It was only afterwards, as they lay cooling down side by side, that they could talk.

'You're bigger – look at your arm,' she said, stroking the one closest to her. 'And your chest – look!'

Danny raised his head for a second, peering down at himself. 'There's all this PT and things called assault courses we have to do. They're forever on at us. Run here, do this, do that. Run five or six miles with a pack on – and that's just before breakfast!'

Hearing the pride in his voice, and how much he was

259

involved with it, somewhere else that she had never seen, Rachel rolled over and looked down into his eyes.

'D'you miss me, Danny?'

'Yeah,' he said. 'Course.' He reached for a strand of her hair and twined it between his fingers. 'Like anything.'

She wasn't convinced. 'But d'you *really* miss me? Not just – you know – doing it, but *me*? D'you miss *me*?'

'I do . . .' he said hesitantly.

'You don't sound as if you do – as if you mean it!' she said petulantly. Her tears came so easily after all the longing and aching and missing she had done. 'I think about you all the time. I live for your letters – they're what's keeping me going. But I s'pose,' she added pitifully, 'you're too busy to think of us much.'

Danny lay back, looking up at the ceiling for a moment, almost as if he hadn't heard her.

'Danny!' she wailed.

'No, listen –' Serious, he turned on his side to face her. 'Thing is, Rach – I was just thinking about it, about you saying "missing you". I mean, I do – course. I want to see you and do this –' he reached round to give her bottom a saucy pat – 'all the time. But when people say they're missing someone, like the other lads do sometimes, the real truth is, I don't know what they mean. I can't honestly say I know what it feels like, missing someone. I think it's . . .' He looked across the room for a minute as if trying to work it out. 'I think it's after being in the home. When you go in a place like that you have to stop yourself missing anyone, your mom, your sisters or whoever you've got, 'cause you don't know if you're ever going to see them again. You just shut it all out. If you missed them all the time, it'd be too much,

sort of thing. So I s'pose I sort of forgot how to do it.
But it ain't 'cause I don't love you, Rach.'

She wrapped her arms around him, touched by the
little boy in him, and hugged him close.

'Glad to hear it,' she said into his neck. ''Cause I miss
you like hell. And I love you, Danny.'

'You, and her –' He nodded his head to where Melly
was sleeping on her mattress on the floor. 'And Auntie
– you're everything to me.'

'What about Jess and Amy?'

Danny hesitated. Matter-of-factly, he said, 'It's not as
if they're coming back, is it?'

'Well, at least you're here now,' Rachel said, trying to
lift his mood again.

'I am.' Danny moved his body against hers again. 'Oh
yes!'

'Danny!'

'Sit on me this time,' he said.

'All right, your majesty,' she laughed. 'Anything
you say.'

Since joining up, he had been home three times. After
his first leave at Easter he had managed a long weekend
in the summer. His last leave had, by what seemed a
miracle, been over Christmas 1942. He arrived on Christmas Eve and all of them decorated the house with what
they could manage in the way of streamers and some
holly Gladys brought back from the market. She had got
a sprig of mistletoe too and Danny stood on a chair and
banged a nail into the ceiling so they could hang it from
a thread in the middle of the room.

'Go on – give her a kiss!' Gladys instructed. She was
in a happy mood. Rachel and Danny cuddled under it

while Gladys applauded and Melanie clapped and gurgled beside her.

That night, when they were in bed, he had laid a hand on Rachel's belly and wriggled up closer to her, mischief on his face. 'Let me stay in you, all the way, Rach. Come on – let's make another one . . .'

Her head whipped round. 'What? A babby? Are you kidding me?'

'No,' he said. 'I'm not.' He turned on his front, half on top of her, and looked seriously at her. 'Rach – there's summat you need to know. This leave I'm on – it's called embarkation leave.'

Suspicious now, she pushed him off her and sat up. 'What d'you mean?'

Danny sat up beside her, putting his arm around her with such gentle care that it made her feel even more worried. 'We're being sent somewhere – abroad. That's all I know – honest. They haven't told us.'

Rachel fell silent. She turned her head away, feeling desolate. She thought about Netta's Francis, with his safe job in the Pay Corps in England. Why couldn't they have given Danny a job like that?

'Rach – I can't help it. It's where we're ordered. The war'll soon be over – it *will*.'

'But how do I know when you'll come back?' she said, her emotion building. This was a new blow, which felt unbearable. 'It's bad enough that you're at all these army camps here. But at least we know where you are.'

'Soon as I get somewhere the first thing I'll do is let you know,' he said. 'I'll write to you as often as I can.'

She looked up at him in the gloom. 'D'you *want* to go, Danny?'

'*No*,' he said. 'I don't, cross my heart. I want to be back here with you – for it to be over. That's all I'm waiting for. But –' he shrugged – 'they give us these orders. There's nothing you can do.'

They were both silent then. Terrible thoughts came to her. What if he never came back from wherever they were taking him? She wondered if he was thinking the same, but neither of them wanted to say anything like that. It was as if saying it might make it true.

'Come 'ere,' Danny said. His hand moved up and started stroking her breasts, kissing her. 'We're here. You and me. Now. You're my girl, and I need you.'

They had made love every night of his week's leave, fully, without Danny having to pull out at the last moment, the way they had tried to avoid a baby before. They had spent every moment together. Even when the Morrison boys begged Danny to come out and kick a ball around with them, Rachel went and watched. Once again, when he left, it was as if he was torn away from her. Later, after they already knew he was somewhere in the east, but not exactly where, Rachel had woken one morning feeling sick in a way that was immediately familiar.

'It's all right for you, Danny Booker,' she muttered, after heaving over a pail in her bedroom. 'All you have to do is make the babbies and then clear off!'

But she smiled a little, thinking of the nights they had had together. No one could take those away. Over the next weeks, she alternated between feeling utterly browned off with Danny one minute and aglow with happiness the next at the thought that another little result of their love was taking shape inside her. Whether she was pleased or fed up really depended on just how sick she was feeling at the time.

Twenty-Eight

June 1943

'I'll come with you today and give you a hand,' Rachel said as Gladys gathered herself to head into the market on a warm Saturday morning. 'I could do with a change. I can keep an eye on Melly, this once, and she's no trouble is she? She'll like coming.'

'All right,' Gladys said. 'We can give it a try.'

Rachel realized that Gladys rather liked the idea of showing off her granddaughter.

It felt very nice to be out and about, travelling into town on a fine day, and Rachel's spirits lifted. Even all the destruction of the smashed-up city, the bomb sites and wrecked buildings, the grey warehouse walls and grimy streets, looked less glum and depressing in the sunshine. Rachel pointed out things to Melanie as the tram rumbled along.

'We're going to the market,' she said, excited. Melanie snuggled up on her lap, looking about her, wide-eyed and happy. She was wearing a little pink-and-white flowery frock and Rachel enjoyed the warm loveliness of her. She stroked the little girl's bare, fleshy arms.

Gladys went round and picked up the basket carriage and the stand she used to hang some of her clothes on and they set up together. The war was pinching everything tight with shortages, but everyone struggled on the best they could with goods off the ration, and there were many people looking for a bargain in these difficult times. Rachel, now six months' pregnant, felt well and was full of energy. It was lovely to be back in all the hurly-burly of the Rag Market. The only thing was, she kept half-expecting to see Danny come in and head across to her with his fast-moving stride. Each time she thought of it a pang of longing went through her. When would she ever see him here again, his eyes seeking her out?

When the big gates swung open, as usual the crowds came surging in, some of them at the front, breaking into a run. The woman who was in the lead, a large matron in a big black coat, her old shoes forced out of shape by bunions, was cackling with laughter, she and her friend elbowing each other to get in front. Her open mouth revealed a few remaining stumps of teeth. Rachel chuckled, loving the atmosphere and excitement of it all, and Melanie shrieked with delight as well, clapping her hands.

'It's nice to be back, Auntie!' Rachel said. 'And you,' she addressed Melanie who was on her hip. 'You've got to behave yourself, all right?'

People kept pouring into the market. In these drab, worrying times of war the market was another place to go for entertainment and to forget your troubles for a while. The place was soon heaving with people. Between them, Rachel and Gladys looked after their pitch. There were more tables in the market now, with metal poles through them and you could hang things between them. They set everything up together and took it in turns to mind Melanie. At times they sat her down for a bit and found her a few things to play with. Gladys had a little cotton bag with some pegs and cotton reels and ribbons in and Melanie loved it. Later in the afternoon when she was tired, they were able to lay her down in a safe spot behind their wares for a nap.

Amid the milling heads and shoulders of the crowd there were a number in uniform, mainly khaki, a few in air-force blues. Gladys nudged Rachel and nodded towards a section of the crowd.

'Here we go,' she said. 'Look who's here. They'll be after a rag or two for their brahmas.'

'Their what?' Rachel said, frowning.

'You know, their fancy bits – girls.'

Rachel saw a cluster of servicemen strolling through the market in khaki, but the uniform was different. And they looked bigger, broader in the shoulders than all the others, as well as nearly all being tall and well-fed-looking. Two were black men, one with a white girl on his arm, dark haired and pretty with scarlet lips, who was looking up at him, saying something. Rachel looked at Gladys.

'Yanks.' Gladys stood tall, trying to catch their eye.

Rachel had only heard about the Americans who had been arriving in the country for months. Until now she had never seen any of them. Gladys had mentioned them coming to the market before.

'Rolling in it, that lot are. Overpaid and over here – that's it, lads, you come over here and spend your money.' She stood tall, hands on her hips, beaming at them and beckoning, to distract them from the other clothing sellers and the woman across the way selling cheap perfume and paper flowers.

Two of the white boys in the group noticed Gladys staring at them. She was an eye-catching person and they were obviously curious. One said something to the other and they peeled off from the group, moving closer in their USAAF uniforms. They were almost the same height as each other, one ginger haired with freckles, walking with a loose-limbed swagger, the other dark haired, with a long, thin face. They nodded shyly at Gladys and eyed her wares.

'Say, Ed,' the ginger one said. 'Look at these, will you? These are really swell.'

He fingered two coats which were hanging from the stand. One was in soft camel, the other black with a smooth sable collar – a bit the worse for wear, but not bad. Gladys moved over to them immediately.

'Hello, boys – looking for something for the ladies?'

'Hello,' they said sunnily. The dark-haired one immediately fastened his eyes on Rachel, who sat perched on a little stool behind their wares. 'Hello, miss,' he said, touching his cap. Rachel nodded back, lowering her eyes, flustered, but she soon raised them again out of sheer curiosity, to see that he was coming round to speak to her. His ginger friend was talking to Gladys, holding up the sable-collared coat, trying for a bargain.

'Hi there,' the darker one said. 'You're looking mighty comfortable down there.' He held his hand out. 'My name's Ed.'

'Oh, hello,' Rachel said. 'I'm Rachel.' To her annoyance she found she was blushing.

'Nice to meet you, Rachel. Him over there, that reprobate's real name's Patrick Finnigan but we always call him Fin. He's after a bargain and the way it looks, he's going to get one.'

He was not exactly handsome, but he had dark, dancing eyes that made Rachel smile. It was nice to talk to a man of her own age again. It felt a very long time since she had had any carefree fun.

'I wouldn't be too sure,' she said. 'Auntie drives a hard one.'

'A hard bargain?' A little frown rippled across his eyebrows for a second, before his face cleared. 'Does she now? Well, never mind – Fin would do anything to get around that gal of his.'

Rachel thought about Gladys's comments about the brahmas, and from her tone she obviously thought they were no better than they ought to be.

'Does he have a girl in America?' she asked. She wondered how old Ed was – not much older than her, she guessed, but he seemed much more worldly wise.

He squatted down suddenly and Rachel found that they were level with each other. She was looking into his brown, laughing eyes and he was searching hers. She tried to look back at him as if she was not aflutter inside at his tall form so close to her and intent on her.

'Oh, maybe – but it's his gal here I'm talking about. A fiery little redhead like him! Great gal.' He looked attentively at Rachel. 'Say, you're a pretty little thing. How would you fancy coming out for a walk with me?'

Rachel blushed even deeper. 'What – now?'

'Well, no, not now,' he laughed. 'You seem to be quite occupied right now. I was thinking of later.'

Rachel realized that as she was sitting down, Ed could not see that she was expecting a baby. And she had certainly not told him she was married. She found herself keeping her left hand, with Danny's ring on it, tucked well down in her lap. She knew she should tell him straight away, that that would immediately break the spell. But it was such a long time since she had had attention like this, so long since Danny left. She was tingling with excitement. It was so flattering to have a man looking at her with frank admiration the way American Ed was looking at her.

'Where're you from?' she asked, trying to delay the end of the conversation. She smiled, patting her hair. Dolly had given it a little trim yesterday and put a couple of rollers in it for her. She was quite pleased with the way it was looking.

'Me? Oh, I'm from Franklin, Indiana,' he said. 'Fin over there's from upstate New York.'

Rachel kept smiling and nodded away as if she knew where Indiana was, let alone Franklin.

'Say, you really are swell,' Ed said, staring into her eyes. 'What d'you say we go out tonight – hit the dance floor?'

Out of the corner of her eye Rachel could see Gladys moving closer with the other Yank. It looked as if she had made a sale and when she turned to look, Rachel saw that Gladys's face wore a satisfied smile. However, a second later she caught sight of what was going on, Ed squatting there like that, the intent look in their eyes. Gladys immediately moved closer.

'I see you're getting acquainted with my assistant,' she said to Ed.

'Oh, yes,' he said easily. 'And a most charming young lady she is too.'

'Well, that there –' Gladys pointed to Melanie, fast asleep at the back of their pitch on her blankets – 'is her daughter. Have you told him about your husband being away in the army, Rachel?'

Ed stood up hastily. The charm with which he had been wooing her dropped away. 'Say, you don't look old enough to be a married woman!' He looked shocked and fed up.

Rachel lowered her head, her face burning. Gladys

took the money from Fin and bundled up the coat for him.

'So long,' they both said, and moved away. Rachel looked up, but Ed did not even glance in her direction again.

'I tripled the price – he didn't even notice,' Gladys said, tucking the money away gleefully. She turned to Rachel and in a sarcastic tone said, 'Enjoying yourself, were you?'

Rachel kept her gaze on the feet passing in front of her, burning with annoyance at Gladys. She'd frightened that American off, as if she was her mother or something! Who did she think she was? She had been about to tell him she was married – any minute! A tantrum of misery and self-pity erupted silently inside her. Would it really do so much harm to have a drink with a man? Danny had been away for so long. She could never be sure if he was alive or dead and here she was, left with their child and another on the way. And she wasn't even eighteen yet – wasn't she allowed to have any fun, *ever*, without Gladys acting like a prison guard?

More gently, Gladys said, 'You want to watch that lot. Here today, gone tomorrow – and far too full of themselves. You can be sure they're after one thing and one thing only.' She shook out a blouse that someone had left in a tangle on top of the other clothes and began to fold it. 'Brahmas,' she muttered scornfully.

When they were clearing up that afternoon, Gladys packing some of the leftovers into the basket carriage, Melanie kept trying to make a game of it and climb in.

'Oh, for goodness' sake,' Gladys said in the end. Melanie became furious every time they tried to stop her.

'All right, madam – you stay in there for now. We'll all go round to Bromsgrove Street together – you bring the other bundle, Rach, and the stand, and I'll push her in this.'

Everyone else was packing up and nearly all the punters had gone. Some pitches were already empty and a man was pushing a broom across one of the largest spaces. It was still a nice afternoon though the sun had sunk low by now. Rachel breathed in the street smells of horse, of fumes from trucks that were grinding along towards Bradford Street and the delicious scents of cooking food. Over her shoulder she carried the bundle they were taking home, wrapped in a sheet, the stand in the other hand. It was made of cane, so not heavy.

'It'll be nice when summer really comes,' she said. She was gradually simmering down and getting over her annoyance with Gladys. She knew Gladys was right really. She had never intended to be unfaithful to Danny, had she? As if she would, ever!

Gladys, pushing the carriage with Melly clinging on inside, made no reply. Rachel sensed that she was very weary. They went up to the pub on Bromsgrove Street and stashed the carriage in the stable, handed over their money for the pleasure and set off again. This time Rachel carried Melanie and Gladys the bundle.

They were aiming to walk across town to get the tram to Aston, which would no doubt be crammed full. The streets were choked with traffic, not helped by the fact that two large lorries were parked end to end at the corner of Jamaica Row. They seemed to loom over the pavement and Rachel and Gladys squeezed past them. Behind the second one, a man was standing with the back open, smoking a cigarette and looking as

271

if he was waiting for someone. They barely gave him a glance, but as they passed they heard him call out:

'Poll! Hey – Polly!'

Footsteps hurried after them and the man was beside them. Rachel saw a burly, strong-looking man with a head of black curly hair and stubbly cheeks walking up close to Gladys. He pawed her arm.

'Oi – Poll. Long time no see! Don't just march on past like that when an old pal's saying 'ello to yer!'

Gladys's face was a mask of bewildered irritation. 'Loose my arm, will you?' She shook the man off with a forceful jerk. 'Get your hands off me! You've got the wrong person, pal. My name's not Polly and never has been. So sling yer hook.'

'Oh, come off it, Poll – I'd know that face anywhere,' the man said, with a laugh. 'You can't just go pretending you're someone else now you've gone up in the world. Not with those eyes of yours. Remember me – Joe the Diver?' He was laughing even more now. 'Come on, Poll – you can't've forgotten old Joe.'

Rachel watched in bewilderment. The man seemed completely sure that he had met Gladys before. But why was he calling her Polly?

'I don't know you from Adam, never mind Joe,' Gladys retorted angrily, trying to push on along the road, but the man was keeping pace with her.

'Come on, Poll,' he joked. 'Don't be like that – where's the harm? Come and have a bevvy with us – and your friend if you want?' His weather-beaten face turned to Rachel and he winked at her.

'Just get lost!' Gladys fumed at him so forbiddingly that he did at last step back. 'I don't know who you are but I'll report you if you don't let go of me. Just leave me alone!'

'Oh, have it your way – you ain't lost yer spirit, Poll!' The man stopped and they hurried on, his voice ringing out behind them. 'Gone up in the world, have we? Well, good luck to yer, wench. But your old pal Joe ain't forgotten you, whatever you call yerself these days.'

'Auntie?' Rachel said, puffing as she tried to keep up. 'Who's that? Why's he called Joe the Diver?'

'That's not summat you need to know,' Gladys snapped. Then, after a moment's pause she added, with sudden indignation, 'I've no sodding idea, have I? How'm I s'posed to know? I've never seen him before in my life – he must be off his flaming head. You get all sorts round here.'

The man had seemed so sure, Rachel thought. He *had* known her, and Gladys knew who he was. But why was he calling her Polly? She had never heard Gladys swear so much before either. She eyed her from the side, but Gladys's face gave away nothing. It was blank and hard, as if set in stone. But it was another thing about Gladys that seemed closed and secret – and she knew she would never dare to ask.

Twenty-Nine

Rachel didn't dare say another word all the way home. Gladys was in a flamingly bad mood.

'Did you get any soap yesterday?' she demanded when they got back. 'Oh, you stupid girl – I told you—'

'They'd run out,' Rachel protested. She was close to tears now out of sheer exhaustion. 'There just wasn't any to be had.' I'm not a sodding magician, she felt like adding, but this was not the moment to push it.

Gladys was tutting about how she had all these things to wash and how was she supposed to make a living if she couldn't even get things clean? Melanie was sitting on the floor grizzling. 'All right, all right,' Rachel said crossly. 'I'm getting you some soup . . .'

'Eh – look what's come.' Gladys's voice changed abruptly. She held out a letter with the mauve censor's stamp on it.

'Oh!' Rachel's tiredness vanished instantly. 'It's from Danny!'

Dolly's head appeared round the door. Her expression held mischief and she clearly had things to impart. 'Back, are yer? You lot've missed a whole lot of carry-on!'

Rachel put the letter carefully in the pocket of her blouse, close to her heart, waiting to savour reading it once she was alone.

Gladys gave a not especially interested sort of grunt, but Dolly was not deterred. She came and sat at the table, smoking, as Rachel spooned soup into Melly's mouth. Each time Rachel felt the rustle of the letter in her pocket, a pulse of excitement went through her.

'Them two over there were at it hammer and tongs at dinner time today,' Dolly began.

'Who – that new lot?' Gladys looked up from folding the rest of her unsold goods away to be stored upstairs.

'Yes. The bloke – he must've been at work but he came home at dinner time – from the pub and tanked up by the sound of things. Off they went, walloping each other – she was screaming like a pig being killed. Those two little girls came out in the yard and hid, crouched down by the wall, poor little buggers.'

'It's quiet now,' Gladys said. She didn't seem very interested in other people's squabbles.

'I know, but you should've heard them . . .'

'You going to open that letter then?' Gladys said to Rachel.

'In a minute.' Rachel wanted to read it by herself first. After all, she didn't get any time alone with her husband these days – at least she could get a first read of his letter! As soon as Melanie was fed she slipped away upstairs with a candle to read it in the bedroom.

She smiled at the sight of Danny's looping, childish handwriting. Then her smile faded. The letter was dated at the beginning of May and the address: '*Not allowed to say where I am.*'

Dear Rach,

I'm in hospital at present but <u>don't worry</u>, by the time you get this I shall be long gone out I expect. I got bitten by one of the bloodsuckers [the middle of the sentence was blocked out by the censor] *arm swelled up like a football! It made me feel pretty bad but I'm on the mend now. Also, couldn't use my arm, so no good to anyone.*

I've been lying here thinking about you and about home and your news about another little one on the way. I can hardly believe it. But I wish the war would just end and I could come home and look after you. We've all had enough. I don't feel I'm very good with words but sometimes when I think of you and little Melly I feel like the luckiest person ever to have found you. You're my everything, Rach. There's a bloke I know here who knows all about the stars and he says you tell everything by where the North Star is because it keeps still. Well, you're my North Star – everything revolves around you, my whole life and everything. All I want to do is get out of this rotten stinking country and come back to you again and be in our room, our bed. You're what I dream about all the time, being home with you and Melly, and it keeps me going.

Thing is, I've been told I'm joining my battalion tomorrow and [there was another missing part here]. *So, I don't know what's going to happen next. All I can say is I'll be thinking of you wherever I go, my lovely. I wish you could just walk in here now, God, I do. Sometimes home feels such a long way away.*

Holding you in my arms and in my heart, and sending all the kisses I can't give you.

Your husband, Danny.

Squeezed in at the bottom right-hand corner was a tiny drawing of Jack in his straw hat and Patch, from the back, sitting at the top of a hill, looking out. The hill was more of a hummock as there was not much space, and in front of them Danny had drawn a little twig of a tree and a bird flying. The dog's black patch on his back was an oval scribble in blue ink. She touched it lovingly with her finger, thinking of Danny sitting in a hospital bed somewhere, his pen moving over the paper, drawing Patch with his perky tail . . .

She was surprised by how much Danny said in letters. He found it easier than talking. She realized that because now they were parted and he had to write, she had got to know him better. She thought her own letters were pale in comparison – we did this, Melly did that, I miss you. She was better at talking.

Tears of longing and love for him ran down her face and she lay back on the bed and had a sharp cry to let out her feelings. Shame washed through her. To think how easily tempted she had been by that American, that she was so easily flattered by his attention! Curled on her side she lay aching for Danny. She felt sometimes as if she might explode with longing. The baby twitched inside her as if disturbed by her sobs. Oh, when would it all be over? How old would this baby be before he saw it? It felt like an eternity already since she had seen Danny, so much so that sometimes it seemed as if only his few letters made him real and brought him back to her just a little bit.

Wiping her eyes she went downstairs. Dolly was still sitting with Gladys and they looked expectantly at her. She didn't want to hand over the letter to them. It was hers!

'He's all right,' she said and read out a few bits.

'An insect!' Dolly exclaimed, horrified. 'Ooh, I bet they have really big nasty ones out there. The poor kid!'

'I wonder where he is, exactly,' Gladys said, half to herself. They all had the idea that he was 'out East' somewhere.

Rachel felt herself tighten inside again. All this not knowing was so hard to bear.

It started up again when the pubs had turned out. Melanie had long been asleep and Rachel and Gladys were off to bed. A voice was bawling across the yard, aggressive and male.

'Oh Lor – who's that?' Gladys, her hair in a plait and her shawl over a nightdress, stopped at the bottom of the stairs. Loud, drunken yells were coming from outside.

'Who d'you think! That bloke – Ray,' Rachel said.

'With a skinful inside him, by the sound of it.' Gladys grimaced.

From upstairs they heard the door of number four being kicked in, followed by Ray Sutton's drunken roar.

Gladys tutted. 'Here we go. Come on – let's get up to bed. There's nowt we can do about it.'

From her bedroom in the attic, Rachel heard smashing sounds and Irene's screams. They kept it up at full tilt for a bit and Rachel lay listening, hating the noises, the high-pitched, hysterical screaming. She remembered a Mr and Mrs Pye from two doors up when they lived in Floodgate Street, the yells and screams that used to ring out of their house some Saturday nights. It always made her stomach knot up tight. She put her hands on her belly and felt the child twitch inside her. Oh, Danny, she thought miserably, trying to block out thoughts of what was going on in the house along the yard. Why aren't you here? Where had he gone to since he wrote that letter? Anything could have happened. He could be . . . No, she mustn't think that either. She mustn't expect the worst before it had happened.

Ray and Irene were both yelling.

Stop it, she thought, trying to bury her ears in the pillow. Just sodding well *stop*. Eventually, at last, it did go quiet.

The next morning, Sunday, she went out to get a pail of water from the yard tap and saw Irene strutting back into her house with a full bucket of her own.

'She's got a right shiner,' Rachel said to Gladys. 'But she's prancing about as if she's proud of it.'

Gladys, drinking a morning cup of tea, made a non-committal noise.

'Why would she be *proud*?' Rachel said. 'God, if anyone hit me like that . . .'

'Oh, I s'pect she's just putting a brave face on,' Gladys said. 'Mind you, she can dish it out, that one.'

Rachel added a drop of water from the kettle to the pail and did her few bits of hand washing. Tepid water and only the thinnest remaining wafer of soap – but it would have to do. A few minutes after she had carried the pail out to the washing line, Irene Sutton appeared as well. She couldn't have been trying to keep out of everyone's way then, Rachel thought. In fact it felt as if Irene had been looking out for her. Rachel eyed her from the side. Irene was wearing her grey baggy dress which was so crumpled and frowsty looking she must have slept in it. Her hair was scraped up behind her head. Rachel thought Irene's belly was sticking out more than her own, even though they were at about the same stage. But then Irene was bigger altogether and she had already had two children.

In silence, they hung their bits of washing together in a patch of sunlight. But as Rachel was coming to the end of hers, to her astonishment, she heard a sob from Irene. Seconds later, when another followed, she didn't feel she could ignore it.

'You all right?' she enquired.

Irene dropped the socks she had been hanging back into the bucket and put her hands over her face. More loud sobs came from behind her hands. Rachel dearly wished she hadn't asked.

'Oh dear,' she said. It wasn't hard to guess why Irene was crying. I'd be crying all right if my feller had gone on like that last night, Rachel thought. 'D'you want a cuppa?'

Irene shook her head emphatically. She removed her hands from her blotchy face and said, 'Come in the brew'us a tick.'

Rachel followed Irene's ample figure along the yard. Her pink, plump arms protruded from the tight sleeves of the dress and her bare feet, the ankles swollen looking, were pushed into her ungainly brown lace-ups. She was a strong, stately-looking person and Rachel wondered how old she was. She dreaded what she might be about to hear.

The brew house smelt of damp and soap and soot. There was ash on the floor from the fire hole under the copper and the spread remains of old candle stubs hardened on the windowsill. At one side was a stone sink which looked to be choked with the remains of something muddy.

'Yow 'eard us last night then? 'Eard my old man, the way 'e goes on?' Irene burst out. Her Black Country accent sounded strange to Rachel's ears. 'Look what 'e's done to my face – I ay gunna be able to go out looking like this! And look at my neck – tried to throttle me, 'e did!'

Tilting her neck, she gave Rachel a view of the bruising over her left eye and cheekbone, which were an angry red and mauve. The rest of her white skin looked tired and dry, down to her neck, around which were red, angry marks. Rachel was horrified.

'He did that? God, he could've killed you!'

'Nah,' Irene said dismissively. 'He day mean it. That's just 'is temper, like. That's my old man when 'e's kalied –' She sounded almost proud. Her voice softened. 'Like a lamb, 'e is, in the morning after. Begging me to forgive 'im.'

Her full lips turned up in a smile, then abruptly she burst into tears again. 'Oh Lord, save me – what'm I going to do?'

Rachel, now bewildered, could only say, 'Oh dear – what's the matter then?'

'It's Ray. I love 'im – I love 'im more'n my own life . . .' Full-hearted sobbing prevented Irene from saying any more for a few moments. Her whole body wobbled with crying. Rachel stood helpless and baffled beside her. Why on earth was Irene Sutton suddenly confiding in her? And what did she expect her to do?

''E's got another woman – I know 'e has,' Irene choked out at last. 'I guessed it but now I know for sure. 'E wouldn't admit it but I know 'im – I know what 'e's like when 'e's got a bit on the side. And last night, he said . . .' She couldn't speak for crying for a moment. At last she gasped out, ''E said that ho 'e's been with's got a bun in the oven an' all! And 'e says if 'er has a lad, 'e's gonna leave me and go with her!'

'No – he wouldn't!' Rachel said, shocked. 'He can't have meant it?'

'I dunno.' Irene looked miserably down at her feet. 'I dunno what 'e'd do. When 'e's kalied he says all sorts. But I just know I've got to give him a lad after two girls. He cor just have girls, he says. I dunno what I'll do if I don't.' She stared at Rachel's belly, pushing out her own blue-and-white dress as if an answer lay in it somewhere.

Rachel struggled to find something to say and came up with the only practical thing she could think of. 'Why don't you come up the clinic with me?' she said. She wasn't at all sure about Irene Sutton. She seemed to be of very uncertain temper. But she thought she must be lonely to have confided in her. 'I go with my pal Netta – she's due about when we are. They're nice up there and they make sure if your babby's all right.'

Irene looked rather blankly at her. 'Clinic? I've never been to no clinic before. But all right – ta.' She spoke with sudden warmth. In fact she seemed instantly recovered, her mood suddenly cheerful. 'Let me know when you're going and I'll come with yer.'

'You must be mad having another one in the middle of all this – and that husband of yours away,' Peggy had said when Rachel took Melanie to see her the next Sunday. She made this not especially helpful comment in a disgusted tone. She had never found a way of mentioning Danny that did not sound contemptuous.

Rachel came close to losing her temper. It had felt a long journey, traipsing over here on a warm afternoon when she would rather have snatched a nap. But Cissy and Melanie were devoted to each other and as well as that, for all Peggy's faults, Rachel did not want to deprive Melanie of the chance to know her grandmother. For herself though, she realized, it hardly mattered what Peggy thought about anything now. She was very obviously having another baby and that was that, whatever Mom thought about it. It was Gladys who felt like a mother to her, who was really her family. Even so, she still hoped, in her heart, that her mother would be nice and encouraging, though she was usually disappointed.

'Well,' she said, sinking down onto a chair. 'I can't send it back, can I?'

Peggy was installed in the little upstairs room with her feet up on a stool, having declared when Rachel arrived that she was exhausted. Rachel could see that her mother had aged since having Cissy. Her face was worn, her skin looser over her bones. Sometimes it was hard to believe that she was younger than Gladys.

'Fred's working himself into the ground,' she declared, picking up a piece of sewing and then dropping it down again as if it was all too much effort.

'What – selling blackout blinds?' Rachel said, trying once again to stifle her sarcasm.

'Oh, and all the other demands of the war,' Peggy said. 'And of course he worries so about Sidney.' So, Rachel thought, disappointed, that greasy sod's still alive then. 'And fire-watching . . .'

'Did you hear what happened at Bird's?' Rachel said, to interrupt the eternal trail of complaint. Gladys had heard from someone when she was in town. The fire-watchers had been, as usual, on the roof of the Devonshire Works in the night.

'One of them spotted this parachute coming down,' Rachel related. 'One of those parachute mines and it was heading straight for them. They all stood there as it came closer and closer out of the sky – right across the roof.

They were all waiting to be blown to bits! And then it just kept going, over the edge of the roof, and landed somewhere down below. It never even exploded!'

'Oh, my word,' Peggy said, fanning herself with a folded newspaper. 'I think my heart would have given out. Ooh – don't tell me any more, makes me feel quite peculiar.'

'Well, it's all right,' Rachel said. Looking at her mother, again it came to her how distant she felt from Peggy. 'You weren't there.'

Peggy gave her a look. 'Why don't you run and put the kettle on?' she suggested. 'I'm parched for a cup of tea.'

Rachel struggled to her feet. Walking to the kitchen she remembered that when Mom was six months on with Cissy they had all been waiting on her, hand and foot.

Thirty

August 1943

'If you don't put that away, babby, the other kiddies'll have it off you.'

Rachel paused with one hand on the heavy door into the mother-and-baby clinic, which stood on the corner of the street of small brick terraces. About to push against it and go in, she looked down at Melanie, who was gazing defiantly up at her. Seeing those big blue eyes – Danny's eyes – turned up to her, filled Rachel with an ache of longing. If only he was back home and she could feel his arms around her . . .

Letting go of the door she held out her hand. 'Give it me, Melly, and I'll put it safe in my bag. Come on – let's go in and see if Auntie Netta's here, shall we? You can have it when we get home.'

'No-o . . .' Melanie was shaking not just her head but her whole body. She had just passed her second birthday, was a good little walker and was beginning to hold her own with words and was becoming mightily stubborn. With both hands she clutched her treasure to her chest. '*Mine.*'

Rachel sighed, quelling her temper. 'I s'pose he did say it was just specially for you.'

'Children only,' the greengrocer said earlier, when she

was shopping. On the counter was a box half full of the glowing fruit, like distilled sunshine. 'Here yer go, bab – get that down yer – do yer good. Don't let your mother go pinching it off yer!' He winked at Rachel, who didn't think Melanie had understood that last part. But now she seemed to be taking him at his word! Rachel could see the bright stripes of orange skin between Melly's chubby fingers.

'All right then, but don't blame me if one of the others tries to take it off you. In we go.'

She opened the door into the dark, cavernous hallway of the building. A latticed window at the far end threw light onto the quarry tiles on the floor. Sounds came from behind the double doors to her right; the chatter of women over the bangs of the children playing on the wooden floor. Overlaying the building's mustiness she could smell the sweaty female odours of the clinic which seemed particularly rank today and she wrinkled her nose. She guessed what that strong smell meant – it meant *she* was in here, old Ruby, heaven help her.

The clinic was like a little world of its own. Out in the streets, in pubs and on the buses and trams, so much talk was about the war – they'd got the Mussolini bloke banged up at last in Italy. But when were we going to open a second front? And as ever there was the struggle with food and rations – even though more was getting through now, thanks to the Americans. In here though, in the clinic full of expectant mothers, everyone was involved with their bodies, their ailments, their worries about children and husbands.

Rachel pulled this second door open by its long brass handle and shepherded her mutinous little girl in front of her. 'Go on, bab – in you go.' She was looking forward to sitting down, the weight of her belly dragging at her today. She had one more month to go and was getting to the stage where she just wanted it over.

The noise grew louder. The smell intensified. The nurses had to heat urine to test it and the smell was acrid. Rachel swallowed. Faces turned to look at her. From the other end of the room one of the nurses, who was ushering a woman behind a screen, gave her a welcoming smile. Rachel liked that nurse. She was red-headed, Scottish and kind. She was the only one who made sure the chairs were arranged for the clinic in a wide circle so that the mothers could sit round and let the children play in the middle.

'So much better than sitting all in rows, wouldn't you say?' she had told Rachel on a previous occasion. 'It's not as if we're in church, is it?' There were a few toys provided and a gaggle of small children were moving about, corralled by the chairs occupied by women in varying stages of pregnancy. Rachel swallowed and looked across to see who was there. Melly stood beside her, cradling her precious orange.

As she predicted Ruby was there, a mountain of a woman, sitting apart from the others. Surely to God she was too old to be having another? It was impossible to guess her age but there was a whole gaggle of kids who swarmed in and out of her house in the next street to where Rachel lived. The Scots nurse had confided that it was the first time anyone had ever got Ruby to come to a clinic of any kind to be looked after. Ruby, in a navy tent of a dress, was heaped on the chair, cheeks the red of raw meat, head lolling forward on her chins as she dozed, looking as if it was a relief to have a chance to sit down anywhere.

'Rach – come and sit here!' Netta was beckoning her towards an empty chair. As she went over Rachel saw to her surprise that Irene Sutton was already there too, with her girls. She had brought Irene along once before but last time she was going Irene said, 'Oh no – I can't be doing with that.' Obviously she had changed her mind. She realized that Irene liked attention if she could get it, and this was one place where it was, at least briefly, on offer. She called out a greeting to her as she went to Netta and Irene nodded back. She was an odd sort, Rachel thought, sometimes friendly, sometimes looking through you almost as if she'd never seen you before. Now, she appeared as if she had a bad smell under her nose and was looking down on everyone around her.

'All right, Nett!' Rachel said, sinking down beside her. 'Oh my word, it's good to sit down.' She looked anxiously at her friend, who she had not seen for a few days. Netta was now very heavily pregnant. 'How're you keeping?'

'I'm grand,' Netta said bravely, resting her hands on her huge, precious bulge. She was still a bag of nerves about this baby. 'You look all in, Rach.'

'Oh, I'm all right,' Rachel said. 'But I've been in one queue or another ever since I went out this morning.' She leaned forward, massaging the ache in her lower back with both hands. Melanie toddled towards some of the other children and stood looking, her hands still up close to her chest.

'I know,' Netta sympathized. 'I'm lucky that Mammy does the shopping. Even though I'm not working.' They were doing everything they could to look after her. Netta had been working in a factory in Rea Street, but she had given up once she got to six months. 'Francis says I've to be wrapped up in cotton wool. We don't want to take any chances.' Her eyes filled as they did whenever she started to talk about this child. She winced.

'Mother of God, he's kicking me today.' Though her eyes filled with tears, she was smiling at the same time. 'But he can kick me black and blue for all I care – it shows what a life he's got in him.'

'Sounds as if you've got a strong little man in there,' Rachel said, full of sympathy. She had had no real problems having Melanie, or with this time around. But for poor Netta it had been such a hard road. Sometimes she had seen Netta looking at Melanie, her face brimming over with longing and sadness, and she ached for her. Surely this time it was going to be all right?

Rachel noticed that Melanie kept turning to look at her, seeming uncertain. The other children were playing all around her and she obviously wanted to join in while at the same time not wanting to put down the precious treasure in her hands.

Rachel was just about to say something to her when one of the nurses came over.

'Mrs Fitzpatrick, we'll see you now, please.'

Netta struggled to her feet. Her frock, despite being a baggy pale green thing, was stretched tight over her bulge.

'There you go.' Rachel smiled at her. 'Check everything's all right.'

'Tickety-boo.' Netta rolled her eyes but she still looked worried to death.

'It's all right, Mrs Fitzpatrick,' the Scots nurse soothed her. 'Everything's going very well this time. But we just need to make sure.'

Rachel watched Netta walk away, her mottled legs looking fragile, as if they would scarcely have strength to carry her.

Her attention was brought back by a screech from nearby. During the few seconds while she was talking to

Netta, she saw that Irene Sutton's girls had gone to Melanie and were trying to get at what she was clutching so eagerly in her hands. Though they were skinny little things, they were tough and wiry. Rita, who was a couple of months off four, had got hold of some of Melly's fingers and was trying to bend them back. Rachel was just moving over to them when Irene boomed across at them.

'Oi – you two – Reet! Shirl! What're yow doing?' She scowled. 'Girls – nothing but flaming trouble. This one'd better be a lad or I'll drown the flaming brat.'

Rachel heard a murmur of disapproval from some of the other women who were looking at her in horror.

'You shouldn't say things like that,' one said. 'That's disgusting, that is.' Rachel was only glad that Netta had not been there to hear it.

'Don't you talk like that,' she flared, going up to Irene. She got really sick of her sometimes, with all her fights with Ray keeping them awake and her changeable moods. She wasn't afraid of her though, even if Irene did try to look intimidating. 'That's no way to talk – especially in front of them.' She nodded at the children.

'Who the 'ell d'yow think yower bossing?' Irene started, but Rachel ignored her because Melanie was now screeching like a pig being killed.

'No-o-o!' she screamed. 'Mine!'

As Rachel hurried over to Melanie she saw Ruby, who had been dozing, wake with a violent start at the screams. 'No!' she cried, her face full of anguish for a moment. 'No!' No one took any notice.

'Oi – you leave her alone,' Rachel said, darting forwards to get Rita and Shirley away from her daughter before things could get any worse. She tried to speak calmly.

'Leave 'er, Reet, Shirl,' Irene called, though she was too heavily pregnant and too idle to get up and do anything about it. 'Gerroff 'er.'

Seeing Rachel standing over her, Rita gave her a fearful look and withdrew her hand.

'I only wanted to see,' she said. The girl seemed cowed. 'What's 'er got?'

There was a pungent smell of orange in the air now. The girls must have caught the skin with their nails. The tangy smell made Rachel's mouth water.

'It's an orange, from the greengrocer's,' she told the child, feeling sorry for her. 'If you go with your mother I 'spect you can have one too.' Fat chance of Irene bothering, she thought to herself.

She looked across at Irene who was watching them, arms folded across her large bosom.

'Leave it, Rita,' she said lazily. 'C'm'ere and sit down – stop mithering me.'

But the girls seemed rooted to the spot, unwilling to move away. Rachel could almost see the saliva collecting in their mouths.

'All right, Melly,' she said to her daughter. 'You come and sit down with me.'

To her surprise, instead of obeying her, Melanie put her arm out, opening the hand containing the orange and offering it to the two girls who she saw as her friends from home. Neither of them took it. They looked confused. Some of the other children were starting to show an interest in the proceedings now.

'Come and sit down,' Rachel insisted. 'We'll put it away for later and you can play with the children.'

Melanie shook her head. 'Have some,' she insisted.

'But it's yours, Melly,' Rachel said, feeling annoyed at the thought of sharing her daughter's precious fruit with

Irene's scratty little girls, especially after she'd stood in that queue for it. 'Don't you want it all to yourself?'

Melanie shook her head. 'Have some,' she said again.

Swallowing her annoyance, Rachel said, 'You want to share it? To give the other little girls some?'

Melanie nodded emphatically. She seemed to feel rather grand now.

'All right if I give them some?' Rachel said to Irene.

Irene, who had been ignoring the situation, looked back at her, astonished. 'What, mine? Reet and Shirl?'

'She wants them to have some.' Although none of you flaming deserve it, she thought crossly.

'Well – if that's what 'er wants . . .' Irene seemed disarmed, softer again. Like a different person. 'D'yow want some, girls?'

Rita and Shirley nodded, their eyes eager.

'Hang on a tick then.' Suppressing a sigh, Rachel rummaged in her shopping carrier for a paper bag and sat peeling the orange on it, using her thumbnail to pierce the skin.

'That smells nice!' some of the other women said.

'I can smell it over 'ere,' Irene said.

It was quite a big orange and by the time Rachel had the skin off it all the adults and children in the room were watching.

'That's an orange!' old Ruby piped up suddenly. 'Orange, that's what that is!'

Rachel separated all the pieces and gave one to Melanie, who put the end of it cautiously in her mouth. 'Shall we give some to all the children?'

Melanie nodded happily. She seemed less interested in the orange now it had been peeled open. Sucking her piece of fruit, she watched everyone with wide eyes. The clinic had turned almost into a party and she dimly realized that she was the one who had made it happen. Rachel handed out orange segments to the children and as there were pieces over, she gave the rest to the adults.

'Ta!' Irene said, taking hers with relish.

Going over to Ruby, doing her best to look as if she was not trying to avoid breathing in the smelliness around her, she held out her hand.

'What, me?' Ruby looked up, childlike with amazement.

Rachel nodded. 'There's a bit each.'

'Ooh – ta very much.' Ruby beamed and guzzled it down.

'Good for the baby,' Rachel said, not sure what else to say to her.

She saved the last piece for Netta. When she came back from behind the screened-off examination area, she was wiping her face. She could hardly talk about this baby without dissolving into tears.

'All right?' Rachel asked, holding out the segment of orange.

Netta nodded her thanks and sat down, nibbling on it. 'She said so. Oh, I can't believe it might be all right.' The tears flowed again. 'Francis is so excited.'

Rachel smiled. It was quite hard to imagine pale, devout Francis Fitzpatrick getting excited about anything.

The nurse came and called big Ruby in. They watched her haul herself off the chair and go along obediently, rocking from foot to foot.

'God now, she's a wreck,' Netta said. 'I'd wait for you, Rach –' she picked up her cloth bag – 'but I said I'd get back and give Mammy a hand.'

'Never mind,' Rachel said. 'See you soon, Netta. Pop in if you can. Look after yourself.'

'Oh – I will!' She laughed and gave a wave. 'Bye now.'

Rachel turned back to the ring of children, where Melanie was now happily playing with Rita and Shirley Sutton who were acting as if she was their little doll. For a second she caught Irene watching her. Irene was sitting with one leg crossed over the other, in that grey, old-fashioned frock of hers. There was a strange expression on her face as if she was trying to work something out. When she saw Rachel looking she turned her mouth down in the contemptuous way she often did, as if to say she was better than all of them, and turned away.

Rachel looked at her. She didn't really like Irene all that much; she was such a moody so-and-so. But she, Irene and Netta all lived in the same street. Their babies were all due within a few days of each other and Melly seemed to be fast making friends with Irene's girls, poor little mites. It looked as if they were all going to be stuck with each other, whether they liked it or not.

Thirty-One

September 1943

Two weeks later, Rachel was walking back from the shops on a hot, sticky day. Everything smelt stronger to her: whiffs of bins from the back courts, of horse muck and metallic factory smells. Fat green flies buzzed about, settling on the vilest things. And progress was slow, leading Melanie by one hand and carrying a bag of shopping in the other. She felt heavy and sluggish and in low spirits. A sharp pain niggled somewhere deep in her pelvis. It seemed an age since she had heard from Danny. Where was he? Why had he not written? But perhaps he had. There was no knowing when letters would arrive. Sometimes it was many weeks before she heard from him. At night she often lay in bed full of dark thoughts and fears that something terrible had happened, awful pictures of Danny injured, or worse, filling her mind, though she managed to banish them in the daylight.

Pausing for a moment as her daughter dawdled, she winced as the muscles of her belly tightened, like a cramp.

'Come *on*, Melly, walk a bit faster,' she urged wearily. 'Shall we sing "Teddy Bear's Picnic" and you walk along to that?'

She looked down at the child, who was idly sucking

one finger, and saw her eyes widen in surprise at something along the street. Rachel looked up to see a tiny, bird-like figure tearing along in her direction, dodging the other people in the street, apparently blind to everything. Rachel felt a surge of dread. Was something wrong with Netta?

'Mrs O'Shaughnessy!' she called to her.

'Oh – it's you, darlin'!' Mrs O'Shaughnessy did not stop. 'It's our Netta – I'm going for the doctor.'

'Has it started?'

Mrs O'Shaughnessy was moving past her now but she turned and scrambled backwards for a moment. 'She's after having her waters go – and there's only our Eamonn there and him not right in his wits . . . And Mrs Brown . . .'

'Shall I go and be with her?' Rachel called.

Mrs O'Shaughnessy stopped for a moment, her watery blue eyes widening. 'Oh, would you, darlin'? Yes, you go to her – God bless you!' And off she scurried.

Rachel scooped Melanie up into her arms, the shopping bag dangling, and lumbered along the street as fast as she could to the entry into the O'Shaughnessys' yard. A woman, outside mangling her washing, called out to Rachel as she hurried along but Rachel ignored her and ran into the house. Even as she came in through the front door she could hear sounds of pain.

In the downstairs room she found Netta half-slumped over the table, gasping. She was barefoot, again dressed in her green frock. Her thin hair was tied back and her face was pink and damp with sweat. Eamonn, seventeen and the youngest boy of the family, was sitting by the unlit range, wide-eyed and bewildered. Mrs Brown, a kindly, thin-faced lady of about fifty, still in her pinner with a pink scarf on, was standing behind Netta, making encouraging noises.

'That's it, bab – oh yes, that's it!' she said, in between frantically chewing at the ends of her fingers and not seeming to know what else to do. Rachel saw that there were already pans of water heating on the stove.

Rachel almost dropped Melanie and the shopping on the floor. 'Netta!' she said as the wave of pain seemed to pass by. 'It's me – Rach.'

Netta looked round and grabbed Rachel's arm, her eyes full of fear.

'Rachel! Oh my God, it's started. Oh, I'm so scared . . . Something's going to go wrong. I'm never going to have a healthy child, I just know it. God doesn't want me to – He must be punishing me for something.'

'Ooh, it's no good talking like that, bab,' Mrs Brown said. She seemed very flustered and uncomfortable. Rachel saw her eyeing up Mrs O'Shaughnessy's Catholic statues and the sacred heart on the mantelpiece. 'I've put some more water on to boil,' she added, to no one in particular.

Rachel put her arm around Netta's back, feeling the hot moistness of her. 'It's all right – your mom's gone for the doctor. She'll be back in a minute. Just hang on, Netta, all right? You're doing everything you're supposed to do.'

Netta was beginning to pant and another pain seized her. 'Oh, sweet Jesus, here it comes again!' As she emerged from it she wailed, 'There's something wrong with it. It's going to die, I know it is!'

Mrs Brown kept tutting helplessly and saying things like, 'No need to keep on like that.' Rachel caught sight of Melanie, crouched as far away as she could get from Eamonn, who said not a word, looking terrified.

'Go out in the yard and play, Melly,' she ordered her. 'Wait for me there – I won't be long.'

Melanie scampered outside with relief, away from all these alarming sights.

'You're all right,' Rachel kept saying to Netta. 'Just breathe nice and deep and your mom'll be back soon,' while the weight in her own body pulled on her and the hard jabbing pain deep inside her grew worse. She longed to sit down.

It felt like an eternity before Mrs O'Shaughnessy came hurtling back across the yard and burst into the house.

'The doctor's called an ambulance!' she announced. Mrs Brown gasped, which Rachel did not think was very helpful. 'He said you should have this one in the hospital.'

Netta dissolved into sobs. 'I told you!' she cried. 'There's something wrong. I'm going to lose this one as well and what'll I tell Francis? It'll break his heart . . .' She was so sure of it, so grief stricken, that Rachel found herself in tears as well, as if the worst was already happening. Soon, two orderlies appeared across the yard carrying a stretcher and Netta screamed and clung to the table, a look of utter terror on her face.

'No! Mammy – don't let them take me away!'

'Come on now, Netta, they're here to help you,' Mrs O'Shaughnessy said. 'To help the baby and make sure it's all right.' She didn't seem too sure though and even as the two ambulance people, one man and one woman, came and spoke gently to Netta, Rachel felt very upset for her. Hospitals seemed frightening places to her.

'Wait!' Mrs O'Shaughnessy cried, running to the stairs. 'Let me get her things.'

Once on the stretcher Netta lay quiet, suddenly submissive. Rachel went and took her hand and squeezed it. 'See you as soon as I can.' She forced her lips into a smile.

But it was a terrible feeling seeing Netta carried away, even if it was meant to be for the best.

'Holy Mother,' Mrs O'Shaughnessy said in desperate tones, sinking onto a chair. 'For pity's sake, let her be all right this time.'

All that day after she got home, Rachel fretted about Netta, wondering what was happening. She told Gladys and Dolly what had happened and they all wondered and hoped for Netta, of whom they had all grown fond. Rachel could not settle to anything.

'It made me feel quite queer seeing her,' Rachel said as they sat around the table. 'I keep thinking mine's starting – sort of in sympathy, like!' Then she giggled. 'You should've seen that Mrs Brown's face. She looked as if she'd walked into – I don't know what – a witch's den! What with all Netta's mom's statues and that.'

Gladys cleared her throat. 'It's not everyone holds with all that sort of thing,' she said stiffly. She held out a little white bag. 'Anyone for a mint?' She put her head on one side. 'You all right?' A pain had clenched through Rachel's belly and she was gasping. 'You look flushed. You're not coming on as well, are you?'

'I don't think so – it's a bit early,' Rachel breathed, as the wave receded. 'I overdid it today though – carrying Melly and everything.'

By the small hours the pains were coming hard and regular, and there was no mistaking the fact that her own labour had begun. Rachel tossed and turned in bed as the pains became so intense she had to make a huge effort not to scream. The room was very dark and she did not like it, being lost and alone with the contractions, unable to see anything. It was frightening and miserable. Between one pain and another she got up and lit the stub of a candle and that made her feel a little bit better. She knew Melanie would not wake. The child slept very soundly once she was off to sleep on the other side of the bed.

She knew she could stand it for a while. After all, she had done this before. But eventually the pain reached such a peak that she could not help crying out, trying to muffle her mouth with the bedclothes. Despite herself, she let out a thin, high shriek and after a few moments she heard Gladys moving about. A wavering light appeared at the bottom of the attic stairs.

'Rach?' Gladys's voice came up to her. 'What's going on – are you having it?'

'Yes – get help, Auntie,' Rachel cried. 'It's coming. I must've set it off, carting Melly about like that . . .'

'Right.' Gladys came upstairs and put her candle down. 'Let's get this one out of the way – I'll put her in my bed.' She disappeared with a soundly sleeping Melanie in her arms. It crossed Rachel's mind that she had never seen the room where Melanie was about to be put to bed again. Shortly Gladys came back up.

'I've got Ernie to run for the midwife,' she said. Ernie Morrison, the eldest boy, was now fourteen and just out at work. 'I told him to stay with her and bring her – they can never find these houses.'

In the candlelit room, Rachel sank into herself, barely aware of anything else that was going on around her. Time passed, during which she was dimly aware of

Gladys organizing things, shifting her over to lay news-paper on the bed, coming up and down the stairs. But the pains were getting closer and the crushing clench of it became her whole awareness. She crouched forward, face turned sideways on the pillow, and she dozed during the short lulls between each contraction and the next, wishing she could just go to sleep and then wake and it would all be over. She felt tired to her bones, and the idea of trying to birth a baby was utterly exhausting.

'You all right, Rach?' Gladys's voice came to her from time to time. She could hear her trying to sound in com-mand, when she was nervous and wishing the midwife would get here.

'Ummm,' she managed in reply. And, as the pain grew again, 'I want Danny . . .' In her mind she fixed an image of his face, smiling at her, urging her on.

Then there was someone else in the room – sounds of activity. 'Well, hello – here we are again!' she heard. 'Now you look as if you're doing very well.'

With pleasure she recognized the voice. Looking up, she saw the dark curly hair and competent figure of Nurse Biggins, the same young midwife who had delivered Melly.

'I've seen you before, haven't I?' she heard her say. 'Well, you're a nice healthy young thing. It was a little lady we delivered last time, wasn't it?'

'She's asleep downstairs,' Gladys said. 'Bonny little thing she is.'

'Well, she's got a nice healthy-looking mother.' In a lull between the pains, she added, 'I'll examine you now, Rachel, while we have the chance. You're an old hand at this, aren't you, young lady? Could you just roll over for me?'

Rachel smiled vaguely. It was nice to be thought a

woman of the world. She endured the examination and the midwife said, 'Very good – you're more than half-way there already.'

And then everything stopped. Rachel did not notice at first. She sank into a doze, waking with a start and no idea how long she had been asleep. She saw Gladys across the room and the midwife who was sitting beside her, sipping from a cup.

'Are we off again?' she said, putting the cup down in an expectant way. 'It's been a while since the last one.'

'No,' Rachel said muzzily. 'How long've I been asleep?'

The midwife glanced at the little watch pinned to her uniform. 'About ten minutes.' She frowned, then brightened. 'I expect there'll be another one along in a minute. You've probably reached the "rest and be thankful" stage. It happens, dear. I should make the most of it while you can. The pains will be back sure enough.'

Reassured, Rachel dozed. Everything went very quiet. The she became aware of voices, low and urgent. She heard the word 'doctor' more than once.

'What's the matter?' She was wide awake suddenly, gripped by panic at the hushed, worried tones.

'It's all right, dear.' The midwife hurried across to her. 'We were just wondering if you needed helping along a little bit. I tell you what –' She looked across at Gladys. 'We'll try something first. That baby seems to be having a bit of a rest and we need to get him moving again.'

Though she spoke cheerfully, Rachel could hear a tremor in her voice. She sat up, her hair tumbling about her face. The bedclothes felt like hot ropes around her legs and she kicked them off. 'There's something wrong. Don't hide things from me!'

'We're not, bab,' Gladys said, though she sounded even more worried than the midwife.

'It's all right,' Nurse Biggins said. 'This does happen sometimes for a while. But it's getting a bit of a long time now. Can you get up and walk about with me a bit and see if that does it?'

Rachel struggled to stand upright. Her bare feet reached the rug by the bed, then the dusty floorboards as she began to shuffle along, holding Nurse Biggins's arm. Back and forth they paced, the words of encouragement becoming more desperate as time went by.

'What's wrong?' Rachel was tearful now. 'There's something wrong, isn't there? Oh, Auntie ... Oh, I want Danny . . .' She started to sob.

'Now, now – don't get all in a state,' Nurse Biggins was saying, when, with no warning, a tearing pain began and Rachel headed for the bed, yowling with pain.

'Here we go,' the midwife said, a great rush of relief in her voice. 'That's woken him up again, hasn't it?'

After that the pains intensified and came so thick and fast that Rachel scarcely had time to recover from one before another was upon her. On and on it went until at last, propped on the bed, the pain tearing at her, she pushed the baby out.

'Oh,' she heard Gladys say emotionally, as the child's limbs slithered from her. 'Oh, thank God!'

Rachel raised her head, desperate to see.

'It's a lovely little boy,' the midwife told her. 'And a good size by the look of him!' A moment later the little lad was wrapped and lying in her arms, and she could feel the solid, convincing weight of his body.

'A boy!' Rachel said, hearing the joy in her own voice. 'Hello, little one! Hello, Tommy! Oh, Danny'll love having a boy!'

Thirty-Two

'You've got a lad then – let's have a look!' Rachel could hear the envy in Irene Sutton's voice as she waddled over towards her.

It was the second day after she had had the baby and she ventured out with him in the corner of the yard to catch the late-afternoon sun. Melly was out there playing with Rita and Shirley. She was very interested in her baby brother but disappointed that he did not quite seem disposed to run around with her yet.

Rachel felt sore all over, and light-headed with weariness. But it was over at last and she had her little boy. As soon as she sat down, Irene had appeared out of her house, now hugely pregnant, the lump of the baby seeming to move under her sack of a dress almost with a life of its own. She came and leaned over, peering at the baby, and Rachel saw that her fleshy pink-and-white face was swollen.

'What's 'is name then?'

'Thomas,' Rachel said proudly. 'Thomas Harold – the Harold's after my father. I just liked Thomas – I want him to be Tommy. He was six pound eight,' she said. 'He came on a bit early.'

'I wish this flaming thing'd come on early,' Irene said,

straightening up. She reached for a packet of Woodbines in her pocket and lit up, pushing one hand into the small of her back. 'Look at the state of me!' She indicated her ankles which were puffy and distended as well. 'God, it'd better be over soon. I cor stand waiting much longer. Was it bad?'

'Well, you know.' Rachel grinned. 'Bad enough.'

Irene laughed knowingly. 'I'm all right with that – having 'em, I mean. Just seem to pop 'em out. It's bringing the brats up after that does me. Shirl!' she bawled suddenly. 'Stop messing with that tap!'

'Have you heard about Netta?' Rachel said. 'She started the day before me and they took her to the hospital . . .'

'No.' Irene shrugged, her ample breasts lifting. 'I dunno where she lives.'

'I must go and see them,' Rachel said. 'I hope to God she's all right.' So much had happened in the meantime that it felt as if Netta going into labour had been weeks ago instead of just a couple of days.

Irene leaned over the baby once more. ''E looks nice, he does. Bonny. I hope mine's like that. Any road, better go and get Ray's dinner.'

Just as she was turning to go they heard the usual whistling and Ray Sutton himself appeared along the entry. He seemed in a good mood, swaggering along with a smile playing around his lips, his cap at a jaunty angle on his black hair.

'Afternoon, ladies!' He stopped as if taken aback at the sight of them and gave a theatrical bow. 'What have we here? The new arrival?'

Rachel shrank away as Ray Sutton came and peered down at Tommy. Close up she could see the five o'clock shadow on his chin and smell sweat and Brylcreem. She didn't like his coming up close to her, uncomfortable with the sort of crude man he was and his fake charm.

'What is it then – a lad?'

'Yes,' she said, holding Tommy closer to her.

'That's the spirit – lads, that's what you want, not all these flaming wenches!' He started to move away towards the lavatories at the end of the yard. ''Scuse me, ladies – call of nature.'

Irene rolled her eyes. 'Making room for the next pint.' But Rachel saw her stare after her husband with a longing look in her eyes. 'That bitch still ay had hers yet,' she said in a low, bitter voice. 'It'd better be a girl – if it's a lad I'll go round and scratch her eyes out.'

'I wonder you don't go and scratch them out anyway,' Rachel said. 'If it was Danny I would.' Would she? she wondered, despite her brave talk. If Danny was carrying on like that with another woman? She could scarcely imagine it. It would feel as if her world had ended.

'He'd kill me,' Irene said. She looked down, seeming shamefaced. ''E would. 'E's like that.' Her chin came up, defiant. 'Any road, sod 'im. I'm gonna go and do the spuds.'

Rachel waited until Tommy was asleep and left him with Gladys. She hurried round to Netta's house. She was longing to show Tommy off to people but she was worried in case Netta's birth had once again ended in tragedy.

It was not comfortable to walk. Her legs felt wobbly and the bloody rags were like a lump between her legs. Thank heavens they did not live far away. As she drew closer to Mrs O'Shaughnessy's yard she felt herself tense up, worried for Netta.

Outside the house everything seemed deathly quiet. Her sense of foreboding deepened. Was it a house of death and grief she was coming to? Not wanting to delay – she felt tied to Tommy by a tight string – she tapped on the door. There was a pause before the door opened with creaking slowness, like that of a haunted castle. She almost expected to see some aged crone peering out from behind it. Instead, she saw Netta's brother Eamonn, vacant looking as ever. When he saw her he pulled the door open and just stared.

'Hello,' Rachel said.

'I want to marry you,' Eamonn announced.

Rachel laughed, taken aback. 'Well, that's nice – but I'm married already, Eamonn.'

'Oh.' He looked down at his feet, on which there were grey socks with potato holes in them.

To Rachel's relief she heard more footsteps across the yard and she turned to see Mrs O'Shaughnessy.

'Oh – Rachel. Hello, darlin'!' she called. A tired smile lifted her face.

'Is she all right? What happened?' Rachel cried, hurrying to meet her.

'She's doing well, praise God,' Mrs O'Shaughnessy said and a laugh of happiness escaped her, followed by tears. She wiped her eyes with her forearms. 'Oh, I can hardly believe it. You should see him – a fine little feller. Netta had a long, hard time of it, but it's all over now and she's happy as a bird. He's a proper lad – she's calling him Patrick. We sent a wire to Francis – he's over the moon, so he is!'

'Oh, thank goodness. I'm so glad!' Rachel said, tearful with relief. It would have been unbearable to hear more bad news from Netta.

'She'll be home with him in a couple of days,' Mrs

O'Shaughnessy said, pausing at the door of the house. 'What're you doing hanging about there, Eamonn? I've told you about staring at people. Now will you come in for a cup of tea, Rachel?'

'Oh – no, ta, Mrs O'Shaughnessy,' Rachel said. 'I'll need to be getting back to my own little one before he wakes.'

'Dear God!' Mrs O'Shaughnessy's hands went to her cheeks. 'You've not had yours already!' She eyed Rachel's waistline. 'So you have now! And you've a boy as well?' She smiled back at Rachel's beaming face. 'Oh, what a lovely thing – the two'll be playmates. I'm happy for you, darlin'. And how's your little girl liking him?'

'Oh, she likes being the big sister. Give my love to Netta, won't you? I'll see her in a few days.'

She walked home with a big smile on her face. There was just Irene's baby now. And what they needed was a hat-trick of boys.

A couple of nights later, after dark, shouting broke out from across the yard.

Gladys rolled her eyes. 'Just when you've got them both off to sleep, Rach,' she complained. 'I s'pose the pubs've come out.'

The shouting and the sound of things crashing to the floor at number four went on for some time, despite Dolly standing at her door and yelling across the yard, 'Pack it in, will yer? Some of us are trying to sleep.'

Rachel carried her sleeping son up to bed and slipped in with him. He was milky and contented and she felt very weary, but the sounds from the neighbouring house grated on her nerves. What was going on? She lay with her arm crooked around Tommy, hearing his little breaths.

Melly was asleep close by as well. Rachel wanted to lie and dream of Danny, that he was here beside her. She imagined him walking in, his first sight of his son. But the shouts and bangs would not let her slip away into her dream world. She thought she could hear Irene sobbing. God, what a pair, she thought.

The next morning it was raining. She saw Irene come out to fetch a bucket of water, head down, her hair loose and hanging around her face. She seemed very subdued – upset or sulky or both. She was so heavily pregnant now that she rocked from side to side as she walked. She waited for the bucket to fill, not once raising her head and apparently oblivious to the falling rain, before going slowly back inside.

Later though, there was a knock at the door. Gladys was out and Rachel, holding Tommy, opened up to find Irene outside with Rita and Shirley. The two little girls looked very downcast and Irene had an angry red mark on her already swollen cheek.

'Can we come in?' she said, advancing in anyway. 'Siddown, you two,' she snapped at the girls, who slunk onto the mat by the range like mice. They looked around the room, seeming amazed, and Melanie stared at them, unsure what to do.

'Melly, you play with Rita and Shirley,' Rachel said. Melanie followed them onto the mat and for a while they all sat very quiet and cowed. Before long though they were nudging each other and giggling. Melly went and fetched her peg dolls and they all started on a game.

Irene sat herself down at the table, legs splayed. She looked grubby and unkempt, her crumpled dress all stains down the front.

'You heard us, I s'pose?' She spoke aggressively.

'Course. The whole flaming neighbourhood heard

you, I should think,' Rachel said, irritable with lack of sleep. Tommy had been up feeding. He did not feed well, not like Melanie. He didn't seem to be able to suck strongly as she had. It was starting to prey on her mind. Was he getting enough to eat?

'That ho's had her brat,' Irene said. Her voice broke then. 'It's a boy.' Sobbing, she gave an imitation of Ray's view of things. ''E's been on about it all night – "I've got a son now, a lad. What're yow gonna do if *you* cor give me a son? . . . I don't want a house full of women – there's too many in this place already. *Your* job is to give me a lad . . . A proper woman would have lads . . ."'

'Oh dear,' Rachel said, putting a cup of tea in front of her, so weak it looked almost like milk and water.

'He's gonna leave me and go to her,' Irene sobbed. 'What if I don't have a boy?'

Rachel wished that Gladys was here. She'd have something to say about it all. For herself – what could she say? She had no time at all for Ray Sutton and his oily charm. He was just a revolting bully, she thought. But he was Irene's husband so what was she to do?

Irene seemed to read Rachel's silence as criticism and she looked across defiantly at her.

'He loves me really – I know he does. It's not like yow think – it's only the drink talking. He's only like that when he's had a few.'

'Well then,' Rachel said, feeling that whatever she might say she was never going to win. 'You've got nothing to worry about then, have you?'

Thirty-Three

A few days later, as the sun was rising, there was more commotion in the yard of a different kind. Gladys saw Ray Sutton hurrying in along the entry accompanied by a blonde-haired young woman in a nurse's uniform. The two of them headed straight for number four.

'Irene Sutton must be having her baby,' Gladys announced, over Melanie's morning grizzling. She was always a grumpy child until she was fed. 'There's that Ray with the midwife – trotting along with her like a lamb. He doesn't look his usual cocky self at all!'

'God, I wonder if she'll have a boy?' Rachel said. She had told Gladys all about Irene's troubles. 'All right, Melly – just hang on a minute. I'll get you some stera.' Tommy was asleep for the moment, thank goodness. She poured a drop of sterilized milk to pacify her daughter, who drained the cup, then looked expectantly at her.

'All right, all right – look, here's a piece, you little madam.' She sawed at the half-loaf on the table. 'Never anything wrong with your appetite, is there?' She tweaked Melly's nose affectionately and the child giggled.

With Melanie eating eagerly, Rachel sat for a moment, sipping tea and feeling washed out and exhausted. It had been another poor night with Tommy struggling to feed and she felt anxious and close to tears. Melanie, as a baby, had latched on and sucked away as happily as anything, but with Tommy everything seemed to take more effort. She was afraid he was not getting enough milk but it was hard to tell.

'It'd serve that Ray right if he has a lad who can knock some sense into 'im,' Gladys said. 'He could do with a bit of competition, that one. Damn and blast.' She was trying to get the range to light. 'I'm sure this cowing coal's damp.'

Everyone got on with their tasks all day, but in the yard there was a restless, listening mood. A new life arriving seemed to draw everyone's attention. While Irene laboured, Ray had disappeared to work and Rita to school, so little Shirley came outside and played with Melanie, out of the way. Soon the two of them were in their own world, taking no notice of anything else.

As she went back and forth across the yard, Rachel looked at the grimy upper window of number four. The window was kept closed, but every now and then through the glass she heard a low moan. Rachel had so recently been passing along the same road of birthing a child that it was easy to feel what Irene must be feeling in her own body. Tears sprang into her eyes and she tried to close her mind to it. Everything seemed to be pressing in on her. There had been no letter from Danny for several weeks now and in her low mood it seemed like forever since she had heard from him, let alone seen him or lain beside him. He wouldn't even know about his son's birth yet. Sometimes it was hard to believe he was real and she struggled to picture his face. She ached for him to be there, for him to be able to see Tommy.

And all the time her worry over Tommy niggled at her mind, though Gladys kept saying it was nothing. 'Babbies don't always feed right to start,' she said. 'He'll get the hang of it.'

Rachel felt like snapping back, *How would you know?* But she chose to try and be reassured instead. How could two babies be so different? she thought. Was this the difference between girls and boys? Tommy's body felt so stiff and strange compared with Melanie's. I must go and see if I can get him to take a bit more now, she thought.

By afternoon, the tension was growing. The women found themselves wandering out into the yard, even if they could not remember exactly why they were there, to stand listening.

Rachel went along the yard to the lavatory and came upon Gladys and Dolly, leaning up against the factory wall. Both of them had their hair tied up in scarves. Dolly was talking about her favourite subject.

'I've told Mo, I ain't going through that lot again,' she said in a hushed voice. 'And 'e said, well, what'm I s'posed to do? And I said, you've got them bikes to ride – you'll have to make do with them instead . . .' Rachel passed out of earshot.

On her way back, though, she found herself lingering beside them.

'How's the babby?' Dolly asked, a smile in her brown eyes. As usual her lips were painted a cheerful scarlet.

'He's all right,' Rachel said. But she could feel the tears rising again. 'But I don't think he's eating properly.'

'Oh, he'll be all right,' Dolly said. 'You should have seen my Wally when 'e was born, and Reggie too –

proper little so-and-so's they were when it came to feeding. They'd have me up half the night, on, off, messing about. I thought they'd waste away. But look at them now!'

Rachel gave a wan smile. She did feel a little comforted. Dolly had five sons – she must know. But the worry niggled on.

'Eh –' Dolly pushed herself off the wall. 'Hark at that! She must be getting near the end!'

Agonized yells came from the upstairs of number four.

'Here we go,' Ma Jackman said, crossing the yard with her stiff hobble. 'Another brat.'

'Trust her – full of the joys as usual,' Dolly tutted.

In a few seconds they could just make out the ragged mewl of a newborn.

'Oh,' Dolly said, a hand on her heart. Her eyes were full of tears. 'Listen to that. Am I doing it all wrong, Glad? Should I have another one?'

Gladys gave her a look. 'I'm not answering that. I'll only have you coming to me when you're six months gone, saying it were my fault.'

Tears were running down Rachel's cheeks at the baby's cries. To her surprise she saw that Gladys, as well as Dolly, was in a similarly watery state.

'Sounds healthy enough,' Gladys said, wiping her eyes quickly.

'Ooh – never again,' Dolly said emotionally. 'But ain't it lovely?'

They hovered about until the midwife emerged from the house looking tired but relaxed.

'She all right?' Dolly called to her.

'All doing very well – a lovely healthy baby.' The young woman smiled.

'What's she had?' Gladys asked.

'Oh – a little girl.' Rita, now home from school, was hovering about with Shirley. The midwife smiled down at them. 'Are you the big sisters?'

They nodded, in awe of her.

'Well, you've got a new baby sister – you can go up and see if you like, but then you must leave your mother to rest for a while.'

'A girl?' Rachel said.

The midwife hesitated. 'I gather she was rather keen to have a boy.'

The other women looked at each other.

'Is there no one to be with her?' Gladys asked.

'No – I gather her family live some way away,' the midwife said. She hesitated again. 'I've given her a wash and made some tea for her, but – well, the place is rather disorganized.'

'Someone ought to be with her,' Dolly said. 'It seems sad, her all on her own, like, no mom or anything. My mom came when I had all mine . . .'

'I'll go in and see her,' Rachel said, thinking with dread, a girl, oh dear. 'Shall I go now?'

'Yes, go up and pop your head in, bab,' Dolly said. 'Tell yer what – I'll come with you. You want someone with you when you've had a babby, don't you?'

'That's kind,' the midwife said. 'She did seem a bit upset.'

'Call me if Tommy wakes, will you?' Rachel said to Gladys.

She was relieved that Dolly was coming. It felt as if someone older and motherly was what was needed.

They pushed the front door open and stepped into a downstairs room which made Dolly catch her breath. A cockroach scuttled across the floor heading for cover.

'Oh, my word.' She tutted. 'What a state. This place must be alive.' She looked around as if expecting to see vermin crawling out of every corner. Rachel shuddered. Gladys was very strict about stoving her house and keeping the bugs at bay, but it didn't look as if Irene ever did much about anything.

The table was strewn with dirty crocks and bits of food, the floor did not look as if it had been swept for days and the range was stone cold and dull with grime. On the gas stove in the corner stood a couple of pots, one with a yellow, sulphurous-looking overspill down the side of it. The other one, which was cleaner, had a half-inch of water in it. The fireplace had rubbish and broken china thrown into it.

'Hello-o?' Dolly called up the stairs. 'Can we come up?'

There was a pause. 'Who's that?' Irene's voice came muzzily down to them.

'It's Mrs Morrison from number one – and Rachel.'

There was no reply. Dolly raised her eyebrows at Rachel and they started to climb, pausing only for a few seconds in the curve of the stairs, to listen.

There was no door to the bedroom, which opened right off the top of the stairs, with a second room leading off from it. With no door to knock on, Dolly tapped on the top step.

'Here we are, bab,' she said, kindness overcoming her other observations about the state of the place. 'We thought we'd come up and see you – and the babby. See if you needed anything.'

Irene raised her head as they came in, her blonde hair

greasy and tousled. Her face still shone with a sheen of sweat. Already, even so close to the birth, she seemed smaller, shrunken, her cheeks a little thinner. Rachel thought she looked suddenly young and helpless and she felt a pang of pity for her. As they moved closer Irene let her head drop back onto the bed. There was no pillow, or sign of any comfort. She was covered by a thin, stained blanket.

'The midwife said you've had a healthy little girl,' Dolly said.

Irene gave a slight nod, apparently indifferent.

'You all right?' Rachel said. The room was so bare and cheerless, she thought. She and Danny did not have much but they had tried to make their attic room a home. Surely Ray Sutton earned a reasonable wage at Kynoch's? Probably poured most of it down his throat, she thought, with a wave of thankfulness for Danny who only ever had a pint or two. The only furniture other than the bed was an old wooden chest of drawers. The middle drawer had been removed and Rachel could make out a little bundle swaddled in it. She leaned over and saw the baby's pink, tensed-looking face, the eyes tightly closed.

'She's lovely,' she said. As she said it, she saw that it was true. The little girl had the squashy face of a new-born, but there was something even and well spaced about the features that promised well for her.

Irene grunted.

'Have you fed her?' Dolly asked.

'Yeah,' Irene said, in a resentful voice.

'Shall us make you a cup of tea?' Rachel asked.

'Yeah,' Irene said again. Adding, 'Please,' as an after-thought.

'I'll go and put the water on,' Dolly said. 'You stay with her,' she whispered to Rachel.

Rachel dared to sit on the edge of the bed. Though Irene was a few years older than she was, in those moments it felt as if the age gap between them had evened out, almost as if she was the older girl. Irene seemed so crushed and upset.

'What're you going to call her?' she asked, for something to break the silence.

Irene jerked up suddenly, resting on one elbow. 'She's gonna be called Eve,' she said. Her voice was harsh and angry. 'Eve. 'Cause Eve was cursed, wasn't she? And she's my curse – I'm cursed by God, I am. The only thing I've ever wanted – a boy. And God says, well, you cor 'ave it - you can 'ave a sodding wench instead.'

'But you can't blame the babby!' Rachel protested. 'Poor little thing.'

Irene's face contorted. 'Little rat. She's gonna be the ruin of me. He'll leave me for *her*, for that ho – she can have boys. But me – I cor do what a proper woman should do. I'm never 'aving any more brats – never!'

Irene turned her face downwards and burst into tears. Loud, gulping sobs came from her.

'Oh, Irene . . .' Rachel tried to think of something comforting to say. But what was there to say about a husband like that, if he would really leave? Surely that could not be true. 'He won't, will he? It's all just talk. He just likes to upset you.' Rachel did not realize at this moment that she had hit the nail on the head when it came to Ray Sutton's cruel games. At that moment she was just trying to think of something to say.

Irene quietened a little. Eventually she turned over again, her face pink and blotchy.

'D'yow think?' she said. ''E won't leave me and go to her?'

They heard Dolly's feet on the stairs.

'I don't know,' Rachel said. 'But how d'you know she wants him anyway?' Why would anyone want him? she wondered. 'Maybe he's just all talk.'

'Here we are, bab – nice and hot,' Dolly said. She looked encouraged at the sight of Irene beginning to sit up in bed. 'And would you like a hand clearing up a bit?'

A tear dropped onto Irene's left cheek. 'What – you help me?'

Dolly sat on the bed and touched Irene's plump shoulder. 'You ain't from round here, are you, bab? You ain't got your mom nearby?'

'No,' Irene said. ''Er's in Netherton. If 'er's still alive.'

Dolly looked shocked. 'Oh dear – like that, is it? Well, we'll give you a hand, bab – won't we, Rachel?'

Wearily, Rachel nodded.

Thirty-Four

The tap-tap of a well-heeled pair of shoes on the bricks of the yard slowed, then stopped at their door.

Rachel was in with Gladys, both of them at the table. Gladys was humming to herself while she stitched a tear in a blouse: 'Oh God our help in ages past', over and over again. Rachel, seated across from her, was trying to feed Tommy. As ever it was a struggle. Her nipples were sore from the attempt and she never thought he was getting enough to eat. She was exhausted and worried. She felt as if her face was set permanently in a frown and her irritable moods were affecting Melanie who was playing up more than usual. Gladys's humming was grating on her nerves. To her relief, the polite knock on the door which followed the footsteps made Gladys stop and look up with a slight frown. 'Come in!'

A round face appeared around the door topped by flat brown hair, cut in a severe bob, and followed by the plump body clad in a brown utility suit of a woman who must have been in her early thirties.

'Morning!' she announced cheerfully, advancing in. Her eyes scanned the room as if there were certain things she was looking for. 'I'm Miss Nolan, your health visitor. I've come to see how you and the little feller are getting along.' She looked at Rachel, then down at the card she was holding. 'It is a boy, isn't it? Tommy Booker?'

Rachel nodded warily. The woman's warm manner and Irish accent were reassuring. After Melanie was born a different health visitor had come. She had never seen this one before. It was nice though, hearing someone say Tommy's full name. It made her being a mother and being married to Danny feel more real.

Miss Nolan put her bag down on the chair.

'Would you like a cup of tea?' Gladys asked her. She always thought it was a good idea to get on the right side of these people.

'Oh, that'd be grand if you can spare it, thank you.'

Rachel could see Miss Nolan taking in details of the neat, colourful room, Gladys's clock and row of knick-knacks on the mantelpiece, the rug by the fire and sense of cosy cleanliness. She seemed reassured. But Rachel hugged Tommy close to her, worried that the woman would find something wrong. Because somewhere in her mind, in all her constant niggling worry, she knew that there was something about him, something very different from her daughter. Whether this added up to anything much she was not sure. But it was not just the slow, defeated way he fed from her that worried her – it was the strange, stiff feel of him. Whatever it was, she had never yet dared to put it into words.

'I'm just after visiting Mrs Fitzpatrick along the way,' Miss Nolan said, laying her papers on the table and fishing in her bag to retrieve a stub of pencil. Her cheeks were round and looked pink and weather-beaten. 'Fine little lad she's got there after all her troubles. I've hardly ever seen a mother so happy with lack of sleep! She said to say hello to you.'

For a moment Rachel could not think who the woman meant. 'Mrs Fitzpatrick? Oh – Netta!' She smiled for what felt like the first time in ages. 'Yes – ta.'

'And you have another child – Melanie, born 1941?' Miss Nolan looked up from the notes. 'Goodness, my dear, you don't look old enough!'

'She's outside,' Rachel said wearily. Her mind felt treacly with fatigue. 'Playing with the other girls. I can call her in?'

'Oh, I saw them. Leave her be for now. Let's look at this little— Thank you,' she interjected as Gladys put a cup of tea down by her. 'This little lad. He's six weeks old now? And where's his father?'

'In the army,' Rachel said miserably. 'We think he's out East somewhere.'

'Good gracious, that's a long way off. You poor girl,' Miss Nolan said. 'Well, it's grand that you've got your mother here.' She smiled at Gladys.

'I'm not her mother,' Gladys told her. 'I'm her husband's aunt.'

'Well, I'm sure you're a huge support,' Miss Nolan said. 'Now – where can we lay the little one down?'

'The table's clean,' Gladys said, rather defiantly, Rachel thought. 'Here – he can lie on this.' She fished out a piece of white cotton sheeting from one of her bags and spread it on the table, several layers thick.

'Well, now that's a lovely thing!' Miss Nolan said, fingering the edge of the clean white cotton. 'It's not often you see a sheet in these rotten little houses, I can tell you – let alone one so clean and new!'

'I sell them,' Gladys said, dignified in the face of such rudeness. 'On the market. Make them up myself. Or I did before the war, any road.'

'Oh, I see – well, it's lovely and I'm sure you do well,

Mrs er . . . . Here we are – now where's our little Tommy then?'

Rachel lay him on it, still wrapped in his blanket.

'Well, hello, Tommy!' Miss Nolan unwrapped him and tickled his tummy. Tommy made a little squirming motion and his left arm shot out stiffly from his side. Rachel thought she saw the shadow of a frown pass over Miss Nolan's brow. But she said nothing. 'There's a lovely little boy now, aren't you? Let's be having a look at you.'

Rachel and Gladys stood side by side as Miss Nolan's plump, capable hands felt round Tommy's head and body. A look passed between them, as if to say, *She seems to know what she's doing.* She bent each of his legs and arms. Then she did it all again. She had gone quiet, Rachel thought – or was she imagining it? She picked Tommy up and gently held him up in front of her, looking up and down his little body. His legs hung stiffly, slightly crossed, as Rachel usually saw them do.

'He feels very different from my daughter,' she said, hoping to place her sense of unease within a cheerful conversation which would banish any of her fears.

Miss Nolan laid Tommy very gently back on the table and he gave a small whimper but nothing more.

'Have you any problems?' she asked.

'He's not feeding well like Melly did, is he, Rach?' Gladys said.

To her annoyance Rachel felt tears rising in her eyes. She saw Miss Nolan register this. 'What's the matter, dear?' the health visitor asked carefully.

'He just can't seem to suck very strongly. I mean, Melly – she used to guzzle away but Tommy, he tries but it takes him an age – as if he's weak. And he sicks a lot of it up again. He cries when he's hungry but then he only manages a bit and then he stops. Sometimes he just falls asleep – and then a bit later he'll wake and start all over again. It takes such a long time to get anything down him. I just don't think he can be eating enough.' Her anxieties and tears spilled out together.

'Oh dear, now – I see.' Miss Nolan was looking very thoughtful. 'Well, I'm sure you're doing all right, dear – he doesn't seem too thin. Every baby's different, you know.' This was what Dolly kept telling her as well. 'Let's take a look at his weight . . .'

She hung Tommy in a white sling from her spring balance and peered at the markings on it.

'Well,' she said hesitantly. 'His weight is down a little but he's all right. I do just wonder . . .' Again she looked grave and thoughtful and seemed to be weighing up what to say. Whatever it was that she wondered, she did not announce it. She put the spring balance away in her bag and turned to Rachel.

'Look, he's very young. We'll keep an eye on him, see how he grows and so on.' She shut up her bag and gave Rachel a pat on the arm. Going over to the window, bag in hand, she looked out and said, with a smile in her voice, 'You're doing well – look at that healthy little girl you've got running about out here. I'll just take a look at her on my way past. But she looks as fit as a fiddle.' At the door she said, 'There are babies coming thick and fast but I'll call and see you again as soon as I can.'

Rachel felt herself relax a little, as if a load had been lifted from her. 'He's all right? There's nothing wrong with him?'

'I'd say he's a grand little feller. But I'll be back to see you both as soon as I can, all right? Now – there's another baby just born in this yard, so I gather? A Mrs Sutton?'

'There – at number four,' Gladys said, pointing through the open door. 'You want to try and talk some sense into her.'

Miss Nolan turned. 'What d'you mean?'

'All I'll say is –' Gladys folded her arms contemptuously – 'she wanted a lad and she got another girl.'

'I see,' Miss Nolan said, not sounding especially as if she did. Her shoes tapped their way across to Irene's front door.

'And she could try keeping her house up an' all,' Gladys muttered. She, Dolly and Rachel had all lent a hand trying to clean the Suttons' house and get some order into it after Evie was born. They had barely received a thank-you for their trouble either.

Gladys stood watching, a dark expression on her face. Everyone else in the yard was appalled by the way the Suttons went on but it seemed to enrage Gladys especially. Irene was full of resentment towards the baby for not being a boy – the son that Ray had achieved with his mistress. Even so, Ray had shown no signs whatsoever of disappearing and was still there, day or night, drunk or sober, playing one woman off against the other. But instead of blaming him, Irene took all her anger out on the baby, Evie as she now seemed to be called. She was careless and sulky with her, acting as if Evie was a burden and nothing else.

'It's wicked, that it is,' Gladys said, shutting the door again. 'Wicked and unnatural. The child might be too young to notice now – but one day she won't be. There's some women don't know they're born. And as for that useless bugger she's married to – they ought to've thrown him in the army, not have him sitting about pouring drink down his throat!'

Thirty-Five

April 1944

By the time Tommy was seven months old he was showing no signs of being able to sit up. On Rachel's visits to her mother with the children, Peggy was starting to remark on it and Cissy kept asking when Tommy was going to come and play. His feeding was still very difficult. She had started him on solid food, slops of soaked bread, but Tommy's tongue forced itself out whenever she put a spoon in his mouth and it only ever seemed by luck that he managed to swallow anything.

Dolly took a motherly interest and kept saying that things would get better. 'Don't you worry – he's a brave little lad. And you want to look after yourself, bab – you're thin as a rake.'

Miss Nolan called round every so often, as she had said she would. Rachel could tell she was keeping an eye on Tommy, though as yet she had not said anything much. But on her latest visit, after she had looked him over, she straightened up and said carefully, 'I think the time has come to have the little man looked at by the doctor.'

'Why?' Rachel said, all her dread rushing to the surface. 'What's the matter with him?'

'Oh, let's hope it's nothing – just a precaution,' was all

the health visitor said. 'But he is a little behind. Just take him along and see what they say.'

Later, though she trusted Miss Nolan, she cursed her for a coward, for not warning her and saying what she had obviously guessed. She passed the job into the lap of someone else.

She left the pram outside the surgery. Everything was brown in the waiting room: the floor, the chairs, the walls. And there was a stale smell of damp wool overlaid with disinfectant and people coughing and groaning. It did nothing to lift the spirits.

'What's wrong with him?' a grey-haired lady sitting beside Rachel asked her. Rachel bridled for a second, as if her words were meant as criticism. But Tommy, wrapped in a blanket and sitting gazing around, looked perfectly normal. She realized the woman was just being motherly.

'He's got a bad chest,' she lied. She did not realize then that this would be one of many, many times that she would be asked this question and that there would never be a time when it didn't hurt.

'Poor little devil,' the woman said. She suddenly began coughing herself, hunching over and laying her hand on her chest. Her lungs sounded like a drenched engine trying to start up. Eventually, wiping her eyes she said, "E's not the only one, bab!'

When her name was called Rachel carried Tommy to the doctors' rooms at the back, feeling as if everyone was watching her. Holding him close, her heart hammering, she went to the second of the rooms as instructed. A little wooden bracket on the door had a groove just wide enough for a narrow slice of wood to slot into it. On it, in white letters, it said, *Dr R. J. Evans*.

'Come!' a peremptory voice barked at her timid

knock. This room, also brown, smelt of stale cigarette smoke accompanied by a sweaty, masculine odour. Dr Evans was middle-aged, with a grey complexion, dark brown oily hair combed flat across a bald patch, and heavy horn-rimmed spectacles. Rachel looked at him with dread. She was not familiar with any of the doctors as she and the rest of the family were usually quite healthy. What she saw did not make her feel confident.

'Yes?' He looked up from his desk, pebbly eyes peering over the spectacle frames.

'I . . .' She heard her voice go faint with nerves. 'The lady from the welfare told me to come and see you. To bring the babby, that is . . .'

The doctor pushed his chair back briskly. 'I see. What's the matter? Cough? Chest?'

'No, it's not . . . He's not poorly.'

'*Not* poorly?' he said impatiently.

'She wanted you to look at him.' All she felt like now was running away. She did not want Tommy poked about by this strange, smelly man with his forbidding look. 'It's just – he's not sitting up, and . . .'

He looked back at her for a moment and she saw herself through his eyes: young, scrawny, ignorant. But what was required of him seemed to be sinking in. 'The health visitor, you mean? All right – bring him over here.' There was a flat, hard bed at the side of the room. As she obeyed he snapped, 'Age? When was he born?'

'September the eighteenth.' Only such a few months ago – it felt like a lifetime.

'Unwrap him then.' He stood with his hands on his hips, like a threatening bird about to take off. 'Right – let me see then.'

Cowed by his manner, she stepped back towards the

door. Dr Evans did all the things she had seen Miss Nolan do, though some of them with more force. He flexed Tommy's arms and legs in and out until the little boy started to whimper and then cry. Even his cry sounded weak. Dr Evans held him up under the arms like a rag doll, his own arms outstretched, so that his cuffs popped out of his jacket sleeves. He stared at Tommy, then put him down again. He tried to sit him up. Tommy flopped back, falling sideways. Dr Evans caught him and laid him down again.

'Feeding all right? He's thin.'

'It takes him ages,' she murmured, feeling accused.

'What? Speak up!'

'He has trouble feeding.' She was close to tears now. 'It takes him a long time to get any and I don't know if he's getting enough. His tongue keeps pushing it out of his mouth. I've been telling her . . .' She trailed off helplessly.

The doctor made no further comment. He felt around Tommy's body some more as the child cried.

'Difficult birth, was it?' he asked suddenly.

'It was . . .' She didn't know what to say. 'No. I don't know.'

'Hmmm.' The doctor straightened up and stood looking down at Tommy. At last, he said, 'Right – wrap him up again.'

She obeyed and stood holding her snivelling little boy pressed close to her, rocking him to try and quiet him. The doctor fished in the drawer of his desk and brought out a packet of Player's. He fiddled with the packet for a few seconds with his left hand, staring down at his notepad. At last he threw the cigarettes down on the desk as if in irritation before finally looking at her across the top of his glasses.

'The child is certainly diplegic – probably tetraplegic, though there is some hope for the right arm I'd say. That's why he's so stiff, can't support himself sitting up and so on. Most likely never will.'

'I don't understand,' Rachel said. A glow of desperate anger lit somewhere in her belly. At the same time she felt helpless and pathetic. Don't cry! she ordered herself. She pinched the flesh of her own arm. Don't cry in front of him. How dare he talk to her in riddles, like some sodding encyclopedia, trying to make her feel stupid? She tried to keep her voice calm, though it came out high and thin. 'What does that mean?'

'It *means* . . .' He sounded as if patience cost him effort. His hand strayed to the cigarette packet again and closed over it. 'That he'll be a cripple. He'll never walk. Possibly never speak. The muscle of his tongue is compromised – that's why his eating is poor. You'll just have to keep doing the best you can with that. There's nothing that can be done.' Still grasping the cigarette packet he got up and went to the window which overlooked an alley, a slimy wall only feet away. Loudly, over Tommy's cries, he said, 'There is some treatment – a bit. Not very effective and it costs more than you could afford, I'm quite sure. All I can suggest is that you try massage, though I don't suppose that'll have any deep effect. My advice would be hang onto him for a bit. There are places he can go when he's a bit older.'

She was trembling. The explosion of rage and upset was swelling in her to bursting point.

'Places?' she managed to say.

Dr Evans swivelled round to face her. 'The city has several institutions for crippled and imbecile children. It's the best thing, very often. You'll be able to get on with your life – forget about it. He'll be looked after – out of sight.'

Rachel could not speak. Clutching Tommy so tightly that she made him cry all the more, she hurried out of the room. She did not even see the other people in the waiting room. She had just tucked Tommy back into the pram outside when a voice shrilled at her from the steps, 'Excuse me!' The receptionist sounded very annoyed. 'That'll be half a crown!'

'Sod you – and sod your half-crown,' Rachel muttered. She did not look up and set off, storming along the street. Running footsteps followed and the woman was officiously at her side.

'You owe—' she began.

'Here's your *money*.' Rachel pushed it into her hand without ever looking up.

Once the woman had hurried away and she was alone, she pushed the pram up against the side of a house and leaned over it, her tears flowing at last, unable to stop her anguish pouring out in the street.

Head down, she hurried along the entry into their yard, praying that no one would be about. She didn't want any questions, however kindly meant. No one was in the house as Gladys had taken Melanie to the shops with her. All she wanted was to be alone with her son, to try and take in the doctor's harsh words.

She took Tommy upstairs and lay on the bed with him beside her. The ride home in the pram had sent him off to sleep and now he lay there drowsily, eyes opening and closing. While Melly looked so like Danny, she knew that Tommy favoured her. From the moment he was born there had been something about him she'd recognized, something beyond his shape or eye colour, that she could not put into words. He was kin in some deep, blood way. She moved her face close to him, taking in the fine, fresh texture of his skin, the tiny mauve veins at the corners of his eyes. Very lightly she laid her fingers on his chest, feeling the breath flicker in and out.

He'll be a cripple . . . The doctor's indifferent tones rang through her mind. How could he be so cold and detached? Tommy would never walk. He might not talk. It was impossible now, to take in, to know what it might mean, except that it felt as if Dr Evans had cursed her. It was like looking up at a cliff that she had to scale, that she could not see the top of as it loomed above her. And no one else could do it except her. All she could see was that her life would never be free of care. She searched her mind for anyone she knew with a child the same. She had seen one or two children wearing calipers on their legs. And a little boy in Floodgate Street who had had a lurching, ungainly walk. A cripple. Some of the other children had teased him, shamed him. What would they do to a boy who could not walk at all?

Another of the doctor's phrases threw itself at her: *You'll be able to get on with your life . . . He'll be looked after – out of sight.*

She imagined wheeling Tommy to some unknown place, a big, brick monstrosity of a building, no doubt. A heavy door would open, a strange face and strange hands would grasp her son and take him away forever, leaving her free . . . She felt a longing for this freedom course through her. She was eighteen years old, too young for all this. What if someone could just take Tommy and give him a life? But even more powerful was the terror of someone taking him away from her, the dread and shame.

'Oh, Tommy . . .' The tears came then, from deep inside her, sobs which shook her, heartbroken for him and for herself. 'My poor, poor little Tommy-babby. I won't let them take you away – I *won't*.'

Laying her head beside him on the rough blanket, she wept for a long time, full of sadness, for him and for herself, and feeling fiercely protective of him. Her sobbing died and she fell asleep next to him. The next thing she knew was the sound of footsteps on the stairs.

'Rachel?' Gladys came into the room, her face stony with concern. 'You all right? What's going on?'

Rachel pushed herself up and moved to sit on the edge of the bed. She felt utterly stunned, as if something heavy had knocked her down.

'What did they say?' Gladys sat on the bed beside her.

'Oh, Auntie!' Rachel burst into tears all over again. 'He was horrible, the doctor! He said Tommy's going to be a cripple. He said things I didn't understand. But he said his legs don't work and his left arm – and his tongue. And then he said I should put him away in a home and forget all about him!'

She heard Gladys's intake of breath. She waited for her to say something brisk and dismissive, that the doctor was wrong, that they should not take any notice and just wait and see. She wanted her to say it wasn't like that.

Into Gladys's silence she cried, 'And what's my mother going to say? She'll most likely be the same as the doctor!'

Gladys laced her fingers together in her lap and looked down at them. It was a long time before she said anything. Rachel found herself waiting. It was another of those moments when she looked at Gladys afresh, and found her utterly mysterious. She could not guess what

333

was going on inside Gladys's head. But at last, gently, she said, 'Tommy's your son. Yours and Danny's. And he's my nephew. He's *ours* – our blood. God knows, we've lost enough of our family . . .' She stopped, hesitating. 'I'm not saying it'll be easy. I don't want to sentence you to . . .' she began, then stopped again. At last she said, 'Your mother's not the one who'll be seeing to him day after day, looking after him.'

'No, she's made sure of that,' Rachel said bitterly.

'None of it's his fault,' Gladys went on. Her voice was low, as if she was struggling with her emotions. 'Or anyone's. It's no good getting in a state about things when you don't even know how it's going to be. We'll just have to take each day as it comes. That's all there is to do – keep going and see. He's your son, Rach. For God's sake, let's look on him as a blessing. He belongs with us.'

With tears running down her cheeks, Rachel looked at Danny's aunt beside her. 'Thank you,' she said. 'Thank you – for being so kind.'

'We're family, wench,' she said. 'That's how it is. You never know how precious it is until you've lost it.' Her eyes filled and for a second she reached across for Rachel's hand, gave it a rough squeeze, then got up and left the room.

Thirty-Six

7 May 1945

They were drawn back to the wireless to listen to every bulletin. All weekend the excitement grew and grew. Hitler was dead! William Joyce, Lord Haw-Haw, whose sinister voice had oozed propaganda through the airwaves all through the war, had signed off a few nights ago.

'You may not hear from me again for a few months,' he slurred.

'He's drunk!' Rachel said. 'Hark at that!'

He finished in a low voice: *'Heil Hitler.* And farewell.'

'He'll need to be more than drunk,' Gladys said with satisfaction.

German forces had already surrendered and, this Monday dinner time, the sound of wireless broadcasts sounded out of the windows into the yard and along every street. Waiting in silent suspense, at long last they heard it: the German Supreme Command had surrendered at Rheims. The war in Europe was over!

Dolly erupted through the door almost before the newsreader had got it out of his mouth. The yard was filling with the neighbours, cheering.

'Did you hear? Oh, I can't believe it – it's over!' She

flung her arms around Gladys, then Rachel. 'Oh, I wonder if Mo's heard – I feel like running over and telling him!'

'They'll have the wireless on, won't they?' Gladys said.

'Oh – it's over!' Dolly repeated, jumping up and down. Then she caught sight of Rachel's face. 'Oh, bab – no, it's not, is it. Your Danny's out East . . .'

Rachel hardly knew what it meant. She was elated but it was hard to take anything in yet.

'And poor Ma and Pa Jackman . . .'

Their faces sobered. The Jackmans had received word earlier in the year that Edwin had been killed during the Battle of the Bulge in the Ardennes.

'There's some won't be celebrating,' Dolly said. 'But there'll be no stopping some of 'em! Not after all this! Ooh – what a day to remember!'

Rachel slipped back into the house as the others stayed in the yard, chattering with excitement.

The factory at the back had gone quiet, as if everyone had downed tools. Lil Gittins had taken their wireless outside and put some band music on. There she was, out there in one of her low-cut dresses, teetering on her heels and calling to everyone to join in.

'My Stanley's coming home! He's coming back to me!'

Irene had come out and danced about with her. She was like a different woman now, no longer pregnant, dressed to kill in a shimmery, copper-coloured frock, hair dyed white blonde. Rachel felt like a bag of bones, a mousey frump in comparison. And she found Irene hard to put up with, especially since she had had Evie and the way she treated the child.

She went to check on Tommy. Dolly had said they could hang onto the old pram for as long as necessary and she had Tommy propped in it, on a pillow, a strap round his body to keep him upright and safe. At twenty months old, he ought to have been up and running about like Evie and Netta's Patrick, a pale, round-faced little lad like his father who Netta doted on. As she walked inside, she saw Tommy's eyes register her arrival and he made one of his spasmodic movements of pleasure, his left arm clenched close to his body. His right arm worked quite well and in that hand he was holding his favourite toy, a little wooden rattle with bells on the end. Whenever she found time she did massage his stiff limbs as the doctor had suggested. She had no idea whether it was doing any good but at least it was something she could do.

'All right, babby?' She sat down beside him, looking into his sweet, round face, his head covered now by a cap of mouse-brown hair like her own. He made a lot of sounds – no actual words yet, but he was trying. His mouth didn't work quite normally. His tongue had a tendency to pop out without him being able to control it. She still had to feed him, though his right arm was strong and she thought maybe one day he might be able to do it himself. But when the food went into his mouth, his wayward tongue pushed a lot of it out again. He had a permanent trail of drool from his lips which made his chin red and sore.

'So you're saying he's not . . . right?' Peggy said, when Rachel first got round to telling her about Tommy. He was about eight months old by then and clearly not doing the things you would expect from a child that age: rolling over, sitting up, perhaps even starting to try and get onto his hands and knees. Although he was still light for his age, in her overwrought, weak state, Rachel found it exhausting getting over to the Coventry Road with Melly walking and Tommy in her arms. It was especially tiring when there was no prospect of support or affection at the other end.

At least it had been a warm spring day and not raining, but she was already at the end of her tether by the time they got to the flat. She waited until Peggy had reluctantly stirred herself to make some tea and they were all in the upstairs sitting room, a faint breeze coming in through the window, before she broached the subject.

'You mean, he's some sort of cripple?' An expression of horror came over Peggy's dainty features.

'Steady on,' Fred Horton said. He happened to be around that afternoon. 'He looks a happy little chappy despite it . . .'

Rachel warmed towards her stepfather in that moment. After all her years of trying to get on the right side of her mother, however mean and selfish she could be, today she felt an immense, bursting rage on Tommy's behalf. She'd had more than enough of it. Mom could be nasty to her but she wasn't having it with her son! She clenched her hands, waiting to see what else Peggy would come out with.

'Well, he may be cheerful enough,' Peggy said. 'But what use is he going to be if he can't walk, as Rachel seems to be saying?'

'Use to who?' Rachel flared up. 'Is that all anyone is – *useful*?'

She could see Melly listening in hard to this conversation, but there was nothing she could do about it.

'He may not be useful to you, *Mother*, but he's *my son*.' She was so overwrought that her voice had sunk almost to a snarl. There was so much more she wanted to say: *You never loved me, all you ever think about is yourself – don't you dare ever let your stupid, selfish attitudes near my little boy . . .* All her rage and tension were ready to pour out, as if from a bursting boil, on the person who most seemed to deserve them.

'Eh now, steady on,' Fred intervened. He stepped over and closed the window, as if he was worried that someone might overhear.

'Oh – I suppose having a *cripple* in the family might be bad for business as well!' Rachel said.

'Rachel, for goodness' sake!' Peggy said. 'All I said was . . . I just *asked* what the state of things is.'

'*Things*? What d'you mean, "things"?' Rachel sat on the very edge of the chair, her arms waving as she spoke. 'Tommy has a . . . a condition where his legs don't work and his left arm as well and his tongue. There – that's *the state of things*. You may not like it – *I* don't like it. But that's how it is. That's Tommy.'

'Oh, for goodness' sake,' Peggy said again. 'There's no need to be so unpleasant—'

'*Unpleasant*!' Rachel heard her own caustic tone. 'Unpleasant for you? Oh, *poor you*.'

As she snapped at her mother she saw Melly move over to her little brother and tweak his nose playfully. Then she put her arm around him where he lay, half-propped on a cushion. Cissy followed her and sat on the other side of Tommy and tried to make Melly laugh. But Melly was staring very solemnly at her grandmother, as if protecting Tommy from her.

'But . . .' Peggy seemed abashed by this outburst, but also confused. 'I can see, Rachel. I'm not blind. We've noticed there's something amiss with him compared to a normal baby. It's going to make your life very difficult, I can see that. So what are you going to *do*?'

Rachel felt the rage swelling large in her again but she pressed it down. She was afraid of what she might do if she let it all come boiling out. In an icy voice she said, 'Do? What d'you mean, *do*?'

'Well – you know. There must be something they can do. Treatments and things.'

Rachel was shaking her head. 'No. Not much. They've said – the doctor and the health visitor. You can't cure it. It's just how he is.'

'I suppose you'll have to put him in a home then, eventually,' Peggy said.

It was not so much that Peggy had said this but her casual tone which made Rachel feel as if she was turning to stone. She simply could not speak. Melanie could not understand exactly what was being said, but she read something of the tone of it and a fierce expression of dismay came over her face. She leaned forward and made a loud noise at her grandmother, a loud snarl, as if protecting Tommy from her.

Rachel thought she had never loved her little girl so much as at that moment. Tears filled her eyes and she looked down, swallowing, her rage redirected into a fierce pride in her children.

'If you don't want to see him,' she said bitterly to Peggy, 'I shan't bring him. But you won't see Melly either.'

'Oh, don't talk so silly,' Peggy said, laughing. 'I was only asking. I don't know what you're getting so worked up about. You always did get in too much of a state about things. I'm only worried for you, that's all, having to bring up a cripple.'

Sitting here now, on this day of celebration, she felt tired to her very core. Even the thought of her mother made her feel drained. Peggy had said that of course she could bring the children over, when she could. After all, it didn't involve her in any effort and they were company for Cissy. But it was becoming more and more tiring. She would have to keep trying though, at least for Melly and Cissy's sakes.

Melly was out running about with little Shirley Sutton. Rita was at school but Shirley was, as usual, having to watch baby Evie. Irene let Evie crawl around in the dirt – anything so long as she didn't have to bother with her. Several times she had toddled right out of the yard and been found sitting in the road. Dolly brought her back once from the bottom of the street. But Irene didn't seem to care what anyone said. Rachel thought bitterly about blonde, big-eyed little Evie. At least she *could* get about, not like Tommy.

She poured a cup of tea and slumped in the chair, hearing the music drifting in from outside and the sounds of the women's laughter. I'm not even twenty yet, she thought, and I feel like an old lady. It was as if all her energy had burned itself out in her fierce protectiveness towards Tommy. She wanted to be young, full of joy and energy. She wanted to long for Danny, to miss him. It felt like a hundred years since she had seen him. In fact she wanted just to feel anything at all. For now, she was numb and worn out.

Like everyone, she could hardly begin to take in that the war had really ended for them. The blackout was gone already, from last autumn. Mo had been stood down with the rest of the Home Guard. They had seen all the changes, the progress, but even so, after nearly six years, how could they really believe it was over . . .?

All through the early part of last year there had been talk of the Second Front. Everyone knew there was a build-up to something – all those Americans and Canadians over here, as well as Poles and Czechs. And in April, Mr Jackman was called down south along with hundreds of other firemen, to guard ammunition dumps. Once the invasion in early June – D-Day as it became known – was over, Mr Jackman had returned, saying that the south had been one 'blooming great army camp' in the build-up before 6 June. He came home via London and had heard one of the flying bombs come down.

'Terrifying,' he said. 'Like a cowing motorbike going across the sky, and then they cut out – and God alone knows where it's going to come down. I don't envy those buggers down London one bit being under that lot.'

The atmosphere changed. There was a lightness: hope, after all the bad news. The Italian campaign was pushing the Germans north. The invasion of France had begun. She had little news of Danny except, now and then, to say that he was alive and that where he was stationed was still a dump and that he loved her and hoped she and the children were all right. He wasn't allowed to say anything much about where he was or what he was doing. He had stopped sending his little drawings and she wondered if he was doing them in his notebook. Sometimes she wondered if he still really existed. It was as if she had dreamt him, her blue-eyed husband. She wondered if she felt real to Danny. She had written to him and told him about Tommy, but she realized he had probably not really taken in what she said. How could he? He was thousands of miles away, in a place she could barely even imagine.

As the freezing winter passed and 1945 arrived, there was still terrible fighting across Europe. And there were further shocks for which they had been unprepared. Only last month, Gladys had been out for one of her trips to the pictures, but she had come home early. Rachel, settled by the fire once she had got the children to sleep, looked up in surprise as she appeared through the door on a gust of icy air.

'What're you doing here?' she said, yawning.

'I didn't stay in the end.' Silently, Gladys took off her coat and hat. She seemed preoccupied and heavy in herself. As she sat down at the table she clasped her hands together and just sat, a haunted expression on her face.

'D'you want a cup of tea, Auntie?' Rachel asked.

'If we've got nothing stronger, that'll have to do,' Gladys said.

Rachel filled the kettle from their pan of water, set it to boil and came back to the table. Carefully, she said, 'What's happened?'

Gladys shook her head, her eyes wide. 'I couldn't face it – not after the news . . . Those German camps they've found. I've never seen anything like it . . .'

'What d'you mean?' Rachel sat down. She had never seen Gladys look like this before.

Gladys glanced at Melly, but she was on the mat by the fire, humming to herself – a habit she had caught from her aunt – and in a world of her own.

'They've had all these people kept in great big camps . . .'

'POWs?'

'Yes – but not soldiers. Just all these people, Jews and

others – thousands, by the look of it. It was called Booken . . . something. My God . . .' She could not seem to meet Rachel's eye as she spoke, and when she did look up, she seemed somehow shamed. 'I knew there were bombs and guns – that's the war. All sorts of terrible things. But this was different. It was . . .' She trailed off again, looking for words. 'I mean, that wasn't war – it was summat else . . .'

There was more to come. As well as Buchenwald, camp after camp was liberated as the Allies pushed across Europe. The even darker horrors that had gone on under the black cover of war were brought to light. Piles of shoes, spectacles, corpses. Rachel never did see the images for herself – hearing them described was bad enough to make them hover in the mind.

The war was ending. With it came enormous relief and jubilation, along with grief, loss and a deep human disgust. It was over.

But for the next two days they were celebrating! Amid all the dancing and drinking of VE Day, the bonfires and parties, the pianos wheeled into the street, mouth organs and songs and flags, there was one other cause for celebration.

The next morning they heard the familiar roar of an engine in the yard and Mo Morrison shot in along the entry on a Norton, a huge grin on his face. The noise of it bounced off the brickwork, immensely loud until he cut the engine. He was immediately surrounded by children.

'I've got a sidecar out there!' He pointed back down the entry. 'Who's coming for a victory lap?'

The younger Morrisons and Shirley and Melanie were all yelling for a turn.

'Can I go, Mom?' Melly ran to Rachel as she came outside. 'Can I have a go?'

'Oh, I expect so,' Rachel said.

'Can Tommy?'

'Tommy's a bit small – you go, and Shirley.'

'What're you up to, Mo?' Gladys called to him. Rachel found a smile spreading across her face at the sight of Mo's exuberance.

'You lot go and wait out there,' he ordered the excited children. 'Make sure no one goes off with it.' They all dashed to the entry to be the first in the sidecar.

Mo was pulling a newspaper out from under his jacket and looking mighty pleased with himself. 'Now I've got shot of the kids – the moment we've all been waiting for!'

'Mo?' Dolly advanced towards him. 'What're you on about?' The other women were gathering round.

'Well – I don't know if I should say,' he teased, his pink face fit to erupt with laughter. 'Not among all you womenfolk.'

There was an outcry. 'Come on, Mo – stop teasing us!' Lil called to him. Rachel wandered over out of curiosity.

Mo held up the paper and proclaimed, 'That wench's done it at last!'

Over Lil Gittins's shoulder, Rachel peered at Mo's copy of the *Daily Mirror*. Within three frames, their cartoon character Jane had been comprehensively de-mobbed out of her uniform and into her birthday suit, her modesty preserved only by a strip of Union Jack.

'Ooh – look at her, the cheeky strumpet!' Lil cackled. Rachel giggled at the sight of it.

'Oh, Mo!' Dolly grabbed the paper and started hitting him about the head with it. Everyone else was laughing.

'Get off me, woman!' He grabbed the paper from Dolly, fending her off with one hand and rubbing his chest contentedly with the other. 'Now that's what I call good news.'

'I hope you're not expecting me to do the same, Mo Morrison!' Dolly called, going off to the house again in a pretend huff.

Mo gave a mock-desperate sigh. 'A man can dream, can't 'e?' he said, winking at Rachel. 'Now – them kids.' Kindly, he said to her, 'How's the lad?' He was always very nice to her and to Tommy.

'He's all right,' she said, 'Ta.'

'Course 'e is.' He patted her on the back. 'He's got a fine mother. Now – I'd better go and give that lot out there a ride. There'll be no peace in our time 'til I do!'

Fondly, Rachel watched his stocky figure take off across the yard in his baggy trousers, his voice booming, 'Right – a few laps for victory round the block. And then who's coming down to the old Salutation with me to get cracking?'

Thirty-Seven

August 1945

'Come in and have a cuppa with us, will you, if your mom's not in a hurry for them?' Rachel said, nodding at the bag of vegetables dangling from Netta's arm. It was a Saturday afternoon and she had run into Netta on the way back from the shops.

Netta was carrying little Patrick on her hip and looked on the point of dropping him. Her cheeks were pink from the exertion of lugging both him and her shopping about on this warm day. But she also looked quite a different young woman from the sad, frightened person Rachel had first met. She looked healthy and much brighter, a ribbon in her hair and laughter coming easily to her. Having little Patsy as they called him, had been the making of her.

'Oh, there's no rush – I'd love a cuppa,' Netta panted. 'His Majesty here decided he couldn't be walking any further. Didn't you?' She looked adoringly at the little lad, then at Rachel again. 'But no – that's silly. We're nearer to mine. You come and have a cuppa with me and Mom – she loves a house full of babbies!'

As usual, Mrs O'Shaughnessy gave them a warm welcome and made a fuss of Melanie and Tommy. Rachel ached with wishing her own mother was a tenth as kind as Netta's mom.

'Bring the pram inside,' Mrs O'Shaughnessy said. 'He'll not want to be left outside and we can squeeze it in. Will you be getting him out?'

'No – he's all right,' Rachel said. 'I've got him fixed in there with the shopping and he likes watching the others.'

She could see Mrs O'Shaughnessy thinking, *What a shame* as she looked at Tommy, the way so many people looked. But she did not say it. Rachel was very grateful to Netta and her mother. Ever since their sons were born the two girls had grown closer and been company for each other.

Melly settled down and played with Patsy, making him chuckle. This made Tommy laugh as well. Melly liked being the older sister and looking after the little ones. The women settled at the table and Mrs O'Shaughnessy moved back and forth to the little stove like a sparrow in her old brown dress, her faded hair twisted into a little bun, making 'tay' as she called it in her Limerick accent. They laughed at the children's laughter.

'He loves other kids,' Rachel said, smiling at the sound of Tommy's gurgles. She felt a strong twinge of love for her sweet-natured little boy.

As usual they discussed the children. Netta was full of Patsy's doings. He was the very centre of her life, so much so that Rachel could not help wondering quite what was going to happen when Francis came back. Netta slept with Patsy in her bed every night and lived and breathed nothing else.

'Is your auntie at the market today?' Netta asked.

'Yes,' Rachel said. 'Dolly's gone with her – Mo said

he'd take the lads fishing. Heaven help him, with all that lot!'

'They'll scare away every fish within miles,' Netta laughed. 'Oh, I do like Mr Morrison though – he's a kind man, he is.'

'Oh – I forgot!' Rachel sat up straighter, laughing at the thought of her news. 'You'll never guess what's happened?' Netta and her mother looked eager. 'The other night Mo and Dolly suddenly started off, at it hammer and tongs . . .'

'He'd never raise a hand to her?' Netta said, shocked.

'Oh no – just Dolly really, having a right old go. We could all hear it. She's expecting and she's only just realized. Well, you can imagine – Mo was really for it!'

The women laughed. Mrs O'Shaughnessy did not know the Morrisons but she had heard all about them.

'Ah, but that's all right,' she said. 'How many's she got – five lads? A sixth'll round it off nicely.'

'It'll look just like all the others, I expect,' Rachel said. 'Blonde and just like Mo. Dolly's always saying she might just as well not have been there!'

Netta was giggling. 'I don't s'pose Mr Morrison'll ever hear the end of it!'

It was good to sit in Mrs O'Shaughnessy's little room laughing and chatting. Rachel found it a comfort and it stopped her feeling too sorry for herself – a battle she was fighting every day.

A few days later, she was out with Tommy in the pram again. While he was very young there had been no difficulty in walking the streets with him. He was just another baby in a pram and even people who peered under the hood to admire him hardly ever noticed anything different about him.

Now he was older, things were beginning to change. As the months passed, Rachel was gradually adapting to the idea that he would always have difficulties. Sometimes she would sink to her knees in the house weeping. Tommy would never walk! He would never grow up and go to school normally. Would he ever be able to speak to her? He would always be stared at because he was different. And, though she was ashamed of her feelings, she cried because she knew that her own life would now never be free. She would be tied to him forever. On these days, when she was low and angry with life, she found herself being impatient and angry with Melly.

'Just do what I say!' she would shriek, like a woman beside herself.

Sometimes she saw her little girl watching her with a steady, wary expression.

'All right, Mom,' she'd say. 'Don't be cross. I'll do it.' Melly was due to start school in the autumn. Sometimes it felt as if she was having to grow up very fast.

On other days, when she had more energy, she felt matter-of-fact and hopeful. Tommy was her son. He had difficulties and she would stick with him through all of them. She would guard him like a tiger and would give him every help. They could survive anything!

This afternoon she was walking through Aston, cutting along a side street to get home. The street was drab and dirty, lined by factory walls and entries into back courts of houses. It was a hot, hazy day and she had pushed the hood of the pram back to let Tommy feel the light on his face. He had slumped to one side and she stopped to hoist him up and make him comfortable.

350

After a moment she sensed that someone was watching her. Turning, she saw a thin, haggard woman standing close by at the end of one of the entries, her body half-hidden in the shade. Faded, straggly hair hung round her thin cheeks. She was staring hard at the pram, and at Tommy.

Rachel was just about to move on when the woman stepped forward, slopping along in old down-at-heel shoes. A frock with faded red and white patterns hung on her skeletal frame.

'That boy of yours . . .' She had a soft voice, despite her rough appearance. Sad, grey eyes looked into Rachel's face. Up closer, Rachel saw that the woman was not as old as she had first supposed. There was an intense feel to her, to the way she was looking at Tommy. 'Why's he still in a pram at his age? What's wrong with him?'

Rachel was taken aback, for a moment thinking the stranger was criticizing her. But she quickly realized that this was not so. The woman came closer and her lined face lifted into a smile at Tommy. Why was she asking these questions, Rachel wondered? She also realized she still hardly knew how to answer, to say what was wrong.

The woman was looking at her with some sort of need in her eyes.

'He's a . . . His legs aren't . . .' She stopped and tried again. 'He can't walk. Not yet anyway.'

'My boy's never walked.' Words rushed from the woman's mouth. 'My Frankie.' She laid a cold, veiny hand on Rachel's arm. 'Come and see him. No one ever comes to see us.'

Rachel wanted to resist this odd request. The woman was gesturing towards the entry.

'The pram,' Rachel protested.

'Bring it. Bring it with you.' She was eager now, ushering Rachel along.

Rachel might have refused, but she could feel that the woman was kindly and that she was desperate for something – company, or perhaps just a kind word. They went along the entry into a yard not unlike the one where Rachel lived, except it was narrower and there was no works at the end, only houses and a blank wall along one side. There was a bleak feel to the place. They went to number four, at the other side of the yard.

'You can leave him by the door here for a moment,' the woman said.

A strange noise came from inside, a kind of howl. For a moment Rachel thought it was a dog.

'That's Frankie,' the woman said, pulling on Rachel's arm again. 'He'll be pleased to see you. You're about his age.'

Inside, as Rachel's eyes adjusted, her nostrils were seized by a strong, unpleasant mixture of smells which came close to making her gag. There were a lot of flies moving around the room as if half-drugged. The woman did not seem to notice these things.

'Frankie, love,' she said in a caressing tone. 'There's a nice lady come to see you.'

To the left of the fireplace, in a strange, sloping chair with footrests, Rachel saw a young man. His body was contorted, his arms clenched up close to him, the hands flopping at the wrists and his twisted face turned to one side, looking to his right, as if he could not turn it to face the front. Hearing his mother's voice, he made sounds which sent his tongue out of his mouth but it was not speech that Rachel could understand. Near the chair stood a bucket with a cloth draped over the top. Rachel realized that the worst of the stench must be coming from there.

'This is . . . What's your name, dear?' the woman said.

Rachel was so horrified by the sight of the man and even more repelled by the stench in this poor, bare room that she wanted to run out and get as far away from the place as possible. But she could not bear to behave in such a hurtful way to him, or his poor mother.

'Rachel,' she said. Then she added, 'Hello, Frankie.'

'He had his twenty-first birthday last month,' his mother said. She spoke factually, without pride or resentment.

'I've just turned twenty – a few days ago,' Rachel said, for something to say.

'Twenty-one years,' the woman went on. 'Him and me – for nineteen of them anyway. His father soon took off. Couldn't face it. No one can. I never take him out. He sits in the yard sometimes, just by the door, but I never let him out in the street. I used to take him out, at first. Children threw stones at him and after that I thought, never again.' Rachel heard the passion in her voice. 'I wasn't having that, not for my boy. He never went to school – no one said anything. I think everyone just forgot about him. My little Frankie –' Her voice was a mix of fondness and utter despair. 'The invisible boy.' She looked at Rachel then with her sad, washed-out eyes. 'No one wants them, you know, cripples. They just want them to disappear.'

Rachel felt that if she did not get out of that house she was going to break open with grief and revulsion. 'I've got to go,' she said, turning to the door. 'Sorry. My auntie's waiting for me.'

Abruptly, with no goodbye – which afterwards she felt desperately ashamed about – she hurried out of the house, away from Frankie's formless sounds, from the smell, from all the things that the poor mother was trying to tell her.

'What's up with you?' Gladys asked when she got home.

'Oh, Auntie – a lady made me go into her house ...' She broke down, relating the story. 'She only lives up the road and I've never seen her before and her son's in that house and never goes out and ... I don't want to be like that!' she cried. 'And I don't want Tommy to be like that! She's shut him away as if he doesn't exist.' She looked up at Gladys, her cheeks streaming. 'I don't want to have to be ashamed of my little boy! I'm not going to let people make him feel as if he's all wrong. Why are people so cruel?'

Gladys looked down at her, her face full of pity. Something in her expression shifted suddenly, as if she had realized something.

'You know, you've turned out a strong sort of wench, you have. Staunch. You stand up to things. It's true, I've known other children hidden away, not let out with the others, as if they've done summat wrong.'

'I'm not going to let them be horrible to Tommy,' Rachel vowed fiercely. In those seconds she saw how much she had changed during the months of her son's life. Her own future had become welded to his. 'I'm going to make sure he joins in and does things and ... and if anyone's nasty they'll have me to answer to – and that goes for my mother, along with all the rest of them!'

VI

Thirty-Eight

February 1946

Rachel stared at the telegram, hardly able to make sense of the words while Gladys stood nearby, looking ready to snatch it out of her hand.

'They're at Southampton. He'll be back today!' Rachel held the telegram out to her, her face lit with wonder.

Gladys sat down on a kitchen chair as if her legs had given way and stared at the telegram. 'Oh, thank the Lord.'

Rachel stood by the table, trying to let the news sink in. Danny had been in the army now for four years so he was one of the earlier ones to be sent home. Four years – twice as long as they had had together before he left. After all these months and years of waiting, of longing for him, of feeling he had become a stranger to her – now, today most likely, he would really be here. And after all this time, he would meet the son he had never seen.

'Tommy –' She went over to her little boy who was sitting up in his special chair. 'Your dada's coming home.' She tickled his tummy and Tommy squirmed and chortled. 'You're going to see your dada today.'

Tommy made one of his sounds which they knew, now, meant, 'Melly!' Melly, his adored elder sister.

'Yes, Melly's going to see Dada too.'

Tommy was two and a half, no longer a baby, and now his difficulties were far more obvious. Rachel had kept up massaging him and Tommy seemed to enjoy it. He often chuckled while they were up on the bed and Rachel was rubbing his arms and legs, trying at least to make him more comfortable. And it was good to hear his gurgling laugh. Melly sometimes came and helped. But for all Rachel's efforts, his little body could not hold itself upright unsupported and he had to be strapped into his chair. His left arm moved as if it had a mind of its own, while his legs were very rigid and he could not walk. The doctor had given him some leg braces to wear at night to try and keep his legs straight. Because his tongue would push out of his mouth, beyond his control, his speech was distorted and eating was a messy, trying business. He still had to wear napkins. However lovely he was – and he was a truly sweet-natured child – however much he was her boy, for whom she would battle and strive and fight off anyone else's pitying glances or rude remarks, there had been many bitter days when Rachel came close to despair. Each dawn she faced the inevitable round of feeding, washing and changing, of sliding his stiff legs in and out of the splints and his clothing, of lifting and pushing him about, of trying to keep him entertained. Once all that was done and she fell into bed, she had to get up and begin the whole thing all over again. Whereas most boys his age wore you out because they were running about with more mobility than sense, Tommy was tiring because he was not. He could not be left. Other than care for him and Melly, in an endless round, Rachel felt she had no life left.

The only real friend she saw was Netta, who to her joy had safely had another baby, a little girl called Clare. Rachel could not work on the market, or anywhere else. Though she could leave Tommy with Gladys for short amounts of time, she knew she was tied to him like a horse to a post. And though she loved him with a passion, what dragged her down the most was that there was no end in sight. This was her life now and this is how it would always be. Sometimes she went up to her room, just for a few minutes, and let herself have a cry, the sobs rising up from the depths of her, before she had to get up, a little relieved for the moment, and soldier on again.

As that day passed she could not settle to anything. She could think of nothing else but Danny. He was on his way home! Was he on a train now, moving closer and closer? Her whole being was aflutter with nerves and anticipation. At long, long last, he was coming. He'd be home. They could be a family again and at last Danny would be here to help.

Everyone in the yard knew he was coming, thanks to Dolly.

'Oh, Danny boy!' she sang, after popping into their house and being shown the telegram. 'The pipes, the pipes are ca-a-lling!'

Dolly was more than six months pregnant now and more happily resigned to the fact than she let Mo believe. Any excuse and she was taking the rise out of him, and Mo, in his big-hearted way, seemed to enjoy his wife berating him. 'He's pleased as punch with himself,' Dolly complained fondly to Gladys. 'Makes him feel proud of his manhood.'

'I hear your old man's coming back,' Irene said to Rachel as they passed outside in the drizzle. 'I hope he don't leave you, once 'e's seen the way that lad of yours is – some men're like that, you know.'

'You mean *your* bloke's like that – not mine!' Rachel fumed back at her. 'You silly sod,' she added under her breath. God, Irene was the pits – what a thing to say! Her Danny wasn't like that, like that sleazy Ray Sutton. He went sloping off having his way wherever he liked and Irene always took him back, even though she lived in a brooding storm of resentment.

But what really caught Rachel on the raw was that, deep down, she was afraid that what Irene said might come true.

When the time came, he paused at the threshold as if afraid to come in. It was already dark outside and no one had seen him come into the yard. As the door opened, Rachel and Gladys were with the children at the table, about to have tea. For a couple of seconds they all stopped as if turned to stone. In the doorway stood a very thin man in a brown suit, double-breasted with wide lapels, a bag slung over one shoulder. His cropped hair, his gaunt, tanned face and that suit all made him a stranger.

'Auntie? Rach?' He spoke very quietly, as if unsure.

'Danny . . .' Rachel put down the pan she had been carrying to the table. Slowly she went to him. 'Oh, Danny . . .'

For a few seconds they stood taking each other in. Rachel searched his face, trying to find the Danny she knew. She was too busy absorbing the sight of him to notice the shock that flared in his eyes when he looked at her.

All of it welled up in her, the relief, the worry and struggle, the sheer joy. As they walked into each other's arms, she was already weeping and she heard him make a sound as his arms came around her, a long, sobbing sigh. For a few moments they stood with their cheeks pressed together, then leaned back again to look at each other. They could not seem to speak. She touched his face, his hair, his neck, as his blue eyes drank her in. Then she held that tall, thin body close again.

Gladys stood watching. Melly and Tommy sat in absolute silence, even Tommy seeming to take in the awesome importance of this moment. As they were at last able to stand apart, Gladys walked over.

'Welcome home, son,' she said, and took him in her arms. 'You're all skin and bone,' she said as she drew back.

'You don't run to fat in India,' Danny said.

He was looking over at his children. In a wondering tone he said, 'Melanie? Tommy?'

'Melly?' Rachel said. 'Come and say hello to your dad.'

As Melly got down, Rachel could already see Danny taking in the chair in which his little son was sitting. It was something Mo had rigged up for them. He had made a lovely job of it, really trying to understand what Tommy needed. He had got a wooden chair, padded the seat and back and attached wooden arms and a sloping leg rest. He had also altered it so that it had two wheels at the back. You could tip it slightly and push it along. It was rough, but it worked. Once Tommy was strapped in between the chair's arms, he was quite safe and comfortable.

Melly went solemnly to her father. She was heading towards her fifth birthday, a rather grown-up little thing, her brown hair snipped into a bob round her ears.

'Hello, babby,' Danny said, sounding shy and tender at once. He squatted down. Melly looked apprehensive. Perhaps she had expected that she would remember this father who vanished from her life four years ago, but she did not. She murmured 'Hello' very quietly.

'You got a kiss for me?' Danny said.

With almost formal politeness, Melly stood on her tiptoes and pecked a quick kiss on his cheek, before scuttling back to her chair again.

'She'll get used to you,' Gladys said, seeing Danny's injured expression. 'It's been a long time, lad.'

'And Tommy.' He went over and Rachel saw his expression as he took in the state of his little boy. He knew. Of course he knew: she had written and told him of Tommy's problems, of some of her struggles. But he had not seen. Perhaps it had all seemed very distant and not real over there. Danny made no reaction.

'Hello, son.' He gave Tommy a pat on the head and seemed at a loss as to what to do next.

'Put that bag over there, Danny, and take your coat off,' Gladys said. 'We'll have our tea in a minute. You came just in time.'

'You mean he sleeps in our bed – with you?'

There was no mistaking the hostility in Danny's voice as Rachel started on the evening task of getting the children to bed.

'Oh, not now you're back,' Rachel said, trying to keep her tone light. 'They can sleep down in the other room. Only it's been easier to settle Tommy.'

Now, at night, as well as changing his napkins there were the dreaded leg braces, contraptions of metal and leather straps. Tommy howled every time they were put on.

'Will they make him walk?' she asked, and the doctor said he did not know. He doubted it, but they would help to keep his legs from deforming further.

'I'll get them to bed – it won't take long,' she said, feeling close to tears as she took the children upstairs. Had she expected that Danny would rush to help her? She carried Tommy in her arms, Melanie following obediently behind. Melanie had learned early to be a good girl, not to make a fuss, and she usually went off like a lamb. But tonight even she was unsettled.

'Am I sleeping with Tommy?' she asked. Ever since Tommy was born, he had been in the bed in the attic with Rachel. Melanie slept on a single mattress on the floor. They had prepared for this. A returning husband needed to be with his wife and Gladys had bought another bed for the children to share. The neighbours had helped them haul it up through the window.

'Yes,' Rachel said. 'Now your dad's home he'll need his bed back. And you'll be a good girl and keep an eye on Tommy, won't you?' But she was heavy with guilt, as if she had just handed Tommy's care over to her little girl.

She began getting Tommy ready for bed, strapping on the braces which tugged at the tight muscles in his legs, making him cry with the pain of it. It astonished her still, the force with which the muscles in his legs pulled against her when she tried to straighten them. All the time she was pacifying him, trying to settle the two of them down, a terrible tension was knotting her up inside. Here she was with her little ones, who she had cared for all these years, who were used to her and needed her. And now here was Danny, who barely seemed interested in them, who was like a sad stranger at their table. He had not said much during the meal. He did not seem very well, in fact. Rachel was torn to anguish by the conflict inside her. She found herself almost wishing he would go away again so that she could long for him as before. At the same time she wanted urgently to get the children quiet, to be with him alone, to hold and soothe him in the way that she knew he needed, that only she knew.

Tommy was a long time settling, his wails of distress carrying through the house, and by the time Rachel got downstairs again to where Gladys and Danny were sitting by the fire, she felt tearful and wrung out with emotion. They both looked up at her. Danny's expression seemed closed, as if she was someone he barely knew. He was sitting forward, tensed, a cigarette in his hand. Gladys's eyes were troubled.

'Tommy gone off now?' she asked, pouring Rachel a cup of tea.

Rachel nodded and sat down silently with them. Her head ached and she felt drained and full of anguish. She had been here all this time, waiting. Now it felt as if it was he who should move towards her and come back to her.

'I was just saying to Danny,' Gladys said, with her hands still around her empty cup as if for warmth. 'We'll have to go out and see Jess and Amy again as soon as we can. They seem to have settled out there and Nancy's been ever so kind to them.'

Danny nodded faintly. He seemed detached from everything. They asked him a few questions but it was as if the subject of four years away was too big to begin on and they ended by talking about small recent things: his train journey to Birmingham, the fact that rationing was going on just as if the war was still on.

Eventually Danny turned to Rachel, though he seemed to be finding it hard to look her in the eye. He spoke hesitantly, as if they had only just met. 'Shall us go up now, eh?'

Thirty-Nine

As soon as they closed the door to the attic, Danny pulled her to him. He made love to her with a frantic, urgent force, not even fully undressed. It happened so fast, without any closeness or gentleness, that Rachel was left far behind, her thoughts distracted. She found herself praying that Tommy would not wake so that she would have to break away and go down. She could already feel that Danny did not understand the amount of time and care that Tommy took from her.

Danny came in her with a convulsion that passed through his whole body and she held him close. She had barely had the time to feel desire herself. Instead she felt protective and bereft, as if he was still somewhere far off and they could not find each other. She held him close as his breathing steadied, feeling how very thin he was. Her fingertips played along the prominent bones of his spine and ribs.

'Danny?' She spoke almost to check he was still there, even though his slight weight was still resting on top of her.

He raised his head and looked down at her in the light from the oil lamp. They looked into each other's eyes, almost as if meeting for the first time. Rachel felt a surge of loss, of anger for all they had missed of each other, so that they were left like this, like strangers.

'You're so thin,' she murmured.

Danny stroked her shoulder. 'So're you. Where've you gone? You look . . .' He stopped, sounding upset.

She had barely noticed, even though people commented on how much weight she had lost. Very occasionally she glanced in the little mirror downstairs and saw a hollow-eyed face which she hardly recognized staring back at her. She reached up and stroked Danny's cheek. 'You're alive. We're both alive – not like some. That's the main thing.'

Danny gave a harsh laugh. He pulled away and lay beside her on his back. She turned to cuddle up to him, not wanting him to move away from her. 'Yes – I'm alive,' he said.

'What was it like?' she said. 'Out there?'

He rolled his eyes to look up at the ceiling. He seemed weary, even at the thought of talking about it.

'Oh – I was hardly right most of the time out there. Does your innards in – the dirt, the bad water. What a hole.' His voice was heavy with disgust. 'Filth, shit – the whole place stinks. It's just dust and flies and beggars. All this war going on and we spent three years in that cesspit. Ten days in Burma and that was . . .' He trailed off, shaking his head. 'A cowing disaster, that was.'

'I don't really see why . . .' She realized how ignorant she was, how caught up she had been in other things. 'The war wasn't really *in* India, was it?'

'Oh – they were worried about the Japs, the little yellow bastards. But we spent most of the time on "internal security" as they called it. All the last year we was in a flyblown hole called Bihar. They want us out, see – "Independence now! British out!" They're always having these marches and shouting about it. Christ knows why we don't just let 'em have it – what do we want with a dump like that? Our job was to keep them down – stop them rising up and slinging us out. It wasn't really war but it felt like it. Worse – it was their country. All I wanted to say was, *You can have the place and all your spit and shit and bloody temples – just let me go home. To my wife,*' he added, glancing round at her.

She squeezed him. 'You seemed so far away. I wanted you back – all the time.'

'That's my girl.' He seemed closer now, just a little. He rolled onto her and they made love again, more slowly this time, and he seemed a fraction closer to her, her body now coming to life with feeling for him, allowing her release that left her weeping, clinging tightly to him.

'It's been so hard,' she sobbed. 'With Tommy and everything.'

Danny held her silently. At last he said, 'He'll get better, won't he? Better than he is now?'

She felt a stab of worry as he said it. Did he really think Tommy could just be cured?

'He'll get bigger,' she said. 'Like any other little boy. But that's all I know. He won't walk, they say – or talk quite right. That's how it is.'

Danny took this in silently. Rachel felt she had lost him again, just as they had drawn closer.

'What about Jack and Patch?' she said, appealing to the little boy she had known and loved. 'Did you do more drawings?'

'We had to cross this river,' he said. 'In Burma. It was in my pocket – I never remembered 'til it was too late. When I took it out, all the pages were stuck together. It was ruined.'

'Oh dear!' She hugged him. 'Have you still got it?'

'Nah,' he said in a flat voice. 'When I saw the state of it I chucked it out into the bloody jungle for the ants to eat. They'll eat anything.'

'We'll get another one and you can start again,' she said. 'You can show the kids. Melly would love your drawings.' It seemed vitally important suddenly that he did this, as if it was a precious link with the past.

'Huh,' was all Danny said.

Danny stayed in bed late the next morning. It was Saturday and horribly wet. Everyone had to stay in, Tommy in his chair and Melanie playing at the table with some little wooden puzzles Gladys had brought her from the market. Danny came down yawning fit to crack his jaws.

'By the look of you, you need to sleep for a week,' Gladys said. Just for once, today she was going to stay home, not go to the market.

Rachel felt a smile spread across her face. It was so strange him being here after all this time. Like a dream almost. But he was home – for good now! She felt like treating him like a prince.

'Come and sit here –' She got up. 'I'll get you a cup of tea.'

'Ta,' Danny said. He sat beside Melanie who looked up at him guardedly, then smiled. Rachel saw Danny smile back and the sight made her very happy. She had dressed in the nicest clothes she had, a swinging black skirt and a blouse and sky-blue cardigan, and she bustled about, almost vying with Gladys to wait on Danny and get his breakfast.

'Are you my daddy?' she heard Melly say in her usual solemn, direct way.

Rachel watched as the two of them looked at each other with the same blue eyes.

'Yeah – I am,' he said.

'You could hardly miss the fact,' Gladys said, 'looking at you!'

Danny looked at Tommy then. 'He's his mother's boy, all right,' he said.

Rachel felt a niggle of disquiet inside. It was true that Tommy did look like her, but she wondered if Danny meant something else. Was he in some way saying that Tommy was not his? Or that he did not want him to be? But she tried to tell herself she was being silly. They all had a lot of getting used to each other to do.

'Can you do my puzzle?' Melly asked.

Danny bent over the puzzle with her and was helping to put a piece in when Melly said, 'Where have you been? In Germany?'

'No!' Danny laughed. 'I wasn't in Germany. Ta,' he added, as Rachel laid a dish of porridge in front of him. 'No – I was a soldier. In India.'

Melly solemnly took this in. Then she said, 'You should have stayed here, not gone there.'

He gave a shy laugh again. 'Yes – I should.'

'You're a big girl now, Melly,' Rachel said. 'When your dad left you were only a babby.'

'Was Tommy a babby?'

'Tommy wasn't born then.'

Hearing his name mentioned, Tommy was making little excited noises. Danny looked at him, and Rachel saw his eyes cloud with confusion.

'Does he know what we're saying?'

'He does,' Gladys said, bringing some bread to the table. On her way back she bent over Tommy. 'You know what we're saying, don't you, Tommy lad?' She prodded his tummy and the boy squirmed and chuckled, his tongue pushing out of his mouth so that a trail of saliva swam down his chin.

'He's all there, Danny,' Rachel said quietly. 'I know he is – whatever they say about him. And he loves other children – Melly and Cissy, and my friend Netta's kids. He's just got some trouble with his body – his legs.'

Danny nodded, staring warily at his son. He put his head down and ate his porridge.

The rain cleared by the afternoon and everyone emerged. Danny was the toast of the yard that day. Dolly hugged him and patted his head like one of her own. Even Ma and Pa Jackman seemed pleased to see him and Lil Gittins exclaimed loudly over him as if he was a pet lamb.

'Your feller's back then?' Irene said, sidling up to Rachel as she stood behind Tommy's chair which she had wheeled into the yard. Tommy was well wrapped up and he liked to be with everyone.

Irene, with her bleach-blonde hair and very tight, low-cut blue dress with a belt that more than showed off her curves, seemed to dress every day like a seductress. Pity she doesn't spare a bit of time for her kids instead of preening, Rachel thought sourly. Then she thought, God, I'm turning into one of those moaning old bags. But she didn't have much time for Irene these days.

'Yes, he's been fighting for his country – in India and Burma,' she announced, adding caustically, 'not like some.'

Irene, who she guessed had no idea where either of those countries was, said, 'Fancy.' Rachel saw her eyes taking Danny in. Although he was very thin, his shoulders were much broader and stronger than when he left and his tanned face and short hair made him look even more handsome. Compared with Ray Sutton who, despite his film-star appearance, now had a drinker's belly and a dissipated look to his face, Rachel thought her Danny was far more fit and good-looking. She felt a swell of pride.

'Oh, yes,' she said. 'He's been right round the world. Seen all sorts. He's a proper *man*,' she said, as if to emphasize her view of Ray Sutton as a pygmy in comparison.

Irene folded her arms at this and looked fed up. 'Each to their own,' she said grumpily.

'Come on, Danny – get yerself down the pub for a pint or two!' Mo commanded, standing in their doorway. 'You're a man now, lad, no good sitting at home with the wenches all your life! It'll send you soft in the 'ead!'

Danny grinned, clearly pleased.

'What're you going to do now you're back then?' Mo said as Danny got up to fetch his cap. 'Back on the markets?'

'I dunno,' Danny said. 'I might. My army pay'll tide us over for a week or two.' He looked at Rachel and Gladys. 'All right if I go?'

'Go on,' Rachel said. 'Go and see the lads.' She was secretly glad that she would be able to get Tommy off to bed without Danny sitting waiting for her downstairs. To her enormous relief Tommy seemed to have settled in the other bed, probably because he still had his sister with him.

'Did he wake up?' she asked Melly.

'He woke a little bit,' she reported. 'Two times. And I gave him a pat, like you said, and he went back to sleep.'

'There's a good girl,' Rachel said, full of warm gratitude for her responsible little daughter. 'You're such a help to me, Melly. You're a real good girl.'

'Come on, lad –' Mo hauled Danny out with an arm around his shoulders. 'You come down the boozer with me and see the lads – we'll have you in a job of work by the time you get home again!'

Forty

After all the years of longing and waiting, Rachel found those first weeks after Danny's homecoming a bitter disappointment.

'He might take a while to settle,' Gladys had tried to warn her. Gladys had seen it all before with the men coming home after the last war. But Rachel had not been able to imagine this, or anything other than Danny coming home and just being the Danny she had known before. And she desperately needed to lean on him, for him to be a strong support for her.

As it was, she spent her days with a sick feeling from all the tension building up inside her. Danny drifted in and out, sometimes almost his old self, but a lot of the time seeming distant and cut off from them all. Sometimes she almost forgot he was home. She felt just as burdened by everything as before, but with the additional pain of this lack in her husband.

Within a few days of his return, Dolly Morrison came round to tell Danny that a Mr Rose along the street was looking for a worker in his watch-repair business.

'That sounds all right,' Rachel said brightly. 'You keep saying you don't want to work in a big factory, don't you, Danny?'

Danny was, as usual, sitting by the fire, smoking and staring at nothing. 'Yeah. All right.'

'He's a nice old gentleman,' Dolly said with a glance at Gladys that said, *Oh dear, this doesn't look too good.* 'Says his eyes are failing him now. But he's happy to take on someone who's been fighting for King and country.'

'Huh.' Danny gave a cynical snort.

The three women all looked at each other. Rachel's eyes filled with tears and she saw Dolly notice this.

'Eh, Danny, come on,' Dolly said, sinking onto a chair as if the weight of her swollen belly was too much for her. 'You know you might feel a bit better for getting out and doing some work, bab. No good sitting here with nowt to do. That'd make anyone feel a bit blue.'

'I'll do it,' Danny said, an edge of irritation in his voice. 'I said I would, dain't I?'

Any hint of anyone telling him what to do and he was full of rage. Rachel found this when she tried to explain to him how to deal with Tommy. One night she had been showing him how she strapped Tommy's braces on. When she corrected something he was doing, he stormed out of the house in a rage. He came back later and lay in her arms, sorry by then, and upset.

'I dain't mean it – I don't know why I feel so pent up the way I do . . . I know you've had it bad, Rach – I just don't know what to do . . .' None of it was making life easier. Melly moved around him with great caution, as if he was some sort of wild animal with claws that might lash out. At times Rachel found herself wishing power-fully that he had never come home.

Danny went to work with Mr Rose in the front room of his little terraced house. Mr Rose began to teach him all he knew about watch mechanisms and jewellery repair. Danny pointed him out to Rachel in the street one day and she saw a slightly stooped man with silver-grey hair and a neat beard, walking with the aid of a stick. She immediately liked the look of Mr Rose. He had a strong-featured, sympathetic face.

'There you are, my boy!' He raised the stick in a wave.

'All right, Mr Rose?' Danny said, appearing to be shy of him.

They were out with the children. Danny had been very unsure about going out with Tommy in that ramshackle chair. 'You don't take him out, do you – in that?' he said in horror.

'Yes, Danny – I do,' Rachel retorted, in a voice of such fierce finality that he did not dare argue. 'For one thing he's too big for the pram and Dolly's going to need it back. This'll have to do for now – I'm not having him shut away like a prisoner for things he can't help. If other people don't like it, they'll have to put up with it.'

But she could see that Danny was embarrassed when Mr Rose came over.

'So this is your family, Daniel?'

Rachel was startled, never once having heard him called by his proper name before. Mr Rose had a very nice voice, she thought, deep and well spoken. He seemed a refined sort of man.

Danny nodded, introducing Rachel. She shook Mr Rose's small, cool hand. He shook hands with Melanie too.

'Hello, little Melanie,' he said. 'What a pretty name.' Melly beamed up at him, enchanted by this elderly stranger.

'And your boy?' Mr Rose looked down at Tommy, a

kindly light in his eyes. 'He has some problem with his legs?'

Rachel saw Danny look away, as if detaching himself from the situation.

'Yes,' she said. 'He was born with bad legs. He can't walk.' She felt tearful at the sight of the sheer benevolence in the old man's eyes.

'That is a difficult thing,' he said, shaking his head. 'And not easy for his mother either.' He looked at her. 'You know . . .' He moved a fraction closer. 'I had a cousin who was much like this. Can he speak?'

'No – well a bit. But he understands—'

Mr Rose raised a hand as if she had said something very important. 'Understands – exactly, my dear! You must never think, as so many do, that poor muscles in the body mean a brain that does not tick along like the finest of clocks! My aunt – she worked and worked with our cousin Sam. And he was such a lively boy, you know, when they took some time with him. He died young, alas, of influenza – only made twenty-five or so. But they took trouble with him and he learned, he responded. I know it is not easy.' He smiled down at Tommy. Danny turned to watch. 'Hello, little fellow.'

Tommy's eyes lit up and he made a happy sound and squirmed with happiness, his mouth working.

'That's "Hello", I think!' Rachel laughed.

'There you are, you see – a mother always knows!' Mr Rose patted Danny's shoulder. 'You have a fine family, my boy. You are very lucky.'

However, Danny worked for Mr Rose for only nine days before coming home saying he had packed the job in.

'*What?*' Rachel erupted, more upset because Mr Rose

had been so kind than she would have been about any other job. 'But why? He's such a nice old man as well.'

Danny shrugged resentfully. 'I've just had enough. There's other jobs. I haven't *got* to stay there.'

He told her that Mr Rose had sat him down, when he said he was leaving, and given him a lecture about how he would never get anywhere in life if he didn't stick at something, a rolling stone and so on. This seemed to have made Danny even more determined to leave.

'Well, I suppose there are other jobs,' Gladys said, trying to smooth things over, as she could see how upset Rachel was. 'And you can come up the market and help me again, Sat'd'y.'

Later, she said to Rachel, 'He's like a lost soul. Tell you what – I'll take him over to see Jess and Amy on Sunday. Change of scene. That might perk him up a bit.'

'All right,' Rachel said, alarmed at the extent of the relief she felt that Danny would be out for the day. 'I might take the littl'uns over to Mom's – she hasn't seen them in a while.'

Tommy's stiff legs would not wrap around her hip so she had to carry him in front of her, cradled in a blanket. He was not too heavy yet but it still tugged at her back and she was very relieved when a man gave her his seat on the tram into town.

'You look as if you need it more than I do, bab,' he said kindly.

Melly stood beside them holding on tight and Tommy enjoyed sitting on Rachel's lap, gazing around at everything. His legs were hidden in the blanket, but his arms were free and his bad left arm was clenched close to his body. As he looked about him, excited by being out, his mouth kept opening and his tongue sliding out and in again. Rachel could see people looking at him, then away, wondering. But on the trolleybus out to Hay Mills, a woman sitting right behind them started making observations to her neighbour with no attempt to lower her voice.

'It's not right, bringing them out where everyone can see them. It's not nice.'

There was a pause, until the other one said, 'He's not a bad-looking child really. It's a shame.'

'All the same,' her friend said in an officious tone. 'There are homes for oddities like that. We don't need to see them. She ought to have more shame.'

Rachel clenched her hands hard on Tommy's blanket, so tight inside with outrage that she could hardly breathe. She saw Melly looking at her sharpened knuckles, then up at her face with wide eyes. Melly knew the woman was talking about her brother. Rachel looked at her daughter's solemn face, then away out of the window. Nasty, ignorant old cow! she raged to herself. She ought to be used to it by now, she thought. But could you ever get used to it – to the feeling of being stabbed by people's stupid, cruel words? The hurt, angry, protective feelings flamed in her on Tommy's behalf every time. And it was not as if her own mother was any better. Getting off the bus in the Coventry Road, still breathing shallow, upset breaths, she prepared herself for Peggy.

'Oh – it's you,' Fred Horton said, without enthusiasm, opening the door. The top buttons of his shirt were undone, his jacket swinging open, and he looked half-asleep. 'We weren't expecting you. You'd better come in. Sidney's coming over later.'

Oh, I'll be long out of here by the time *he* comes round, Rachel vowed, following her stepfather's burly figure upstairs to the flat. To her great disappointment, the Germans had not succeeded in depriving her of her stepbrother. He was back, full of himself and soon to be married. Peggy had mentioned that Rachel must come to the wedding with Melly – but of course, not Tommy. She was determined not to go at all.

'Oh – Rachel,' Peggy said, rousing herself in her chair by the fire. 'I thought it might be you – though it'd be nice if you gave us warning. You could send me a post-card if you're coming.'

'Yes, I s'pose I could,' Rachel said, without the intention of doing anything of the sort. Was her mother planning to pay for the stamp? she wondered sourly, sitting down with Tommy on her lap. She winced at the pain in her back.

Cissy, who had been sitting quietly at the table with a picture book, came running over. Cissy spent a lot of her life being quiet. 'Now just sit there for a bit and let me have some peace, Cissy ... You be quiet now, your father needs a rest ... ' Cissy was six now, a cheerful child with pale, carroty curls, parted on the left side and pinned back off her face. She was obedient – Rachel could see that it had never occurred to her not to be – and had a nice nature. She absolutely adored Melanie and was always doting and sweet with Tommy. Cissy was the main reason now that Rachel kept up any visits to her mother and Fred at all.

'Here, Ciss –' She held out a little bag. 'I saved my ration of rocks for you two. Look, there's a few Dainty Dinahs and a bit of liquorice.'

The girls took the toffees and liquorice off into the corner and were soon giggling away, sharing them out, cheeks bulging. Rachel glanced affectionately at them. They could make a game out of nothing, those two. Tommy watched them and gurgled excitedly. Rachel was longing for a cup of tea, but she obviously wasn't going to be offered one.

Fred made himself scarce, down to the shop, and Peggy sat back in her chair with a sigh. She was wearing her Sunday best, a brown wool suit and cream blouse, which she had made herself. Not that she ever went to church. She was still a pretty woman, her frizzy curls of hair pinned back in a bun and arranged softly to frame her face. She's ageing well, Rachel thought. Not like me. She felt thin and scraggy in comparison. Not that Peggy ever asked how she was feeling.

'Does that child really have to dribble so much?' Peggy said, giving Tommy a look of distaste. 'It's really very offputting.'

'He can't help it – it's his tongue,' Rachel said, wiping Tommy's chin with the rag she kept in her pocket. It was already soggy in her hand. Instead of the anger she often felt, she had a shrinking, defeated feeling.

'So – how are you?' she asked mechanically, wondering why she ever came here or hoped for anything from Peggy.

There followed a long list of complaints about the tiresome details of Peggy's life, the shortages of everything, rationing, how very tired she was with all the work she still had to do, the way things seemed worse than when the war was on.

'Mom,' Rachel interrupted after a time. 'Danny's home.'

Peggy sat up straighter. 'When? Why didn't you say?'

'You never asked,' Rachel retorted. 'He got home two weeks ago – a bit more than.'

'Well, about time,' Peggy said. 'You need a man to keep you – I hope he's got a good job. I've had enough of worrying about whether you and that gypsy woman are looking after my grandchildren properly.'

Rachel almost laughed at this. When had Mom ever worried about her and the kids, or lifted a finger to help in any way? By now she was used to Mom being rude about Gladys. She ignored such remarks.

'He is . . . all right?' Peggy asked.

'How d'you mean?'

'Not – injured at all?'

'No,' Rachel said. 'He's all right.'

'And has he got himself a job?'

'Yes,' Rachel said. Of course he had found a job. As soon as he'd packed in the last one, he'd been taken on by another older man, Mr Jones, whose business, making carts and basket carriages, had also expanded to include filling accumulators for wirelesses. It was when they took Gladys's wireless to him to be fixed that Mr Jones said he could do with a hand.

Dolly laughed when she heard Danny had gone to work for Lofty Jones, a tall, gangling man in his fifties.

'Old Lofty's carried a flame for Gladys for years – no wonder he's taken Danny on!'

This was news to Rachel. She also wondered how long that would last – Danny said the stink of acid for the accumulators was horrible and he came home smelling of it.

Cissy and Melanie came over then, still chewing, their breath full of sugar, wanting to play with Tommy. They stood each side of him, chatting to him and tickling him, and Tommy was in heaven at all the attention. Cissy looked up, pink cheeked.

'He's funny,' she said, giggling and stroking Tommy's cheek with her finger. Rachel looked lovingly at her. Dear old Cissy! At least someone appreciated Tommy.

'Mom –' Peggy looked as if she was falling into a doze across the room. 'Is there any chance of a cup of tea?'

Peggy looked at the clock. It was half past three. 'Oh, I don't think we need – not until Sidney gets here.'

'I've got to go soon,' Rachel said. She could see what her mother was after – that she would end up making tea for Sidney. That was going to happen over her dead body. 'I'll make it if you like – only it takes me a good while to get home. I could really do with it.'

'All right, if you must,' Peggy said languidly. 'I must say, I do feel so terribly tired today.'

In the kitchen, while she waited for the water to boil, Rachel looked out at the same old view over the yard which was hemmed in by the adjacent row of houses Nothing much had changed – the place was as it had always been, only all the drabber from the war years. She thought back to living here with her mother and Fred and within seconds she was filled with a bursting desire to escape.

Thank God for Danny, she thought, and for Gladys. A wave of desperate love filled her for her husband. She thought of them over in Sutton Coldfield and hoped it would help Danny feel he had come back home. She ached for the old Danny, the boy with the dancing blue eyes, so full of life. The Danny who had come home seemed so lost and distant. She knew she must try harder to find out what was troubling him. She could see that he had no idea what to do or how to feel. However exhausted she was herself, she knew she had to try and try or they would lose each other. As the water began to boil for the tea, she wiped away the tears which had started running down her cheeks.

She arrived home before the others and set about feeding the children.

'I wish Cissy lived next door,' Melly said as she spooned up her watery mince.

'Yes, that'd be nice,' Rachel said, though thanking her stars she did not live next door to her mother. 'But you've got Rita and Shirley to play with – and Evie.'

'Ye-es.' Melly put her head on one side. 'But Cissy's nicer – and I don't like those girls' mom.'

'Well, you don't have to play with her, do you?' Rachel said.

'Poor Evie,' Melly said suddenly.

'What d'you mean?' Like everyone in the yard, Rachel was uneasy about Irene's attitude to her youngest daughter, whom she had taken against on sight.

'Poor Evie having a mom like Mrs Sutton,' Melanie said. 'I'm glad you're *my* mom.'

'Well, that's nice.' Rachel thought she'd better change the subject. 'When you and Cissy're big girls you'll be able to go and see each other, won't you?'

They were chatting about Cissy, who Melanie was in love with in the way that little girls sometimes adore each other, and she was still talking all about their games when Gladys and Danny came in. Rachel pulled all her resolve together. She was going to be the very best she could for Danny! She *had* to make things better.

'Oh, you're back!' she cried, getting up. She went and kissed Danny and said, 'Tea's ready – and the kettle's on. I've nearly finished feeding his nibs.'

Gladys sat down with a groan. 'Ooh – feels a long way up there and back.' She looked pale and exhausted.

'Here – I'll get you a cuppa . . . Danny, love – could you take over feeding Tommy while I make the tea?'

Danny looked panic-stricken. 'I don't know how.'

'Just feed him a little bit at a time – gently. He has a job getting it down – you've seen me do it.'

I mustn't stand over him   I must just let him do it, she thought. She went to mash the tea. 'How are they all?'

'They're all right,' Gladys said. 'Jess is courting again – they say he's a nice enough lad so we hope it'll last this time. And Amy's leaving school in a few weeks.' Her face clouded for a moment. 'She's an odd child. I hope she'll be all right.'

'What'll she do?' Rachel asked. She glanced over at Danny, who had so far said not a word. She saw him try to spoon food into Tommy's mouth. Tommy writhed and spat all of it out down his chin. She saw a look of disgust come over Danny's face.

'Here,' she said gently, taking the tea to the table. 'I'll do it, love. I'm used to it.'

Danny nodded and got up. He said he needed the lav and went out of the house.

'How was it really, Auntie?' Rachel asked as soon as he was out of earshot.

Gladys shook her head sadly. 'It was all right. Nancy and Albert were marvellous and the girls are doing all right. But they're no more his sisters than any other wench out on the street. None of them said a word to each other all day.'

Forty-One

'Danny – are you feeling any better?'

Rachel slipped into bed beside him as he lay in a restless doze. He had barely looked at her all evening and Rachel had thought he was upset about Jess and Amy. But he did not want to eat and eventually admitted that he didn't feel well.

'I've felt bad all day,' he said. 'My head's thumping. I'll have to go to bed.'

Rachel and Gladys exchanged glances. 'I thought he wasn't looking too good,' Gladys said as Danny climbed the stairs.

Now Danny stirred and turned over to face her in bed.

'I'm all right,' he said. But it was obvious that he was not. He was shivering and boiling hot at the same time.

'I brought you some water,' she said.

'Ta.' Sitting up seemed a huge effort. He took a few sips and slumped down again. She could feel him waiting, though, as if for her to say something.

'Was it nice to see them?' she said, turning to embrace him. 'Danny – you're shaking!'

'Yeah –' His teeth were chattering. 'Got a fever coming. I feel bad. Had it before. My head – it's bad . . .'

Suddenly he clung to her and she held him, soothing him as his body shuddered.

'I love you, Danny,' she said, desperate to leap over the gulf between them.

'Love you, girl,' he said between chattering teeth. He sounded very drowsy and ill. He turned away from her and seemed to fall asleep, though he kept twitching and muttering.

Although she was exhausted, Rachel felt too pent-up to sleep. She lay with her eyes open in the dark. Tonight she would have welcomed Tommy waking so that she could go and comfort him. She felt very alone. Tears seeped from her eyes into her hair. Talk to me, Danny, she wanted to cry to him. But he was sick and in no fit state. With her new intentions of that day, to get close to Danny again, to find the boy she loved inside this troubled man, she had thought they would lie and talk for hours, that she would gradually draw him back to her with all the love she could pour over him.

So far, he had talked very little about the war. He said it was so vile and tedious that all he wanted was to forget it.

'Four years down the toilet, that's what it was,' was mainly all she had got out of him. He didn't seem to have much more to say about it. 'All I ever wanted was to come home to you.'

Every so often, when she had the energy, Rachel persevered and asked about India. And didn't he say he had been in Burma? Some of the stories which were coming out about what the Japanese had done were so extreme that she was almost afraid to ask. Was there some terrible secret he was hiding?

But Gladys asked sometimes as well. One evening, once the children were in bed, he had talked a little bit.

'We were only in Burma a couple of weeks.' Danny picked up the poker as he spoke, prodding at the floor with it, as if avoiding looking at them. It was this not looking that made Rachel feel worst. Where had he gone to, her Danny? Who was this Danny who could no longer meet her eye?

'They signed us up with one of the Indian divisions and sent us in when everyone else was coming back the other way.' He shook his head. 'It wasn't that long after I got out there. We had a bit of jungle training – huh, so much for that! May forty-three they sent us into Burma and told us to hold this pass called the Ng . . . Ngakey-dauk . . . summat like that. The Okeydokey, we called it. It was so all the rest of them could clear out – the Japs flushing all our army back into India. Six days . . .' He jabbed at the floor and shook his head with a cynical smile. 'Jungle training . . . As if you could train for that hellhole. We weren't in all that much fighting, not as such. But it felt as if they were there, all over the jungle, creeping up on you, every minute of the day and night. It was enough to send you round the bend. And the lads were dropping – sick as dogs. We got the hell out of there after that, those little yellow bastards chasing the lot of us out.' He looked up at Gladys. 'So yeah – Burma. Then it was back to Bihar and more bloody Indians.'

She could not imagine India or Burma, or how it must have been. And it really did not seem as if Danny had much more to say about it. And yet, it was as if between the time she last saw him, in December 1942, and his homecoming, the real Danny had been stolen and re-placed by someone else. His light-heartedness, his electric energy, all seemed to have vanished.

Reaching out in the bed she laid her hand on his hot back. Eventually, she slept.

She was woken by him vomiting over the side of the bed.

'Danny!' She leapt up. 'Oh, no – I'll get the bucket!'

She stumbled downstairs, barefoot, returning with one of the buckets and a cloth. Upstairs again, she lit a candle and sat beside him, wiping his forehead as he strained and retched. He was shivering even more violently while he remained alarmingly hot at the same time. At last when he had finished he lay back, limp and feverish. Rachel wiped up the floor and crept down to empty out the bucket and rinse it with water from the pot on the stove. Then she took the bucket back up.

As she reached the top of the attic stairs she saw that Danny was getting up.

'I've got to go . . .' He stumbled across the room. 'The lav . . .'

'But . . .' It seemed such a long way.

'S'all right . . . Used to it . . .' he murmured.

She heard him go out of the door. For a moment she sat there, stunned and queasy at the shock of being woken suddenly, and panicked at seeing Danny so ill.

I might as well go out and get some more water, she thought, while I'm waiting. She took her shoes this time. Downstairs, the door was ajar. She paused behind it to slip her feet into her shoes, picked up the other bucket and went out to the tap.

The lamp shed a dim light. The night was cold and damp, the sky thick with cloud. With just a cardigan over her nightdress, she was soon shivering. As she stood filling the bucket, even the slow flow of water from the tap sounded loud in the dead hours of the night. But as she turned it off and was going back to the house, she heard a little whimpering sound.

Her heart beat faster. Surely that wasn't Danny? She stopped, listening, the bucket weighing down her left side. The sound came again, from her left, a thin, desolate wail. Then a high voice said, 'Mo-om . . .' and a grizzling crying followed. It was coming from the direction of the Suttons' house. As she moved closer, she saw that there was a tiny someone sitting in the shadow of the doorway, curled up on the step.

'Evie?' She left the bucket and went to bend over the little girl. 'What on earth're you doing out here, babby?'

Evie raised her blonde head from her knees. Rachel saw there was something draped over her legs, a coat or bit of blanket. Her face was stony with woe. Rachel sat beside her and put her arm around her. She knew the little girl well. Evie often came into their house.

'Why're you out here, Evie?' She was beginning to simmer with rage at Irene. What in the name of God was she playing at, leaving this little one out on the doorstep? Had she got drunk with Ray and forgotten about her? 'Evie?' she repeated, when there was no answer.

'Mom said,' Evie hiccoughed the words out between sobs.

My God, Rachel thought furiously. So it was no accident!

'Did she say you'd been naughty, Evie?'

The child nodded.

'Why did she say you'd been naughty?' The little girl did not seem to know, or remember. It was nothing, probably, Rachel thought, knowing Irene. Looking down she saw that Evie was barefoot. She wrapped her hands round each of her plump feet for a moment. They were icy. The poor child was freezing cold.

Rachel got up and tried the front door. It was locked. They had gone to bed, deliberately locking Evie out. By God, she fumed, she'd be having words with Irene in the morning! She wanted to hammer on the door and demand that they get up and come and get their daughter. But she knew if she did that she would wake everyone else, even if Irene and Ray were stupefied with drink. And if they did wake, there was no telling how Evie would be treated.

'Come on, babby,' she said. 'You can come and sleep with our Melly. Holding Evie's hand, fetching the bucket as she went, she led her into the house. As she tucked her in at the other end of the mattress from Melly and Tommy, she started to worry about Danny. He was taking such a long time. Had he passed out in the lav? Her heart thumped harder again with fear.

'There you go, littl'un.' She stroked Evie's hair and tucked the blanket around her. The child was giving tired little sobs. 'You go to sleep now, babby, all right?'

As she crept out again she heard Danny come staggering in downstairs. To her relief she could hear Gladys giving off little snores from her room. Thank goodness Gladys was such a good sleeper! She slipped her shoes off and hurried down again. Danny had sunk down onto a chair.

'Danny – love?' Panic-stricken, she laid a hand on his back. He seemed so terribly poorly. She had never known him as sick as this before. 'Come back to bed – it's cold.'

'In a minute.' Head down, he was gathering his strength. 'This is malaria,' he said. 'You'll have to go to the doc – get me the medicine.'

'Malaria?' She knew something about it being a

disease people had in foreign countries. No one had it here, surely?

'Got it in Burma, first time.' He gathered his breath. 'It comes back. Need quinine . . . Oh – I'm gonna be sick again!'

Rachel seized an empty bowl just in time, panicking as Danny heaved and retched. Malaria – what did it mean? Was he going to die?

When he was finished at last, Rachel cleaned the bowl and went back to him. Danny held out an arm. 'Help me back to bed. Feel bloody terrible.' Side by side they shuffled and squeezed up the narrow stairs to the attic. Holding him as they climbed, stopping often to rest and whispering words of encouragement to him, was the closest she had felt to Danny in a long time. He fell back into bed, shaking and shivering. She held him, warming him as he gradually slipped away into sleep.

Forty-Two

'Mom – why's Evie in our bed?'

Rachel opened her eyes blearily. It had been a terrible night. Danny had been up several times being sick and staggering out to the lavatory. He was sleeping more peacefully for the moment, completely worn out, his face drawn and sallow. Rachel felt she had barely slept at all. Melanie's serious little face looked over the bed-clothes at her.

Evie! She had forgotten all about that. Anger drove her up and out of bed.

'Evie just had to stop over with us,' she told Melly, not wanting to start a long discussion about why and how. 'I need to go and see her mom.'

'She's asleep,' Melly said. 'And Tommy's awake.'

'She'll be all right, let her sleep,' Rachel said. 'You leave them both and get ready for school.'

I wonder if Irene will even notice she's gone? Rachel thought, pulling her dress over her head. She felt frayed with exhaustion and nerves. Was Danny going to be all right – should she get the doctor? Could he die of it? All the time as she got Tommy up and fed him, the worry jangled inside her, making her jump at the slightest thing.

'Auntie!' she cried as Gladys appeared downstairs.

'Danny's ever so bad – he's been up all night being sick and he says he's got malaria and he needs the doctor to give him some medicine . . .'

'Malaria?' Gladys said, bewildered. She stood hugging her shawl around her, over her skirt and blouse. 'That's some foreign thing. He must've brought it back with him.'

'He says he needs the medicine . . .' Rachel was almost crying. 'And I found Evie out on the step last night and she's been up with Melly, and I don't know how I'm going to—'

'Hang on, slow down – *what*?' Gladys held her hand up. When Rachel explained about finding Evie outside she saw a cold, enraged look come over Gladys's face. Her jaw clenched.

'My *God*,' she hissed, turning away to see to the stove. But a moment later, under control, she turned back to Rachel. 'I'll go for you – to the dispensary for Danny, soon as it opens. You'd best deal with Irene – I don't trust myself.'

But a few minutes later, Irene was out, bawling across the yard.

'Evie? Get in 'ere – where've yow got to?'

Before she even got to the door, Rachel heard Dolly's voice.

'What's up with you, Irene – lost 'er again, have yer? You want to keep a better eye on your kids, you do.'

'Who asked yower bleeding opinion?' Irene retorted. 'EVIE! Come on, babby – get 'ere, now. Stop messing about!'

Trembling with rage at Irene, both for her treatment of Evie and at hearing the way she spoke to Dolly, Rachel burst out into the yard.

'I'll tell you where Evie is,' she announced at the top

of her voice. 'I found her out on your doorstep in the middle of the night – and the door locked – as you know perfectly well. She's in bed with my Melanie and that's where she's staying – although much you care so far as I can see. You ought to be locked up, the way you treat that child!'

Irene bridled. She was dressed in a flowery frock, all pinks and pale greens and belted tightly at the waist, her hair newly peroxided, and a pair of black heels. Her stocking-less legs were lardy white against the shoes. All in all she was looking smug and self-satisfied. Things must be going all right with Ray, Rachel thought, so the stupid bint was full of herself, preening and prancing about.

'Always got pennies for a new frock, haven't you, Irene? It's a pity you don't spend it on feeding your family.'

'So you've taken 'er, you interfering cowbag!' She came marching across to Rachel. 'Here'm I worrying myself to death about 'er and yow've been hiding her all the sodding time. Who d'yow think yow are? You get 'er out 'ere – now!'

'Hey, you!' Dolly came striding over like a steamboat at full speed, magnificently large with child. Her wavy dark hair was all hanging loose as she had been in the process of brushing it out, which made her look younger and rather wild. 'Who're you talking to like that? Our Rachel's been looking after your babby when you and that feller of yours are too kalied or idle to bother – you should be thanking 'er, not shooting yer mouth off!'

Irene, already in the wrong and faced by two furious women with their arms folded, could see she was beaten.

'All right – well, now you've got *my daughter* you can cowing well give 'er back!'

'She's asleep,' Rachel said. 'And that's the best place for her. How much sleep did you think she was going to get sat out on the step all night with next to nothing on? You're a lousy mother, Irene – your kids'd be better off in a home than with you, the way you carry on.'

She hadn't really meant to say that, but she was tired and overwrought.

'Oh-ho!' Irene drew herself up, relishing the insult she was about to deliver. '*My* kids ought to be in a home? *My* kids're all right. It's that halfwit babby of yours should be shut away in a home – with all the other cripples.'

Rachel had no idea she was going to do it. She just found herself launching her whole weight at Irene, her knuckles smashing into Irene's cheek, her other hand coming up and slapping her face the other side. The pain from the punch jarred all down her arm, but she didn't care. In fact it felt glorious! Irene screeched and Rachel felt her head jerked agonizingly to one side as Irene grabbed handfuls of her hair and yanked on it with full force. Rachel went mad – she was screaming, lunging at Irene with her nails, her fists, feeling blows landing on her as both of them yelled and flailed at each other. Rachel barely even knew where she was – she was full of crazed energy, a mass of kicking and hitting limbs, like a whirlwind with fists.

'Eh, you two – pack it in!' Dolly yelled, wading in.

'What in heaven's name is going on?' Gladys hurried out into the yard. 'Dolly, you keep out of it – you're in no state . . .' All the same, both of them set about hauling the two scrapping women apart.

Rachel stood, panting and tugging at Gladys's arms as she tried to hold her back. She could feel the burning from her cuts beginning and a hot trickling sensation down her right cheek, but she couldn't care less. She stared triumphantly at Irene, who was scratched all over her face, her hair dishevelled and a bleeding cut over her left eyebrow. None of her own pain mattered in the slightest – she was full of a delicious, swelling ecstasy, of having let all the tension erupt out of her. To make it even more satisfying, she knew she was in the right – so sod Irene!

'You're a stupid cow, Irene!' she bellowed as Gladys hauled her back towards the house. 'You'll get your daughter back when she wakes up and not before!'

'I should've thought you'd've had more sense,' Gladys said, back inside. 'Look at the state of you! But by God, that one's had it coming to her.'

Nothing seemed to shatter Rachel's momentary, carefree mood. She peered in the glass on the wall. Her hair was wild as a madwoman's and her gaunt cheeks were smeared with blood from cuts and punches. 'God – what a mess!' she said, but then found herself laughing at the sight, unable to stop, until tears ran down her cheeks.

Gladys was buttoning her coat. 'I'm going out,' she said, with a disdainful sniff, 'to get *your husband* his medicine. And by the time I get back I should've thought you'd have pulled yourself together.'

'Danny –' Rachel shook him awake. 'Here – Auntie's got this for you. You'd better take some.'

Danny opened his eyes, utterly bewildered for a moment. He was still feverish but seemed calmer.

'You haven't been sick again?' she asked.

'No –' He accepted the water she was holding out to him. 'I think it's stopped.' He peered blearily at her. 'What the hell's happened to you?'

'Irene,' she said, measuring out the medicine for him. 'We had a bit of a barney.' She sank down onto the edge of the bed. 'Here – open wide.'

'I was dreaming I was back there again,' Danny said, lying back, exhausted. He sounded vulnerable, almost tearful. 'It's being sick, like this – just the same. I had to keep walking along that road . . . So hot . . . Dust . . . Never felt so bad before . . .' He was drifting off to sleep again. Rachel leaned over and kissed his cheek.

She crept out of the room and down to the one below, where she found Evie lying in the bed, looking around her.

'Hello, bab,' she said. The little girl brought out a special tenderness in her. Rachel had never felt that her own mother liked or wanted her and for Evie it was even worse.

Evie sat up. 'Po,' she said.

'Come on then.' Rachel sat her on the pot to relieve herself. 'We need to take you back to your mom,' she told her as Evie looked up at her. 'Would you like a piece first?'

The little girl nodded. Rachel led her down to sit at the table, near Tommy who was in his chair. Mo had fixed a wooden tray across it for him to play with things on and he was fiddling with some tin soldiers Gladys had bought him at the market. He brightened up at the sight of Evie and made his noises of welcome. He loved having other children around. Rachel cut her a piece of bread and scraped margarine over it.

'Here you are – get that down you.' And then we'd better go and face the music again, she thought, full of dread now that she had calmed down.

Holding Evie by the hand, she knocked at Irene's house. Irene came to the door, her own face dotted with angry red welts and scratches, though she had tidied up her hair. With satisfaction, Rachel noticed that Irene looked worse than she did. She wondered if Irene would start on her again, but suddenly she was all wheedling charm.

'Thanks ever so much for looking after her,' she said. 'I never meant to leave her out there – it was a mistake. Course it was! Come on, Evie,' she called in honeyed tones. 'You come inside and we'll do summat nice, while those other two're out of the way at school.'

Evie looked especially confused by this offer and still seemed dazed. She wandered up the step into the house. Irene leaned her voluptuous body against the door frame.

'How's your husband?' she asked ingratiatingly. 'Mrs Morrison said he's poorly.'

'He's got malaria,' Rachel said, feeling rather important. 'He caught it fighting out east.'

'Fancy,' Irene said, determinedly unimpressed.

Rachel paused. 'Look – Netta's coming round this afternoon with her kids.' Netta, to her joy, was expecting again now and well on into the pregnancy. 'Just for a cuppa, when school's out. You can come too if you like.'

Irene considered, a haughty look coming over her face for a moment, but if she was going to make a rude retort, she thought the better of it. 'All right,' she said grudgingly. 'Ta.'

Forty-Three

That day Danny started sweating like nothing Rachel had ever seen before. It poured off him, soaking the bedclothes. His face was shiny with moisture. He assured her that this had happened before, was part of the illness.

'It's horrible,' she said, when she went up late that afternoon. The room reeked of sweat. 'I'd better change the bed.' One thing they did have was sheets, thanks to Gladys. But she felt exhausted by the thought of all the washing.

'Not 'til this bit's over,' Danny said, shivering. 'No point. They'll be soaked again in a few minutes. This is how it goes. I've just got to keep drinking.'

Rachel brought him more water. 'I've never seen anyone sweat so much,' she said. 'If you don't drink, you'll end up looking like a prune.'

'Ta very much –' He gulped down some more water and lay back. 'Who was that here – I heard someone.'

'Oh – it was Netta, my pal. Came round with her kids. And Irene.'

'Irene? I thought you said you'd just socked her one?'

'Yeah –' Rachel was heading for the door. There was so much to do, Tommy to see to. 'She socked me one an' all – but . . .' She shrugged. 'You know.'

'Stay –' Danny reached out his arm. 'Talk to me. I want you here.'

'I can't stop now,' she gabbled, feeling under pressure. She could hear Tommy shrieking downstairs. 'I've got to get the kids their tea, massage Tommy and get him off to bed – and Auntie wants me to help her with a load of stuff needs ironing.'

Danny dropped his hand and turned away, closing his eyes.

'Danny – love? I'll be back a bit later. I will – there's just so much to do.'

But there was no reply.

'Why did Evie sleep in my bed last night?' Melly asked while she was having tea.

Rachel paused, holding up a spoonful of potato for Tommy. He was not eating well today. There was already a mess of spat-out food on the tray of his chair and down his front. Her head was throbbing with tiredness and she was stiff with tension. There was the usual worry that Tommy was not getting enough to eat, combined with burning impatience at the slow, revolting process of trying to get anything down him. Rachel knew that Gladys, who was sitting nearby, sewing, was waiting to use the table.

'She just needed somewhere to sleep,' she said.

Melly looked severely at her. 'But *why* did she need somewhere?'

Rachel thought of Danny's turned-away face upstairs, looked at the swamp of spat-out food on Tommy's tray. She took a deep breath, feeling she was about to explode.

'She just did – all right?' she snapped.

401

Melly tightened her lips. 'Why did you have a fight with Mrs Sutton?' she asked, not for the first time.

'Come on, Melly,' Gladys said. 'You want to shake yer feathers and get that tea down you. I've got things to do.'

'But—' Melly persisted.

'Just eat up,' Rachel told her. 'Or the mice'll have it.'

Melly frowned even more at this.

'I think Tommy's had all he's having for today,' Rachel said briskly. 'Let's get you cleaned up, young man – ups-a-daisy! Out you come.'

'There aren't any mice,' Melanie was muttering. 'Only in the brew house. I saw one in there.'

The evening seemed endless. Rachel was just longing to sit down with a cup of tea and close her eyes, but there were all the usual chores. She went up and down a couple of times to check whether Danny wanted anything. The sweating had worn off and he seemed quiet and drowsy. When she finally got to bed her head was still throbbing and she was longing to lie quite still and sleep. But she was churned up over Danny, feeling he was sulking and disappointed in her.

He was turned away from her as she got into bed, but his body was cooler now. She lay a hand on his back. 'Danny? You awake?'

He made a faint, drowsy noise and seemed to shrink away from her hand, though she was not sure if it was deliberate.

'I love you,' she said tearfully. If only he would turn to her and be the old Danny, so sweet and so hungry for her!

But there was no reply. She lay, feeling more alone

than she had when he was away. At least then she had been able to concentrate just on the children. Now she spent her whole life feeling torn in two.

As Danny recovered she tried to spend more time with him. But if she was upstairs she really had to take Tommy as well, not leave him on his own. It would be a chance for Danny to get to know him, she thought.

A couple of days later, when Danny was sitting up, she carried Tommy up so they could be with him. Danny was even thinner now. His hair had grown out of its military crop but his face looked yellowish against the sheets. He was beginning to eat, though, and he was definitely on the mend.

'Look, Tommy –' She made a joke of them peering around the door. 'There's your dada!'

Tommy squirmed and waved his good arm, a trickle of saliva running down his chin as he made his happy chirruping noises.

'Look who I brought to see you!' she said to Danny, and she got onto the bed with Tommy and propped him up between them, in the curve of her arm. She leaned round to kiss Danny.

'All right, son?' Danny turned to look at him. He was wary with Tommy, as if he did not know what to do with him.

'You look a lot better,' she said.

'I'm all right. I'll be up soon.'

'D'you want a cup of tea?'

'No, it's all right. Stay here.' He seemed worried that she would go and leave him alone with Tommy.

There was still an awkwardness between them which she tried to fill with chatter.

'You should've seen Dolly this morning – she's a right one. Ever since she found out she was expecting again she's been ordering Mo about, making him do everything for her. It's all, "I can't possibly do that, Mo, not in *my condition*." She's even sending him down the shops! I mean, I know she's joking, sort of, but poor old Mo – he's like a donkey ever since they knew they're having another one!' She turned to him, joking, 'I'll have to try that one, won't I?'

But Danny looked fed up. 'We're not going to be having another one, are we, at this rate?'

She looked at him.

'We're never on our own, are we – there's always some babby or summat getting in the way!'

'But Danny –' She looked across Tommy's head. Tommy was looking from one to the other of them, intrigued by this new situation. 'You've been so poorly – I mean, you haven't been in a state to . . .'

She was wracking her brains . . . When had they last made love? But they had, before he was taken ill. Almost every night, in fact. What on earth was he on about?

Danny made an angry gesture. 'But he's here now. Why does he have to be up here with us? Can't we have five minutes' peace?'

Rachel felt her own anger surge to the fore. 'He's a babby, Danny – they don't just look after themselves, especially one like Tommy. And he's your son, he's—'

'Is he?' He choked out the words as if they had been waiting there. 'How do I know he's mine? No one in my family's ever been like that before.' He gestured towards Tommy's legs. 'Not a cripple.'

Rachel gathered Tommy to her. She had such a huge, aching lump in her throat that she could not speak. Without looking at Danny she got off the bed and, holding her son close to her, protectively, she took him downstairs. Gladys was out. She strapped Tommy back in his special chair, putting his little bricks and toys on the tray. Sinking down by the table, Rachel lay her head on her arms and wept until she was empty from crying.

Forty-Four

By the next weekend, Danny was up and about again, though still looking tired and a faint shade of yellow.

'You'll be able to go back to work tomorrow, won't you?' Gladys said on the Sunday night. 'Lofty'll be glad to have you back after all this.'

'Oh – I'm not going back to Jones's,' Danny said.

Gladys looked up quickly. 'What d'you mean? You've only just started! Lofty Jones gave you that job as a favour.'

Danny shrugged. 'He can give it to someone else as a favour then. I'm giving him my notice.'

Once again, Rachel had a desolate, shrinking feeling. Danny had become a stranger who none of them could reach.

'You want to settle to summat, lad,' Gladys retorted. 'You can't go on like this.'

'Everyone's very good at telling me what I want!' Danny flared up, getting to his feet. 'I'm off down the Salutation. At least there'll be no one nagging me there!'

'Oh, yes – on whose wages?' Gladys roared after him. 'Life's what you make it, lad – it's not going to fall in your lap.'

'Danny!' Rachel protested. 'Don't go out.' She had

406

been hoping for a cosy night in, to go to bed early and make it up to him, to try and get close to him again.

She flinched as the door slammed and he was gone. Danny seemed to want to be with other men whenever he could. There was no one else in the yard who had been away in the forces. Rachel now felt as if she didn't count for anything with him. Her tears rose to the surface again but she swallowed them down. Gladys was not a person who invited emotion.

'He'll have to knuckle down sooner or later,' Gladys said. 'The world doesn't owe him a living. And he's got a family now.'

Though she was trying to sound tough, she really sounded upset and bewildered.

Danny went and got himself another job, in assembly with Coronet Cameras in Summer Lane.

'Is it better than the other jobs?' Rachel asked. Nowadays she found herself asking him questions she did not really want answered, just to get him to talk to her. *Are you all right?* she'd ask, or, *What's it like out?*

'It's all right,' Danny said. Everything he said sounded on the edge of anger. She was becoming almost afraid to speak.

By the Friday night he had at least held the job down for the first week and received a pay packet.

'Right,' Gladys ordered him. 'I want you helping me on the market tomorrow. I could do with someone to bring in some stuff for me.'

Rachel hoped the market would do Danny good and as he went off with Gladys on Saturday with various bundles of stuff it felt almost like old times.

It was a nice day for March and after they had gone

she wheeled Tommy outside, well wrapped up, to watch the other children play. The younger Morrison boys were outside and they ran back and forth and up to his chair – 'All right, Tommy!' 'Hello, Tommy!' – touching his nose, making him blink and chuckle. He loved it and was all smiles. And Rachel adored every little blonde one of the Morrison lads, for being Tommy's allies. She knew they would stand up for him out in the street too, if there was ever any trouble. Sometimes they wheeled him about for fun.

She took a chair out and sat beside Tommy, turning her face up to the weak sunlight. After a moment she noticed Evie, wandering about by herself. She had one finger in her mouth and was scuffing along the yard staring at her feet, looking very subdued. Her skimpy frock was all stains, and she had only one scruffy old pump on her left foot, the other bare. Her hair was a bird's nest of tangles.

'She must be cold,' Rachel said to Melly, her heart going out to the little girl. 'Go and see to her, love, eh?'

Melly went over in a motherly way and took the little girl's hand. 'Where's Rita and Shirl – ain't they playing out with you?' Rachel heard her ask, but Evie just shook her head. She never said much at the best of times.

'Take her inside and put your old cardi on her,' Rachel said. 'And give her a piece as well, Melly – she looks half-starved to me.'

As the girls disappeared inside, Dolly appeared. 'Ooh, you've got the right idea, bab – I could do with a sit-down, I can tell yer.'

Dolly plonked a chair down next to Rachel. Despite being heavily pregnant she seemed active and fit, whatever she might protest to Mo. As ever she looked lovely with her dark, glossy hair pinned back each side of her face and red lipstick. Her belly was a rounded cliff under her baggy dress with its royal-blue-and-white swirls of pattern. She descended onto the chair with an outrush of breath and leaned back.

'Oh – it's good to sit down!'

'Don't you need more on?' Rachel said. Dolly seemed to be dressed for summer, while Rachel, who had borrowed Gladys's shawl to wrap around her, was still shivering.

'Nah – this one's keeping me warm.' Dolly stroked her belly. 'Any road, I'm not such a skinny whippet as you. You need to look after yourself, Rach, you've got that scrawny. Hello, little feller,' she said, leaning over Tommy. His tongue slithered out and he gave his lopsided smile.

Dolly fished in her pocket for her ciggies and matches and lit up, taking a contented drag and blowing out the smoke. She seemed about to speak when something else caught her attention.

'Oh, my *word*, look what's coming,' she said. 'And after all that flaming carry-on last night.'

Rachel saw the apparition that had appeared from the door of number four in the shape of Ray and Irene, arm in arm, all dolled up to the nines. Ray, hair Brylcreemed back, was in a sharp black suit and Irene in a scarlet frock and hat, each trimmed with white. Irene came tottering across the bricks on high navy heels. In their wakes were Rita – in pale blue frills – and Shirley – pale yellow frills – managing to look both mutinous and self-important at the same time.

Miraculously, Irene's face seemed unscathed, as she and Ray had had one of their noisiest ding-dongs ever last night, yelling and crashing until so late that Mo went and banged on the door and told Ray he'd fetch the police if they didn't knock it off. This had a measure of success, as Mo guessed it would.

Arm in arm they advanced across the yard.

'Ray's brother's getting wed,' Irene announced loudly. She half-turned to the girls: 'Reet, Shirl – come on now! We've got to get along to the church!'

'What about Evie?' Rachel asked indignantly.

'Oh, we're not taking Evie, 'er's too little.' Irene waved a dismissive hand.

'Well, who the hell d'you think's going to look after her then?' Rachel demanded.

'You'll keep an eye on 'er for me, won't you?' Irene said as the two of them sashayed off along the entry. 'Yow'm not going anywhere, are yer?' And off she went.

'She's the flaming end, she really is!' Rachel erupted. 'Fancy just going off like that and leaving Evie! She'd never've even said if I hadn't asked. God, it's a good job Gladys isn't here.'

Dolly's eyes followed Melanie and Evie as they re-emerged from the house, Evie chewing hungrily on a crust of bread.

'Good job you're here, bab,' Dolly said. 'That Irene knows you've got a soft spot for Evie.' An impish grin escaped her. 'Fancy wearing that outfit to a wedding, though – talk about red hat and no drawers!'

Rachel managed a laugh. 'P'raps his other missis is going to be there – Irene wants to stand out.'

'She's going to do that, all right,' Dolly giggled. 'I mean, I like a bit of colour . . . She's a case that one, and no mistake.' Dolly took another long drag on her cigarette. 'Silly cow.' Her face sobered again and she looked at Tommy. 'How's he getting on, Rach?'

'He's all right,' Rachel said with a sigh in her voice.

Dolly took in her tone. 'You all right, bab? It must be a job, looking after him.'

Rachel nodded. In the face of Dolly's sympathy, the tears came. She leaned forward, hugging herself. 'It's not Tommy . . . Well, it is in a way, but I'm so used to him. It's Danny . . .' Her hurt and upset really came out then. She was glad that the other neighbours were not within earshot. Ma Jackman was up the other end, wearing a spotty pinner and beating the guts out of a rug that was hanging over the line. Rachel didn't want the whole world to hear her woes.

'Is he finding it a bit difficult to settle?' Dolly asked.

Rachel looked into Dolly's kind, pretty face. 'He doesn't like Tommy,' she sobbed. 'He said to me the other day that he didn't think he was his son. And he's – well, he's so angry and unhappy. I don't know what's the matter with him. He's not the Danny I married. I don't know him any more. And I thought he'd help me . . .' Her pity for herself welled up. She longed to feel that Danny was on her side, and on Tommy's! Letting her tears flow, she added, 'I want my old Danny back.'

'Oh, love –' Dolly dropped her cigarette stub, grinding it under her heel, and put her arm around Rachel's shoulders, her eyes full of sympathy. 'I can see it's not easy for you – either of you. You look worn to a frazzle. But there's something else I don't think you've faced up to, bab.'

Rachel looked up at her, wet-eyed and startled.

'If Mo had gone, if he'd been the right age, it might've been the same. But we're both older – 'specially him, of course, the old bugger. At your age, four years is a life-time. The way Danny sees it, you're not the woman he married either. You *are* different, Rach. You're both four years older, you've been bringing up two little ones on your own, one of them giving you more to worry about than most. Look at yourself – you're not the kid you were when he left, are you? Just think about it.'

Rachel sat feeling dazed. Had she changed? She didn't feel so different. She was still the same old Rachel, surely, though thinner and more worn?

'You're a woman now, Rach. When Danny left you were still kids. You've both got a lot of catching up to do and it's going to take time.'

'I do love him, Dolly,' Rachel said in a heartbroken voice. 'I do.'

'I know you do.' Rachel could feel Dolly's warm hand stroking her back. 'Course you do, bab.'

'I don't know what to do to make things better.'

'You'll have to give him attention. They like that, fellers do. They're like big kids. Even ordering them about – it makes them feel important. Danny's a lost child as well, Rach, remember that. You'll have to not let this little man get in the way of everything.' She reached over and stroked Tommy's hand. 'However beautiful he is.'

Forty-Five

'Feeding him a bit early, aren't you?' Gladys said as Rachel sat spooning food into Tommy.

'I just thought I'd try and get him fed before Danny gets in,' Rachel said.

It was Monday. They had spent an uneasy Sunday with Danny out a lot of the time and withdrawn when he was at home. Rachel had taken Dolly's words as gospel and was doing everything she possibly could to make Danny feel that he was the centre of her attention. When they made love last night she was as affectionate as she knew how to be and they had cuddled each other. But she found that while she could get a bit closer to Danny in bed, holding him, trying to show him how much she loved him, he was still withdrawn from her and any closeness soon wore off when they had to get on with daily life.

Gladys gave her a straight look. 'He's got to get used to being home,' she said. 'Whether he likes it or not –' she gestured at Tommy – 'this is how it is. Look, go and meet him. I'll finish feeding Tommy.'

'Oh, thanks, Auntie!' Rachel's spirits leapt. She caught a sudden glimpse of being young again, as if going out courting.

Quickly pulling on her coat and hat, she went out into the overcast afternoon. As she walked along the road it felt very strange to be out without the children. She felt a sudden sense of freedom, but also as if a large part of her was missing. She headed towards Summer Lane, picturing herself standing outside the camera factory and Danny catching sight of her there, waiting for him. She wanted his face to light up the way it used to when he met her out of Bird's Custard.

She was so busy daydreaming that she did not notice the little figure walking along towards her, head down, in a royal-blue coat. It was only when she was up close that she said, 'Oh, hello, Mrs O'Shaughnessy! I didn't see you for a minute.'

Netta's mother looked up and Rachel saw a terrible distress in her eyes. She was not weeping, but her whole face was distorted by grief.

'Oh, now Rachel, I was on my way to find you, darlin'. Come with me to our Netta, will you – such a terrible thing . . .' She took Rachel's arm.

'What is it? Is she having the baby?' Rachel said.

Mrs O'Shaughnessy shook her head. 'She's after having it this morning – in the small hours. The poor wee thing never uttered a cry. There was no life in it. Oh, it's a terrible thing seeing them like that!' Tears started in her eyes as she said this. 'Come and be with her a while, will you? She's not in a good way.'

Very torn, Rachel glanced along the street. How could she refuse to go and see Netta? And there was no sign of Danny yet.

When they got into the little house Mrs O'Shaughnessy whispered, 'Patsy and little Clare are next door with Mrs Flynn – I'll have to be fetching them in a minute. You go up, darlin', and I'll make us a cup of tea. Our Netta's in her bed.'

Her heart very heavy, Rachel crept up to the bedroom.

'Mammy?' she heard Netta call, in a small, desolate voice. 'Is that you?'

'It's me – Rach,' she replied softly. Going into the room she saw Netta lying on the bed. All signs of the birth in the night had been cleared away. Netta's face was raw with crying and she looked very small and limp with sorrow. Rachel sat down and took her hand. 'I'm ever so sorry, Net. So sad for you.'

Netta's brows pulled into a frown. 'I'm never doing it again,' she said, as more tears trickled from her eyes. Rachel's own tears flowed in sympathy. 'Not ever, not after that. I've lost all heart for it. Francis'll have to get used to it.' She looked away, her face full of pain.

'You've two lovely children, Net,' Rachel pointed out.

'Count your blessings? Is that what you're saying?' Netta's voice was bitter, but only a little.

'No. Well, yes. I s'pose. Before you had Patsy you never even knew if . . . Well, if you'd have one at all.'

'I know.' She sat up, reached for a hanky and blew her nose, then stared bleakly ahead of her. 'It's just the saddest thing in the world, thinking there's going to be a new life, and then there isn't. Even when you've already got fine children.' She wiped her eyes again. 'I know I'll just have to get over it. I just need a little time – and not to hurt so in my body. Every twinge reminds me.'

'Oh, Net,' Rachel said.

Netta looked at her. 'Supposing your Tommy . . . I mean, I don't mean to be nasty, but d'you ever wish you hadn't had him?'

Rachel wanted to rush into saying, *No, of course not!* She searched her heart. 'There have been moments,' she said. 'Yes, there have. I suppose really, I don't wish I'd never had him – he's my little man and I can't imagine life without him. I just wish he'd been born different – just normal, with a better chance so I wouldn't have to worry so much about him.'

The two girls looked tearfully at each other. When Mrs O'Shaughnessy brought the tea up, she found them holding each other in a sympathetic embrace.

By the time Rachel got home, Gladys told her that Danny had been in and gone out again.

'Down the pub, I think,' she said, sounding very annoyed. 'I thought you'd gone out to meet him. Where the hell did you get to?'

Rachel explained what had happened and Gladys's face softened. 'Oh, the poor wench,' she said. 'She's not had a lot of luck, that one.'

When Danny got back later, fresh from beer and male company and a degree or two more cheerful, she explained to him what had happened.

'Oh well, can't be helped,' he said, whether about her missing him or about Netta's baby she was not sure. She thought they might make love later, at least be close for a little while, but as soon as he got into bed he fell into a deep, snoring sleep. She sat and looked down at him feeling as if she couldn't win, as if every time she tried to meet him, she missed him.

The week went on like that. Tommy had a cold and was restless at night, waking because he could not breathe through his nose and she had to get up and pacify him. Once it was just as she and Danny had begun kissing in bed. Hearing the grizzling sounds from the floor below, Rachel stiffened.

'I'll have to go,' she said. 'He won't stop now.'

Danny rolled away from her cursing angrily. By the time she had settled Tommy down, Danny was asleep once more. When they got up in the morning, they were like strangers and did not speak. As the week went on Danny became more silent than ever, yet she sensed that something was building up in him. She felt as if he was a ticking bomb, just waiting to go off, and however much she wanted to try, she had no idea what to do to make him feel better.

On Sunday morning they had some time alone together. Danny had been out with Gladys at the market the day before, but Sunday meant church. It was a horrible day, the rain tippling down and the yard filling with puddles. Gladys put on her best frock, her coat and hat and off she went under an umbrella. Rachel looked out glumly. She had hoped they might get out, go for a walk, that maybe Danny would carry Tommy. Pushing the chair was slow going and she knew Danny hated being seen out with it. But there was no hope of a walk either way.

By the time the bit of breakfast was cleared away, the morning seemed to yawn ahead with nothing to fill it.

'What can I do, Mom?' Melly moaned. 'I'm bored.'

Rachel took a deep breath. She felt exhausted and tense. Danny was just sitting smoking, in his own world, not making any attempt to join in with the children or responding much to anything she said.

'I don't know, Melly,' she snapped. Melanie was usually such a good girl but she was picking up everyone else's tiredness and the tension in the room. 'You'll have to sit quiet for a bit. Get your little pad of paper out and do a drawing – or play with Tommy.'

'Tommy can't play,' Melly said mutinously. She sat at the table with her head on one hand and a sulky face. 'I wish I had a *proper* brother.'

Without really meaning to, or knowing she was going to do it, Rachel lashed out and slapped Melly hard on the arm. 'Don't say that about your brother! How dare you say that? You know he can't help it.'

Melly started to cry. 'I dain't mean it,' she sobbed. 'Only I wish Tommy could play with me and he could run around. I wish Cissy was here! I got no one to play with . . .'

Tommy was starting to snivel now. He was sensitive to other people's moods and on the whole if they were smiling he was too.

As she started to comfort Melly and say she was sorry for hitting her, Rachel saw Danny get up and go to the door. He lifted his coat from the hook.

'Where're you going?' she cried, panic rising in her. Of all weeks, when she was trying to get through to him, she needed him to stay here. I'm trying to get to you, a voice screamed inside her. Only things keep getting in the way – can't you see that?

'Out,' he said, without looking at her. 'I'm going. I've had enough.'

'Oh, Danny, don't,' she pleaded. 'Please stay – I need you here.'

'Do you?' He turned to her, holding his cap. His face was hard and aggressive. 'What d'you need me for, eh?'

'I just . . . Of course I need you here . . .' Her voice was high and tearful as she went to him. 'Just stay in and help me,' she begged. 'Just be with us, Danny – please.'

'I said, I'm going.' He seemed like a complete stranger.

'Going?' she said, not understanding. 'Oh, Danny, *please*. Tell me what to do to make things better. You're so . . . You've changed . . .' She burst into tears.

'*I've* changed?' he said furiously. 'That's rich coming from you. You're not the woman I married. You're just . . .' He struggled for words and they burst out angrily. 'You don't need me – you don't need anyone! You're . . . You're like someone else – and as for him –' He nodded at Tommy. 'He's all you ever think about! *Look* at him! He's a wrong'un – what use is he ever gonna be to anyone? He's never gonna be able to even wipe his own arse!'

'Danny! How can you be so . . .' But she was choking on her words and Danny was turning away.

'I can't stand it.' He spoke with his back to her. 'For four years, every day of that, all I dreamt about was coming home to you. To my girl – the girl I married. And when I got here – nothing's the same. You're not the same . . .'

'Danny,' she pleaded. 'I know some things've changed, but I've not changed really . . .' She raised her voice as her own hurt and rage poured out. 'I've had to do all this on my own. And I did my dreaming too, you know! I dreamt of my husband coming home – a husband who'd help me and look after me. The man I married who was kind and who'd be at my side . . . And where's he gone – eh?' Her voice rose to a shriek. 'All you ever think about is *you* and how *you* feel! What about me? What about your kids, Danny? You're not the only one who went through the war, you know.'

Danny stood very still. Then he reached out for the door latch.

'Daddy . . .' Melly said in a small, frightened voice.

Danny pulled the door open. The sound of rain came suddenly louder. 'I can't.' He stepped outside.

'Go on, Danny –' She was still shouting, beside herself now. 'You be a *real* man and run away – just bugger off and desert your kids. Who cares, eh? Someone else'll look after them. Not your sodding problem, is it?'

But he kept walking. Rachel went to the door and, past caring who heard, screamed after him. 'That's it, Danny – you go! Just like your dad did. Just like your own bloody marvellous father did!'

She flung her words like rocks at his departing back. And then he was gone, down the entry.

Forty-Six

'Well, I can't say I'm all that surprised,' Peggy said. 'Although it's absolutely disgusting. But if you marry from the other side of the tracks the way you did, Rachel, that's often what happens – you can't say I didn't warn you. I never liked the look of him – and as for that aunt of his . . .'

Rachel sat opposite her mother, numbly listening to this with her head bowed. It was a fortnight since that rainy morning when Danny walked out. In that time Rachel had not seen Peggy, or told her what had happened. Eventually Gladys said to her:

'Look – you ought to go over to your mother. And Melly ought to see her cousin.' Cissy was in fact Melanie's aunt, but they always called them cousins. 'Leave the lad with me and take her over. You'll have to tell them sometime.'

Of course at first they all thought he would come back the same day, when he had cooled down. When he didn't, Rachel had gone to Summer Lane the next afternoon to wait outside Coronet Cameras for the workers to come out at the end of the day. Her heart banged like a crazed drum as the first ones appeared. But though she waited until the factory must long have been empty,

Danny was not among them. She walked home, despair seeping through her. It took several more days, still expecting him to walk into the yard, before she really saw that he was not coming back. With every day that passed, she knew this with more certainty. All her anger at his lack of care and understanding towards her seeped away. Every moment of every day, she ached for him to come back to her, Danny, her darling Danny who she loved and had waited for all these years. Surely he could not really have gone forever? She was constantly in a state, every moment expecting him to appear at the door.

Sitting here now under the barrage of her mother's words, she had no defence to offer for herself or for him.

'Rach?' Cissy came up to her, her round, pink face full of a question she wanted answered. She leaned up against Rachel's shoulder and looked winningly at her. Rachel found this comforting, but Peggy admonished her.

'For heaven's sake, Cissy, don't go throwing yourself on people like that – they don't want you.'

Cissy froze, a hurt expression on her face, and started to withdraw, but Rachel put her arm around her little sister.

'It's all right, Ciss,' she said. 'Course I want you.' She gave her sister's plump body an affectionate squeeze and Cissy brightened a fraction again. Rachel burned inside at the memory of their mother's capacity to hurt and reject. Fred Horton still doted on his little girl but now that Cissy was past the baby stage and the novelty had worn off, Peggy was reverting to her true colours. Rachel felt very protective of her little sister. Melly had come up as well and the two girls looked as if they were plotting something together.

'What, Ciss?'

'Can I come and sleep at your house again?' Cissy pleaded. She had come back with Rachel once, some time ago, to share the bed with Melanie and Tommy and thought it a great adventure.

'All right, maybe next time I come – in a . . . a couple of weeks?' She looked at her mother, glad to get off the subject of Danny, about whom there seemed to be no possibility of anything good to say. Every mention of him felt like a stab wound.

Peggy nodded. 'I suppose,' she said wearily. 'I don't know why you want to go and sleep in that slum of a place, Cissy, but I suppose, if you must . . .' Rachel knew that whatever Peggy said, she was glad of a break from mothering and as often as possible.

Cissy and Melanie were all smiles. 'I'll bring Lolly!' she said. Lolly was her raggy doll. The two of them scuttled away to make plans.

On the way home, Melanie, who seemed happier for the visit, looked up at Rachel as they were waiting for the bus.

'Mom?' she said cautiously. 'Is our dad ever coming back? Only I don't know what to say to Cissy about it. Or to Mavis.' Mavis was her best friend at school.

Touched on the raw again by this question, Rachel wanted to scream back at her – how the hell should *I* know? Rage and hurt welled up in her. She took a deep breath and tried to be kinder, and more reasonable. God forbid, however bad things got, she should start acting like her own mother.

'I don't know, Melly. I wish I did. But it doesn't look like it, does it? I suppose you could tell your friends that he's had to go away for a bit – for work. If you have to tell them anything.'

Melanie's eyes filled with tears. 'Is it because of

Tommy?' she asked. 'Is it me? Did I do something bad?'

'Oh, babby –' Rachel squatted down beside her as the traffic rumbled past. 'No – it's not you.' This was true, she knew. 'You're your dad's little girl. It's just . . .' What could she say? Grief swelled in her throat. 'The war did some bad things to people. Made them different from how they were before. I think the war did bad things to your dad.'

Melly was listening, her eyes wide and hurt.

'It's not your fault. I don't think it's mine, or Tommy's either. It's just something that's happened, that's all.'

But deep down, she did think it was her fault. She had not been understanding enough of the state Danny was in, or of how much she had changed herself. And she had been so wrapped up in Tommy that she had not put Danny first. She had ruined everything. But she never meant to, she kept thinking as she cried herself to sleep in bed every night. She had just been trying to do her best.

Everyone in the yard had been kind, in their own fashion. Even Ma Jackman said in her acid way, 'I'm sorry for yer, bab. You're back where you started.' Rachel knew that she meant as if the war was still on. The way Ma Jackman was herself, only now she knew that Edwin was never coming back. The odd thing was that although Rachel was full of pain and the deep hurt and disappointment of it, it was all so familiar. She and Gladys and the children were back where they had been before, just trying to keep going.

Gladys was alternately full of grief, anger and shame

for her nephew's actions. Rachel had never seen her so upset.

'I never thought I'd see flesh and blood of mine behave like this,' she said to Rachel, soon after Danny went. She was brim full of emotion, finding it hard to settle to anything. 'If I could get hold of him now . . . By God, I'd give him what for. He's his father's son, all right – and I hoped I'd never say that. Mary'll be turning in her grave, that she will.'

Dolly was full of kind indignation. Netta was sweet and upset for her, while suffering her own grief as well.

'You'll let me know if there's anything I can do, won't you?' she said sweetly. 'Anything at all.' Rachel knew she meant it, but what was there that anyone could do? There was no one who could repair her lost love – all the dreams of the future that she had clung to through the war now lay at her feet like a pile of ashes.

The only person who was not kind or sympathetic was Irene.

A few days after Danny went, when it became clear he was not coming back, she waltzed up to Rachel in the yard, when she was out hanging washing.

'What's this about your feller taking off?' she demanded.

Rachel turned to her, already tense with fury at her tone of voice.

'What's what?' she said, angrily shaking out a frock she had just put through the mangle. She felt geared up to belt Irene one. She could feel the force of her temper rising in her.

'I heard he's cleared off – days ago.'

Irene sounded smug, as if she was enjoying all this as

a piece of gossip. Rachel rammed a wooden peg onto the line at each shoulder of the dress. Behind Irene, she saw Evie wandering across the yard, looking cowed as usual.

'Well, has 'e?' Irene crossed her arms.

'What's it to you?' Rachel asked. 'Look –' She nodded at Evie who was squatting down, pushing something into her mouth. 'Why don't you look after your daughter for once instead of keeping on at me?'

'Evie!' Irene yelled at her. 'Gerroff of that – what're yow putting in yower mouth? You put that down or I'll lamp yer!' She went over and gave the little girl's hand a vicious slap. Evie dropped whatever it was she had been about to chew and slunk away down the yard. She did not cry, Rachel noticed.

'So,' Irene said again. 'Your feller's taken off then, has 'e? I hear 'e's been gone a few days now and no sign of him coming back. So – about time yow stopped looking down your nose at me and Ray, I'd say.'

'What the hell're you on about?' Rachel said, finally losing her temper. 'What's any of this got to do with you and Ray? I couldn't give a kipper's dick about either of you so leave me alone. You want to stop keeping on about your cowing drunk of a husband and look after that kid of yours!'

She picked up the bucket and started to move away.

'Well, at least I can keep my feller,' Irene bawled after her.

'Oh,' Rachel mocked. 'Really? He may be under your roof, but how many other women's beds is he in and out of – eh?'

Dolly appeared at her door. 'What's going on?' she shouted, hands on hips.

'Nothing you need to know about, yer nosy cow!' Irene retorted, with a furious shriek.

Before Irene could come back at her, Rachel stormed into the house and slammed the door. Sitting at the table, she allowed the sobs to rise in her.

Forty-Seven

21 April 1946

'So you mean, you're having a bit of a celebration, a year on, sort of thing?'

Dolly was sitting at the table and watching with a puzzled expression as Gladys poured cake mix into two tins, brown and sticky and dotted with raisins and sultanas, the fruit of saved rations and scrimping. Their delicious aroma was already filling the room.

Gladys licked a finger. 'Yes – sort of thing.' She stared at the cake tins, as if her mind was on something else.

'For Easter, you mean?' Dolly said.

'That too. Just a bit of a party.'

As Rachel passed behind Gladys, Dolly gave her a look as if to say, *Party? What on earth does she think there is to celebrate?* It seemed very strange. Danny had been gone now for over a month. It didn't seem like a time for festivities. And – the first shock of the day – Gladys had stayed home and missed church *on Easter Day* to bake cakes! This was unheard of. Dolly had drifted in mid-morning to see Rachel and exclaimed in surprise at seeing the baking in full spate.

'Well, I'm glad you've got the energy, is all,' Dolly said, sitting back, pushing her ribs out to try and catch her breath over her very swollen belly.

'Are we having a party?' Rachel heard Cissy, who was staying over with them, say excitedly to Melanie. They were watching the cake preparations with great interest. Tommy was in his chair as usual. 'Is it someone's birthday?'

'It's the end of the war, silly,' Melly said.

'What're you on about?' Rachel said. 'The war's been over a year!' She thought of Danny. 'Well, months, anyway.'

'Is it going to be a street party?' Cissy said, bouncing on her toes with excitement. 'With tables and jelly and fizzy pop?'

Everyone laughed at this, but Rachel said, 'It's not for the whole yard, is it, Auntie?' So far as she was concerned she didn't want to go anywhere near flaming Irene Sutton. She felt hurt that Gladys thought there was anything to celebrate while she spent every night crying and struggled through each day feeling leaden and hopeless.

'No, *no*,' Gladys said. 'Nothing like that – just us.' She straightened up from sliding the cake tins into the oven and looked at Dolly. 'A little way of saying thank you, that's all. For all you've done for me over the years.'

'Oh, Glad, don't talk daft,' Dolly said. 'We're pals. Nothing to say thank you for.'

'The boys can come.'

'What – *all* of them? Are you sure?'

Gladys smiled. 'Course. If there's cake about they'll be here anyway, won't they?'

'They can sniff it out miles away,' Dolly laughed. Then she grimaced, laying a hand on her belly. 'Ow – it's kicking me! Not long now, thank God – I bet the little so-and-so'll be late coming though.'

*

By tea time, two large cakes sparsely dotted with fruit were on the table, surrounded by thinly cut sandwiches. It reminded Rachel, painfully now, of the day she had gone round, the day of Dolly's birthday tea. That felt like another life now. She was bewildered by the whole occasion. Gladys had not warned her before that morning that this was what she was planning, nor had she asked for any help. She had sprung it on them all and then got on and prepared everything with a quiet, almost reverent determination. She had even bought a tin of salmon for the sandwiches. Her best embroidered cloth was on the table. The big crock teapot had been brought down from the shelf and the pretty one, like a country cottage, and all the best cups and plates were laid on the table. Dolly promised to bring a few extra ones.

Before anyone came, Gladys went upstairs, reappearing later in a peacock-blue frock that Rachel had never seen before. Her hair was brushed and swept up high on her head and she was wearing deep-red lipstick. As she came into the room, Rachel and Melly both gasped.

'Auntie – you look *ever* so nice!' Melly cried.

'Ta, kid,' Gladys said. 'There's no need to sound so amazed.'

To Rachel's surprise, she noticed that Gladys seemed very nervous. She was sorting out cups and knives by the table and several times she dropped something. One of the cups dropped to the floor and, by a miracle, did not smash.

'Let me do that, Auntie,' Rachel said. She was trying to put two and two together in her mind, but when she did she was not sure if she was getting four, three, or some other completely different number. She wondered, with a dawning of possibility, whether, on the quiet, Gladys had a new man she was about to introduce them to, a surprise guest. After all, Gladys went out and about, to the markets, the church, often on her own. And plenty of men were interested, Rachel could see. Was that what all this was about?

'D'you want me to get changed – smarten up a bit?' she asked. 'And the girls . . .?'

'Oh – only if you're in the mood,' Gladys said. She seemed absent-minded. 'There's no real need. I just . . . I wanted . . .' And she trailed off and never finished the sentence.

'All right,' Rachel said, thinking that she would maybe just tidy everyone's hair instead. She did not dare ask any more. 'Come on, girls –' She beckoned to Melly and Cissy, who could not seem to stop gazing at the table and the food on it. Their noses were twitching like a couple of terriers. 'Come and have your hair brushed.'

Dolly was the first to appear at the appointed time of four o'clock.

'Mo'll be here in a tick,' she said. 'But I thought you might need a bit of a hand, Glad?' She looked at the newly tidied room, the beautiful table, Tommy all scrubbed up in his chair and the little girls and Rachel with ribbons in their hair. 'It doesn't look as if you do, though! Ooh – this looks nice! And don't you look a picture, Glad –' She stood admiring Gladys's dress. Rachel could see the baffled look in her eyes but she did not ask any more. 'That's beautiful, that is. Sorry about the state of me – I'd've dressed up if I could fit into anything!'

'You look lovely as ever, Dolly,' Gladys said. 'Come on – you have a seat. I'll brew up in a minute.'

The big kettle and another pan of water were steaming

away on the stove. Gladys warmed the teapot and started spooning tea.

'So come on, Glad, put us out of our misery – what's all this in aid of?' Dolly said, obviously deciding on the direct approach.

Gladys had her back to them. The vivid blue dress showed off her voluptuous curves, and she had an apron tied over the top.

'You'll see,' she said. Once again, Rachel could hear the nerves in her voice and Dolly picked it up too. Their eyes met and Rachel shrugged. Dolly rolled her eyes.

'Well, you are a woman of mystery,' Dolly teased. 'Come on, Glad – there can't be much you can have kept a secret from me after all this time. Spit it out then – who is 'e?' Dolly had obviously had the same thought as her, Rachel realized.

Gladys laughed suddenly, turning to them. 'A feller, you mean? Ach – no. Tried a few of those, dain't I? Never again – oh, no. Not worth it. I want a quiet life, I do. Anyone can bend down and pick up nothing.'

Rachel and Dolly exchanged glances again, as if to say, *Well, that's telling us.* Gladys popped the lid on the teapot, slipped the cosy over it and carried it to the table. At that moment a bedlam of Morrison boys erupted into the yard and a few seconds later they were clustered around the door. The youngest, Freddie, was now eight.

'Hang on, hang on, yer little buggers – wait for me . . .' They heard Mo come lumbering along behind. 'Now you watch your manners or you'll be out on your ears . . .' He and the eldest boy, Ernie, had each brought a chair with them and Reggie, the middle boy, was carrying an orange crate. 'Look, you can't all fit through the door at once. Have some sense . . .'

'Come on in, lads,' Gladys said. 'Come and have a bit

of tea.' She went and switched the wireless on and big band music streamed out in the background.

'Cor – look at all them cakes!' Freddie exclaimed with all the food-obsessed glee of an eight-year-old.

Rachel watched Tommy as the boys crowded into the room. His face lit up and he started squirming in his chair with excitement. The girls, however, retreated to one corner of the room as if rumours of plague had just arrived. The Morrison boys were good-natured, all of them, but as far as Melly was concerned, and Cissy especially, they were *boys* and best avoided.

'Well, this is very nice, Glad,' Mo said, easing his capacious backside down onto one of the chairs as if he was afraid it would collapse under him. 'Very nice indeed. Knock it off, Reggie,' he instructed number three, who was fourteen. 'Leave Freddie alone. Right, lads –' Mo held up a thick finger in admonishment – 'I ain't going to say it again. Mrs Poulter has made us a very nice tea and you lot can sit down and behave yourselves, or –' He jabbed his thumb towards the door.

The youngest children sat on the rug by the fire and Gladys poured tea and everyone munched on the sandwiches, egg and jam for the children, the tinned salmon ones reserved for the adults, while the music played softly from the wireless.

'You make sure you get one or two of those, Dolly,' Gladys said, holding the plate out to her. 'It's good for the baby.'

'Ta, Glad.' She looked down at herself. 'It's getting to the stage when there ain't much room in here for food!'

'You eat, wench,' Mo instructed. 'We've got to keep you strong.'

'Huh,' Dolly said. Then she smiled, looking around. 'It's funny to think – this time last year the war was still on and we never knew when it was all going to be over, did we?'

'We knew it was coming by then,' Mo said.

'Yes, but that waiting – and then, when the news came . . .'

'Ah – that were a good day,' Mo said. 'All the lads down the Salutation . . .'

Dolly rolled her eyes. 'That sounds like any other day to me.' She and Gladys smiled. Rachel was sitting beside Tommy to help him enjoy the party. No one mentioned Danny. What was there to say that they had not already said? She looked across at Gladys. Beneath the smiling and celebration, she could still see the tension bunched up in her.

'Cissy, Melly,' she whispered. 'Offer round some of the cake.'

Cissy looked very reluctant and Rachel realized that her little sister really needed to come over more often. She was shut up in that flat with their mother and Fred far too much. Melly was used to the Morrison boys. She got up and took a plate of cake round, bossing them about. 'Only *one* bit, Eric . . .'

They sat enjoying the spread and reminiscing about the war, some of which, now it was all over, took on the memory of an adventure – the nights in the shelters, the wreckage they found when they ventured out in the mornings, all the anxious, frightening times they had lived through.

As the children ate, the noise in the room increased more and more.

'It's no good feeding 'em,' Dolly said, smiling round at her bunch of now very lively lads. 'It only gives 'em ideas.'

'You lot,' Mo ordered. 'Out – go and have a run-round.'

Melanie came over to Rachel. 'Can Cissy and me go out too? Rita and Shirl're outside.'

'Yes – off you go,' Rachel said.

The room went suddenly quiet, only the adults remaining, and Tommy, still slowly eating scraps of his tea. He could feed himself well now, with his right hand.

Rachel looked at Gladys, seated at the head of the table. She was taking in shallow, nervous breaths. After a few moments, she drew herself up straighter, as if collecting herself.

'Right,' she said. Everyone looked at her. 'Now all the young'uns have gone, I'd like to tell you all summat. I dain't ask you all round here just to talk about the war.' She got up and clicked off the wireless. It felt very quiet. Gladys laid a hand over her heart and took another breath.

'What's up?' Dolly leaned forward. 'Are you all right, Glad?'

'I will be,' Gladys said. 'Only I want to tell you summat that I should've done years back. Rach – go upstairs for me, will you? On my bed you'll find a little box. Bring it down for me, bab.'

Forty-Eight

This was another shock. Rachel had never had reason to go into Gladys's bedroom before. Pushing open the door, which was always kept so firmly closed, she wondered for a second whether she was going to walk into some surprise, some secret Gladys had been keeping all these years. But what she saw, glancing around, was a simple, tidy room which Gladys had always kept as her most private place, in the way that she seemed to keep so much about herself private.

Dark blue curtains hung at the window. There was a small, rectangular rug on the floor of a Chinese design she had seen sold at the market, a dressing table with Gladys's tortoiseshell hairbrush and comb laid on it alongside a box of talcum powder. There were a few hairpins and kirby grips lying about and several strings of coloured beads dangled over one corner of the mirror. There was a dark wardrobe, one wooden chair and the bed, covered by a spread of deep red chenille. Resting in the middle, in the slight sag of the mattress, was a cardboard shoebox, plain and battered at the corners. Not wanting Gladys to think she might be delaying to peep inside, she picked it up at once and carried it downstairs. It had a certain weight, but was not heavy.

Everyone else's eyes fixed on it as she came in and placed it on the table in front of Gladys, resplendent in her exotic blue dress. Rachel felt her heart beating fast, as though Gladys's nerves were catching.

'Well,' Gladys said, her cheeks flushed. 'There's a few things I want to get off my chest.' She didn't open the box. For a few seconds she closed her eyes and Rachel couldn't decide whether she had suddenly changed her mind, or was perhaps praying, composing herself. At last she looked up again, across the room, not at anyone in particular.

'It's almost to the day, but not quite,' she said. 'Thirty years. It should be the nineteenth of April, not the twenty-first, but I kept it for the weekend. But on the nineteenth, last Friday, my boy would have had his thirtieth birthday.' Seeing their uncomprehending faces, she went on: 'April the nineteenth, nineteen sixteen, he was born. His name was Alfred John. Alfie, he always was to me. My little Alfie.'

Tears rose in Gladys's eyes for a moment, but she wiped them swiftly away, as if to say, *No, not yet – I haven't finished.*

'Glad?' Dolly spoke gently, but there was a hurt bewilderment in her voice. 'You had a boy, of your own? Is that what you're telling us? And you've never said, in all this time?'

Rachel felt things jolting into place in her mind. No wonder Gladys knew exactly how to care for a baby, was so fierce about holding onto family . . . She sat listening, stunned.

'His father never saw him,' Gladys went on. 'We married in 1915, but by the time I had Alfie, he'd passed on.'

Immediately, everyone's eyes turned to the faded photograph on the mantelpiece, of the pale, smiling soldier. Rachel saw Mo shake his head sorrowfully. Two of his brothers had gone away in 1915 and never come back. She noticed that the black crêpe was no longer draped around the picture. At last, perhaps, Gladys was going to talk about him.

'Your Harry,' Dolly said softly.

'I know what you're all thinking.' Gladys's voice was quiet and very sad. 'And I've let you because – well, I couldn't stand to talk about any of it. It was just to let you think . . .' She paused a moment. Looking at the photograph she went on: 'That's not Harry. My Harry looked nothing like that. That picture's of my brother John. There were four of us and he was the oldest – John, Mary, me and Albert. John was killed on the Somme, in 1916.'

Mo made a tutting sound and shook his head sadly. No one knew what to say. The only sound came from Tommy rattling his little toys on his tray and the distant shrieks of the children outside.

Gladys lifted the lid from the box and laid it carefully to one side. 'This was Harry.'

She brought out a photograph and they all saw a broad-shouldered man with thick, dark hair, a bushy moustache and laughing eyes. Immediately, Rachel could see that he looked a match for Gladys in a way that the slim soldier on the mantelpiece did not. He was dressed in a suit, not an army uniform.

'Harry never went to war – they needed him here,' she went on. 'He was at Kynoch's – he knew all about the chemicals that went into the bombs. That's where I met him. I worked there at the beginning of the war, until we married and then I got out – thank the Lord. It would've finished me off like it did some of the other girls. I never felt properly well when I was there and your skin'd go yellow ... None of us felt right after a spell there. Any road, Harry and I married in September 1915. I was already expecting.' She looked down for a second, embarrassed. 'I'm not proud of the fact – it just ... Well, that was how it was. That winter, we had the blackout – we had it in that war too. Harry was coming home from work and he was knocked down and killed by a tram. I'll never know how he didn't hear it coming. No time to say goodbye, nothing. Married five months and that was that. We were living in Erdington. We had quite a nice little house on his wages – better than this anyway.' She glanced around the room. 'I had to get out, of course. I couldn't keep up the rent on my own, so I moved back in with my mother and father. Albert, my brother, was still at home – he was ten or eleven. My Alfie was born in the April. We would have been all right. I was grieving for Harry, but my mother was a good soul. She looked after Alfie and I went back to work – not at Kynoch's, though. I couldn't have stood it, thinking I saw Harry everywhere.'

For a moment she looked around at them, as if needing reassurance. Everyone was listening, rapt.

'Oh, Glad,' Dolly said.

'Things went along all right for a bit. Then, within the year both my parents died. My father's heart gave out. My mother was never the same after. She died of the Spanish influenza. If she hadn't been so low in herself I believe to this day that she'd have withstood it – she was a strong woman, our mother.' She was talking swiftly now, as if not wanting to dwell on those times. 'By the end of the war there was just me and my sister Mary, with Albert and the baby. Mary was keeping us by and large. I had Alfie at home and I did outwork and bits of anything I could. We moved into a much poorer place

– a little way from here. Mary was doing factory work, and Albert left school and started work at thirteen. We were getting on all right. And then it came back – the influenza. Just when we thought it was over.'

Rachel felt a cold dread grip her as Gladys spoke. She could see what was coming. Echoing through her head suddenly came a skipping rhyme from the school yard:

> *I had a little bird,*
> *its name was Enza.*
> *I opened up the window*
> *and in-flu-enza.*

'I was the only one who never got it. Mary and Albert were very bad with it. I thought we were going to lose Mary. Alfie was all right to begin with. And then he went down with it as well. There was no money coming in. I was at my wits' end.'

'Oh God,' Dolly breathed. 'How on earth did you manage, Glad?'

Gladys kept her gaze on the table. Her face flushed. 'I got by for a time. This and that.'

No one asked, but in that moment Rachel saw the man near the market, calling out in that nasty, familiar way, *Polly*. He would never forget Polly, with those eyes of hers. Polly, working to feed her sick family and keep her baby alive. Rachel felt choked with sadness. She sought out Gladys's eyes and for a moment they exchanged a silent look. She could see that Gladys knew she remembered. And she knew that they would never speak of it.

'I did everything I could. I had the doctor in, found the money for all that. Mary and Albert came through it. But my little Alfie . . . I was up with him day and night.

440

But the Angel of Death wanted my little one. He breathed his last in my arms.'

Gladys reached into the box and brought out another picture. 'Here he is. My little man.' She laid the picture carefully on the table. 'And these were his.' Beside the picture she placed a soft little pair of black leather infant shoes. Finally, from the box, she brought out a locket and opened it to show a dark brown curl of hair.

'I moved away,' Gladys went on, 'to the other side of town, to Ladywood. I left Mary and Albert. I never saw them, not for several years. And I never said a word – not to anyone. I thought if I opened my mouth, started telling anyone about my Harry and Alfie, I'd fall to pieces. Everyone was forever on about the war dead. My Harry was one of them, but there was no child marching for him on Empire Day, up at the front of the procession. No child left to do it . . .' She picked up the picture of Alfie and held it up to them. Rachel saw a big-eyed child's face, a corona of dark curls, a little lad dressed all in white. Danny, Rachel thought, with a wrench of pain inside her. God, he was so like Danny . . .

'That was my war baby,' Gladys said. She nodded at Rachel. 'I know – our Danny's the image of him, almost. Later, after Mary married Wilfred and we were back in touch, I started to help out with her kids. I'd moved over here by then to be near them. I've always looked out for Danny, poor lad.' In a desolate voice she added. 'And now he's gone.'

Rachel heard a snuffle to her left, then the trumpeting sound of a man blowing his nose, and she realized, touched, that Mo was in a watery state, wiping his eyes. Dolly, also very emotional, hauled herself up and leaned over to embrace Gladys as she sat at the table.

'Oh, Glad,' she said. 'Fancy you keeping all this in for all these years. But I'm glad you've told us now.'

Gladys leaned into her and closed her eyes. 'Oh – I'm sorry,' she said, as her own tears started to flow. 'I just . . . All this time. I don't know why really. I thought one day I'd tell everyone, once we were all together, Danny home, and everything right somehow . . . But now he's gone again and I can't bear it . . . But it was Alfie's birthday again and I just wanted you all to know . . .' She couldn't manage any more words. Leaning her head on the table, as Dolly lovingly stroked her shoulder, Gladys sobbed from the bottom of her heart.

When things had calmed, they sat chatting, the room full of a gentle atmosphere of love and sympathy for Gladys.

'I wish you'd told me, Glad,' Dolly said, her own eyes still red from crying with her friend. 'You didn't have to shut it away all this time – it was nothing to be ashamed of.'

'It was a terrible, black time,' Gladys said. 'I didn't want it all dug up again, or have pictures about to remind me . . . I knew if I kept that photograph of John on the mantel, everyone would think I was a war widow and that'd be that. No more to be said. I wanted to put the past behind me. And when Mary had her family – I was very fond of those kids, Danny especially. When Wilf took them all off and wouldn't say where – well, it was like the same thing happening again. As if they'd all died.'

Rachel ached with sadness. Did Danny have any idea what Gladys felt for him, even now? Or of what he had done to her, to all of them, by disappearing once again? Hearing Gladys's story, she was now full of a warmth of gratitude for her own life, for her children. She reached out to stroke the soft skin of Tommy's arm. Even though her son was not like other little boys, his body not working the way it should be, even though his prospects were not bright, here he was, alive and so lovable. And she had Melly, her sweet, solemn little girl. Despite everything, she felt overwhelmed by good fortune compared with Gladys, and grateful to Gladys for all she had given her.

As Dolly and Mo got up to leave, they said their goodbyes tenderly. Mo squeezed Gladys's shoulder.

'You always know where we are if you need anything, don't yer, wench?'

Gladys nodded and smiled up at him, almost shy suddenly. 'You've always been the best, Mo. I'd never leave this yard while you're here. I don't know what I'd've done without you and Dolly.'

'See you tomorrow, bab.' Dolly kissed Gladys and they gave each other an emotional look. 'And don't bottle it all up next time. We know you're upset about Danny, both of you –' Her troubled eyes took in Rachel as well. 'It's not a crime to let on, you know.'

They left, and Gladys got up and started briskly clearing the table, her back to the room. Rachel watched her, aching at all she had told them.

'I wish you'd said, Auntie,' she dared to begin.

'Well, I have said now, haven't I?' Gladys replied. Her voice was still thick from crying. She didn't turn round and she obviously didn't want to talk about it any more.

'I'll have to get Cissy back to Mom's,' Rachel said. She had told Peggy she would bring Cissy back that Sunday evening in time for school the next day.

'Yes – you go on over,' Gladys agreed.

'I expect Melly'll want to come . . .'

Normally Gladys might have quibbled about spending another fare unnecessarily, but she just nodded. Rachel went to the door to call the girls inside. The sun was going down and the yard was now full of shadows, stirred up by the energetic movements of children. Cooking smells were coming from the other houses. She thought she saw a cluster of girls up at the far end.

'Melanie, Cissy!' she called. Two figures broke away from the little group of children down near the wire factory and moved, with seeming reluctance, along the yard. 'I've got to get you home, Ciss,' Rachel said.

'Coming . . .' They hurried a few steps. Then they slowed, as they reached the lamp post in the middle, then stopped. For a second Rachel thought they were trying to defy her, but then she saw that they were riveted by the sight of something. Whatever it was, it was coming along the entry and Rachel could not see from where she was standing. She stepped outside.

'Come on, you two,' she called, more loudly.

Cissy started to move, but Melanie was completely rooted to the spot.

'Dad?' she breathed.

Rachel felt the hard prod of her heartbeat, the way it speeded up. In the uncertain light of dusk she saw a figure come round from the entry. She noticed three things: the unkempt hair, the froth of something white in his left hand, and some other thing, tucked against the right side of his chest, something small and partly white. She, herself, could not seem to move.

'Dad!' Melly ran forward. 'Dad!' She flung herself at him, her arms around his waist.

'Danny?' Rachel breathed. 'Oh my God – Danny!'

Other emotions would come later: sorrow and anger and questions would pour out. But in this moment, here he was, her Danny, and all she could feel was a huge rush of relief and joy.

'Oh!' Melly squealed. 'Look, Ciss, it's a puppy! Oh, Dad, is it ours – can we keep it?'

'Hey, hey – steady.' Danny squatted down and Rachel saw the little creature leap from his arms, a stumpy little white tail wagging madly as it jumped up at everyone in sight. Melanie was giggling ecstatically and Cissy came to join in. Soon all the children in the yard were crowding round the little Jack Russell.

'He's for you, Melly,' Danny said. 'And your brother, of course,' he added.

Melanie was beside herself with excitement. 'Oh, he's lovely! He's mine, Cissy! What's his name?'

'Patch,' Danny said. 'Look – on his back.' The little dog's face was mainly black and his body white, but for a lozenge of black fur all across his back, almost like a saddle. 'That's got to be his name, right?'

'Patch!' the girls chirruped.

'Careful with him,' Danny instructed. The little dog took off across the yard, the girls squealing behind him.

Danny straightened up and saw Rachel waiting, her arms folded, smiling a little in spite of herself. No matter about all the hurt, the rage, the grief, the sight of him was what she wanted, what made her smile.

'Rach?' He came closer to her.

'So –' She put on a stern voice. 'You're back, are you?' She nodded towards the dog. 'Well, if that's Patch – are you Jack now then?'

A vulnerable, sorry look came over Danny's face. He looked down, then back at her and said, 'I dunno, Rach. But I hope so – I really do.' He held out the white froth of blossom to her – lilac, in perfect bloom. 'Here – I picked these for you.'

Rachel took them, smelling their strong perfume, and cradled them against her. She went to their door. 'Auntie,' she called. 'You'd better come out.'

Gladys appeared at the door. She took one look at Danny, who stood shamefaced before her, folded her arms and in a tone of enraged affection, said, 'And where the hell d'you think *you've* been?'

Forty-Nine

It was quite late by the time Rachel and Danny managed to talk properly. Cissy, on seeing the puppy, declared that she was not going home, that she was in fact never going home again and Rachel had to march her, glowering, to the tram stop. Melanie did not beg to come – she was full of the novelty of her father and the puppy.

When they got to the Hortons', it was Peggy who answered the door.

'I don't *want* to come home,' Cissy fumed, still full of outrage. 'Melly's got a puppy and I want to live there forever.'

Peggy pursed her lips disapprovingly, but before she could say anything, Rachel said, 'Danny's home. He's just come back.'

'Oh, really – and for how long, I wonder?' Peggy said contemptuously. She took Cissy's hand and began to drag her away along the hall. 'Go on – upstairs, Cissy, and stop your blarting.' As Cissy thundered off upstairs, Peggy came back to the door. As usual, she was smartly dressed, in a black, swinging skirt and cream blouse. 'Well,' she declared, 'if he takes off again, don't come running to me for help.'

'Running to you?' Rachel flared at her. She felt

stronger suddenly, knowing Danny had come home. 'Why would I come running to you, *Mother*? When have you ever offered any help – to me or to anyone?'

Peggy drew herself up, stung. 'I don't think there's any call to talk to me like that,' she said. 'When I've strained every sinew in my body to be a mother to you.'

Cissy's voice bawled suddenly from the top of the stairs: 'I don't want to live here. I want to go and live with Rach and Melly and Tommy!'

Rachel glared at her mother in triumph and started to turn away.

'You ungrateful hussy!' Peggy called after her. 'You've never known what it is to struggle, that's your trouble.'

Rachel did not bother either to turn round or to reply.

She found everyone gathered around the fire at home. The little dog, having long been the centre of attention, was fast asleep on the rug. Just opening the door, seeing Danny there, she had to stop for a second and take it in, to remind herself that this was real – he actually was *here*.

'There's tea in the pot,' Gladys said. She seemed to have recovered her temper. 'Now – Melly. Up the wooden hill with you. And you, young man,' she said to Tommy.

'I'll help –' Danny sprang up.

Rachel looked at him in amazement. He seemed like a different person.

'I want to,' he said hesitantly. 'I want to make things better.'

Tears came to her eyes. She was still smarting from her mother's self-obsessed fury. 'You *can* make things better, Danny,' she said humbly. 'Every other day, from now on. But maybe not tonight. Let me just get them off, shall I?'

He nodded. It would be smoother for now if the children did things in a familiar way.

'Can Patch sleep with me and Tommy?' Melanie asked, gazing at the puppy with whom she was obviously already head over heels in love.

'No, not 'til he's a lot older,' Rachel said.

'He'll be up in the night,' Danny told her. 'And you don't want him cocking his leg on your bed, do you?'

'Ugh, no!' Melly giggled. 'Will he sleep by the fire?'

'He can sleep just where he is now,' Gladys said. 'Now go on, off you go – he'll still be here in the morning.'

Rachel lifted Tommy out of his chair. He already looked sleepy. Having a lot of people about delighted him, but also exhausted him.

'Goodnight, son,' Danny said. 'And you, Melly – goodnight.'

Rachel carried Tommy upstairs, her head still spinning with astonishment.

In bed together, at last, was the first time they embraced, as if all evening something was holding them apart – a need for privacy, hesitation on his part, and hurt and anger on hers, however much she wanted them to be close.

They did not make love – not straight away. There was too much between them for that. Danny had talked, as Rachel and Gladys sat with him by the dying fire. He had told them things – how he had done odd jobs in Birmingham for the first couple of weeks, earning enough for a cheap lodging room, how he had walked out of the city and worked on a farm, planting potatoes and cleaning out ditches.

'That's where the dog came from,' he said. 'They had ratting dogs and one of them was almost ready to have her pups. Mr Blunden, the farmer, said he might keep one but he'd drown the rest. When she had them, I saw the one with the patch –' He looked down at the tiny puppy, a smile on his lips. 'I knew he was the one and I said save that one for me – I'll work for you for a couple more weeks 'til you wean him. And then I came back here. It was a bit soon for this little'un to part from his mom, but we'll have to look after him . . I had to get back to you.'

Now, as they lay in candlelight together, she on her side, facing him, he said, 'I haven't told Auntie – not yet. I will. But – Rach . . .' He turned to face her and she could see the intensity in his eyes.

'What?' she said. She was not full of softness – not yet. She needed him to explain himself.

'I'm sorry for leaving you. More than sorry, Rach. I hardly know how to say it – I'm *ashamed*. When I got back, from out East . . . It was just, everything was all the same as before, too much the same – these old streets, all cramped in, never anything changing. But it was different as well – the way you'd moved on without me, as if you were more grown up than me. And Melly – well, she was all right, but Tommy – it was a shock.' He looked away for a moment. 'What I said, about him not being mine – it was a terrible thing to say. I know it's not true. I was angry. I was in a state. And I'd sort of shut myself down. That's what you did out there, all that time, just to get through it. Trouble was I'd forgotten how to stop doing it.'

Rachel swallowed. She didn't speak.

'I just needed some time to sort of get adjusted to it all – to come to my senses if you like. On the farm it was good – I was working outside, in the quiet. It was a bit like, sort of being on the boat home, only without all the other lads, just me and the sea. Only it was me and the rows of spuds, or digging all the muck out of a ditch and just the wind blowing. It was like travelling home – because I knew I was coming home. It just needed to be right.'

'You knew you'd come back? Why didn't you let us know where you were – or something?' Her voice came out tearful, resentful. 'I thought you'd gone for good, Danny. After the first week or so, it was back to me on my own again, like the war – just the kids, no father, no help or wage coming in. If it wasn't for Auntie, all the way through, we'd have gone under, and I'm not even her flesh and blood like you are. My God, you owe her, Danny – you owe her far more than you know you do.'

Quelled by the passion in her voice, Danny looked even more contrite. 'I know. I *know*. The thing was, I—'

'You were waiting for the dog?' she said scornfully.

'No. Well, yes – but that wasn't really the reason. I could've gone back for him. I just needed to know something – something that made me sure about myself. The thing I haven't got to yet is . . .' He seemed to be struggling again, had to force the words out. 'When I was still in Birmingham that couple of weeks, working on the buildings, I saw him.'

'Who?' she said, bewildered.

'The old man. My father.'

She raised herself up on one elbow. '*Did* you? Where? Did he know you?'

Danny made a contemptuous sound. 'He could barely tell his own arse from his elbow, never mind

451

knowing me. It was in this place I'd been staying in while I was in Brum. I asked on the buildings where I could go, cheap like, and the Irish lads said to go to the workhouse. Rowton House they call it. There was a nice lad, Seamus, who was lodging there and his girl was working at the hospital – it was just 'til they could find a room.' Danny shook his head. 'Bloody huge place – and God, it didn't half hum.'

'The workhouse?' Rachel breathed. The very name inspired dread. She lay down again to listen.

'That's the one. Rowton House. Some of them were young'uns like us, good lads. They'd come back of a night, get scrubbed up and go out to enjoy themselves. But there were these old men, broken-down old fellers, hardly knew where they were, stinking of piss and drink. A lot of them were Paddies, but not all. I passed him when I was going up to the room. My old man – looked just like all the other old wrecks in there.'

'Are you *sure* it was him?'

'I'm sure, all right. He's my dad. I'd know him anywhere.' There was a silence. When he spoke again, there were tears in his voice. 'I never knew if he'd gone to Australia – that's what he was always on about. I'd never set eyes on him from the day he dumped me in the home. And that was the worst thing. I used to think that p'r'aps he'd gone over there, right to the other side of the world, and maybe he was rich now and he'd made a good life in the sun with a big house and fields around and was thinking about sending for us all. I wouldn't've gone to him,' he added quickly. 'But it was summat to dream about. That it had all turned out good and he might want to do summat for us all in the end, me and the girls. And there he was, still in Brum all the time – and in the workhouse, a broken-down old drunk. I took a good look at him – he was so kalied he couldn't see straight and he took no notice of me. And I thought . . .' Danny's voice cracked now. 'That's going to be me. I've gone and done just what he's done – I've run off and left my missis and my children – and it'll damn well serve me right. And if I go on like this, I'll be in the cowing work-house all my life, just like being back in the home where I started – only worse, 'cause it's the end of the line in there.' In the quiet that followed she felt him sobbing, and she gently curved an arm around him as he wept.

'I'm sorry,' she heard, muffled by the pillow. 'I'm sorry, Rach . . .' She held him, waiting.

When he could speak again, he said, 'The thing was, as I say, I knew I'd come back to you. I just had to get away and think – see everything different. I needed to sort of make the journey home again, only longer, slower, knowing what I was coming to. And wanting to be here.'

'You'd better want to, Danny,' she said bitterly. 'For all of us – not just for you. Because if you don't, I'd rather you went, right now. I need a husband, a man who can be a proper father to his kids. I can't dance round you forever – life's hard and it's even harder with that kind of dancing to do. I haven't the strength and I don't want to have to try and find it.'

'I know,' he said. He wiped his eyes with his arm. 'But it will all be different now, Rach. That's what I found out – that you're my life. Not just you – everyone. You, the kids, Auntie. And Tommy – I keep telling myself, what does it matter if he's a bit different? If it's a struggle . . . How he is . . . I've had to get it straight in my mind, Rach – that he's not going to be a *man*. But I've been the biggest kind of stupid fool there is. I've lost all my other family – Mom, my sisters – and here I was throwing away everything else. Tommy's our lad and this is home. I want to be the best for you, girl – you're everything. You're my love, and that's all there is to it.'

'Promise?' she said, still wary of giving in to the hope he was offering.

'I do promise. With all my heart, Rach. I can't promise I'll know what to do and that – but I just want us to be together. That's all that matters.'

'I've always loved you, you know,' she said, still rather crossly.

'Yeah,' he said. 'I reckon I've always loved you, too – from the day you came and bossed me into giving you a bargain on those comics.'

Laughing, crying too, at last she allowed him to take her in his arms, and she embraced his strong, thin body. They clung together, loving, hoping, into a fresh beginning.

VII

Fifty

One week later

Rachel walked along Alma Street early on a sunny Saturday morning, a bag of shopping in each hand. Melanie walked to one side of her, Danny the other, pushing Tommy's chair. Danny paused, as he had a number of times on the walk, when the wheels snagged on something on the road.

Danny still could not come to terms with the idea that Rachel refused to have Tommy hidden away. 'You're not taking him out, are you?' he'd said, before they set out that morning. 'Not in that? Not right out – in the street?'

'Yes,' Rachel said firmly. 'Now and then. It's hard work, with that chair. But I don't want him stuck at home like a prisoner, Danny. Why shouldn't he get out and see things?'

'But what do people say? And what about other kids? They can be wicked like that, kids can – one or two of them in the home, their lives were hardly worth living.'

'I know.' She stood in the doorway, and looked sadly at him. As if she needed telling. 'And some of them think you're deaf and can't hear what they're saying. But at least round here people can get used to him. Dolly and

Mo's lads are golden – they'll always stick up for him. But as he gets older – we'll have to see, won't we?'

'We've got to get him summat better than this,' he said rather crossly, as the chair wheels stalled again. 'It's hopeless, going along.'

'I know,' Rachel said. 'But I don't think Mo thought I'd ever take it this far – it was just for round the house.'

'It were nice of him – it's good in its way,' Danny agreed. 'But he ought to have a proper pushchair or summat, not this flaming thing – especially now he's getting big.'

They had gone out early to get the shopping, to be in time for Danny to get to the Rag Market with Gladys. Melly was going with them as well.

'Proper little market kid your nanna says you are,' Danny said. He gave Melly a wink and she looked delighted. 'Just like we were, Rach. Auntie says she can haggle with the best of them.'

Rachel walked on with them, the sun on her face, with a feeling of miraculous happiness. There might have been difficulties, things to get used to, but it felt so much better now. The Camera works had taken Danny back for the time being, though he was not keen to stick there. And best of all, he was really home, not just in body, but *with* them, unlike the absent figure who had first appeared.

One evening last week, when she felt the time was right, Gladys had sat Danny down and told him, as she had told the others, about her little Alfie and all that had happened. Almost all. When she was alone upstairs with him later, Rachel told him about 'Polly'. She saw the shock register on Danny's face.

'I can't believe it,' he said, shaking his head. 'Not Auntie. No – she'd never do that.'

'You mean you *won't* believe it,' Rachel said, suddenly furiously angry. 'You don't know what a woman will do for her children to keep them from going hungry. Why wouldn't she do it? *I* would.'

Danny looked at her, startled. 'Would you?'

'If that's what it took, yes. So don't you go judging her!'

'I'm not!'

'Yes, you are – I can see.'

Danny blushed. 'It's just – Auntie's always been so . . . You know, sort of religious and *upright*.'

'Don't go saying anything to her.' Rachel found a grin spreading in spite of herself. 'She evidently wasn't upright *all* the time!'

'Rach!' But they lay helpless with laughter for a while – the thought was so outrageous.

'I wouldn't say a word,' Danny said, once he could speak again. 'Wouldn't dare.'

But she noticed that for a while afterwards he was especially tender with his aunt.

Walking towards the entry to their yard with their shopping, Tommy's chair rumbling along the pavement, they saw that there was a horse and cart pulled up at the side of the road. The cart, a flat, open thing, was empty and the horse stood with its nose down, dozing in the warmth. A blond-headed boy was standing near it, holding a galvanized bucket and staring intently at the horse's rear end. As they approached, the boy slipped his hand in his pocket and went to the horse's head, offering it something to eat. The horse suddenly revived and started munching.

Danny chuckled. 'Eh, Jonny! What're you feeding him – laxatives?'

Jonny, Dolly and Mo's fourth boy, now eleven, looked round guiltily. 'No – I weren't, honest. It were just a bit of carrot!'

Danny peered into Jonny's empty bucket. 'You've got a way to go there, son. Still, I s'pose it's the time of year for gardening—'

'Jonny! Quick!' Reggie, the next Morrison boy up from Jonny, came tearing along the entry, his face full of urgency. 'She's had it! Our mom's had it!'

Rachel felt excitement leap in her. 'What – Dolly? Has she had the babby – already?' It was news to them that Dolly had even gone into labour.

'She's had it real quick!' Reggie gabbled. 'Our dad'd only just got the midwife. And it's a girl!'

'A girl!' Melly jumped up and down, clapping. 'A girl, a girl!'

'Oh, Dolly'll be so pleased to have a girl to dress,' Rachel laughed.

'She's gonna have to be tough with all of that lot,' Danny said.

They hurried in along the entry, Reggie and Jonny dashing on ahead. There was a general air of celebration about, the neighbours outside chatting, and when Mo came out he was clapped on the back and looked suitably proud and bashful at the same time.

'Right!' he proclaimed, wiping his forehead. 'God, I'm exhausted, I am, I can tell yer . . . Time to wet the baby's—'

'Oh, Mo!' Rachel interrupted. 'You can't just disappear off to the pub. Let's wet the baby's head here – later on!' There were nods of agreement from the women. 'Come on, Mo – you live most of your life in the Salutation!'

Mo looked crestfallen. 'Why not both?' he asked hopefully.

Gladys, who was looking very happy on Dolly's behalf, said, 'All right then – you go off now and get yerself back here for when Dolly's ready to face the world. And wait 'til we're back from the market – don't start without us!'

Mo scuttled off happily along the entry.

Irene, who was leaning in her doorway watching the proceedings, announced, 'That's one thing I'm never cowing well doing again. Over my dead body.'

Everyone ignored her. This was Dolly's moment and they were delighted for her.

Mo did them all proud that evening, with bottles and jugs brought along from the outdoor at the pub, and everyone crowded into number one. The Morrisons welcomed Tommy's chair inside even though it took up precious space. Some of the neighbours, the Jackmans and Lil and Stanley, and a number from the other yards around, came for a quick look and chat and left again, the children spilling out into the yard as soon as they had got a glimpse of the new baby and grown bored with her. Dolly brought her down for a bit and seemed in very good health and spirits. The closest neighbours stayed.

'It was that quick I hardly had time to turn round!' said Dolly.

'Oh, Dolly – she's the image of you!' Gladys said tearfully. She was more emotional about everything these days, as if she had finally allowed her feelings to show.

'About time an' all!' Dolly beamed down at the little

461

girl, all seven pounds three of her, with a dark thatch of hair, sleeping soundly in her arms. 'She and me'll have to stick together. We even look as if we might be related!'

'Isn't she beautiful?' Rachel murmured to Danny who was standing beside her. He smiled and nodded. 'Have you got a name for her?' she asked Dolly.

Dolly looked at Mo and he gave a nod. 'She's going to be called Donna,' she said. 'It's a pretty name and it means "woman" in Italian. Any road, she's going to need to be all woman in this house! And her second name'll be Elizabeth, after Mo's mom.'

'A toast!' Mo announced, standing up and trying to look solemn, though a man with such a comical face and generous belly faced a challenge with this. 'To Donna Elizabeth – our little wench!'

'To Donna Elizabeth!' they all chorused, sipping from an array of crocks that had been brought in for the purpose.

'Now you come to think of it,' Gladys said, as they quietened down, 'she's the first babby born in this yard since the war ended.'

Everyone thought for a moment.

'That's true,' Rachel said. 'The last one was Evie Sutton.'

'Poor little bugger,' someone muttered. 'We'll all have to keep an eye on that one.'

'Well – let's have a further toast,' Mo said, raising a teacup full of ale. 'To Donna Elizabeth – child of the peace!'

'Child of the peace!' everyone joined in.

Rachel and Danny clinked cups. His wide blue eyes looked into hers and she could see the love and happiness in them. 'Here's to the peace,' he whispered. 'And to us, love.' And they reached for each other's hands.

Acknowledgements

As ever, the research for this story involved tracking down a great many small pieces of information from an even greater number of sources too numerous to mention. But I owe particular thanks this time to Iris and Gordon Parker and their daughter Nina Jennings who shared with me their memories of working on the Birmingham Rag Market. Also to Maureen and Fred Hyde for hospitality and more memories. And, once more, many thanks to members of the Birmingham History Forum for all their memories and for answers to questions when needed.

Keep in touch

Are you on Facebook? If so it would be good to hear from you. You can follow my author page on Facebook at **www.facebook.com/Annie.Murray.Author** or search for 'Annie Murray Writer' on Facebook. You may also like my website **www.anniemurray.co.uk**.

My Daughter, My Mother

BY ANNIE MURRAY

**Two daughters. Two mothers.
The secrets of two lifetimes.**

*In 1984 two young mothers meet at a toddler group in
Birmingham. As their friendship grows, they share with
each other the difficulties and secrets in their lives.*

Joanne, a sweet, shy girl, is increasingly afraid of her
husband. The lively, promising man she married has become
hostile and violent and she is too ashamed to tell anyone.
When her mother, Margaret, is suddenly rushed into hospital, the bewildered family find that there are things about
their mother of which they had no idea. Margaret was
evacuated from Birmingham as a child and has spent years
avoiding the pain of her childhood – but finds that you can't
run from the past forever.

Sooky, kind and good-natured, has already been through
one disastrous marriage and is back at home living with
her parents. But being 'disgraced' is not easy. Her mother,
Meena, refuses to speak to Sooky. At first her silence seems
like a punishment, but Sooky gradually realizes it contains
emotions which are far more complicated and that her mother
may need her help. Meena has spent 20 years trying to fit in
with life in Birmingham, and to deal with the conflicts within
her between east and west, old ways and new.

This is the story of two young women discovering the
heartbreak of their mothers' lives, and of how mothers
create daughters – and learn from them.

ISBN: 978-0-330-53520-5

The Women of Lilac Street

BY ANNIE MURRAY

Troubles in life. Strength in friendship.

*Birmingham, almost a decade after the end
of the Great War, and the women of Lilac Street
have had more than their fair share of troubles . . .*

Rose Southgate is trapped in a loveless marriage. Shy and isolated, she makes the best of life, until she meets a man who changes everything.

Jen Green is struggling to make ends meet, with a sick husband and five children to support. Aggie, her eldest daughter, is twelve years old and longs for excitement. But prying into the adult world shows her more than she had bargained for.

And Phyllis Taylor is a widow who has managed to put a dark and traumatic past behind her. But the return of her daughter Dolly threatens all that . . .

These women find strength in friendship, as they discover that the best way to solve their problems is to face them together.

ISBN: 978-0-330-53521-2

Meet Me Under the Clock

BY ANNIE MURRAY

**Two Families. Two Wartime loves.
Their lives changed forever . . .**

*Growing up in Birmingham, Sylvia and
Audrey Whitehouse have always been like chalk and
cheese. When the Second World War breaks out,
Sylvia is still dreaming of her forthcoming marriage
to fiancé Ian while Audrey jumps at the career
opportunities the WAAF throws her way.*

Audrey joins the ranks at RAF Cardington but soon finds
that her new freedom also brings temptation. When she
goes too far, the consequences ripple through the Whitehouse family. Meanwhile, Sylvia is doing her bit as a railway
porter, much to Ian's dismay. Ian thinks the job is unfemi-
nine – unlike Sylvia's new friend Kitty, who is as sweet and
pretty as can be. But Kitty's innocent nature hides a dark
secret . . .

As the pressures of rationing, bombing raids and sleep-
less nights grow, the two sisters must decide what they
really want from life and if they're brave enough to fight
for it.

A heartbreaking yet inspiring novel, perfect for fans of
Margaret Dickinson and Katie Flynn.

ISBN: 978-1-4472-3374-9

FOR MORE ON

ANNIE MURRAY

sign up to receive our

SAGA NEWSLETTER

Packed with **features, competitions, authors'
and readers' letters** and **news of exclusive events,**
it's a must-read for every Annie Murray fan!

Simply fill in your details below and tick to confirm that you would
like to receive saga-related news and promotions and return to us at
Pan Macmillan, Saga Newsletter, 20 New Wharf Road, London, N1 9RR.

NAME

ADDRESS

POSTCODE

EMAIL

☐ *I would like to receive saga-related news and promotions (please tick)*

*You can unsubscribe at any time in writing or through our website where you can also see
our privacy policy which explains how we will store and use your data.*

At Bello, we believe in the timeless power of books, and our extensive list of classic fiction has something for everyone. Whether you want to indulge in a heart-warming tale of life in the Hebrides from Lillian Beckwith's *The Hills is Lonely*, read a classic Yorkshire saga from award-winning author Brenda Jagger, or escape to the scandalous world of Renaissance Italy in Sarah Bower's *The Sins of the House of Borgia*, we've got the book for you.

BELLO

panmacmillan.com/bello

🐦 @bellobooks   f bellobooks